Far, deep into the moment we stood. It was grave cold, a breathless misty late night had drawn on us. Naturally, the unrefined roughness of early European summertime showing off its' potential and will. We had been held to a standstill on a lone dark Tuesday. To each other, we were noticeably unperturbed over the circumstances that our situation had brought forth, but I was genuinely inwardly upset that we had to deal with this mishap in our tired and somewhat drunken state. My backpack was heavy, and full of needed weight. My traveling partners too, struggled to stand erect under the weight of what they had been carrying for so long now. There was no sign of activity outside besides us. The dark crept in on us. Lights from inside the empty train station flickered, struggling to illuminate the scene, making it seem more surreal and murky than it appeared in the daytime light. The seeping wet wind was in revulsion. It was moist and thick, pushing materiality around. Thunder lay growling, snapping its whip and stretching it, in check, but ready to attack.

Behind us, the South bound train that we should have been on was sluggishly leaving the station without us. The train did not make any whimpering sounds because we were not aboard it. A victorious conductor stood proud, solid like a statue, protecting the departing train from just such stowaways. His mustache covered his whole snarling face. He looked on us as vagrants to his peace of mind. A calamity, our situation was not, but it required a certain concentration that I personally was empty of. Regardless, there was very little choice about our next move, at least for the time being. With a jump that was above the red line of our energy levels, Arlo, our want to be jester, ran back inside the station. I stared with blank eyes out into the night, not stopping him, not worrying about what he was doing, sighing, as the rain commenced its downward procession upon us. Our fate, unsurprisingly, had brought us into another nervous moment. Tensions arose, trying to find a place to lay blame. The three of us, outside, held our tongues carefully, speaking only because of necessity. We could have well begun to argue, although that hadn't really happened at all on this trip, now would have been the perfect time for it, ruining the beautiful ending that was so close. Rainwater seeped in between my toes, loosening the grip my feet had on my sandals.

Beezley came stomping back outside with his dignity held high, as the yells and calls from the jubilant provocative conductor followed him out. Arlo enjoyed taunting the authority that the man owned up to. It wasn't exactly the smartest thing for him to do, this conductor seemed like the type to call the cops on travelers like us. He handed me a plastic bag to cover my drum with, keeping it from the spoils of the rain. His drum was already sheltered within a hole-filled plastic bag as well. Arlo stated boldly, with a look like he wanted to pat himself on the back, his unnecessary new piece of information, "There's a train out of here at nine o'clock tomorrow morning fellas!"

No one answered him directly. Our thoughts were on more immediate questions. Where o where are we going to sleep tonight, I thought? And can we get a ride there! Unpleasantness was happening with strict suddenness, it was late and getting cold, quite quickly. Idling, with our backs to the train station, the four of us, darkened within the fall of the rain, talked loudly over the sound of the brewed storm.

Arlo screamed as he flashed us a big ring of keys, "Check this out, I stole his keys!"

Jules looked over to the brass bundle swamped into Arlo's hand, "You know how much of a pain in the ass it's going to be for that bastard to replace all those keys!"

Marvin looked over to Arlo, he struck his pointer finger against an air post putting another notch in it, "Oh, You're one step closer to hell than me now Arlo, Yeah." Sarcasticly stating.

"Yeah, if he's lucky I'll leave them in the toilet after I take a shit, before we leave tomorrow." Arlo said.

"You go girl," I said, pointing three fagot stiff fingers at him. Marv looked up out of our conversation to the world around us, drawing our attention to it as well. As if it wasn't happening, or perhaps it was a welcomed pleasure, we became drenched by the pouring dense water. It really made you feel the cold of the night. Water streamed down my face, I licked my lips, wishing there was an aftertaste of some pleasure still on them. Decisions were rapidly and somewhat incoherently made about the course of our present movement.

Sadly I said, "Well, I guess we'll have to catch the morning train to Madrid," then reassuringly I uplifted my tone and stated confidently, "Don't worry Jules, you're not going to miss your flight home!"

"I'm not worried," he said, laughing off my statement. More likely, he was hoping to miss his flight. A cool worn look from his stature, his confidence, passed itself off of him.

"When's your flight?" Marv blurted out curiously.

"Tomorrow night sometime, from Madrid."

"Ah, there's still plenty of time to get there, man." Marv spoke excitedly, uninterrupted by the wetness that covered him. Water started to bead up on his glasses, but you could still see his eyes shining with the strength of the sun's vibrance. Granted that the way that we traveled, we should at least make it there within the next day, I hoped.

Arlo started bragging, thinking he was some sort of troubadour, "Shit, you'll make it with plenty of time to kill at the airport. But me, I only got two days to make it all the way down to Seville for my flight home, now that's cutting it close!"

"Why are you wasting you're time with us then?" Marv cut him up.

"Yeah you better start walkin right now." Jules laughed at him. I pushed him in a direction opposite of South.

"Beezley, if your not careful, you might not make it out of this town, so you better play your cards right."

"I could live in this town for a while!" He claimed like a fucking politician.

And then the capping statement from Marv, in which Arlo had no response, "Yeah, but you'd be livin' shacked up with some faggot Spanish sugardaddy, lickin' him from head to toe for your dinner, you little bitch!"

Jules laughed and pushed Arlo and he moved three or four feet almost falling to the ground, slipping and sliding on the water under the weight of his backpack, the ring of 100 keys jingling in his thief hand.

"We're lucky we made it out of Cannes," I said to myself, not necessarily under my breath, but covered up and mumbled by the sound of the coming water all around us, "Anyway, what are we doing, huh?" I asked speaking up, bored and soaking wet, not bothering to try and light a cigarette. "Why are we just standing here, gettin rained on?" I was thinking it so I said it. I wondered why nobody else cared about this fact? Where had all our booze gone, I thought?

"Seek shelter, out of harms way. Quick men!" Arlo played out the thought that ran through all of our minds'. Without looking back, but knowing full well that we would follow him, anytime, anywhere, to face his fears even, which I imagined to be quite severe, Julian Shivers picked up and started moving. Marvin, with a suddenness, put a sweet tightlipped smile on his face. He looked around to see if we left anything laying about, then with eyes gleaming hard behind his glasses, which took all the attention away from the smile on his face, he walked into Julians' footprints, which by now were hidden deep into the splash of growing puddles. I reached over and put my loafish wet arm around Beezley's slippery dirty neck, above his backpack, and pushed him along, complaining about the burden and a pain in my leg, letting him bear my weight in a jokish style. We both tapped away on drums, muzzled by the loose bags that protected them from the falling water, and all the while Arlo used the keys as a tambourine. A marching beat, and laughter only from Arlo and I. He had a weird sort of look, like reckless glee lacquered to his face.

3

We walked on, following along in different worlds, Marv dodging the drops effortlessly. Julian's hips twitched as the weight of his guitar leaned him to one side. I was trying to count rain drops, going mad with thoughtlessness just to keep my mind occupied. I was so wet and dirty. We were all expecting some sort of salvation from our dilemma. But it did not show up. It appeared that we would be spending the night here, in another small town in Spain. Hopefully, we wouldn't have to sleep out in the rain. With a tired lack of hope, I prayed for shelter. Thunder crackled above. Walking in the rain we were; unhurriedly and not complaining, carrying our houses and all of it's necessary and extravagant furnishings, now about a week into our journey. Less than a day left until we went our separate ways. Still and all, the road that we traveled to get there, long ahead of us, our gear only to feel like more weight was being added to it with each step. Soaking and growing mildew from the exposure to the bursts of rain, and the lack of adequate drying.

Our movement across the *terra de Espania* was now in abeyance, in this pleasant town called Victoria, just below the northern border, west from the *Catalan* region. Our journeying taking us into Spain from Cannes, France, then through Erun towards San Sebastian. Aesthetically, The towns and lifestyles along the Bay of Biscay and the Atlantic Ocean are so perfectly unpretentious in their veer towards awe. There was a deep and hidden contentness in all of us, knowing that we had been to some of the most extravagant places in the world of status. No matter if it seemed to me, that we weren't welcome there, we were there experiencing it, at least we weren't stuck in our little home towns in America, not knowing what else was out there. None of us bored or tired, we were totally deluded by our every new experience, becoming more of ourselves, allowing ourselves to grow out of uncertainties' offerable nurturings, yet making things happen that couldn't possibly have been charted on any of destinies' maps.

The travels of this trip were initiated from London, England, which seemed so far away. We made good time, especially through France, down to Cannes for the film festival, what an experience that was. Then we headed down into Spain. My traveling companions and I, had become now a solid working instinctual unit. Our timing was tight, and we knew each other's mannerisms and feelings without necessarily verbally sharing them. Needless to say, the four of us traveled well together.

Momentarily, we were chilled and somewhat tired. Spain grew cold at night, and the rain added to the falling temperature. It was going to be nice to lay down in my sleeping bag tonight and dream. We had all been through a lot together on this voyage, all of us able to understand and fulfill the roles

necessary for surviving our particular style of traveling. We walked along
getting more wet on a main street. I looked up to see if there was an end. In
the distance I saw a light barely staying lit near an entrance to a building. A
bar we were in, earlier this evening. A fat man with short legs and stubby
arms came out from the doorway attempting to hold a newspaper over his
head. He was running in the rain toward us and sheets of the newspaper were
ripping and falling all over the place from the weight of the water. Arlo's ears
perked. "I'll be a six footed son of a bitch, yo, this is the guy who stiffed me
on that hash we bought earlier." He pointed up ahead.

That got Marv's attention, he slowed down to check him out. The fat
man was walking quickly toward us, looking down the whole time, not
noticing us as we stopped walking.

"Are you sure?" Asked Marv. Jules stopped and turned around to
look at us. I started getting excited, I was feeling some sort of repercussive
payback building.

"Hells Yeah! That's the guy, look he's even got glasses."

"I bet he's got even more than that on him," I said as I started walking
into his path. He looked up, and his depreciation of speed in his stepped
implied that he had noticed us. Arlo ran right passed me. He started a
crescendo of screaming and he ran right up to the guy and tackled him. They
both hit the floor, Arlo on top of him and all's you could hear was the smack
of the fat mans head hitting the terracotta sidewalk. The poor man's glasses
flew off into the night. Marv started busting out laughing. The fat man
wasn't moving. Arlo scrounged around under the weight of his backpack to
get up and gain his balance.

"Jesus, did you kill him?" Jules asked with sincerity.

"Arlo don't answer that question." I said, "How much money did he
get us for?"

"Probably forty five, fifty American." Arlo turned around. You could
see a big bruise swelling on his forehead, and blood on his face gleaming
amongst the sweat and rainwater.

"Shit, Arlo, what did you do, head but him?" Marv asked.

"That's the only way to take them down quick!"

"No wonder you're always forgetting stuff." Jules joked.

"Ha-ha," I peeped. "Arlo, are *you* bleeding. I asked as I walked over to
the guy to check him out. Marv followed me. Arlo touched his face to check
for cuts. I looked at the fatty, laying there, he looked like a proud sneak of a
sort of man. He was snoring. That was a good sign. I could see blood mixing
like sangria in the puddle of water around him, he had a cut on his face, but I
was assuming the major damage was to the back of his head. I looked over at

Marv. "This guy deserved this shit right?" I asked, "I mean Marv, he even deserves to get mugged right now, yeah?"

Marv shook his head quick to the right, splashing rain water off in layers. He looked dead on at Arlo and asked seriously, "Arlo you conniving little thief, now listen cause what's happening right now is going to affect all of our Karma's in a bad way, if you lie to me, so," He grabbed Arlo's arm and squeezed it tightly, hurting him-

"Hey," Arlo tried to pull away but only managed to get drawn in closer to Marv's grasp.

"Shut up and listen, cause I ain't about to rob a guy if he doesn't deserve it, yeah, I want you to answer only yes or no. Ok?" Marv's eye's opened up absorbing and radiating all the surrounding light, a ferocious look of seriousness crossed his face, "Did this guy really short you on that hash, or were you holding out the rest of it so you could have some on you're way down to Seville, and you wanted us to rob this guy cause you know he had much more hash and cash on him than you?

"Man, what do you take-" Marv squeezed his arm even tighter, "ooooouuuuch, shit, you're gonna rip my arm off!" Arlo cried in dispair.

"Like I said, answer only yes or no," Marv said calmly.

"Fuck yeah he shorted me, yeah!" He looked at Marv, obviously trying to hide his lying bluff.

Marv stared deep into Arlo, "You're a fucking prick Arlo." He said and let go of him. Rain still kept coming down, Jules wiped some water off his brow and slightly pulled Marv away from Arlo.

The moment was stale and silent. "So what's up Marv? Do I take this guy or what."

Yeah," he replied, calmly in a high pitch, "But Arlo's soul is the only one who's gonna get more tainted black for this."

"This moment is spinnin'. That's allot of fuckin blood. Is he gonna die from our hands?" Jules questioned with greedy ambition.

As if it was meant to be, Marv stated, "He shouldn't have shorted Arlo on the hash deal, and if he didn't, Arlo shouldn't have lied to me. Either way fuck him."

"He's in the wrong place at the right time for us, yeah." Jules said.

"That's right." I said, and I bent down to check his pockets. His forehead was swelling up bad. I avoided the puddle of blood and the blood on his face, now running down his neck, as I ran my fingers all over him. He smelled of hard booze, "This guy's been drinkin hard. He'll probably wake up thinkin he just passed out again on his way home." I had hoped to find a flask full of something to drink, but allas I only found a serious block of hash,

6

and a roll of Spanish note. I left the guy a couple of bills and a piece of the hash, so that he didn't feel too bad, and I let him keep his watch. He's lucky none of us cared what time it was. Arlo and Jules moved in on him. Arlo kicked him in the gut, calling him a bitch, and Jules pulled up some fleghm and spit it onto his face delicately. We all stood around the passed out and bleeding fat man admiring the stream of buggered fleghm on his face. After about a minute, Jules sighed and looked up. I handed him the block of hash, then I gave Marv the money. Jules smiled and turned around and started walking. We all followed him, somewhat bored, one at a time, seeming sad, as if we just lost a corporate softball league game to a much weaker team. Arlo didn't even complain about his forehead and he had a pretty big knot growing out like a tumor above his face.

Jules strode ahead, cutting through the thickness of the turbulent conditions impeding us, leading the way with the flare of a lasting torch, persistent, standing high for all to see. We came across an inlet to a couple of stores. Big windows displayed a dark showroom and closed signs in Spanish.

"This is perfect!" Marv claimed with true sincerity.

"Yeah, it's the fucking Ritz Carlton! Lets order room service." I said with non comical wit over a brazen wet face as I walked in.

"Ha ha." Came from Arlo, a high pitched stupid Simpsons' character laugh that was the underlying theme of our experiences' together. "Hey, we should stash the cash and the hash tonight, just in case that guys knows the cops or something."

"Sure," Marv said as he and Jules handed over the evidences. Arlo grabbed them deviously then ran out into the dark to hide the gear. He was back within seconds. "Where did you-"

"Underneath the trashcan around the corner." He smiled, as he held a little ball of hash up, "We got enough to get us to sleep tonight though." He passed the hash to Jules.

We went in to the open vestibule, out from under the rain, and set down our gear on the side, away from the front door. Dripping wet we all were, and apparently not bothered by it. I was so glad to take my backpack off. I stretched, elongating my crushed and crumpled spine, yawning loudly, and turned to watch the fall of the rain. Now appreciating its display. It didn't seem like there was anybody else alive besides us in the world. The only sounds I could hear was nature falling to the ground and its utilities, lightning and thunder, bragging in the sky above. Marv rolled out his sleeping bag, and got comfortable. He started to produce poetically, sonant echoing euphony with his harmonica. Always with a twang of the blues, the instrument vibrated the notes under his soft rasping breath. Jules sat down and started rolling a hash joint. Arlo was in an excited fashion. He was making up his bed to sleep in and was drawing J. Shivers into trivial chatter. With emphasis on his words he tried to catch Julian's eyes directly, but he was looking down at his work purposely avoiding Beezley's glare.

He talked fast, excited, and unsure how to show it, " Man, we had a good day of busking today, huh Jules? Shit those kids loved the puppets. They couldn't get enough. And how about that Mom, God was she hot, she definitely dug us." Stopping for a second, thinking that he should rephrase the last statement to himself more specifically, but then with a kink in the skin of his forehead, he went on disregarding it, but knowing that she was checking him out more so than the rest of us. "And when Mcmanis was miming for that one kid and you pulled his pants down, Man," All drawn out, slapping Jules on the back a little and laughing purposely at what he must have thought was my little dick, "Now that's comedy!"

"Yeah, I should have been wearing an orange handkerchief as a jock strap, or a peanut shell, that would have been funnier than almost getting arrested for flashing a child." Thinking about it for a second I said, "Man, I could have went to jail for that if a cop showed up at the wrong moment."

Jules said thinly, with a little bit of mirthful laughter, "I'm sorry Welton, I forgot that you weren't wearing any underwear." Our lifestyle being stamped by such innocence.

Arlo laughed probably thinking about how hard it would have been to break me out of a Spanish prison, or maybe he was laughing at the attention I'd get from the other inmates in jail, being labeled some sort of clown American pedophile bum. He was enjoying the way he was living, sleeping on the streets. How could he not, this was merely an experience that he could tell a high tale about one day, and one that he would never ever have again. Besides, he wasn't alone out here; that would have been damaging to his sense of self. Also, he was going home soon, to a safe and comfortable suburban lifestyle. There were people in his life that would make sure that homelessness wouldn't ever be an option. And if he traveled again ever, you could be sure that he was going to use real hotel rooms.

We were all young and immature, and aside from Arlo, none of us started this trip with any real money. But that wasn't going to stop us from traveling, we just wouldn't fall under the advantages that Americans that could afford more than one night in a hostel would have. So we did what we had to do, we slept on the streets, on beaches, and sometimes, if they didn't throw us out, trains or their respective stations. To survive living on the streets of Europe was a test and challenge to all of us, we measured ourselves by it. Adopting new roles to adequately rise above new situations presented to us, shedding the comfortable confines of our mastered and well understood personas, and the familiarity of our boringly known surroundings, the thrill of adventure chased us, forcing us to move on. I had this deep feeling that for me, this type of road I walked on, was not just a test, perhaps it would never really end. The straining sounds cried out of Ellowin's harmonica. This whole experience was making Marvin as humble as the ancient spirits. Jules finished rolling the hash joint and he passed it to me to light it.

"Welton Mcmanis Spells, would you please do the honors?"

"Sure!" I said and I pulled out my lighter to burn the excess paper off and then put it to my lips to light it. Even Beezley grew quiet for the ritual. For that second, I couldn't even hear the sound of the rain falling. I took a couple of deep drags and passed it around. Thunder capered and lightning almost came and got us. I jumped. Practically leaping onto my mates. We laughed, taking the edge off of the moment. Julian, who always looked distant from the scene, had been down similar roads, on and off, for most of his life. He was ok with our scenario, and could have called his mother and sincerely told her he was doing fine, without out a hint of a lie in his voice, totally proponent to this way of life. He would have walked down this road alone, unafraid, no insecurities holding him back if he had to. Probably ending up in a better position without us. I loved him for that.

The hours that lay ahead, I considered to be downtime, and although it was late, I wasn't quite ready for sleep. The joint passed around and around. Restlessness crept within bones that lacked calcium, aching with withered marrow. I had too many questions unanswered, too many more questions unfolding in front of me, and no where to find solutions. There was nothing in my mind that I could put a solid grasp on. The rest of my life lay in doubt. I looked out at the rain, it was loud, falling hard and creeping in toward us. I felt like I was still getting wet, I wiped water off of my face with my shirt tail. The harmonica echoed in the space, as smoke from Marv's exhale came out with the crying notes.

Questions in my mind led not to their answers but to more questions asked. Visually imagined incandescent fireworks lit up bright iota and particles in the open sky of my mind. I breathed heavy and looked introvertedly through a stale wide eyed trance. Unwanted thoughts were spoiling my peace. Breaths of hyper-ventilated air told of my desperation. Oh dear, what have I made with this life I've been given? Could I live with myself, if I was nothing, a nobody? What is the truth? Rene Descartes, the man who turned on the light for intellectual culture, was upset enough with the limitations of his own ignorance that he went mad. Centuries of learned minds devoted to the study and understanding of philosophical doctrine produced only uncertain skeptical answers; non-answers. Who the hell really knows what God is? Descartes freed himself from the mental sustenance of others past and sought to gain the truth from within himself. His mind died, forgetting everything it ever knew from the contemplative intensity of one of his physically torpid ritual trances. Some say even he failed to wholly find the full entity of the truth. Or maybe he just couldn't explain it, even to himself. But if he couldn't do it, how was I to prevail? So, who was left then to answer my questions for me? Me? I felt helpless, upset that my comrades didn't have the answers either, yet glad that they were there with me sharing this, in all likelihood, mistaken fate that we had chosen. It would have been a hard struggle to go at it alone, and these guys weren't the types to slow me down. If anything, I would not have made it this far without them. In many ways, my companions diminished the labor of my burden, as I added to it.

Deep down inside my stomach, a fear lay eating away at the surrounding walls in which I had confined it in. It was a draining engagement to maintain its concealment. Pecking, with every chance, it trying to push itself out. I consciously tried hard not to show it, especially to myself. In my mind, I always told myself, 'Don't look down'. Tears swelled up and dripped out of my reddened crazy eyes, strolling down my cheek blending into the rainwater and sweat that I had failed to wipe away. I looked at my friends, Marv was smiling behind his harmonica. They all seemed so happy and content, lounging about as if we really were in the Ritz Carlton. Man what was wrong with me? I thought. I sighed, trying to give up thinking about it.

I untied my soaking wet sleeping bag from my backpack and rolled it out, I got stuck sleeping on the outside, which meant I would probably be the first one to be haggled by an oncoming threat of some sort. It was the chance you took, sleeping on the streets of an unknown town, in a foreign land. You really never knew what to expect the night to bring. Danger was always possibly calling out, keeping you alert, testing you, making you feel alive. It was an unfair thrill that chased away the conservative views that my upbringing had taught me. My mother wouldn't be happy with me right now, but this was the price we paid for not letting our lack of money persuade us into not traveling. I yawned again, searching for daylight, not really knowing what time it was. It didn't even matter, none of us even had a watch. We now had nothing better to do, than to wait out the rain, or at least the night.

We had been in Victoria, Espania throughout the day, arriving by train, on a whim. Well, more likely, we had been thrown off the train, by a well fussed, and irritated conductor. It was a typical response to us from train conductors. We weren't in the habit of paying for train rides during this trip. It was no matter, it was always a pleasure to be thrown off a train, and left, anywhere in Spain. I couldn't say that about certain countries, but down in Southern Europe, everything was *tranquillo*. Nobody sweat the small stuff in Spain, and simplicity was the normal way of life. It was never that bad, even when it was at its worst.

The day had brought us genuine delight. For survival and to earn money, we performed street theater, putting out a hat to collect money. Mostly, we played music, and performed marionette and clown routines. Clowning, I had learned in the states from one of the grander circuses, and I showed Marv and Arlo, and they had picked it up pretty easily. The marionetting, Marvin and I had caught onto in Amsterdam some months back, and man has it been paying off (By the way, if your reading this, John Paul, you are truly a superhero). Jules usually supplied the music with his guitar. Our shows were highly esteemed by those who witnessed them. We would not have done nearly as well on the streets of America, there isn't as widespread an appreciation for street theater in the states as there is in Europe.

Everyone who past us enjoyed what we had to offer, and steadily coins were pitched into our hat. We had a solid, entertaining street show, with much variability, but all in all, it was the puppets that we performed with that got the most attention, and made the most money. Clowning got a lot of attention, but it didn't make as much money as the puppets, Raymond and Pablo. Also, I used a lot more energy clowning for a crowd than I did manipulating a puppet. So I preferred working Pablo, my puppet, for a crowd rather than miming or doing a clown routine with Arlo or Marv. We were not decrepit beggars, hoping for help or free money, we were tightly knit performing entities, we gave people a show that was worth paying for. This, we were very good at, taking it for granted sometimes and probably not really developing it to its fullest potential. We treated it too much like an avocation, not exploiting it enough perhaps.

Earlier this day, we had made enough money performing on the streets of Victoria, to buy four tickets practically to Madrid. But we had spent it, or a good part of it, copiously on domestic wines, grand food platters, and party favorites in which we got stiffed on, but now, being later recompensated! It was fine with me, my preferences were in the order that I liked them to be. Besides, it had been a while since we had any real food. Maybe we still had some money left from our day of work, who knew, who cared right now. And most likely Marv was gonna give the money we took off of that fat man to a bunch of little kids in the village tomorrow before we leave. It didn't matter. It was time to celebrate anyway, in less than a day we would all split up and go our separate ways. These guys had real lives to get back to in the states.

What was I going to do for the rest of the summer, I wondered? For the time being, I let the question slip away unanswered. In my head a cool hum waved in and out and around, soothing the drawn out traffic of nonsensical thought. I was somewhat pleased to lay low, at least for the time being.

The night howled with racing thick presenting winds, buoyantly however, discriminating whom it jostled, careful not to disturb the locals. Bringing with it the secret stories and the luscious stale scent of centuries old buried treasures. I couldn't help but feel nostalgic for the past and what this country had known. Ah, if I could just understand the earth when she talked. How much in life I have not learned, or known to be true. How much I have not seen or done. And what of all I have done? Was it worth it? Was it all a positive stepping stone in the advancement of my success? Am I really having any fun? Maybe I've learned to fail myself. And if so, who was going to save me from myself? I felt haunted by the weight of unsolved doubts. Bondage wrapped itself around my minds' eye. Life entertains some, lavishly and handsomely. This did not seem true of my existence. Was it too much to hope for something out of life that was beyond my destiny? What was I doing traveling like this? Is not the adytum of inner peace available and open to the lame simpleton as it is to the just and the righteous? Ah, what a long slow road it is to reach contentness. What is the purpose of my life anyway? Did anything really matter? Suspense and incertitude strayed into my mind, provoking depression within my contemplation's. Waiting around for something seemed to be all I ever did, it was so tedious. I was interrupted in my thoughts, Jules passed me the joint, I wasn't looking and it fell and burned my arm.

"Ahh, shit man!" The pain felt good actually, it made me realize that either I wasn't supposed to worry about a thing, or that there was a million other things I should be worrying about as well. Anyway, it couldn't have come at a better time.

Jules apologized sympathetically, "Sorry brother."

But I accepted the blame, "Don't worry about it," as I picked it up off my sleeping bag before it got all wet.

"Is this still the same joint?" I asked with dumb curiosity as I yawned.

"No, it's another."

"Damn, I didn't even notice you roll another. Where the hell have I been?"

Marv spoke up with a relaxed intonation, "In the lost land of your mind!"

"Yeah Welton, you think too much sometimes, I mean what the hell do you have to think about all the time, it's as if you think you're the only one thinkin for the team." Arlo broke in from his comfortable position under the covers of his sleeping bag, adding less than his two cents to the conversation, rubbing his forehead.

Jules smiled, "It's better than you Beezley, speaking without thinking!" He winked at me implying that it was good to have as many people doing the masterminding for this trip as he could get.

"Ha ha," I blurted out, ceremoniously. I laid back smiling, as we all grew quiet, sleep coming over us. Silence quickly became the main sound outside of the noises of nature beyond our sleeping spot. Jules seemed still a bit alert, as if he had something on his mind.

"Cannes was pretty fucked up, wasn't it?" He said, not even necessarily asking the question.

"Yeah," I lingered out through some smoke. Stalling for time, I then said,"
Jules, do you think you made a mistake on the beach that night?" I asked.

He didn't reply for some time, then he smiled and said, "Naaaaa." All negative connotation about my existence passed as I saw Julian's beautiful reassuring face. The disruption of my inner peace was lost to the forgotten. Puffing away, the hash making me mellow, a smile made its way back onto my face. Tranquility crawled through my veins, rushing to my head, making me dizzy. Giggles burst out involuntarily through exhausted breath. I reflected in a nonjudgmental way, on our journey, as it lay up to this point. Trying hard not to bash and make ill-worthy our experience. Wondering if it all really happened. Dancing fragmented memories past by in soliloquized shadows, as the candle of my minds eye wavered, yielding barely flickering light for me to see the stream of my consciousness. I pushed away worrying thoughts attempting to penetrate my ease. It rained, hard, with thick dense drops upon the disturbed, upset night.

The shelter we had found was decent enough. For the time being, we were safe, and so what if we were basted with dirt, which was the only real souvenir of my travels, (as well as some sand that lay trapped in my backpack) at least we were still healthy and young. Sprawled out in my sleeping bag and my backpack tied to me with an alarm string, I sighed empty shallow relief. I sat back comfortable within our temporary abode. My smell as haunting as it was, was ever so powerful and probably only personally attractive. Giving myself a signature purer than most other forms. I could recognize myself anywhere with my eyes closed. All's I needed was my olfactory system to stay strong, hold up and not give in. Only a dog could have spent time smelling me and liked it. But the smell now arose not just from my body, but the bag that I slept in. It was moist and putrefied from the spoiling rain, and also permanently drenched and stained from unending perspiration from intimidating nightmare dreams.

I laid my thin, long, wooden drum, a piece of living life, behind my head as my pillow. I scratched it's head surface through the plastic bag, not petting it, more shaking it's hand, saying, 'Thanks for being my friend', in a respective manner. Apologizing to it however, because it wasn't sitting comfortably in a display case. Content on our situation and comfort, my mind relaxed and drifted long and deep, seeking a deliverance that hopefully I could find from within the recent past.

I Chapter

In my earliest expectations of this particular voyage along with my crew, I had no doubts or worries as to what would come to be. I was traveling with three very adept friends. Three growing men that I could rely on in a tensioned situation, those of which I knew would be many to come our way. A scent of wonder stops short of gainful insight when one knows certain things strongly. So as a rule of thumb, even when I know something to be true, I still question it again, just to make sure I haven't missed anything. I knew if a problem arose we could handle it, but what I didn't know, what worried me, was perhaps I was the only one looking ahead trying to avoid dangers that lay waiting to come upon us. I thought maybe these guys would blindly walk into the trap of a dilemma, and then be forced to deal with it. The trick is to elude hazards, not prevail the source of them. In all honesty though, all of us were alone out here, no matter how much we could rely on each other.

Days full of tremendous pain filled the heart of my most cherished comrade, Jules Shivers. He has an invariable kindness, a natural devotion towards chivalry and sincerity. Perhaps out of all three of them, if he fell back from the end, I would want to stay peacefully and content, there with him. As for Marv and Arlo, they would be forgotten about within their own vices. However, I should say that Marvin wouldn't ever fall prey to defeating circumstances, it was questionless. He is more powerful than the baby of a sorcerer bred from the rapaciousness of a pack of wild stallions on the mountain of the divine. So if he ever stopped walking with us, it was because he no longer wanted it to be the way it was, which was respectable. Arlo was another story, I would let him suffer.

It would be good for him. He would worry, and if he didn't fold his cards and start whining, he would realize the severity of the circumstances. And if he understood them, which I think he would, then revelations would sing and his eyes would water from joy. So then and only then would he not need or seek to acquire the help of others to learn for himself. But it was not my job to make him comprehend the complexities involved in his self-realization. If he or any of us in this life could not find personal sanctuary, then we suffered the consequences of our own faults. There was not patience enough in our lives at the time to teach a student who could not learn. It was just the rules of the game, and we were all expendable to the winds of chance. Well, I was pretty sure that these guys were old and mature enough so that I wouldn't have to look after them on the road.

Yet still, the mentions from my mind gave rise to concerns that had obvious clarifications; I had no problem thinking more so than not, that I would leave any of them behind if they couldn't make it anymore. Marv felt the same way, he was better at homelessness than even me, and I was pretty much the greatest bum. Hey, they didn't call me *Uncle Lefty* for nothing. This wasn't a vacation we were going on, it was an odyssey to survive our fears. We were expecting to travel across the lands of three different countries with very little money. As soon as we left, I would be unable to worry about what would happen to them. They all chose this for themselves, each personally asking to travel with me. Reality is life and death and I was nobody's mother, nor they mine either. But I loved them, honestly, for being as excited as me about my lifestyle. So as for our voyage, I treated the matter simply.

In life, I had to realize and fulfill my destiny. It hides sultry and forlorn addicting me all the while. Perhaps it truly is suffering I am seeking. Life I tasted with greedy lips upon each and every scene that passed. They say that God helps his children, but I was all by myself in my mind, and the plans read that I was going at the struggle alone. I felt this constant need to beat myself up, and throw myself to the ground, just to see if I would get back up. I enjoy standing on the edge of the cliff of danger, but yet, I worry that I may perhaps throw myself off. Not in a suicidal attempt, but more a stupid anal reflexive spasm. Even though I am afraid of fear, I ran on its path, forcing myself to run faster, allowing my courage its escape, if it will not come with me.

My mind called at me, telling me that I was on the outside of the looking glass, the windows painted yellow to hide what was going on inside from me. White colored guards with electric lime green shoes and blunt black shielded helmets forcing me to a restrained distance. I was and still am, a stranger, even to myself, a true confusion of nature. Maybe on purpose, I don't know, but that's how it is, and this is the story that I was given in life. Experiences sometimes having seemingly little or small consequencing effects, at least consciously, but this journey would forever shape and dominate the will and nature of my future. I knew this for sure. I had been down this road too many times, and actually, I was looking forward to being able to call myself a veteran. I felt stupidly accomplished because of simple expressions; when I put pressure on my left foot, it yielded strain, then victory smiles crossed my face with black and white checkered blood shot eyes. Scars and wounds from the road left granted visions of waked beautiful moments that have been and also those which would soon come to be. I held the stare and wrinkled forehead of a professional upon my face.

This especial adventure started out in Ealing, London, England. The four of us were American students studying abroad at the same school in London. It was the end of finals week and the days were growing hotter with ambulant intentions making us all perspire tasty salted sudation. We'd been spending too much endearing time together while living in London, and it was a fanatical doubtless illusion that the ride we were on would never come to an end. After all, we were young and full of revolution, aspiration, and uncanny dignity. Marvin and I had known each other for years past now, going to the same college in America. The rest of all of us had just met this semester. I had been in London for the full academic year, and Marv had surprised me this last semester by showing up in London to study. He had studied in Rome for the fall semester prior. From what I could gather of it, was that he not only took the classes, he lived them as an experience. The art, architecture, seen through the daily view of and interaction with the Italian culture turned him into, not necessarily a 'new man', but a better, more dignified and well round '*old* man'. Marv told me he had gotten eighteen credits out of his first semester in Rome and eighteen out of London this semester. It seemed well worth it, the way Marv and I went to college, spending a year studying abroad. And to tell the truth it costs about as much as a regular semester of college at any state school. And you have just as good a chance to fail out and not get any credit, but at least you got to go to Europe. Thus, probably a good idea for any and all child students in an American university. Studying abroad, I would say is the best solution to the limits of institutionalized education. It opens up more than just your mind, it expands the horizons of your boundaries. Both of us talked the whole time that we weren't ever going back to the states. By now, we almost didn't even consider ourselves Americans anymore. This spring semester of study, we had met up and lived with some very unique characters. There was about eleven of us who lived in this one house, and I don't really have the time to talk about that ordeal now, but perhaps another time. The Spring semester of school had ended, it was early May, 1997. Summer vacation in Europe, it sounded like a thing only money could afford. Tourists were coming into London by the boatloads already.

I got out of a bed, damp and stained with rapture, early in the afternoon on the day of our departure. Some of my housemates had already left for their travels. But there was still a good few of us lingering around, about eight of us, most likely unwanted there by the landlord of the house. I was doing some last minute rearranging in my bag, still with my eyes closed tired, while Cherissa lay naked, breathing softly in the bed we both slept in. I was going to miss her, but I couldn't afford to let myself regret leaving her. I stopped myself from taking her love one last time, I turned from looking at her, crushed, wondering what was wrong with me emotionally. Sensitivity lacked itself within me, there was no deep feeling that I could find intimately for her. What was it about her that I could not love? Was it me? Indifference slapped me in the face rudely. Other matters came to mind. I had places to go, and people to see, and the world called me into its sea of destiny. I heard her rustle and wake as I scampered downstairs, testing out the weight of my bag.

I found Jules sitting still, in a slouch, on the sofa in the living room waiting for me. He was vibrant, with the taste of unknown excitement written all over his face, anticipation making him shake and shiver. It seemed like he had been there all night, watching, making sure I hadn't slipped out late in the darkness of the moon, by myself. "Jules, what are you doin'? Waitin' for me?" cynicism clasping to the words, "Or have you been guarding the house for intruders, not escapees?"

He laughed, "Ha, ha, ha…Something like that."

"Don't you know that if I crept out in the middle of the night like an Arab, I would have grabbed at least you?" He nodded his head, unsure and serious. I exclaimed with expression and sound, "What?"

"I can never be too sure, especially the way your mind works Welton. Ideas changing directions quicker than the process it takes to think them up!" His face betrayed his emotions. He looked at me trying to see if I could see his enervate nature. The right side of his mouth quivered, perhaps from a momentary nervous tic.

"MAN, I know-" taking the time to exaggerate the upcoming words, "*FOR SURE,* solidly, that I would have grabbed you. Shit, that'd be like leaving without my clown gear and Pablo." He made me feel such anguish. It had been long since I had known the feeling of caring so deeply.

"Yeah that's what you say now, but I know how you get, you know, Cherissa nagging you about going with us, and how you don't like to say good-bye and all, some times you leave the most important things behind when you're in a furious rush."

"Hey, shit does get lost brother, like that fucking pawn that day in the park, right?"

"Ha ha, I know right, Marv looked for it for like a fuckin hour, swearing up and down the whole time saying he'd almost found it."

"Man I accepted its fate when I realized it was just a pawn, it could be replaced with a bottle cap."

He said with a frown, "Yeah but it's a shame to lose a piece from such a nice set," knowing that some of those pieces were made by his hands too.

"I know, and to tell you the truth, it's not really Marvs' style to go losin' shit like that, but what are you gonna do." Saying it knowing that it was a piece that I had made that Marv had lost.

"How about go to France?" and the question lingered, coming off his lips from no where, it took me by surprise. I skipped a breath.

"Oh, Siiiiiiccckkk, France! Sure, I'd love to!" I yelped. Thinking for sure he meant the film festival.

Smiles, joy, and laughter came out all in one, "Ah ha ha! He he he he he, man…" as he put his backpack on. We stood growing strength together. It was quiet in the house, held in behind blacked out windows. Not even the colored light bulbs hummed their listless, repetitious dissonance. It was apparent that Marv and Arlo, and some of the remaining girls were not in the house, most likely at school tying up loose ends. The awkwardness of it all finally making me realize the strength of the moment. I looked at Jules, completely astounding he is to look at, I smiled as he pulled a little ball of hash out of his pocket. He wrinkled his face, suggesting that I should roll up a joint. We stood facing each other, like looking in the mirror I coveted his advocacy. We stood silent for a good while, barely breathing. He then walked over, with a step of morning excitement to the steps and called up to Suzette and Cherissa upstairs. He hadn't slept at all last night I thought. The girls were barely roused, and still unpacked, leaving it all to the very last minute. I rolled up the hash and started smoking it, getting the smoke all over me, then I passed it on to Jules who accepted it willingly. Eventually, as we stood waiting, like usual, the girls ran down, through a cloud of confusion; dense, more so than the hash smoke had created. Pieces of luggage falling out of Suzette's hands, tumbling down, leading the way to the front door.

"Oops, oh sorry, oh Welton, hmm, wait! I'll just be one more second-" as she turned around and ran back up the stairs, passing Cherissa, who was strutting downward full of cat passion, dividing the distance between us with a cold sharpened unseen claw. She didn't even look at me as she walk on passed toward and out the door. She sat on the step and lit a cigarette, she kept her backpack on, and I could barely see her behind it. She was definitely waiting for me to go out there, but I didn't. I stood frozen, as if I was waiting for Suzette, I looked up the steps. Jules didn't say a thing.

Finally I said, "Come on Suzette, we gotta go."

"I'm coming," She yelled back from her room, "I just gotta get my hair dryer and oh, did I pack my iron?" I heard her stop to wonder, breaking up the commotion of her ruckus. "Hey, Jules, can you check to see if I packed my iron in my bag?" She yelled louder. "I'm going to need that." We heard

19

the nature of a high maintenance women coming out of her. Jules grinned and shook his head.

"Yeah, its in there," Not even really checking, but knowing she wouldn't have forgotten it.

Sitting there, standing, I realized that we were never again to come back to this house. This would soon all be a part of the past. There was no time for nostalgia. God forbid the landlord should show up right now. Inward qualms gave me a nervous feeling in my stomach.

"Come on Suzette!" I screamed with overtaking spastic physical emphasis, my left hand going up then shaking, as I jerked to one side, my backpack pushing me further into a lean.

She came back down the steps with two more smaller pieces of luggage. Jules the gentleman that he is, helped her with her stuff as he escorted her to the door.

"OK, Gee, I hope I haven't forgotten anything?"

"Oh, man!" I cried. She was fussed and it agitated me, so I said, "Let me just double check then." Actually it was more like triple checking. I rushed through the house looking at everything, making sure it was nothing important. Nothing else was coming with us. Clandestinely, at the door, I threw the keys in the house and shut the door on the dense odors of our most recent past. Walking quickly, excited, yet still groggy, I wiped the cold out of my eyes. Although they were not traveling with us, the girls weren't going back to America just quite yet. Cherissa followed from far back, as I led the way, speeding to Jay's house up the street. Jules and Suzette stumbled along between us, like a common clutter of junk mixed in with pretty colored fabric. Fortunately, we were able to leave our excess luggage and living oddities from the past couple of months, at Jerome's house, in his garage, while we traveled for the next couple of days, weeks, or months.

He lived with his parents and two sisters. His whole family was beautiful, each in their own way. They were of an ancient blood, a noble family, who's fidelity and allegiance to the heritage shown brightly through the gallantry of highly dignified characteristics, and complete respect for their ancestry. Jerome was from South Africa, but he had lived and been to so many different places. They all spoke about six or seven different languages, but they usually spoke to each other in French. He was tall, lean, blonde, and very sincere. Jerome was dedicated blindly to anyone he befriended. Solid was he in his acceptance of your friendship. He was a friend of the house, and of all of us personally and individually. Days would pass, not even attempting to lead toward our separation from each other during the past couple of months. We had the love of devoted intensity for each other, for those of whom spent time in our house, and now it was over. There was no going back. Aside from Jerome and some other friends, there wasn't really a great longing to remain.

In Jerome's garage, Jules and I double-checked the things that we wouldn't be taking on our travels, making sure we didn't need anything else with us. There, we said our good-byes to him. He endowed upon us, the wellness of a blessing, and anticipated our return. We knew the next time we'd see Jerome, we would have tales of grandeur from our voyage. Blonde brilliance shone out of his eyes as he cast our predetermined fate upon us, "Gentlemen, and you are dignified in the reserves of the term gentlemen-be that as it may, shall you go peacefully, and gently into your awaiting discovery."

The girls stood in awe of his kindness. They were probably going to stay at Jay's for a day or two. Truthfully, only Jules attempted to muster out some simple words, which should have been verses of poetry that he and I transcribed throughout the night in expectance of this departure scene. Staring blankly, Shivers mumbled under his breath that he loved him, but Jerome cut him off putting his arm around Jules and walked him out laughingly. The girls and I processed behind them, taking in the perfume of the glory of what the moment instilled.

Jerome was excited for us, more so than we were. I was glad to have known a man like him in my life. Some men really were good and just in this world. It was nice to know that a good person actually thought me to be someone worth caring about. There was so much about Jerome to love and envy. One day, he had exchanged a story with me about the rainfalls in South Africa, and how when he was little, he and his very attractive sisters used to shower outside in the warm wet storms of nature. My imagination soared at the thought of his sisters, all wet, standing outside naked in the rains of the dry barren lands of South Africa, covered in soap. The way he told it, with his debonair accent and his appealing staring eyes, made you feel like you were reading it directly out of the bible, and that that was what heaven was like. Jerome was a firm person, with duty and a strong sense of responsibility. He was tied up with some family obligations that summer, or he would have traveled with us for sure.

Finally through unnoticed and inevitable dry tears, Jules, truly entrusted with emotional charisma said, "Jerome, you better be good, because the Devil watches out, looking to recruit people like you!" We all laughed, Jerome a bit more sinister than the rest of us, probably having had similar types of conversations with the devil already. Hugs embraced, with a kind smile, Jerome let us go into the adventures ahead of us.

A long slim delicate finger pointed in the air ahead of his next statement, wagging at us, "Wish well upon the others who join you boys along the way, and keep an eye out for Mr. Arlo Beezley. A bit with reckless knavery is his attempt to hold his cards out of sight from his opponent's eyes!"

Sun came down with potent blinding rays, brighter in front of our steps. Bold, with our travel gear strapped to us, the party girls following on our heels, we headed to school to make our final closing statements.

"See you later Jay?" Suzette questioned, wondering if it was ok to stay with him tonight.

"Yes, invite all the beautiful women that these boys have left behind!" Smirking with a weird smile and eyes that implied an orgy with honeydew juice.

Cherissa didn't say anything, but all she really needed to get a message across was a swing from her hips and a slant in her lean. Her torso suggesting wildly, such body language lust. Wow, I had to get to school, hopefully, Marv and Arlo would be there waiting for us.

I wanted to get out of England. I had been there for too long already. Toward the end, the perspective of London that I was perceiving was basically nothing but school. I was burning out of studying and perhaps blaming London for the bitter taste that was growing from my assiduousness. School was incongruous to my realm, it was no longer in need of any attention. I got all my credits and then some. It was nice to have a clean exit out. My grades were perfect. I was and am a dedicated student, obliging responsibility when needed. I had no need to worry about slacking off that past semester, which is an accomplishment in itself, I had completed a successful semester. Hard was the decisions' to go study, when all were playing in an enticing sandbox, but I persevered. I now could go roam, and have fun this summer, without feeling the crushing guilt of not deserving it. Most of the other Americans were walking out of the study abroad experience with maybe six credits of electives. Not me, I earned above average grades doing top level coursework in psychology and English literature. Julian on the other hand, a dedicated student of sorts was only getting three of the credits he had signed up for. He stopped going to all his classes, and only corresponded with our English lit professor, Jonny O. He was writing something and toward the end of the semester, he started locking himself in, on the third floor of the house and set forth with tremendous determined demeanor to finish what it was that he was writing. He kept reassuring everyone, even himself that he was going to get more than just credit for what he was writing. Aside from him, most of the other students, including the girls that lived in our house spent time travelling further through in Europe instead of going to class, but that's better than sleeping off a hang over in your dorm room in the states. Ah, school was out for summer, and we were in Europe, a far and away place. It was such a cliché, especially noticeable when I looked around at the college, at the other American students with their backpacks and Euro-rail tickets.

Most students were now going traveling. Everyone was going somewhere. They would become, or attempt to successfully fill the role of backpackers. What mystery lay ahead of us all. At school that day, an American had all his stuff stolen. I heard stories like this all the time from other Americans traveling in Europe. It was typical for those who didn't really understand the road that travels to be taken of their property, and perhaps if they were unlucky, their dignity and will as well. One had to be careful in foreign lands amongst the other trespassers. Like children they were, running around checking and rechecking their Euro-rail tickets, and queuing up to phone away for hostel reservations.

Everybody asking where everybody else was going, "Where are *you* off to?" A direct question from a rich suburban queen aimed at a simple boy.

Shyly, the poor Alabama kid said, "Well, um, I-I'm goin up to-" The princess heir wasn't waiting for an answer, She merely just waited 5 seconds before she spoke again. She started blurting. She might as well have been talking on the phone. Her destination triumphed all scenarios.

Oh, gee, that's nice, *but*, I'm going to spend a week in Paris, I don't know, perhaps I'll stay in the hotels, I have to see, After all, I don't know if I could spend the whole week with Lancia at his estate, we'll see." The boy was frozen, unsure how to react. He felt lame and it showed in his posture. "And plus, if I stay in the hotel, I'll be closer to the stores, and I have to shop, I barely have any cloths!" Her proud confidence, false as it was, was no match for his humble ignorance and modesty. He stood clueless to her gibber, glad that his baseball cap wasn't getting blown off his head from her wind. I think he was just happy to stare at her body from such a close personal space. Both of them, so different, yet both still stereotyped as Americans.

Aside from my advisor/ Literature professor, Jonny O, I didn't really talk to or say goodbye to anyone of the other Americans or European students at school. Besides, I had already said goodbye to good friends, Europeans I had met, most of whom had left school or maybe even London the past couple of days prior. I would probably never see any of them again, oh well, I guess. After finishing off briefly with Jonny O, Jules giving him a huge hug, we went to the coffee shop. On the sidewalk patio of the café, at our table, Marv was sitting there telling a story. Vivid and descriptive was he, it was more of a poem being recited than conversation. Arlo was nodding his head up and down, smiling. He had one arm around partygirl #3, Natalia. What beautiful women we surrounded ourselves with. It was nice, I mean these girls were even attractive morally and mentally. Natalia seemed more interested in Marv's story than Arlo's sexual passes with his other hand underneath the table. Later, she would look at a bruise that had formed on her thigh, because of how rough he was and also because she has such soft delicate skin and tender meat on her bones. We walked up, Marv's back was toward us, and Lesley our fourth party girl sat sideways on his right with her hands in his lap, and her legs over his. Her hands were visible, and stroking him softly. Twirling his leg hair instead of her own curly orange hair.

The boys' backpacks' were at their feet ready to go. We were in the sun of an almost ending day. Fun was at the beginning of every thought. Adrenaline and excitement insulting my devastation, practically curing my hunger. Adventure themed in and out of it's frequency. Static raised the hairs on the nape of my neck. Sweat trickled and danced along my beading forehead. A crescendo arose in Marv's song as he felt us behind him "and I was lookin up at the comet, it moved in the sky, alive… the moon was on fire. Fog and smoke surrounding the light, Yeah, juggling fire, man, *IT* was the moment. The beach shining from the glimmer, and the lightning changing colors along this dense pale horizon. Splashes of red and green, encased in white smoke burning out of the heat, it was beautiful, ahh ha ha ha."

"We got a picture of that night," Jules said, breaking in. Saying nothing more, knowing he didn't have to say how truly beautiful those moments were.

There were seconds of silence. Marv should've finished the rest of the story. I waited just enough seconds. Obviously, he wasn't going to so I spoke up, "Yeah, oh man, Yes! That was cool man," with high and well hidden sarcasm, then my posture changed, I slouched low, ready to leap, throwing up an arm and some hand signs, "but did you forget about the storm comin through and the tide rising…the *flood*? And we had to dig a cave in one of the back sides of the sand banks and wrap ourselves in our sleeping bags, our backpacks and the tarp covering us to survive the night."

"Shit, I was just getting to that part, man. Jules went to sleep standin up in that outhouse, remember? There was only room for two of us in the cave! Ah ha ha ha."

Arlo laughed it up, "Ah he he he he ha ha. That sucks."

"It's because the cave fell apart and the flood tried to take my guitar downstream… so I rolled the scene."

"Jules man, you should have tied it to you that night!"

"Yeah…Hah, great." I was becoming so cynical in London.

We all sat down, Cherissa grabbing Natalia to tell her something important, and saving her from Arlo's grasp. The owner of the café brought us out free cappuccinos. It was nice of her, She knew we were leaving, and after all we were regulars, maybe we were a regular pain in the ass, but we did spend some of what little money we had there. And we could have spent that down the street, and not at her shop. Also, she liked us, because our presence brought other business there. I looked at the four of us; men, through the talks, yells, women, and daydream wine, a long hard stare at each of them, merriment in the air, fragmented seconds went by in fractions. I felt the sweat beading up on my forehead. At the end of this odyssey, I would look at them again, but I knew it would be different and much older men that I would be looking at. Ah, were we all willing to accept it? It was too much to hold back the tears. I looked away into the distance. Life is so hard to accept sometimes, it makes me feel something, but it doesn't describe itself to me, what it is that I feel. I looked back to my people, and Cherissa was staring at me, blowing smoke at me from a deep sensuous drag of Natalia's cigarette. She saw that I was crying, I saw then an amazing beauty in her eyes, a tear rolled down her cheek. I cried harder in my mind, and my eyes swelled up. It became silent, as everyone felt the passion of what was to come to be.

Instantly, Arlo, who was the best of us at getting excited publicly, initiated the move onward, but he did so with body language, keeping a firm grasp with his teeth, on his tongue, because it was dying to speak. He jumped down to his backpack and ruffled around, pretending to look for something. "I wanna just make sure I got..." and his head bent down further to inspect, under the table, "Oh," and then you could hear lavish breathing, "Ok, got it!" I think he was licking Natalia's leg, but her express didn't change to show any differentiation in her feelings. He came up smiling, zipping his bag up, looking at me. "Yeah, I think we're ready to go." He said, his whole face was a smirk.

The girls started crying, one by one. Tears said their good byes. Suzette grabbed Lesley for sympathy. It brought unwanted tears to her face. She reached over and grabbed Marv. He kissed her neck, while stroking Suzette's hair. Then we all got up to gather the proper space. Hugs embraced our women with manly tuffness, saying we'd all keep in touch. We put our bags on. Marv was tapping away, playing light beats on my drum, which he had brought with him; another piece of the equipment. Cherissa came over, she didn't hesitate to cry in my arms. We didn't speak. Her love almost knocked me over, and we almost fell together, my backpack pulling us down under the force of gravity. Her craving heart seeped out as I kissed her, tasting and loving her tongue and her tears soiled the saliva on our lips. I wasn't going to miss her, I thought. But I loved her, in someway, in somehow. I smiled. It made her smile.

"Mcmanis?" Came a chirp from a pigeon dove. Deep desiring eyes peeped out at me through sad tears. But I did not have it, what it was that she was looking for.

"Shhh, don't say anything," I tried to sound confident. "There's no room for words." Rather I probably showed my true weak self. That's most likely why she loved me. Women, who understands them? It was blinding to look up, the sun must have been at its peak. I had a feeling that I'd see Cherissa again. She and her mates were determined. They knew at the time that they would soon be traveling with secretive desire throughout the night to catch up with us in Cannes, France. So why all the tears? For outward display, of course. But we lapped it up, why not? It made us feel more attractive about ourselves. But about five minutes of standing around saying good-bye was making me impatient. I finished off my cappuccino as everyone was putting closure on their little culminative rituals.

Destination calling with lunatic cravings scratching at my ego hid behind maintained control of a calm bored look as I said out loud to every one, "Well Julian, their waiting for you at the film festival". After all, it was his idea to go there. He looked up as he was finishing writing something for Suzette, he winked with smiling ecstasy coming out of his pores then returned his attention to his pen. I glowed without saying anything more, taking it all in.

"Yeah baby!" Arlo couldn't hide his excitement. Why was he so excited, I thought? What were we doing going to a film festival? We didn't have a script to sell, and Arlo was acting as if we already sold one and we were meeting up with our agents. If anything only Jules was actually going to come out of this with some sort of hope or at least a realization, he was the one who had something well written, that was worth looking at, besides his beautiful face. And here we all were, being egged on by Arlo, thinking that we were going to walk up and someone was gonna think that we were the next supermodel or world actor. It was wrong to condescend and deceive ourselves, but we provoked the thought that we would be accepting an award that evening. It was mad and the desperation of the idea would let us down, depressingly, in a sad moment of the evening on the night of the awards. It was inevitable, after all, we were going to, not a costume party but a masquerade, as bums. Who invited the bums? They would say, in regards to us. Regardless, Marv and I were indifferent as to where we could have went, anywhere South, and eventually, definitely Spain. And if Jules was going to Cannes for whatever reason, then we sort of felt obliged to get him there. And besides, we didn't have anything else to do. Why not hang with Mr. Shivers, he's the best guy I've met in a while.

Arlo, on the other hand, who at that time was being referred to as 'The Sloth', was fortunate we let him travel with us. It had been a simple conversation between Marv and I one day in the back yard of the house we had lived in that semester, just prior to the end of school. Marv was standing, almost hovering, looking, and exploring the horizon. I walked outside half drunk and barefoot to ask him what was going to happen when school let out. Not even glancing over to look at me, he told me to pack, then he said with an uncertain waiver, "You know, Arlo could come in handy along the road".

"Oh, 'The Sloth'?" I mimicked. I really didn't see how, but I knew better than to question his foresight, so I agreed, "What ever". As I was walking away with my back toward him, I told him, "and I'm already packed." Then I stopped to turn around to tell him my next thought. I said greedily laughing but comically laying responsibility, "Yes but *you'll* have to carry him then, if he gets tired and can't make it anymore." He didn't even stop what he was doing or thinking about.

I didn't wait for a response because I knew Mr. Ellowin wasn't going to give me one on the subject. He too would leave Beezley along the way if he had to, but I bet he would leave him more comfortably situated than I would have. At the café I was watching Arlo, recalling that moment in which we decided his fate. He was whispering into Leslie's ear. Probably something along the lines of, 'I'll come visit you in Florida when I get back to the states, baby'. She was chewing on her necklace, wishing it was gum so she could blow a big bubble in his face that would force him to take a step back from his awkwardly close distance to her. I worked the conversation about bringing him on the road with us over in my mind. He had never in his life slept on the streets before. Was he absolutely sure he knew what he was getting himself into? Did he really think about it? He had chosen this, willing to learn the ways of the beatniks and the hobos'. Did he fully know what in all of plausibility could arise? Would his attempt to behest his might to deal with an emergency lead with a feeble intensity? I was hoping that he could adapt quickly, because this wasn't going to be the kind of environment where any of us could afford to baby-sit someone, let alone teach him the tricks of the trade. From knowing him the past couple of months, I wasn't exactly sure. But I was willing to take the chance, even though I knew it was more difficult to travel in larger numbers, at least he would bring relief, with his sense of convivial and facetious wit to situations fraught with desperation. We would soon see.

In the midst of my thoughts, we rechecked all the gear we had attached to ourselves, making sure all was secure. And there was much, with the musical instruments and performance pieces that we carried. There was not left, any room for the weight of needless extra ware, such as underwear, shirts or pants. Not even an extra sock. Besides, there was no need, for I walked this trip and many before, in the comfort of well worn, but re-sewn and strapped flip-flops, feet exposed to the air. This foot apparel, when I had come across them, weren't in any way or shape, accustomed to the ordeals of use that I would put them through. After considerable amendments to their structure, they were ready for the road. I should have become a Shoemaker, it was and is something I am fond of; footwear. In these flip-flops which now could be called all-terrain sandals, I bounced, jumped, and glided, not losing any of the agility of my acrobatic sense of movement. Ahh, a hint of my old circus days came crawling through my veins, rushing, like what it must be like, the initial rush of heroin. Euphoria, sweltered by the sadness of the color blue causing me to ride it's wave in my mind.

Cherissa broke in on my thoughts, curled into Arlo's hips, rubbing up against each other, like cats, she looked over to get my attention. But it was her words that broke me out of my wandering stare into my mind. "So when do you guys think you'll be in Cannes?" Looking directly at me. A languish posture and seductive glance accompanying the words from her lips.

I turned in, still unfocused and said in a daze, "What?"

She was looking at me for an answer, but not from the question, but from some jealousy that she thought that I would have when I saw her clung onto Arlo.

He had to speak up, bouncing yet still holding on to her, gaining strength and confidence, "Shit, if we really wanted to, we could be there tonight, VIP service all along the way!" Not even stopping for a pause but still nodding his head, "But we're gonna take our time making the run, you know, enjoy ourselves a little, *Yeah*!" He kept nodding his head, but only once every four or five seconds. Holding his breath, or his smile would have deflated.

I shifted my eyes to my girlfriend, but before I could say anything aloud to Cherissa, like; I love making love to you, Marv spoke up, "Awe well," exasperating, "You think it's gonna be that easy getting through *France*," and his tone was more than patronizing on all his words, "with *No* money?" He laughed loud, probably remembering the time he peed on the French soil from eight thousand feet, out of the open door of that noisy little single engine clunker we had caught a cramped ride on, with that thin bony, whisker of a guy named Pierre, to London from Spain. Man, did he really have it then, the full might of his power, ready to jump out, if he had heard his voice telling him to; for he knew that he would have hovered and glided to the boring safety of the ground.

"Hey if we really need it, I have some cash stashed away!" He drew his right eye lids together, and wrinkled both his lips upward, not quite giving a wink or a smile. Proud, knowing he was in possession of something so solid, with the gal of a financial investor with strong American currency.

"Man, you really come prepared don't you Arlo?" I said, letting it sink in a bit.

As he said with a lisp quickly, "Hey, I'm just glad I can look after my boys properly!"

I hit him with some cynicism, "You should be gladder that we're looking out for you, like when you finally decided to take Marv's advice, and you went and got that sleeping bag. That's something that's more important than money on this road."

"Yeah, Sloth, you know, if you were really looking out for us, you wouldn't go hittin' on our girlfriends the moment we leave the room!" Jules shouted at him.

My body stopped dead. "Damn!" I let out. I was totally taken aback, My face moved longly, rolling on my neck. I couldn't believe Jules had said that, "Ha-ha!" I laughed in a sentence.

"Alright you guys," Suzette nervously bellowed with uncertainty, giving and catching glances with Cherissa.

Jules started laughing, blowing it off like a joke, just busting on 'The Sloth'. He leaned through our crowd and punched Arlo's backpack, making him swivel about seventy-eight degrees, knocking Cherissa, almost out of his arms. Jules knew that Arlo got shot down by Suzette, in a friendly way, at least once a day. Arlo leaned back into our circle, still wrapped into Cherissa, and she wasn't letting go of him. I had known, as soon as it had happened, that they had had some sort of sexual encounter behind my back, several months ago. It was only once, and apparently, Arlo must not have been as good a lover as I, not that I'm that good, I just don't think that he tasted all of her lips fully with his tongue, that's all. Me, I love to cover myself with the lustful juice and passionate sweat from a beautiful girl, becoming a part of her. So I didn't care what had happened between them, because she never went back to him, although he had persisted afterwards. I passed the buck. I looked over to Marv, but still while looking at Cherissa out of the corner of my eye, "Anyway, Marv, anything else we gotta do in London?" I asked, trying to look sharply, as the heal of my foot starting having a spasm; the moment was on.

"I gotta make one stop." Jules broke in as Marv was nodding no.

"Well ok then, that's no problem!" And with no maps or understanding how, we left; walking, bitten by wanderlust, not even knowing really, how to get where we were going. A simmering silence fell. Tears, chuckles, and sniffles filled the faces of our bearing women. It was fairly easy to leave, saying goodbye was the hard part. Not one of us looked back as we inched our way along, slowly. Careful not to lay prints in our thickened remains. My eyes drew to Jules, who was ahead of me. Ah, to look upon him was to enter a world, so hard to reach, so full of helpless passion, more depth than romance could ever be. What a prize he is to be traveling with I thought; an accolade notion from all that feel his touch from mere eye contact. He walked on coldly, business matter like. Marv walked in the whisper of his shadow, with a mellow delighted foot. No harm ever daring to lay into his grasp. It sounded quiet, silence filled the air around us. I couldn't even hear the streets talking its' murmur. Even Beezley became overtly small. All of our emotions were perhaps blanketed with inhibitedness, because of all the excitement of one day. We were just sort of taking it all in, the moment feeling more intense because of our respect for it. We were not in any awe of our future. Nothing could have happened that could have seemed like a surprise.

Sitting on a bench in the center of the town, a not quite obese homeless woman with elderly white ragged hair, was peeing with her pants down around her ankles as if she was on the toilet. Her head was bent over so I couldn't see her face, and she was laughing in a dirty drunken fashion, lolling her head. Like a black cat crossing our path, we stepped over the fresh flow of urine dripping and streaming on the slanted slate sidewalk, heading toward the street gutter. Was this an omen, I thought? A foresight of what was to come to be? Marv, with an extraordinary hold on the comfort of our aura, probably considered this to be good luck. After we passed her, the poor decrepit woman started talking to herself, almost crying. Definitely unusual, but we treated the situation as if it was an everyday occurrence, which was worth taking for granted, we kept walking, minding our own business. When we reached far up ahead and turned the corner, the party girls absorbed in the distance, still standing there looking at us, unmoved, Arlo gave a quick glance rearward. He had a creepy smile, yet his eyes seemed full of ignorant mirth. It was a fruitless attempt at nostalgia, as if he would one day recall with happy tears this great moment in his young life. Then he noticed me watching him, and tried to cover it up with some bawking. He sped up and started bouncing with joy, saying. "Yeah, oh yeah," swaying his head, clasping his hands together and turning them, massaging them in a mischievous burglar sort of way. He was thinking in his heart that he was important, well then, so he was.

We walked into the Ealing Broadway Tube Station, a suburb of London, England. A nice quaint, but busy place, where the end of the work day held the greatest hours of the day. It was when everybody went to the Pub for one. Yeah right, it was never just one. But that's what everybody would say, 'Hey, I'm goin to the 'Pub' for one, Yeah?' Saying it as if they meant it no matter what or if you'd respond, but putting the 'Yeah' on the end, therefore asking you the question. Kind of like; Ealing was apparently an old movie industry town for England, Yeah? And like, it went belly up, right? But its bin' getting busier around here Yeah? With all these Americans pourin in n' spendin cash, Yeah? That's how some Turkish colored Pakistani who was born an Englishman would say it, in his proper English slang dialect. It's true though about Ealing, there were many aspiring small business running out of rented shops. Mostly real estate agencies with 'flats to let'. Of course, we met with some of them, when shopping for a flat. The agents were either stupid, lacking the information and zeal to sell the property, or they were the sneaky type, looking to scam you and the landlord out of more of both your pounds. Either way, they were nobody you could trust, so when we shopped for a flat, we ended up taking some matters into our own hands, and actually, we acquired a better living arrangement than pretty much everybody else that I knew, even most locals. What can I say, we got a deal that we didn't have to pay for. Stupid English landlord/tenant laws and homeowner laws, set up that were amendable according to ones' interpretation of them. Whatever.

There was always a steady flow of business employees walking in and out of the tube station. Smells of baked goods, reheated, filled the air outside the station where would be beggars, and definitely homeless squatter types sold 'The Big Issue' magazine. This was a magazine that they could buy from the government for like twenty pence and then turn around and sell it to people on the streets for eighty pence, or something to that effect. It was better than having them beg for change, and everybody got something out of it. A pretty good idea I'd say. I was never approached by anyone trying to sell one. They could see it written all over me, that I had less money then them. Well, better yet, they were weary of me from the perspective they got of me from those special mornings, when they found me crouched in a clump with the rest of the trash, at the gates of the Tube station. Passed out, sleeping in some fresh vomit, which could have been mine, most likely, but who knew; I should have been selling their magazine too. While pretty finely gelled gents and ladies came out, off the Tube, and queued up for the bus out side the train station, standing, not wondering if I was dead. It was a busy intersection.

This little town also had a couple of cool nightclubs that I was going to miss. And now we were leaving, not to come back anytime soon. We were heading for the center of London, where even more dazzling nightclubs held my frequent patronage. The dancing scene, going out at night, I was going to miss, London is a fun town at night. The girls, dressed in barely nothing, the dark pulsing bass, strobes of funneled lights, and action for everyone who entered the dance floor. I danced reeking of a freakish nature. I always managed to gain space on the floor, no matter how crowded it got. And you didn't even need to be on ecstasy to feel high. Although everybody was. It didn't matter or bother me. I just don't do it, and I bet I've gotten higher than most of the junkie hustlers who hung around, spinning to the feeling of music crawling upon them. Ah, London, what a great party town. And it's not true, that the city closes at 11:00 o'clock at night. The Pubs may close, but the clubs stay open, sometimes well into the morning, if there were a lot of people still there, which there usually were.

I'm definitely going to spend more time in London, I thought. One day perhaps, when I was older and more mature. Wow, I looked over at Jules. He seamed like a dog with its ears up, alert. He wanted to get strings for his guitar somewhere in Soho. I didn't even think about getting a train pass. In London, we were the only Americans that I knew that got away with it, almost unconsciously. Arlo, slowed down and let me go ahead, wondering what to do. I walked by the guard putting my hand up, flashing a joker from a deck of cards, real casual like. He didn't even acknowledge me. He was tired and he wanted to go home. On the platform, we all waited silently for the Tube. Tensions and nerves were wrestling among us all. Such curious excitement, did my anxiety stir. Our ride was literally, starting. The Tube arrived, shaking slowly to an idle, yet still moving forward. All the waiting passengers unconsciously moved towards where they knew from everyday experience with Ealing Broadway's peculiarities, where the train doors would be when the train finally stopped. Blaring voices mixed in unison from all the train authorities on the platform, "Mind The Gap! Mind The Gap!" A tourist was probably buying a T-shirt with this statement on it right now, somewhere in London. A little pudgy Arabic man with a rough accent was running around, pacing with quicker upper body motions than his little legs could move him, he looked like he was revving up. His energy shifted the crowd, and along with the vibrations from the train on the ground, coming through from my feet, it made my anxiety shoot through me, making my eyes bulge.

We got on the tube, letting all the business men, but mostly women, on first. We stood proud, instantly I was convalesced from the disease of my fear. The four of us stood facing each other in front of the doors. I looked at Jules and he smiled, then he looked at Marv and laughed. The excitement turned a bit to buffoonery as we haggled Arlo. "Are you ready to go Sloth?"

"Hell yeah! We just gotta pick up some booze, I'm out." As he pulled the pint of gin out of his pocket and finished off the last shot.

"No problem yeah." I said as we started to move. I jerked to lean into the motion. We were on our way. Beautiful songs sang in my head. The moment was bright and clear, swirling more from the wind of our joy, than the jumpy buzzing movement of the train.

We stood out among the English working class. Even if their gazes and bewildered looks crushed our courage, we did not show it. For we held our selves high and proud. And although our excitement level was up, we managed to maintain and act in a reserved and polite fashion. However, this could only last so long. The Tube was getting more and more crowded as we approached the center of London. It smelled potently from perspiration and body odor. The smell of us, thickened from tarred spoils upon us, meshed in, at least a little and disguised itself amongst the body odor scent of corporate perspiration of the English working class. If you must know the truth, the reason we, or at least I smelled so bad from the beginning of our journey, was that the water had been mysteriously shut off by an unknown source for an unknown reason in our house for the last week before we left. It wasn't a problem any way, the shower had been broken for a while, and I was used to those kinds of living situations. Anyway, usually nobody talks to each other on the tube. English people are very cordial at face value, but they usually don't engage anyone they don't know in extraverted conversations. The tube vibrated as we moved along not speaking. Loud wisping sounds of the movement of the train flogged out attempts to have polite conversation. One had to speak up and become noticed in order to talk.

We managed to maintain a wide space around us, no one interfered with it, unless we gave some of it up. We had so much gear that we really did need a lot of space. A simple content looking lady who announced to no one in particular that she was from Reading, England looked our way with focused interest. She asked a question that no one took the time to hear, She repeated it louder until Jules looked at her, with his forehead wrinkled curiously into a question implying her to repeat herself again written on his face. She was from far outside of London, and was greedy for some attention. Her kids must have been all grown up, and barely had time to call her. She spoke up and almost rose out of her seat, but the shaking of the tube held her from an attempt at balance. Jules leaned in to her as she asked us if we were first time travelers to London. Jules who was closest to her, not just physically, but with his patience level, told her we were Americans, studying abroad, and were traveling for the summer.

"Oh, really, well uh, you like England then? I can see that you do. Yes, now, You do." She wasn't asking us, she was more telling us.

Jules said with extreme politeness, "Yes madam, we have even gotten out to the countryside's of North England on school trips."

She sat happily reassured and giggled, she was pleased that we were enjoying her culture. With the effect placed heavily on the inquiries of her questions made it seem as if she would have taken it personally if we weren't having a good time in her country. As she got off at her stop, she wished us luck on our travels. All of us held stern smiles on our face yet said nothing. She was expecting something, she hesitated getting off the train, using her time wisely.

Jules bowed his head, I heard music that wasn't even playing outside of my mind, "Mind the gap" spat out of Arlo's dry lips as the doors closed her out. Marv was translucent within the scene, tapping on my drum, which was strapped to me over my shoulder. I turned the volume up in my own little world as we screamed through the tunnels. The tube finally, had reached our stop. Jules led the way out, off the tube. Marv had a slit smile, and a keen sense of wit. He was already spreading out and looking for his avenue of approach. Here in the center of London's underground, you needed a ticket to get out through the tube station turnstiles. Normally it was no problem, but, with all our gear it was going to be hard to skate through unnoticed. Security picked out backpackers as plausible prey. Somewhere up ahead, a Sax was jamming the same song as it had yesterday, and the day before, and so on. It was busy and there was a rush of afternoon tourists, business execs, and doll faced girls. Some walking hurriedly, others drifting along with the current.

Always, you saw someone with a map of London, mostly its underground system, but along with over ground features and information of site whereabouts. I had a brief twang of anxiety thinking that I was going to get caught going through the turnstiles without a ticket. I looked up trying to find my answer. Ahead, an American tourist had his all day pass in a hand with a big improperly refolded, map of London. I noticed the ticket gleaming off the brightness of his gold watch, as he shook his hands and arms up and down, in a complaining fashion. He was wearing sunglasses, he was short and well rounded, plump, and all alone. He had a money belt that was hidden, obviously intended to be concealed but more noticeable than his gold glaring watch. You could tell that he just arrived for the very first time in London, and from the concerned look on his face, he already had the feeling that this trip was a mistake. He had no sumptuous luggage, only a well broken in backpack, that was definitely borrowed from one of his sons. Probably he was trying to resolve a mid-life crises by deciding to throw caution to the wind and do what he should have done when he was younger, he was going to rough it and backpack through Europe. He looked like he was going to give up before he even started and high tail it to a cozy expensive, but worth it in his case, hotel.

He was flustered and was looking at the different corridors which led to different connection platforms and exits. He didn't know which way to go. I could have taken his ticket right out of his hand as I walked by, and diverted his attention, by trying to help him, one American to another. I thought better of it and chose to take my chances without his ticket. Besides, it would have cast bad karma upon the rest of our trip, which was soon going to turn into a devouring crusade. Well, I thought, at least the day ahead of us would have been ethereally soiled, if I robbed him of his ticket out from underground. The security guards would have charged him double the regular fine, threatening to send him to jail if he didn't pay, and they would have gotten away with extorting him too. I would have felt bad for him if that happened, so I didn't take his ticket. Enticing is thievery only for someone with little or no consequence on his mind. I didn't need to deter my plans. And I didn't need to steal his ticket to survive this scene, so I didn't, but I could have, easily. I walked by him silently, not looking at him, forgetting about it.

As we were walking upward, I didn't really have the proper time or focus to scrutinize the exchange Jules had with the Saxophonist as we past him. But I could feel the Saxophonist looking at us with interest. I could hear it in the blows from the horn. The escalators, continuous in their monotonous climb upward, brought us onward. Marv was already through the turnstiles. Man, he was good. I crouched low and got up close to the person in front of me. It was a lengthy man in a stripped business suit with a briefcase, and fragile non-descript glasses. He was reserved with curly styled hair, average height, reading the paper. This guy wore a bowtie regularly. But then again, you could get away with that in England. He noticed the smell that had enveloped his personal space before I actually made contact with him, he looked up questioning what was behind and around him. I pushed him and me with all my gear threw on his ticket.

"Pardon me, Sir!" I said in a full English accent, "Cheers!" as I smiled a devilish smile. I moved ahead of him without thinking about his concerns.

He wasn't going to even ask what happened, he didn't want to get involved, but he checked his back pocket to see if I had mugged him. The Security guards, big black Englishmen with smiles full of boring one line jokes, but searching eyes, were at a distance. They treated this like sport. I imagined that more than a few not even necessarily daring youth attempt to use the public transportation system for free everyday in London. The guards, who would have been successful linemen for American football teams, were thrown off and didn't see me directly make the transition into freedom because Marv had made some commotion after he was through. They wondered though if I had slid a ticket into the turnstile machine as I walked by them. Ha, ha, ha. They fell for that same stupid trick every time. I looked over and Jules was talking and smiling beautifully with an attractive, classy woman, as he was walking up to the sun light. Beezley came up beside me. He got real lucky getting through, but he acted as if he was so cool and suave. We all still think he is a dork.

Up, on the streets, We stood looking for our direction as if it had left us. For a minute, Jules had to gather his bearings as to the whereabouts of the road that sold all of the guitars and the various wares of the music business. He was getting steamed, because he couldn't solve the puzzle. "Hey man, don't get frustrated, Yeah! You need these strings to play, right? I mean, it's not just extras you're looking for, 'cause we can get them in Cannes later."

"No my High E string is broke, shit... I'm tryin' to think..." Stalling, his fuse getting shorter.

"Well, it's ok. Listen, I'm gonna go get some gin. You guys gonna wait here?"

"Yeah. Hey there's a store over there, and get some cigarettes."

"Anything else?" Marv doesn't even smoke cigarettes, but he smokes more hash joints than all of us. "Arlo, you need somethin'?"

"Nope, just the gin. I got plenty of papers."

"Cool, I'll be right back." I took my drum off and handed it over to Marv, who was in the process of sitting down, "Hold this?"

"Sure." He started tapping away, as I walked down the street to get some booze at the spirits shop. I didn't even know how much money I had on me. I started thinking about the guy who was playing the Sax in the tube station. He looked at us as we were walking by in the movement upward on the platform in between the escalators. We were heavy with gear, pulling it up the hill out from the underground. Arlo at the time was giving light taps on his drum as he let the escalator move him. Looking back, I felt as though the saxman almost wanted to stop and take some money out of his case and hand it to us. But Jules, of course, beat him to it, and dropped a pound and some pence into his case. His sax flared and tweaked along with the beat from Arlo's drum. It was apparent, not only that we were in the same line of work as he, but we worked on the same level within the business. People like us, street performers, were officially referred to as buskers. Now, as I write this, I sit and wonder if he is still there, playing song for all the regular faces of the Tube station traffic, busking for his living.

Not that that is all you do if you're a busker, I mean, most other buskers I had met while living and busking in London had other jobs of various curiosities as well. They did it not only for money, but for the thrill of the impromptu performance you need to have while working on the streets. There is, in many cases a necessary need to involve the people walking by. You needed to have a lot of zeal, earnestness, and a lot of comical yet highly skilled ability to perform and interact in a show, if you were going to get someone to give you money on the streets. It was a lifestyle that most others, secretly envied, wishing that they were humble enough to perform street theater. You could see it in peoples' faces as they walked by pitching pence into your hat, when you were busking. But because of how certain lights are cast, they would not be able to maintain their elegant stature within society, being labeled a street busker, so most hold back and live behind the fear of igniting their passions. Not that buskers are low-class people, you just didn't find any explicitly rich folks performing on the streets for pence.

"Big Issue!" Coughing, sounding old, "Getch ya 'Big Issue!" I heard consistently from a ruff gent. It was a busy time for street and pedestrian traffic, a good time to busk. Lots of different people were walking about, tourists, families, but mostly execs in suits. All unfamiliar people, but I bet the boys and girls in suits probably walked by each other everyday. I walked into this opened up façade of a store. I squeezed through this tight short isle of candybar shelves and postcard racks. I looked over the shelves behind this hairless meaty guy with a striped shirt, half unbuttoned, showing off a sweat stained white undershirt. He was holding onto a stubbed out cigar in between fat but long fingers of his right hand.

"How much is that pint of gin?"

He looked me over, judging a price. He must have been Moroccan, from a line of peddlers. "Eleven pounds."

I didn't even change the expression on my face. Things were always too expensive in the center of London. "You know, I'm no tourist." I didn't say anything else. I stared at him harder with a cold, deliberate glance, my eyes unmoved, forcing him to get nervous. I tried to seem like I was about to rob him if he didn't come down a bit in his price. I wasn't going to let this guy schiester me. I waited, not deflating. Seconds went buy, and I could see him start to fold. He exhaled.

"Ol'right then, seven pound fifty, then." He was shocked at what he had just said, shooting so low. I pulled out the pence in my pocket. He started moving side to side on his feet. I looked down at my hands below the counter, not letting him see what I had. It was only about three pounds.

"How much for those camel cigarettes?"

"Ff-Three pound ten." He was about to say five pounds, I looked at him shaking my head up and down, with the patrony of an officer letting someone go with a warning.

"Hold on a sec." I looked quizzically to the right, and turned around and shot through the isle spinning the postcards on the stand. I needed some money. I wondered how quickly I could make it. Outside, it seemed real busy on the streets. Tourists, and well dressed English people on their way somewhere. Perfect. I had to make some quick cash. I looked down the street. I could see Marv and them sitting there, laughing, not in any flustered impatient wait. They were smoking a joint, right there on the street, man, I can't leave them alone for a second, I thought. I dropped my bag and turned around to get some tools out. Time to get to work. I smiled as I pulled out some balloons, my juggling balls, and my nose. I stretched the cord of my nose over my head, and instantly, I was in clown mode. Such awkward desires came over me. They were no normal wishes, everything was strange and innocently beautiful. I was proud of my senses and train of thought. The blood rushed through me, I held all my energy on the balls of my feet. I could shift the world off its axis, power grew in me, and I started to shake nervously. My face was enveloped by the look of idiocy. I took a breath, then I looked at the guy in the store, he didn't know what was going on. I perceived him to be very worried; looking down, and shifting side to side. I had this quirky smile and wrinkled looking face on. Trying to look like a cartoon moron.

"Duh, A yup a, Ihhh, duh, ok George, time ta go to work ahhh." Talking to myself, getting into character. I put a hat on my head. It was easy to feel reason enough to have a silly weird smile of a face. And besides I love wearing a clown nose. I zipped up my bag. I stretched my back, arching, I turned around, still bent low, I started juggling two balls in my left hand. I was looking down, and I started making weird bird noises, rolling my head on my neck from side to side. No one could see my face yet, it was covered by my hat. I didn't even think anybody had stopped to look. I looked up with crossed eyes and a whacked face, still crouched down, to discover that some people had stopped.

Tourists, great! Americans that have never seen street theatre. I
smiled, "Ooooohhhhh!" with a baby language. "Hhhheeelllllwwwwwooooo,"
as I started waving with my other hand. And slowly, two of the ladies waved
back. A fat guy was smiling, impressed and pushing his little daughter closer
into my show. Good, I had them where I wanted them. I felt strong as I grew
confidence and strength. I was still waving and I laughed like a stupid ogre,
"Huh,m, ahuhuhhhhh." Breathing, "Huh?" I looked over at my hand, it was
still waving. In its own world, totally separate from the rest of its body. I
tried to stop it but I couldn't. I tried pulling it down, but it shot back up. It
had a mind of its own, and then it slapped me in the face. I shook my head all
over the place, screaming out, "Whooooaaaaaahhhhhh!" More little girls
crowded around and giggled. More people were stopping to watch. A little
boy was holding onto his mother, a bit nervously.

I acted like I was wondering what to do. I was full of life. I felt like I
would live forever. I looked over at my left hand and it was still juggling two
balls. My face turned bright as I came up with the solution. I started shaking
my smiling head up and down, counting my timing. "Ooookkaayy, watch
dis!" I took a second for the people to unconsciously draw in tighter. I threw
the two balls up really high, perfectly. Then with my left hand I reached over
and slapped my right hand. All in the nick of time it took the balls to come
back down. I caught them and continued juggling them, not missing a beat.
While my right hand shook and I made whimpering sounds as it went to hide
behind my back. The people liked that, it was an easy trick, but it had a lot of
appeal.

"Ohhhh!" Came the cry from the crowd as they inched inward,
gurgling and wanting more. As natural as a hurricane forming, they formed a
circle around me. I smiled again, having solved the problem. Still juggling
the two balls with my left hand. I shot this bored look onto my face, my lower
lip covering my upper lip. Then I changed expression, coming up with a
bright idea. You could see the light bulb go on, on top of my head. My right
hand came out from its hiding spot and felt its way to a crank on my side. I
started cranking myself up, making quirky clicking noises, bumps and beeps,
while miming spinning a crank. First I elongated my back, then I started
raising up, only on one leg, as my right leg went up with the rest of my body, it
started to drop slowly toward the ground, from the pull of gravity. It was
part of the visual effect of being winched upward. I was yapping and chirping
like a baby pterodactyl breaking out of its egg, looking for food and it's
mama. My head swinging and jerking around and around with turrets
syndrome muscle reflexes. My eyes were bulging, redder than a vampires, or
the devil himself. I loved it. I tried to look at everybody hard in the eye. A lot

of people had gathered, even some English execs that see this kind of stuff everyday, that was good. I reached my full peak and a look of worry came over me because I couldn't stop my hand from cranking.

"Whhhhhreeeaaaaaaaakkkkkk!" I screamed, and then, "Look oooouuuttt! I'ma falwin out o da nest!" As I jumped from a perfectly stretched out position, dropping the juggling balls, into a swan dive of elegance, and at the last moment I rolled into a head stand. All within complete control, not endangering any of my viewers. But they all jumped back in shock, someone dropped a full can of soda or something on the ground in the crowd. And then they all laughed spontaneously at their over reaction. I was standing there, on the gracious space of the pavement, in a headstand for a full beat. Letting it sink in. I was using a lot of energy, and already, a layer of full sweat crawled on my skin. Then I threw myself up in a half circle, onto my feet. They crowd applauded. The hat was left on the floor, the open part facing up, asking to be filled with coins. I smiled, raising one eye brow, pointing to my hat on the floor. I was ready to end the show, everyone got the message. It was a very quick, but clean, besides I was on a time schedule. You could hear people going for their change, as a little girl came up shyly, and picked my hat up and gave it to me. The crowd went wild. I was shocked. I looked shock. I acted like Humprey Bogart saying, "Thanks, you, you little..." I put my fist up, waving it at her. She giggled and I turned her around and shoved her forward with complete clownesque posture.

Then I dropped my hat on the other side, still smiling and pointing to it behind my back with one hand, while moving the girl forward with my other. When another little girl ran up and picked it up. She started tugging at my shirt, and I looked over still nodding and shaking my head. I did a double take. I pulled up into a 'what's going on here' posture. My hands on my hips, elbows outstretched. Hesitating, shaking my head, sweat spitting out, like a dog shaking off water. I gave a smirk, looking clowny tuff. I swiped my hat out of her hands and said, real rough like, "Thanks kid, now scram," as I put the hat back onto my head. There was no money in it yet. A middle aged woman, fat with big rimmed glasses and three quarter inch thick lenses laughed loudly, slapping her stomach. I guess she couldn't reach her knee. I got the impression that this was just as good as 'America's Funniest Video's'. Laughter from the crowd consumed the street. No pedestrian could walk by. It was a sidewalk handsome with space, a railing separating it from the street. I laughed. This was great. I loved it when these kinds of things happened. The little girl didn't budge. She kept giggling and holding on to my pant leg. I tried to shake her off, and the crowd lost it. She sat down and wrapped herself around my leg. I looked up to the crowd, "What am I supposed to do with this, I mean, this wasn't in the script." A fat man laughed, spitting out some beer on some one in front of him.

"Hey!"

"Oh, sorry man, but that was funny." I heard, worried that a fight might break out ruining my show. I increased my volume.

I laughed, "Ahhhhhahahahahahahahaha, ok then." The little girl held on as I lifted her off the ground and started walking.

"Well, I guess you're comin' with me!" And I started walking through the crowd in mechanical slow motion, slurring a long slow speech of the word, yes. Totally contorted, in my face, and my movement. My feet grounding me, using the weight of the girl on my leg as an opposition to my energy. I was in slow motion, perfectly. The girl now wrapped around my leg, probably having done this with her mommy thousands of times, was making it easy for me to walk around in slow motion. The crowd loved it. I reached to my head with my hand slowly, more with my facial focus, letting the people guess my destination before I actually got there physically with my right hand. I then, very slowly, and with clownesque posture, dropped my hat in the center of the circle and I walked like I was running real fast in slow motion, to the outskirts of the crowd that had formed. It was always a good idea to walk through your crowd. It made your show more personable. Somebody patted me on the back. I got to the end, walking stoutly, like a champion thoroughbred. Nodding courteously, my hands moving to my hips, acting as proud as a general, nonchalantly walking out of the ether of my slow motion. Exaggerating highly the step I had to take with the leg with the little girl attached to it, starting to laugh, loudly and more than normally. Then I turned around to come back into the crowd.

I was smothered into the crowd walking quickly back to the center, when the leg with the baby girl on it got stuck. My body was jolted backward. Everyone drew around to look. I looked questioningly at the little girl, "Huh?" She giggled harder, squeezing, not about to let go. I started trying to pull free from what must have been gum underneath my sandal that had caused me to stick to the spot. I tried to pull free, my whole body moving up and down, except for my leg. My face making a straining look, like a mover carrying an armoire, while I made heave ho noised through my lips. Three times, pulling and straining on my leg. It really looked like my leg was stuck. I tried to walk away from it, but got pulled back like a dog at the end of his rope because my foot was glued to the ground. I took some clown breaths, panting portraying how out of breath I was. I got another idea. I showed it, pointing to the sky and saying, "Hey!" I pulled out this saw, the way captain caveman does it. I started sawing my leg off, making hustling and whistling Lamaze type noises.

"Look out, she's gonna fall!" I yelled. "Timber!" And in somewhat slow motion, with a stiff erectness clenching my back, I fell leaning, using the weight of the girl to let me rock slowly down, straight like a board, to the ground in what seemed like slow motion. There was applause. Then the little girl, got off my leg and she ran through the crowd. I smiled, shivers ran down my spine, and a tear came onto my cheek perhaps from joy, but possibly from fear, I couldn't tell. It ran down the side of my face into my ear. I laid there laughing, about to jump up, when the little girl came back and put the hat on my face, open end facing the crowd. There was already a few coins that I could feel, heavy against my face. The crowd went wild with applause and cheers. I said through the mask of the hat. "That's all folks!" And I froze. Then through the murmur, laughter, and applause, I felt money going into the hat. I didn't move. And the longer I laid there with the hat on my face. The more I could feel people gathering to put money in the hat. It got heavy and fell to one side. Coins rolling all over the place. I got up and opened up the hat for the people. Man, I could see a couple of bills in the hat. Little girls ran around collecting my change for me, then running up and putting them in the hat shyly. That one little girl was perfect, you couldn't train someone to do what she did. There was so many babies around I couldn't figure out which one she was. I was gliding high, shaking and sweating; breathing heavy. I couldn't think, or even remember my name. I was on such a rush of adrenaline. Oh well. I would have liked to have thanked the little girl, given her a balloon or something. Anyway, the crowd had died down and I collected my hat and juggling balls, saying thanks to the tourists still lingering around wanting more. Marv, Beezley, and Jules had just walked up.

"What are you doin, Welton? Goin solo?"

"No, I just didn't have enough money for the booze." I was sweating and panting, shaking all over, totally filled with adrenaline. I weighed the hat with my estimations, and looked at my friends. "Now I do!" Smiling, I took my clown nose off. "I'll be right back". I didn't say anything more as I bounced, full of my adrenaline into the shop. I was so high and shaking from nervousness.

The guy looked at me, some what with respect. He had seen my display.

"You ever work in the Garden?" He asked nonchalantly.

"Yeah, everyday." Not looking at him, I counted out the correct change, using the smaller coins. Man, there was a lot of money in here, and three five pound bills, nice. The guy didn't say anything more, he pretended to be polishing something. He didn't even count the change I gave him, he just dropped it all into one slot of the register. What organization he had. I got the booze and smokes and I left, "See ya."

He nodded, not saying anything. What else was there to say. I walked out to my friends. I threw Marv the hat, naturally, he was our bank. He once carried twelve hundred thousand lire in small coins from the deep South of Italy, all the way to Florence. It must have been an extra eighty pounds in his bag. We contemplated throwing some of it out, but we ended up keeping it, not even suggesting paying for the train ticket. I opened up the bottle of gin and took a sip. "Ahhh, that's good stuff." I passed it around and pulled out the cigarettes. I packed them and threw the wrapper and aluminum foil part on the street. It was a normal thing to litter in London. I lit a cigarette and bent down to put my juggling balls and clown nose in my bag, in which they were all standing around.

"You know where we're goin?" I asked Jules.

"Yeah, I think." He said, putting his free hand in his pocket. He was carrying his guitar with his right hand, and he pulled it up, using the guitar case to point, "That way."

I put my bag on. "Let's go, then," I said, seeming really excited.

It was such a rush to have such a great show at such a key moment. Now, I could even buy Jules a ticket to France if I had to. As we walked off, through car exhaust, a newspaper swirled and clung to me from the force of the wind. The streets of London, which were constantly being swept and cleaned by employed gents with either a broom and pan, or a machine driven sweep truck, were always covered in trash, candy wrappers, and way too many cigarette butts. Newspapers being separated and whirled around by the wind, glided at different heights off the ground. Once, I had a conversation with someone who was street sweeping, I was commenting on the non excess of trash cans. This government employed fellow with crooked teeth told me to just throw it on the ground as he was cleaning the area momentarily. If there was a trash can, he would have been out of a job, but the excuse given by him was that someone may perhaps want to put something more than just trash in the can. He held his broom tightly, wrenching it, reassuringly securing the feeling that he still had his job. As I was sitting on the street at the time relaxing, I was glad that he didn't sweep me up along with the rest of the trash.

While we carried ourselves along, hiccups came from a growling mad shrunken stomach, I burped empty gas, having nothing to release. I took another swig from my bottle of gin and past it to Arlo. People past us on the street like it was nothing. There was usually as many backpackers, given the season, as there were English locals, in the center of London. Everybody always seemed like they were coming and going to and from London. Then again, France was but few hours away, and relatively cheaply gotten there, if you had the money. London is a highly cosmopolitan and very international city. More a tourism host than a melting pot, I got the impression that few people actually lived inside the center of the city, as they did work there, via a commute from a little town like Ealing Broadway. However, deeper in Soho, in and around Carnaby street, with it's queer and outlandish attitude, there are quietly held places of habitat that I had come across, that gave court to well established eccentrics. Those of whom are all artists in one way or another of various arts and crafts. Walking through the streets of London, For the last time in a while, we found a row of stores selling hand made and specially crafted musical instruments lined up one by one, competing prices along with each others dexterity.

Jules stopped, causing us to stop, he was accepting his, either, blind faith or intuition. He chose one of the stores and went in without wondering if any of us were going to follow him. Arlo was the second to enter, wishing that he himself had chosen and led the way in. Marv was drawn in by the perfume that the instruments gave off. It was a separate and distinct world in there. The space was emanated with the possibility of creating, with soaking wet perseverance, sweat, and passion; musical harmony. As my comrades perused the guitar store, which had some astronomically priced and configured guitars, I waited outside. Well, from the doorway, I bought a pick, I stepped in for a bit to drop some pence on the counter, just as Marv was staring, wanting to touch a bass which looked like it was created with the utmost respect to authenticity and craftsmanship. It shone gallantly, creating light, not merely reflecting it. The instrument was held in place on a wall, by what seemed like a natural opposition to gravity. Its price was more blinding than the fragile detailed coursework that went into its creation.

Famous guitars were displayed everywhere, on the walls, and on stands on the floor, which was wide and completely covered by all sorts of instruments. I tiptoed back outside careful not to knock anything expensive over with my backpack, or my drum, which was swinging on its leather guitar strap that was hanging around my shoulders. As I exited Jules picked out some strings and a couple of the more expensive picks. He looked around to all the guitars one by one, He sighed out all of his depression, dreaming of knowing the true secrets of the guitar, that are held in the minds of only the greatest who knew, and mastered the being of the instrument. The atmosphere in that stored produced this kind of impression among all of its visiting customers.

Outside, it was a warm sunny day. For once, the grey clodden and silkless backdrop, which sat always still and pale, encumbering the horizon of this illustrious city, was smothered and hidden, obedient to the white shine of the sun. I looked around at the busy clattered streets. It was loud, yet there was no one talking that I could hear. People were walking by in tall cosmopolitan fashion. Bright and conservative business dresses and suits streamed together in a rush of blurred movement. A couple of English youths, teenagers full of rebellious attitude, walked by staring, hoping to be provoked, forcing everyone who passed to step out of their way. A group of old and accentuated aged countryside citizens of quiet simplicity walked by slowly looking at the city of London as if it had all been made new since the last time they were here. It probably had been given their age, and considering the substantial damage the bombing from the last war had done. Street traffic consumed all peace, yet retained a calm unanimity. A daring mini car rode on, stealing the lane from one of the red oversized double decked buses. Both drivers accelerated, logically comfortable with the movement of traffic. An infamous black cab crept to a stop, a passenger with big feminine shopping bags full of new clothes became its passenger. In an outlet by this alleyway, there was a couple of big pieces of cardboard on the ground, and a scattered pile of dirty rags. Underneath the rags, on part of one of the larger cardboard pieces, there was a person sleeping. A breeze carried some moist polluted air my way.

"Shit." I said, nodding my head and looking down.

I took a drink from my pint of gin. Everyone was at least living some kind of life, what and however it maybe. Visions of granted repercussive glory sat quietly within my sheltered thoughts'. What was going to come to be? A question that haunted me, following me around, forcing me to accept it's responsibility, or laying down in front of me, blocking my movement if I didn't. Was I truly a waste of a bum? Should I have been a miscarriage? Such terrible questions to ask oneself. No time to think about their answers either. The rush to get as far out of London as we could today, came feeling it's way back into my conscious. I knew that it wasn't going to be as easy to get through France, as it was the last time I had traveled there. Besides, this time we had more cargo, we had Arlo 'The Sloth' Beezley.

I looked back into the store. I saw Jules focused in on this one guy who was sitting down with a guitar in his hand, tuning it. Jules was excitedly asking him questions. His body language looked like he wanted to pat the guy on the back. He had the bag of strings in his hand and he was fanning the space with them wildly. I walked in a bit to catch what they were talking about.

The English dude with the guitar was getting frustrated. His long hippyish and grayed hair seemed like it was sweating through the tightly wrapped pony tail it was in. Jules kept saying, "Come'n man, show me somethin." Expressive with exaggerated kindness.

The pot-bellied beer drinking wanna be Harley rider replied in a quite abrasive manner, "I usually get twenty-five pound an hour to give tykes a lesson yeah."

""Just a couple of chords, macdaddy," Arlo back Jules up.

"Yeah, come'n," They mustered up together. The guy rolled his eyes, getting pissy, but then started jamming out some wild bluesy riffs. Arlo and Marv started moving to it. Marv was ready to put his harmonica to his lips when Jules broke in from a deafening stare at the guys left hand.

"Wait, can you slow down a second! What cord was that you used after the A-" totally taking mental notes. The English dude got so flustered that without even finishing the musical progression of notes, he just ripped all six strings off the guitar with his right hand at the base of the guitar. He straightened up as if he was going to scream showing that he was expecting Jules and us to leave his space in a hurry, the free lesson was over.

"Wow," I heard Arlo say as he stopped bluntly out of his digging on the music. Marv grabbed Jules and started pulling him. He didn't understand that the guy was pissed at giving free lessons to people. He was trying to earn the title 'instructor'. I stepped back out into London casually.

"OK," I said to myself.

"That guy was fucked up," Arlo said as they came out.

"That was crazy!" Jules beckoned. "What was that all about?"

"You know how many people must ask his advice. He was probably having a long day." I said trying to reassure Jules as we walked down the street quickly, bouncing along between the other people around us.

"Jules you were like asking him to write it out for you though, what did you expect him to do?" Marv said as he turned the corner and we followed him.

Scratching his head with the bag of strings he said, "I think I got it, I gotta try it out on my guitar. I need to put this string on." He stopped in the middle of the street and dropped his guitar case and started opening it up. I turned around from my movement ahead of him and was about to question him, thinking that he was not going to try and figure out the melody right now. But then he looked up and smiled and answered my soon to be asked question, before I could ask it. "Relax, I'm just putting the strings that I bought in my case. Ha-ha!" He quirked and got up and ran ahead of us all.

"What about the picks you bought?" I asked catching up to him.

"They're in my backpack!" He said speeding up.

Arlo pushed me from behind saying, "Lets go, lets get out of here!"
And I picked up the pace.

Eventually, we got to Waterloo Station, running. The moment was on.
We headed for the schedule board of departing trains. Waterloo station is
generous with space, The ceiling yielding high above the second floor and its
balconies, with a ponderous open space in the middle for passengers to wait
for trains. We walked through the crowds of standing and moving people
passably in single file, the most disheveled looking travelers any one had seen
that day. Coffee shops and food restaurants, 'Burger King', sat with opened,
elongated French door facades, along the walls. Bells rung, and train
schedules scrolled and updated themselves. People were standing around
waiting for all reasons. There was a dirty clothed bum, standing off the wall,
near the corner, mumbling to himself, not looking outward, with strict
straight posture, and hair wet down, hand combed to one side. He was
holding just the handle to a briefcase, and he had a torn in half, newspaper
folded underneath his other arm, pressing it up against the side of his chest.
What the hell was he waiting for? There was huge crowds moving to and
from when trains arrived.

We were in the station for about six minutes when we found two
suitable possibilities of trains to approach. Up until now, I didn't even think
of going to Victoria station to catch the speed line. But an instance of
indecision caused some reflections of high class travelling like in the movies.
But even if we stole the ride to Paris quickly and in a more luxurious fashion,
Jules would have thought it a total allegiance to the Bourgeoisie. Besides it
was harder to sneak onto a train at Victoria Station, than it was here. And
none of us wanted to mingle with the higher classes, or richer snotty people
anyway. The kinds of people you found on first class trips like the speed line.
Travelers with Euro-rail tickets and one hundred and fifty dollar sun glasses
would all be present there. So it was either to the port of Dover or South
Hampton we went via Waterloo Station. We talked out loud trying to decide,
nearby people listening to our conversation curiously.

"There's a train leaving for South Hampton in three minutes!" Arlo
was jumping around excited, kind of like a dog when it wants you to throw the
ball, desiring to retrieve it. The thrill of the run, catching the ball in mid
bounce, then slamming on the brakes, making dust rise into a cloud around
you. Then turning around and trotting like a winner, finding it hard to smile
with a ball in your mouth, you come back to your master and ask him greedily
to throw it again. "Let's go! C'mon! Hurry!" He played right into the part,
man it was hard not to laugh at him. He jiggled and shook, like an addict.

"I've never been out of London through there. There's ferries to France?" I said with schoolboy quietness.

"It's a fucking port, what else would they have there?" Making me feel stupid, still jumping around, now more like he had to go to the bathroom.

"Oh." I said and then I shut up, lost in the decision of the moment, hoping somebody else would make the right choice.

"Hey, Marv you been there?" Jules asked.

"Na, but I don't think it's a bad idea. I mean, when is the train leaving for Dover? In like an hour, Yeah? I don't wanna' sit around here that long."

"Yeah, shit, there's gotta be somethin' goin outta there, right?" I said.

"Yeah, even if it's a fucking rowboat, that hasn't stopped us before."

"And we'll let Arlo row this time."

"Yeah, you'll get plenty of exercise," as Marv shoved Arlo.

"Unless you don't wanna' go with us?" I egged him on.

"Shit, I'm like your fucking compass, you need me." He stood up taller, laughing, playing along.

"More like our ass." Jules said through laughter, "Don't slip on your own piss!" That made us all laugh.

"Ha ha," and Arlo broke from the circle, "I'm catching this train." He said astutely, and was about to start moving. And we were about to start chasing him when all of a sudden someone who looked like he was from the south, by the ports, tall, thin, and course like a fisherman, said in humble country English slang, "Ferries to France is the cheapest they come from South Hampton". He must have been able to tell that we were contemplating the price budget.

"Oh yeah? Well thank you then," I said, being courteous. "I say we listen to this guy, he sounds like he knows what he's talking about!" I said, taking away any credit from Arlo. And we bolted with lightning fire for the departing train. "See ya later, Arlo!" As he was following up the rear.

On this unknown man's suggestion, more so than from Arlo's pressure, like a surge, we decided to go there. Mr. Ellowin, Jules, and I were somewhat certain of the kinds of situations that lay immediately ahead. Arlo, who hadn't actually earned, even his name until later, was about to lose what was left of his chastise . In the most obvious fashion, we ran to the platform of our soon to be departing train. Mechanical noises echoed and mingled with the blurred sound of the crowd's bustling and conversation. An Arabic accentuated voice filled the air in spurts, over the house megaphone, announcing arrivals and departures. We ran down the platform to the end , bags bouncing up and down, my drum swinging hard. We got clumsily aboard, me being the last to enter, checking our rear, looking to see if any officials were looking or talking into radios. Breathing hard, I felt like a dork, trying to act like I was in an espionage thriller novel.

We walked through the isles of the train, acting like we had tickets. Creaking sounds and fluted gurgling arose as the train, bent and tattered, yet still new looking, whistled, and like a very old man getting up from his chair, set off on its course of motion. We walked a bit through the cars until we had found a place to settle. I saw a ways down to the other end of the train, four or six conductors, splitting up to go pacing in opposite directions. They had an aristocratic air about them. Arlo was babbling about a sweet female traveler going to Paris, and how he was going to get her. I looked at Marv, who was the main recipient of the 'Sloth' gibber, and I could tell that he was thinking that Arlo wasn't worth bringing on this trip. Marv was staring blankly, but I knew he was paying attention to everything. I was wondering if he had a plan, or were we just going to bump and grind along, 50km here, another 25km there, and eventually with slow steady progress we would arrive to our destination.

I looked out the window, ah, the English country side, so lulling and drab. Sighs rolled down my spine. I tingled with stupid worry and angry curiosity, as I received the gift of frustration from my relentless psyche. Jules sat down with leisurely confidence. I looked around, inside and out of the train. The now grayish late day sky and green rolling hills were what was left of London. I looked back at Jules, wondering how the fuck he could be doing, what he was about to do here, it was an even worse spot than on the streets. He was literally in the process of replacing the broken high E string. I mean, his backpack, or rather, 'The Office' was on the floor and opened, papers starting to catch the wind and blowing away. The guitar was out of the case. Shit was sprawling out all over the place. A deodorant stick fell out of the office and hit the sheet metal floor, and started to vibrate along toward Arlo's foot. It reminded me of some stupid board game. "Anybody seen those picks that I bought?" What was he thinking? We were in this lounge near the food car, already miles out of zones 1, 2 & 3. The way we traveled the mind was never allowed a moments rest. For me, and definitely for Marv, it was a game of chess to the end. Jules had disorganization seeping out of him; that wasn't good, because this ride was coming to an end.

"Jules, pack that shit up man, this scene is gonna move quick," as I pointed at him, not from above, but from a lower left angle, by my thigh, practically snapping my fingers together and making noise.

"Huh?" As he looked up, wondering what was going on. As if he was saying, 'What? The parties over so soon?' He had a mad curious expression of wonder on his face. One of his eyes looked lazy. "I just gotta tune this so I can get that riff down that dude was playin, or I'll forget it." He promised out loud, trying not to stop what he was doing.

"Yeah man, we're about to get thrown off of this train," as Marv gestured with an upward nod toward the door. He had his arms elongated, holding his hands together, a bit lower than his waist, standing on the balls of his feet, not being interfered with by the vibrating train. Jules looked up and realized the situation and quickly got it together. Three conductors were coming for us, not even stopping to check anybody else's' tickets. Arlo bucked up with a plan, gesticulating lividly. What ever it was, I knew that these conductors blatantly had it in for us. They entered our traincar. I tried to feel invisible.

A fat boy, the bald man, and a crewneck came stomping into our space, with the skills of a VP, an executive, and a clerk full of English pale skin covered with bright red pimples on top, on their way to merge upon their corporate prey. The tall man, with a loud dry scalp, who had so much nervous energy, he looked like he could have been doing flips while he was walking, jumped upon us. He was trying to impress his; what was in his mind, his superior being and lord ruler. The fat boy had a lot of gay confidence hiding his insecurities.

"Tickets! Got your tickets?" Came the sound that arrested my motion. It was high squeaked notes from a trumpet, making my insides cringe. Arlo stepped up. He tried to explain to the lads that we were dumb Americans and that his dirty three day old, all day pass, was a genuine ticket for four, straight to South Hampton, England.

"Here ya go fellas," as the bald guy pulled it out of his hand, in disbelieve. He studied it extensively, at first not understanding, and then he chuckled, trying to reassure himself. The fat conductor was staring at us, waiting to see the verdict of the bald guys' dismay. The clerk wimp pulled at his collar, sweating and quiet, looking around, trying not to look at us. He had no power, and if they would have sent only him, this would have been a free ride all the way to the port. I was being thrown around a little by the train. The fat boy was standing squat and firm, immune to the vibrations of the train.

The bald conductor was still studying the ticket, shaking his head, when Arlo broke his concentration, "It's for the four of us," and he pointed around us in a circle as if he was talking to someone who didn't speak the same language.

The bald guy looked up, nodding his head no, fiercely, but waiting for his superior to say something first. The fat boy stared at Arlo without replying for some time. The invigorated conductor looked back and forth at us then at his superior hoping he'd do something, but he didn't move. He was holding his breath, transfixed in a moment in his mind, he looked like he had fallen asleep with his eyes open. The train shook us to the left as it made a turn. I leaned into it, careful not to have to take a step outward.

The bald guy broke the silence, he couldn't take it anymore, "No no no, I mean, are you guys mad, or what?"

"Huh? What's the problem?" Arlo was genuinely curios, as if everything was valid. Marv was still standing there, watching to see how it would all play out. If this was the states, Marv would have pulled out something more than his gun by now, calling everybody on their cards. Jules was just looking down, standing there wishing he could be fixing his guitar while we sorted this out.

The fat boy let out a huge breath, coming back to life, nodding his head now and snorting, "Nope! no no no no! That's right boys." He didn't even look at his mates, "Ol'right, what's the problem then Jenkins?"

The desperate bald conductor, was now finally at ease, the case against us was underway, "Well sir, first off, this ticket expired three days ago! And it's only for one person," as he shoved the ticket in Arlo's face, giving him a snotty look, "for zones one, two, and three."

Were these Americans really that stupid? The thought was protruding from all of them, except for the clerk, that looked like he didn't know what was going on. He was being bounced around by the train to the point where he had to hold onto the side rail. I was going under the assumption that because of the stereotypical characteristics us Americans get labeled with in England, it was totally possibly that we were. I tried to look even more stupid, I tried to think about something a backwoods inbred redneck would be thinkin', while holding an ax in his hand, late in the early morning of another day in the woods, while chewing tobacco drool foamed up in my grizzly beard. I couldn't think of anything, but I had a hard on.

The fat conductor spoke up, with his arms crossed above his chest, totally disapproved, "You lads have any money?"

"Money?" Arlo accused him in his answer, the rich boy coming out of him. "For what?" His knees were bent and he had the posture of a defensive back ready to rush the quarter back. Marv gave a look at Arlo, it was a like saying, 'good answer Beezley!'

The bald guy lost his composure, and sunk down practically to his ankles, shaking his head, saying no five or six times. The head conductor sighed, tired of his job. "Ok, let's go mates," and he lifted himself out of his spot. Needless to say, we were being asked to leave the train. Once it was over, it was nice and cordial. The fat man was used to train jumpers with no tickets. And he was the one who could have really enforced the law upon us, if we pissed him off enough. But he just wanted us out of his way. The tall conductor was parading his victory as he lead the way down the isle, acting as if he was escorting us to a prison cell. The fat conductor, who looked more pudgy than fat when he walked, was ahead of us as well, and the pimply boy lead up the rear. A lot of passengers turned to look at us. Arlo was saying hi to them, smiling like he was going to the first class section. I was a little bit embarrassed for us. We couldn't even afford a ticket to travel. What a shame I thought. Oh well, what are you going to do? Worry? When we reached a suitable exit platform, the fat man stopped and turned to us, feeling the need to lecture. He was quite direct, assuming the responsibility of a traffic guard.

He started talking with blunt undisturbed emphasis, "So, you boys from America, I see! Well, that's a far off land from here. Don't suppose you're worried about paying English fines, are ya now lads? Hmm, or prison, now!" Stopping temporarily to look at us with paternal disgust. Making a clicking noise with his mouth meaning no, no, no, no, no! "So then, how far exactly are you little lads going?"

Marv said with words only, "Cannes, France."

Jules smiled. The fat boy conductor shook his head, unbelieving it. He didn't think we'd make it. The bald guy was struggling to insist that they should call the cops. But the fat man kept putting up his hand to cut the bald guy off.

Then he turned to the bald guy and said, "Go an check everybody's ticket before we get to the next stop. There could be more of em!" The bald conductor shot a surprised look on his face. What a good idea, he thought. He put himself in tracking mode and went quickly, without acknowledging or saying good bye to us. He lunged onward, pushing the pimpled face boy out of his way. He was holding on to the side rail, but still he fell into the wall. I was pissed that this guy didn't think we would make it to Southern France on the trains for free.

So, I exchanged a story with him about the three of us, leaving out all the colorful adjectives, "Man, me and these two guys," pointing to Shivers and Ellowin, " made it to Paris from London on four pounds."

Arlo sat, bewildered, he was configuring a story that he did and how he was going to share it and its wild exaggerations with us, at some strategically planned and plotted moment.

The train was vibrating harder now, gearing down for the stop up ahead. "Four pounds huh? It costs more than that by a lot, just for the ride outta London to the port." The fat man looked around feeling the train with his feet, I could see his toes wrinkle in his soft skinned shoes.

Arlo smiled and said, "yeah, oh, yeah, ah, ha ha ha. Yes!" thinking that he was Jack Kerouac. The conductor looked at Arlo not trying to condescend him but feeling sorry for him.

The fat man stated factly over the increasing sounds of the train at it's attempt to decrease its speed, "Well, if that's the case then, gentlemen, you'd better not let him do the talking next time," as he pointed to the Sloth.

The floors started to vibrate hard, as the train completely geared down. The clerk with the pale skin and pimples was holding on with both hands, but he was still being thrown about. We came to a halt. Jules laughed out loud as he pushed Beezley off the train, onto the station platform. Marv and I followed them, not saying goodbye to the conductors. The train carried on without us. There was no one or nothing on this platform. Not even a conductor inside the station. Arlo saw on a billboard that it was a fifteen minute wait for the next train. I contemplated walking but I knew we would do plenty of that on this trip, so we waited.

Arlo pulled out some hash, "Sick!" wagging his head, taunting us. He started kicking some verse, proclaiming wild exclamations. "Man, we're gonna meet some hot chicks in Cannes," as his hands went to work, breaking up the hash and tobacco, with the skill of a surgeon. "Damn, are we in for a party. I'm gonna fuck on the beach every night, then swim naked with French girls who don't speak English. I love it, Yeah!"

None of us even threatened to take our backpacks off. Jules was standing there, leaning over to one side, still holding his guitar in his hand, telling Arlo with mere laughter that he couldn't run any game. He must have forgot about the riff he was trying to remember because he didn't dive into his guitar case. Marv was holding firm, his arms crossed, swaying at the top like a high-rise using fully, the play of the structure. He was there like an animal in nature, always alert, yet totally at ease and tranquil; a hunter. I wanted to take my backpack off, but I didn't.

"Arlo, the only sex your gonna git is from yourself. Man, chicks at the 'Cannes Film Festival'" and I used my hands to mime quotes around the phrase, "only dig guys with money. You know, the kind of guys that are shaven, showered, and have a hotel room to go back to." He wasn't looking at me, he was looking at the joint rolling process his hands had undertaken, but he was still listening. He was shaking his head, trying to say I gotta aim higher in my standards for myself. "And besides, it's not like your gonna be out all night at the clubs, or schmoozin' with film execs at high class parties with the celebrities." The atmosphere out side of our circle was so plain that if I closed my eyes, we could have been anywhere. But we were nowhere.

Marv spoke up, trying to make Arlo understand, "Arlo, I mean look at us, you ain't exactly vacationing with your parents. You're like a hobo man, a bum."

"Yeah, what the fuck are you thinkin', you little spoiled bitch, like, you couldn't even get laid in London on your own, I had to help you out!"

"Oh, shit! Ha hah ha ah ha ah ha ha!" Jules couldn't hold back his laughter.

"What ever," he broke in, finished with the joint. I'm gonna get a fine lookin' girl. And she's gonna take me to her hotel room. And if you guys are lucky, I'll bring you the scraps from room service."

"Yeah, great, we'll be waitin' for ya, now light the joint bitch." Marv wanted to get high. He gets a little cranky when he's sober. My bag was really heavy now, I was shifting my weight around on my feet, trying to lessen the strain on my back.

Arlo burned off the excess paper and took a couple drags. He held in his hit and passed the joint. We all became silent as the joint went around and around. Jules pulled out the pint of gin and passed it around the other way. How'd he get it? He cleared his throat.

"Jonny O-" Jules started to say but was interrupted by an uproar.

"O, who? Jonny O?" Marv questioned laughingly.

"Who's that guy?" Arlo cried.

"Jjjjjjjjjooooooonnnnniiiieeeee OOOOOOOOOOOOOO!" I screamed. We all laughed at our quirky yet intensely smart English literature professor.

"Seriously," Jules tried to go on, "He gave me this guys name to look up, a real strong friend of his that he said could introduce me to some literary agents at the festival. It seems like a solid connection." He said insecurely.

"Yeah, Jonny O wouldn't steer you wrong Jules," Marv said through a cough, "He told me he liked what you wrote and it had tremendous potential to sell. And I quote, 'It's exactly what the film market needs today' he said!" Marv quoted with his hands.

"Yeah," Jules said, staring at the ground." I wondered if he himself even thought it to be good writing. He hadn't let any of us read it. I didn't say anything. It was quiet everywhere in the world. The voices of worry started yapping in my mind. Desolation hits hard on empty train station platforms. Especially if you know that they might not even let you on the next train. I wonder, does worry constantly remind everyone of its whereabouts. Reality hit me. My back ached out in coughs. Questions were shooting out violently in my mind. Would we make it in time for the overnight ferry? How were four of us going to smuggle ourselves over, to the other side. Then, deal with the Frenchmen. I figured we could save ourselves by making them laugh, if we had enough patience to create the right moment. We were still standing there finishing off the joint as the train arrived. The pint of gin was almost gone. Out of all of us, I had the most hash burns on my shirt. It was pretty much the only shirt I had. I wasn't planning on trying to keep it clean anyway. I found it a little bit crazy that none of us had taken our backpacks off the whole time, I mean, mine was really heavy. I wondered why nobody had initiated the idea. Maybe their backpacks weren't as heavy as mine? I don't know. Maybe it was the knowledge that we had to be ready to move, because anything could change instantly. Jules didn't even change his strings though, and it was the perfect place to do it. Crazy, I thought.

"Mind the Gap"; All four of us said this phrase in our minds as the doors opened to let us on the train.

Our entrance added a new color to the traincar. We walked into a barely empty traincar and grabbed all the excess space. We through our bags down on thoroughly empty seats, ferociously. I sat down within the luxury of the vacancy. Shivers took his guitar out of its case. We were moving. No conductors. He replaced the broken string somewhat immediately, and started tuning the instrument up, as ash fell onto him from his cigarette. His ear told his hand to make a few adjustments, and then to our happiness, music filled the air. We were loud and happy. There was two youthful English students who were going home on our traincar. Both of them were dressed in conservative school uniforms. They were very pale, not just the color of their skin, but their dry timid attitude. They always had a look of boredom on their faces.

Arlo burst out with our parade, he was standing in the isle, jumping up and down the rows, "Boys and girls, Aah! Let the light shine on this moment! Ah ha ha aha aha ha ha ah ha ha, Yeasa!" His energy, powerful with the indication of vast presentative fashion.

Marv was playing on the two drums, secreting sweat from his palms, sacredly. His eyes were closed and he was rolling his head around. The girl smiled. The little boy kept silent, but he was real curious. They enjoyed our American ways. They were obviously brother and sister. I walked over and pulled a balloon out of my pocket and blew it up. It was purple, and it elongated about five feet. I tied the end of it and reach out and grabbed it by the middle. I started twisting it in half. Then with clownesque body movement, shooting down low, then slowly swirling up, taking a step closer to them I got right in front of them. I put the balloon up in their faces, and pulled it apart, in two, as I held on to each untied end. They were impressed like it was a magic trick. Their eyebrows raised in awe. I then slowly, like a nice guy, handed them the separate balloons. They were quite reserved, unsure if it was ok to accept the gift. Eventually they both reached, one waiting for the other to go first, then both together. But before they could grab the two now separate balloons, I let go, and the balloons went whizzing into the air, deflating, reaching almost the other end of the train car. They shot back, but then laughed involuntarily at the joke. They became our friends instantly. The little girl being more talkative than her brother, who kept pushing up his glasses.

Arlo pushed me aside as if he had something to offer, he was drooling and panting, but he froze up. He was still smiling, stalling... thinking... but he didn't say anything. As if something grabbed him in the mind, then escaped him, leaving no trace of what he was about to say. His mind must have went blank. It happened to him sometimes, when he was so excited, and he's been babbling and spitting. His words start to slur, maybe his tongue swells, I don't know, but then he shuts up, and he's still redlining his engines. The same thing happened to him now. His face was turning red and embarrassment flooded his pants. Maybe his mind is working so fast he blows a fuse? It started to feel like a nervous moment.

The little boy began to wonder and he looked at me for an answer, so I started to speak up, but Arlo broke in, starting to breath and say something, but the little girl spoke up shyly, cutting us all off, "We have an American cousin somewhere in America!"

Arlo was stunned, but he answered her kindly, "Oh yeah? Well so do I!" And they laughed at the obviousness of his statement. They giggled, and were reassured. I could tell that it was one of the first times they had ever really interacted with American strangers. And with Arlo along, we fit the classic stereotype. It was definitely the first time they had talked to any strangers on their own volition. But they had now, something curios to comment about when their parents ask of their day. They got off long before us, and without words they walked in a single file line to the exit platform. The boy leading the way, hesitated at the door. The train slowed down abruptly, trying to make better time. Without words they both turned half way around, and put up their hands, palm open toward us, they showed their sincere good-byes. Arlo put up the piece sign, and that was all that needed to be said. I smiled, taking a swig of the gin after they left. They both had nice comfortable warm beds with clean sheets to sleep on waiting for them at home, not to mention dinner.

We past through towns that seemed populated, yet inactive. People must have all been inside. Old churches and unstable looking houses were cluttered along long roadways. As we neared South Hampton, the conductor finally came around to check our tickets. He was generally upset looking, he had a stomach that was full of something, making him appear overweight. Then he became even more upset when he found out we didn't have any tickets. He went red, holding his breath, pissed that he couldn't throw us off at the last stop. Now his peers and possibly his superiors would be at this final stop checking his quota.

"Uhhh, you boys are getting at me hard today. Shite!" His stomach was bobbing up and down, his neck getting squinched in between it and his fat head. He pulled up his pants. We didn't pay him any mind. We didn't even stop singing when he came into our traincar. If he was going to throw us off, it would have been at our stop. He let us know that he made it his intention to notify security. He left, pants sagging, walking toward the front of the steaming train, and we never saw him again. We hung around senseless, for a bit of time, feeling caught.

"You think he's gonna call the cops?" I asked. Everyone taking a breath before an answer was said.

"Nah, I doubt it."

"Cool," I said, figuring that it was the end of his day of work and he had chosen to forget about us. Not wanting to deal with the politics involved in accursing us. So we exited the train, we walked toward the ferry ticket agency entrance. We had set our gear down outside right by the entrance, and we were taking turns watching it while the rest of us went in and around to use facilities and inquire about possible venues of travel. Inside I found bright walls of advertisement packages, and just a few English ticket agents in brilliant colored vests. Our ride was not there. Apparently they had stopped doing ferries to France seven months ago. News didn't travel as fast in England as it does in America. There was a ferry leaving for Belgium however, momentarily. I left the building, upset, but more disturbed.

I was outside with the gear, careening my drum. At the time, and still now, I knew little of the power of the musical device in my hand. It helped take my mind off of my worries. It was louder than normal, the volume of everything that made noise seemed turned up. Wind blew heavier, almost sheeringly by the port. There were snack food and soda machines right by the entrance, where we had set up our camp of luggage. We had dinner; a round of snickers and sodas, and a couple cigarettes. It was a nervous moment, lost in a cloud of doubt. What to do, and how to do it were popular questions in my mind.

"Well?" I asked through chewing the chocolate and soda mixture.

"Well what?" Jules asked.

I swallowed, stalling an answer, "Do we still have any hash left?"

"Oh, Sick!" A high pitch squeal from Arlo, as he pulled out the little ball and threw it to Marv, who caught it without even looking. He wasn't eating dinner with us, he was just standing there waiting for us. "Roll that shit up Mr. Starv, I mean Marv."

"Ha ha, by the way how's that poem go? Did I Eat Today?"

"You don't remember?" He asked, curiously, maybe upset because I didn't. He started rolling the joint, not even looking at what he was doing.

"Hey Marv," Jules broke in through his chewing, exhaling smoke at the same time, "You'd better hurry up, we should get back to the trains."

"Nah, fuck that," I said, then I took a swig of the soda, "Let's walk from here." Having a quake in my stomach, from a subtle feeling that I had just gotten, as if a really good song had just started playing on the radio.

"Walk?" Arlo demanded, insultingly.

"Yeah, walk!" saying it with rushed excitement and confidence, "I got a feelin' about somethin'."

Marv fired up the joint, we were still outside the agency. There were no customer travelers going in to get tickets to Belgium. We threw our bags on, but stood in our spot, finishing up. "At least we still have hash left."

"I gotta a feelin' about that too!" I said, trying to encourage Marv. "We're gonna be fine, the next train we get on will be in France. How about those fuckin guys lookin' at us without tickets, huh? That'll be a laugh!" And I took a deep drag from the joint, letting my presentment sink in fully. "Let's just get to Ports Mouth, we gotta get on a ferry tonight!" It was another port that allowed access to France via the English Channel. "Let's go, we'll hitch a fucking ride to Ports Mouth! "

"Shit, how far is it?" Marv asked, estimating our timing.

"Well it can't be that far."

"Yeah, the guy at the counter said we can catch a ferry to France from there." It was advice from one of the nicer English agents who figured we should go bother his mates at Portsmouth. Arlo mentioned that he did say, in a genuine fashion, that they would take care of us down there more generously. We must have looked like we needed his pity. "But he said to take the train there."

"So what, what he said, Sloth!" I screamed, with my finger in my mouth, trying to dislodge a piece of chocolate from behind my back teeth, almost biting my finger.

"Whatever."

"Yeah fuck it, it can't be that far," Jules added, trying to reassure Marv.

As we left, we walked down the road toward the town. Figuring things out as they came along our path. We were moving quickly because time was against us. Salty air clung to the wetness of my skin. I breathed heavier with each step thinking that the weight of my gear was tripling. I was about to start complaining, when this little noisy car came crashing along, slowing down at an intersection we were walking by, not intending to stop. The muffler was blowing loud, frustrated and annoyed farts of smog. I stopped four steps off from the end of the road. Using my friends behind me as a barrier for its movement. I looked at this car as if I was looking at a car I had in a past life. Either we were going to car-jack this guy, or he was going to give us a ride. There was question about it. It could have went either way, my intuition was on the line. Marv and the driver exchanged contesting glances, he was practically right up on the driver's open window. The driver was mesmerized by something. His hat fell down over his eyes, and for a time, he didn't push it up. Arlo stopped to put his hand on the hood, breathing heavy, resting.

Marv, as nice as he possibly could, which was usually always how he asked for things, told him, "We need a ride to Portsmouth."

The driver looked at us as if we had interrupted his next thought, he seemed about twenty nine years old, and it pained him to do us service. Then, as if he was being coerced to do a good deed by the hand of God, which was how everybody looked after they had been asked a favor from Marv, he looked over at his friend. He was silent, totally accepting of what was about to happen, but choosing to be mute, waiting to see if he was right in his prediction. The ruffled looking driver, with a worn out uncolored beetles hat, sighed hard, and struggled within himself, "Oohhhh, uuuuggggghhhhhhhaaa!" Then he told his friend in the passenger seat to get out.

"I have been sayin' that I've been meanin' to visit good old Flora lately, right? So here I go. She's in Portsmouth. Besides I gotta give her the CDs she ordered." Without thought or comment the passenger allowed the driver to reach over, once, twice, the steering wheel getting in his way, then readjusting himself in the seat, he swallowed, and the third time he finally grabbed onto the door handle, and dis-fastened the door. He then rested his arm on the passenger's knee for a couple of breaths, not looking at him, pausing, went for a fourth push, swinging the door open. The driver sat back and took a couple of deep breaths, feeling sweat in his pants. The passenger looked both ways, first at the open door, which amazingly held open, which was more encouragement for him to leave, then back at the driver, who looked like he had a solution sprung across his face, not giving out the answer.

The driver nodded his head, saying, "Get on mate, it'll be ol'right Lenny, You didn't want come to Ports Mouth anyway, you said yourself that you didn't like it there!" Lowly, the passenger did as was requested of him, he stepped out of the car, slowly, but fully intending to. He did as he was told. The driver also got out without directly saying anything to us, and helped us shove some of our gear into the trunk. The moment was very rush-rush. The driver stirred around the car surreptitiously, yet innocently, looking down the whole time. Then we all got in, and the driver yelled out the window, over the sound of the blown muffler, as he was pulling away, to his friend that he would be back soon to get him. He was holding onto his hat, keeping it from the pull of the wind. His friend, a tall quirky Englishman, was left standing there, uncomplaining, like a dog tied up to a pole.

Marv, Jules, and I fit extremely comfortably together in the back seat of a car. We all looked at each other and agreed upon the moment. All of us still now look back and laugh about this fact. Arlo was up front talking to an excited driver. He was a cherry cheeked fat man with weathered skin. We had more room in his little car than he did. He sat over the steering wheel as he drove, fussing with his oversized hat the whole time, in between shifting gears. He wheezed almost as loud as the motor.

"Sure lads, I'm actually glad to get rid of that guy," looking back through his rear view mirror, then his side mirror, making sure that he wasn't being followed. Then he leaned closer into the rear view mirror, as if he was getting more intimate with us in the back, "You know, he doesn't like music," and he paused, seeming disturbed with confusion, screaming above the sound of his car, "Have you ever met anyone who doesn't like music? I mean, isn't that mad? I know right," shrugging it off and snorting, his hat flopping around on his head, "it's crazy right, and I've been trying to sell him onto the idea of getting some CDs, but like he don't even like when the birds sing. He don't like any kind of music, but he doesn't mind noise. It's crazy not liking music, I mean it's absolutely mad. Must've been something his poor mum did to him when he was little. It is an utter annoyance to have to give him a ride anywhere. Can't listen t'music wit 'im in the car. I can't stand him actually, so it's nice to be rid of him. Anyway, what are you lads into? I like meeting new people. You're Americans right? Of course," and then he stopped, straightened up a bit in his seat and asked with a stern seriousness, "You lads like music right? Sure," not letting us reply, as he looked at Arlo, then at us through the rear view mirror. "Great, check this out then, I just installed it yesterday, I've been blowin fuses left and right, but I'll show you right quick," and with mischievous intensity he pushed a button on his dashboard, looking around creepily.

Then hydraulic noises, which couldn't be heard over the muffler started to maneuver this black panel. Then out came the face of a CD player, "I paid more for this little gizmo than what you boys have ever seen and it's totally worth it. Got it from my mail order catalog actually. A lot cheaper from the States it is. Listen to this!" He pushed the play button and man I almost jumped out of my seat it was so frightening loud. We all cringed at the vigor, force and depth of the sound. It was so loud, I couldn't even tell what kind of music it was. I was about to jump into the front seat to ask him to turn it down, as he was banging his head against the air when all of a sudden, it went off. "Damn, I blew anotha one, shite! Oh well. Sorry boys, I ain't got no more fuses, I'll have to get some in Portsmouth. And it's alright goin there, I mean, I don't mind given you boys a ride, cause I have to give someone some CDs that she ordered through my mail order catalog anyway."

Marv spoke up loudly, above the noise of the car's movement and also probably his temporary deafness, "How far is it to the Portsmouth."

The cheery gent replied in quick verses, "Oh, not that far, I say, it's a just a bit more now. Not that far. After all mates, we are goin there!"

"Oh!" Jules and I said, laughing.

I started to talk about our fate, itching my inner ear with my pinky, "See we could have made it even if we walked!"

"Yeah, sure," Marv said as he sat back, fixing himself into a comfortable position in the car. And then with intent, turning around, bobbing up and down, then turning back around and beaming his eyes in the rear view mirror, forgetting that he was driving, the lad overheard our conversation in the back about making it there if we would have walked. He seemed amazed at us, somewhat almost patronizing as he cut in on our conversation. Several times he repeated himself about our chosen method of travel.

With wondering emphasis, he said "You can't walk all the way to Ports Mouth! Awe, get a cab or a bus, a train even! It's cheap! You can't walk! Why would you do a thing like that, with all that stuff you're carrying mates? Walk? Are you mad lad?" Asking the last question to me, as he looked in his rear view mirror at me, his hat falling over his eyes as we hit a bump.

"Mad?" I said, "Ha ha ha ah, those are my initials! Ah ha ha aha ha ahaha aha aha a!"

Fog crept in through the air vents of the car. The whole scene was etched with a cartoon tint. The driver looked on to what he was doing, with a rag, he wiped clean the face of the CD player. He kept looking at me through the rear view mirror, curious about me, in a doctor/patient sort of way. He settled in and after a short time he asked Arlo, who was proclaiming himself as our leader, what we were going to do in France. Arlo drew him a story of notorious fame and cruel wealth, abundance, and opulence waiting for us at the Cannes Film Festival. Ostentatiously, the driver didn't disagree with our success, he smiled and shook his head up and down. However then, with a patronizing look at his passengers, he wondered what it was like to have such youthful ignorant confidence. I bet he was glad he wasn't American. If he was smart, he would have been wondering if we were planning on letting him finish out the ride with us. I didn't necessarily think about anything at the time I just allowed the moment to move on. Fame, Success, Yeah... The scenery was curving around us as we whipped up and down on the winding road. My ears were still ringing from the burst of screaming sound that came through his hidden speakers. I was held snug into place by my backpack on my lap.

When we arrived at Portsmouth, our driver explained to us that this guy, named Guy would give us discount tickets. He was rushing his words, and said something about mentioning his name to Guy, which he never gave us, even though we asked for it several times. He would just divert the question as if he didn't hear it, and he would just keep blabbing about Guy. Anyway, we said our thanks, and Marvin dropped him two pounds for the ride, although he really didn't have to. He let us off right at the entrance doors. He was polite, but it was hard for him to move around, he was unproportionately surrounded by his weight; full of fat roles. He helped us take our stuff out of his trunk, his hat falling over his eyes several times. Couldn't he tighten it, I thought? Then this amazing looking blonde woman, completely well built, probably just from outdoor activity and maintenance as opposed to working out, came over to say hi to him.

"Smiley!" She yelled from across the lot, getting closer within seconds. We all looked at her with silent desperate stares. Who ever looked at her, thought that it would have been really nice to know her more intimately. "I saw you drive in. Coming to talk to Guy again? Maybe sell some CDs?" nagging him with body language, and finger taunts, "Speaking of which, have mine arrived yet?"

"Got them right here Flora!"

She looked at us, well, mostly at Jules. As she looked us up and down, I could see a twang of jealousy. We were as free as the road ahead of us. Adventure spun around us tight, like saran wrap. Even the simplest things were a joy within our space. "Actually Flora, I just brought these lads in. They're from America, catchin' the ferry to France. I was goin to stop n see ya on me way out. I was gonna bring ol' Lenny but I couldn't take ridin wit' him, so we was just driven around listenen to nothin'."

'Check out her wrists and ankles,' I said to myself in my mind, 'God they are exquisite. Damn look at her collar bone, jeez.' I was going nuts in my brain, this woman was definitely sexy, my eyes walked all over her body.

She asked inquiring, wishing she could drop it all and come to where ever it was we were going, even if it was no where special, "Well where in all of God's fate are you boys off to in France? Paris?" She had excitement glazing in her eyes, choosing to talk directly to Jules, as our interpreter.

He could not speak. Neither could I. Arlo started making an incoherent gabble of an attempt to an answer. The mind confused itself when surrounded with the presence of feminine eminence. Marv was the most cohesive of all of us, even Smiley, who was staring at her without blinking, not tired of looking at her even though he probably saw her a lot. Marvin Ellowin told her softly, with the delicacy of a baby kitten "Cannes, France for the film festival."

"I've been to France several times, but only down South just once for a couple of days in Monte Carlo. It was a very beautiful experience."

'You're a very beautiful experience,' I said in my mind, wondering if I had said it out loud by accident after I had said it, but no one looked at me in shock. Marv looked at me plainly, wondering at my confusion, as if I was following the course of a flies movement with my eyes, bugging out. I shook my head, disregarding anything he was thinking. He exhaled.

She didn't have to say it, but she did, "You boys are in for the times of your lives, so enjoy it while you can."

"How can we not, meeting generous people like yourselves, "Arlo rebutted, looking at both of them. What ass kissing he is good at, he was trying to get in good with the woman. The driver would have been lucky to get a thanks out of him if she didn't show up.

Blatantly, our presence created an aroma just because we were foreign travelers. Not like traveling salesmen showing up on your doorstep to sell you a vacuum cleaner or CDs, we were Estranieros. Which, loosely interpreted from small town Spanish dialect means, from a foreign land; strangers! It sounds so much better when it is said in Spanish. Home was wherever our feet were. She, on the other hand probably had to go and fix dinner for her children. How many times had she seen people coming and going from this town. She was somewhat older than any of us. Being now, the mother of a family, earning a living and raising children weighing her down, keeping her from floating away. Her destiny was sewn to her soul just as much as ours was and still is. Who knows maybe she did have little rituals in her everyday life that she held secretly, deeply within her, that made her feel life, Ingesting it like she was immersed in an ether. And after all, there is a simple and pleasant contentness, in stability and order. Besides, how long can one person really stay on the road? Although this was technically just a vacation, was I planning on living like this when I got back to the States? At the time, I was sure that I could answer no, but who knew the kinds of loss I would suffer, breaking me of my will to live. Anyway, besides it all, I could definitely never ever tell my mother where I was sleeping, or how I was living.

The only thing is, which is my own fault, is that I liked this style of living so much. Free, travelling, poor and dirty. People really did have to look through a lot to want to attempt a relationship with us. Much to my amazement people did approach us, wanting to ask questions in a kindly curios way. It must have been easy to tell that we were humble, peaceful travelers, especially with Jules along. He is naturally just pleasing to look at, like watching a unicorn graze and snort in a field of sunflowers, knowing full well that you should only stare from afar, quietly, less it hears you and flies off. Well, our driver and the girl were definitely non-discriminatingly kind to us. We said goodbye to them and they wished us well. Everybody wishes you well in England. He reminded us to talk to Guy. Then the lady said that she had had lunch with guy to Smiley. He nodded, most likely having already heard all about it. Every body knows everybody else's business in small towns.

"I let him hear one of the CD's I bought from you the other day, but I told him I got it at Pico's. It sounds great-"

"Ohh, Flora, Picos' is so expensive, Guy'll come around eventually and buy from me! Especially because I can get it cheaper and I have a bigger classical selection than crummy ol William and his dirty little store."

"Yes, I know, but..." she noticed us starting to leave and she waved, smiling and for a second we all stopped, not one of us moved. Secret wishes and longings desperately calling made me want to give it all up, if she would have me. I tilted my head, looking at my feet. How dungy they were, with long uncut crumbling nails, I sighed. Rare winds stirred magical spells at the creation of this ravishingly desirous species of a woman. To be with her must have been what the breeze felt like in paradise. I turned and walked toward the agency door with my head down, defeated of my purpose in life, at least momentarily. Slowly, my comrades followed, The Sloth being the last to leave the sweet women's presence. Taking as much of her in as he could.

The inside of this ports ticket agency entrance was relatively bright. It was big, spacious, but bare. People looked at us as we entered, in the normal curious custom to anyone entering the scene. There was mostly children and kids travelling with their parents. French families going home from their English vacation. A few French executives standing around waiting to go home after their international business affairs. Other people were coming and going. Nobody wanted to stop to help anyone, they all had to get somewhere. We set our gear down and I decided to head the mission to inquire about our passage.

"I'll handle this. Jules you hang with the stuff, and Arlo and Marv'll come with me. Ok?"

"Sure," as he sat down, glad to have a break.

"Marv you got-" and I didn't say anything more, his eyes were ever alert to the scene, he was holding what I was asking for, knowing the routine well. We may have to pay something for the ride, but it wouldn't be much. After all, if I really wanted to, I could sell sand to the Arabs. "Ok, let's go, and Arlo keep quiet."

"No problem!." He said excitingly, running his hands through his short dark hair. Wondering and waiting to see what I could stir up.

We walked over to the English side of the agency. All the agents staring at us, hoping to get a commission, I guess. Arlo was drooling, ready to buy a ticket on his daddy's credit card according to the prices displayed on the advertised packages on the wall. I looked around at the agents. I picked him out, Guy, how did I know it was him. I looked at Marv and he agreed, smiling, thinking this was going to be easier than he thought. He crossed his arms. We walked up and a girl, tall, with a beanstalk quality, especially around her neck asked, "Welcome to…"

"Actually lady, we're here to see Guy," sounding real ruff, putting an elbow on the countertop, sliding in closer to her, pointing with my other finger at Guy, who was with his back toward us. My eyes attacked her, and she blinked nervously. He perked his head up, his movement froze as he heard his name being used by a stranger, but he did not turn around.

She took a step back, my beard most likely offending her, "Um, uh, Guy? Well, I could help if it's…"

"No, you can't help, Lady, you see, we have to talk to him!"

And she was real scared, backing off a bit more, as I switched elbows on the counter, "Uh, Guy?" He was hoping that he had mistaken what he had heard, or hoping she would take a message for him, because he didn't turn around. It took her a couple of attempts to get his attention. He was intimidated, and was hoping we would go away. He probably didn't like confrontations of any sort. "Um, Guy, some gentlemen are here to see you!"

"What? Who? Me?" And he turned around practically over spinning. I had a real rough look on, initially, to set the pace of things, then I smiled grandly, standing straight and upright, saying, "Guy, come on over here!" Waving my arm inward, reeling him in. He stalled, hesitating his steps, still holding a piece of paper in his hands. He was trying to keep it from shaking, but his nervousness showed like the sun. Then he started to shuffle his feet. "Good boy, come here."

He smiled without knowing why, trying to hide his insecurities, but failing. His curls came down in front of his face and he kept accidentally biting on them as he chewed on his lips. His upper front teeth stuck out a little bit. He wouldn't stop smiling. He looked like that cartoon character who knew something you didn't know and went around singing that phrase, except in this case, he didn't know anything you didn't know.

He kept saying nervously, "Oh, uh, ok, um, oh, let me see, Uh, ok, um, Oh, ok," then all of a sudden he burst out, "Uh, hello lads, wh-wh-what can I do you for?" Asking, not even professionally. He must have forgotten that he was at work. All the features of his face were working at once, distorting his ability to see in the same direction with both eyes. I had no choice but to take advantage of his capability to help us.

"Well Guy, here's the story, you see. Now we're all friends here," and I reached over the countertop and squeezed his shoulder. He was frail, and he cringed as I did it. "Sure, we all know the same people. That's right Guy, now, I'll tell you, you see," going off on this tangent, sounding like a monologue, with utter confidence. Marv and Arlo were around me, closing into the space, getting into Guy's face a bit. I could hear Arlo laughing through his loud breaths. My straggly beard, Arlo's excitement glazing his forehead, and Marv, looking down on everything, with judicial quietness, we hit him with it, "I'm a very good friend of a friend of yours. Actually you're a very good friend of a friend of mine, you see, it's like this," and I looked upwards seeming to initiate a long proverbial speech, "Well, I and Flora have been…"

"Uh, um, ok, y-y-you know F-F-Flora?" He didn't hesitated to but in, that was a good sign, as he wondered incessantly, how could it be?

"Huh?" I stopped, pretending to be aloof, I looked at him as if it was a brilliant question, "Oh, Flora, well of course, you see, we have been writing letters back and forth for some time now. You see, well, actually," and I leaned in closer, lowering the volume of my bullshit, making things more personal, I took a pause, allowing him to draw in closer as well. He did, his curiosity had the best of him. I took a breath, and turned slightly to look at Marv, he nodded, signaling me to go on with the story, I looked back at the frightened little man in front of me, "I was originally corresponding with Smiley, you know Smiley right? Yes, so we were corresponding, because, I was sending him CD's, yeah. Mostly Led Zeppelin and the like, but then Flora wanted some stuff, and I was getting it real cheap in the states, I'll tell ya, so sending CD's over to England to good friends was no problem. And I know the prices you guys pay out here, and bein' such good of friends of mine in good old England, I figured why not. I mean after all, we did needlessly dump all that tea into the river didn't we? Anyway, Flora wanted some classical music, in which I'm sure you've heard..."

"Oh, uh, Y-Yes but she said she bought it at Pico's record store..." I gave him some space physically. Arlo rearranged his posture, shuffling his feet and running his hand through his hair again.

"That's just what she's tellin' you Guy," and I leaned in close again and squeezed him on the arm, "you see, she has a surprise for you, or..." I stalled, pulled back a little, looking at him, pretending to be scrutinizing him. He became embarrassed and looked away shyly. He couldn't take the inquisition.

"Hmm, or did she give you your present today at lunch?" My arms were crossed, and my face questioned him.

"Lunch?" How would I know about that, he thought? I didn't give him a chance to think.

"Yes of course, she did give it to you today, and wow, your speechless, I can see that we have a changed man..." My arms were flailing and I reached around and patted Arlo on the back. Marv started speaking, wanting to laugh, "Yep, she gave it to him, what a lucky man he is!" And we all started congratulating ourselves.

Guy interrupted us, and for the first time speaking up loudly, "Wait, uh, oh, Well uh, no, she didn't give me anything at lunch. She has a present for me? What could it be?" The girl with the beanstalk neck looked in our direction from behind Guy, I could feel Marv raise up to stand on his toes. Then a look of fear crossed her face and she shot her eyes back to the papers on her desk.

"Oh. She didn't give you the CD's? Oops I said too much, she's gonna kill me." Arlo slapped me on the back and nodded his head in disapproval. "I'm sorry, I shouldn't have said anything."

"Yeah Welton, you ruined his surprise!"

"Well jeez Marv, I just thought that she gave it to him already." I looked down to my feet nodding my head, and Arlo and Marv did the same thing.

"She has CD's for me. Oh, she really was listening to me when I told her my favorite radio programs." And he got lost in his memory and nostalgia, and for a second, he was in the glee of an impossible moment of his hopes, but I snapped him out of it. I looked up, now forcefully.

"Yes well, that's the reason I am here, Guy, back to business, you see, since Flora got such a price on the music, I was assuming that you would give us a good price on the ferry ride! To France, for four people. What do you say Guy, it's not everyday that you run into good friends that you never met before."

"Um," still thinking about Flora.

"Boy, that Flora is somethin' special, taking the time out to transcribe over seas just for a present for you! You must be pretty important to her. After all, she has mentioned your name several times in the letters."

"She has, oh. Well, uhm, uh, what did she say? She mentioned my name? Oh, wow, tell me, please!" I stood silent for a time. I let him speak up, as I held my breath. What the fuck was going on, and how much longer did I have to deal with this weakling. He adjusted himself, and cleared his throat, "Well, she does care for me, I knew it! Oh thank you gentlemen, thank you, oh, how could I repay you..." He stopped talking, not even thinking of how he was going to repay us, He was lost in his mind somewhere, in a field with Flora, but I was just about to remind him, how he, could repay us, for all we've done for him.

I stood erect, I felt an interrupting hunger pain in my stomach but I dismissed it, "Well Guy, we need a cheap ride to France, and it's been a real long day, so let's stop playing around here. What's our situation look like from your end?"

"What?" Now back in reality, "Well, uhm, we do offer rides, if the ferry isn't full," and he took a second to look around to see if anybody was listening to him, "at a minimal rate. We don't like to offer the deal, but sometimes we do." Standing tall, proud of what he was about to say, he spoke up, "I can give you tickets for fifteen pounds each!" And he stood taller, thinking this was a good deal. Marv was courteously quiet, strictly business was he, in his demeanor, demanding respect from merely his physical presence, not to mention the sinister look in his eyes, unhidden, behind his glasses. Arlo breathed in quick and tight, pulling in some drooling saliva, making an unpleasant noise, holding in his breath. I stopped him short of speaking up, he was about to bust out his credit card again, thinking this to be a steal, after looking at the prices displayed on the wall. I didn't even turn around to look at him, I simply just put my hand up, halting and silencing his movement. If Guy was going to play ball and offer us a special deal, I was going to get him to give us the best deal possible, because, frankly, it was possible.

I started to get pissed, "Now wait a minute Guy, I came all the way to England to do you a favor and this is the best you can do? I mean that's still about one hundred and twenty dollars for the four of us. Now that's just great, you can't help anybody out, because you never get any help in return. Great," and I turned around and started off, pushing through Arlo and Marv,

"Well boys, looks like were gonna have to swim," Pausing, not turning around to look at Guy, "Or maybe we should stay a while in Portsmouth?"

"What? Stay? Here! In Ports Mouth!" And I didn't say anything, still with my back to him, he must have assumed I meant stay with Flora, because that was exactly what I was going to let him think. For a second I wondered if he was going to question me more intimately about Flora, but instead, and to our advantage, he asked, "Well uh, oh, umm, how much money do you have?"

And I turned around slowly, smiling, "Marv?"

"Twenty eight pounds, and we need four of it for tomorrow."

"Geez, twenty four pounds, for four tickets, I-I can't do it that cheaply mates, it's just impossible-"

"Oh well," and I started to turn around again saying, "That's ok, we'll go back over to Flora's, actually, that sounds like a good idea, we were thinking about staying awhile, after all she has been really nice to us, hasn't she fellas?" Looking to my mates as they nodded, not having to say anything but smile, "and I have been meaning to get to know her better…"

"Get to know…wh-wh- what are you talking about, I mean, you're going to stay with her, here?"

"Sure, I kind of like it here, and besides I don't have enough money to leave so," I had this guy, just a little more, "And she did offer us a place to stay, and she has been meaning to introduce us to you, and we could all get to know each other, and man it would be a thrill to get to know her!"

"Oh, no, Flora!" He was beat. He looked down and shook his head. He reached deep inside himself, and was about to do something for her honor, he looked around again to see if anybody was listening to him, he sniffled and said, "Ok, ok, um, oh geez. I can put you lads on the next ferry, f-f-for six pounds each. A-a-a-and it's without return, it's just a one time deal. I-I-I mean don't come back lookin' for another deal like this, because I'm giving you my ticket rate, and I'm not really allowed to do that, unless it's for my immediate family."

"Oh don't worry Guy, we won't be back, we're going to sell some CD's in France, and by the way, you're goin to enjoy your present, boy are you gonna." I wagged my finger at him, "But don't forget to look surprised when she gives them to you, ok. Great. Marv, pay the man, Arlo, get the tickets, I'm goin to go see if Jules is still here. Great to see you Guy, and thanks a lot pal!" And I walked off, tired of having to take that guy for a spin, but it was easy. What are you going to do, we didn't have enough money for our travels, but we had to keep moving. You got to do what you have to do. Actually it was a surprisingly good deal. Guy just needed a little egging on, and he was glad to help. So without disagreeing, Marv paid in our last remaining English currency, barely able to make the quota of his estimation. I was getting the feeling that having connections was how these things worked. It's either that or we were getting really lucky, and our karma was good. It couldn't be that I was really good at conning people, because I'm not.

I didn't mind paying for the tickets. They were cheap. But to us, even cheap was expensive. What were we going to do though, we were on a time schedule. This ferry would travel throughout the night and arrive south in France in the morning, via the port of St Malo, closer to our destination than Calais where the ferries let you off in France from Dover, England. We had over an hour of time until the ferry was available to board. Jules was camped out like a slob, laid out on our stuff, which was in a mound, but seemed all over the lobby.

"Where are the fellas?"

"Getting the tickets. We're sorted."

"Cool."

"Yeah," I sat down just as Arlo and Marv came up.

"Nice work Mr. Spells."

"What'd he do?"

"Nothin'," I said, "Arlo bought us the tickets on his daddy's credit card."

"Really? Thanks Arlo."

"Yeah well don't thank him too much, after all, it's his dad's card, you should thank him."

"Well I will, next time I talk to his mom, I'll tell her to thank the big guy."

"Damn Jules, what the fuck? Ha ha Arlo, you faggot." And we all laughed, even Arlo. Marv and him sat down. Marv was wearing the now empty hat.

"Well, boys, we are on our way to France! And maybe we'll even be in Cannes by tomorrow night!"

"Whatever, I mean, however long it takes. I think the awards ceremony is the day after tomorrow, at night, and I kind of have to make that, I gotta see if somebody showed up."

"Who? Jonny O's boy?" Asked Marv, wondering innocently but we all started to smirk at his name again.

And Jules became mischievous, "Ahh, nobody man, I hope it works out with that guy, I'd love to sell this thing and get on with life, but I can meet him anytime. Jonny O said he'd be there all week."

"Who else you gotta meet there Jules?" I questioned.

"Nothin, I mean, my mom mentioned somethin about somebody she once knew, way back in the day, who's pretty famous now, and almost had a thing with him, but then she met my dad."

"Oh, that's cool," and I didn't press the issue, besides, the more that I thought about it, the more Cannes was beginning to feel like a good idea. Anyway, I mean, a lot of important people would be there. Even me! Ha ha, what a joke life is.

We lounged, killing time, drinking gin. One of the more bold French boys veered from his family. He came over and climbed through our mountain of gear and started trying to untie some juggling clubs that were tied to the outside of Marv's backpack. I tried pushing him away, but he went over to my drum and started banging on it, in an attempt to put a hole in the sensitive head. I took that away from him as well. He had an arrogant smile, which meant he knew he was being mischievous, and he thought that he was still cute enough to get away with being spoiled at the publics' expense. It began to get more hectic as other children came over to inspect our commotion. They wouldn't leave us alone, asking us to juggle for them and play music. Well, instead of moving the brats along, we ended up doing a light juggling routine in the lobby, taking up the space gregariously71.

Arlo played his drum, but not annoyingly, softly, braising the head, not beating on it. Marv and I passed juggling clubs between us, as Shivers played our favorite song on his guitar. I dropped passes every once in a while. I was bored, stopping and starting, sometimes swinging them around in a spinning pattern, wishing that the clubs were on fire, it would have been more impressive and intense. Everyone liked us, probably because we had paid for our tickets, and maybe because we didn't put out a hat to collect money for entertaining their children, while they waited for the ferry. It was not really the place to perform a show, let alone ask people for money. So, free it was, but totally in a laxadaisical fashion. Four Americans sitting around drinking from a pint bottle, passing it around, falling over and smelling of spotted rot. In the interim, we juggled and played music. What a sight we must have been. However, I saw smiling faces looking in our direction so it couldn't have been that bad. Regardless, we were just as legitimate a passenger as anyone else waiting for the ferry.

I went upstairs to use the bathroom. This place was huge. I walked down this tall long fluorescent lighted corridor, silently. I heard murmured echoes distantly reflecting along the hall, coming from behind me, following me. The men's room was clearly out of reach from anyone instantly in need of it. At the end of the hallway I found it, the ladies room being placed at the beginning of the corridor, by the steps. I walked into an immense bathroom, fully capable of handling a rush of many handicapped users at once. It was empty, with little air left to breath. The mirrors were deserted of any activity. I walked over and put myself into the mirrors' force field. Staring at myself, unsure whether or not I should look into my eyes. Hoping that the mirror wouldn't crack.

I looked myself wholly over. Jules had cut my hair attentively short a couple of days ago, and I could see a red irritated scalp glowing, showing bumps that weren't supposed to be there. My beard was way past the stage of decently kept, and I couldn't even see my face. My shirt was caked dirty from lack of laundry, and it was sore with hash burns all over the mid-section. It was only attached by two solely remaining buttons, a 50's short sleeve suit shirt, discolored, stained, and broken. I wasn't wearing any underwear, and my jeans were just as dirty as my shirt. At least my jeans weren't ripped yet. Actually, it was Jules' clothes I was wearing. Only the sandals were mine, but who knows who's they were before I had come across them. They were holding up, solidly fine. These exact clothes I had chosen to wear on many a previous escapade, while in Europe. They were the perfect comfort to travel in, providing the weather was suitable. The washing I had done on them in between voyages wasn't sufficient enough to displace the layered in dirt and stench so they weren't exactly clean from the get go on this trip, but I was guaranteeing that they would last forever, or at least outlast me. I had been wearing these clothes for the past week now, in preparation for a moments notice departure.

I opened up the faucet and splashed tepid, distasteful water onto my face. I stood straight and let the water dribble onto my chest, I took off my shirt to aid the process. This place was remarkably clean. For the first time today, I washed myself with soap. Mopping my bearded face, hair from all over, falling off my body. I soaped up my stomach, neck, armpits, arms, and as much of my back as I could. I was well lathered. Looking like a costume in the mirror, I washed it all off with splashes of water from the running faucet. My lower body could wait, after all, I wasn't exactly in a shower, I was out in the common middle of the restroom, totally exposed to anyone walking in. My sandals hydroplaned on the slippery puddle water on the tile floor. I dried myself off with some paper towels. I took a better look in the mirror. I perceived myself to be still just as dirty as I was before my clean up session. Smiling as if I had expected it, I walked over, bouncing and a little hung over to my left side, swaying drunk, to use the facilities toiletry system.

In the roomy stall, I felt soft nostalgia from a mystic source, as the smell of my penis consumed me. I held myself as urine flowed out of me with sweet relief, thinking that no just woman would put her lips on it, how it was looking. Even though it was not riddled in disease, it was however, dirty, and full of dried stained cottage cheese looking schmegma from the extended sexual venues I had recently had with Cherissa. It also had been a while now since my last real shower. Somehow though, I seemed comfortable with my scent in this condition. My penis and I really were dirty, but the smell was intriguing to me, full of the dense odor of lustful greedy sex and soiled salty sweat. I accepted it, knowing fully that this was no way to get a decent woman's interest, but I had other things to deal with right now. I zipped up carefully and I left without looking into my eyes through the mirror. I tracked water all the way down the corridor as I whistled a tune, appreciating the echoing effects.

Back in the lobby there were other newly arrived passengers of vast differences standing near each other, but not mingling. In places of arrival and departures, people tend to congregate within tight personal spaces peaceful. They were all sort of just there, like pieces of luggage themselves, set down and keeping to their own distinction. Our mountain of gear and equipment seemed the most interesting out of all the other passengers. The kids had dispersed and Marv had packed up the juggling clubs and he was now standing, leaning on a knee over Jules, talking and laughing about something Arlo had done. There were some groups of people all travelling together getting really drunk. They were mostly French students. We wisely didn't mingle with any of them. An announcement was made; first by the French agents, in French then repeating it in English. Then by the English agents only in English. The English girl, with the beanstalk neck, looking now, like a giraffe because of the way she was holding the microphone to her mouth, her head facing the ceiling. She sounded confused at her attempt to show up her French rivals public speaking display. They had both expressed in the same exact words that it was time to start boarding the ferry. We loaded up our gear and queued up, letting everyone pretty much go in front of us. Slowly, we came into view of our next form of transportation.

A Monty Carlo casino style cruiser; a mini ocean liner. It was no little ferry. It was a ship; big, broad, and glaring white. We walked up some caged in platforms on the port to get onto the entrance platform high above on the ship. Excited at the impressive hunk of welded metal. Cars were crawling into the mouth that lay open as tall as it was wide. It stood opened, enormous, swallowing even flying birds. Everything you could possibly want was on this ferry. It was no way near full capacity when we all boarded. You could have fit the population of a small state onboard. It was getting cold, and nighttime was falling on our last moments in England. We got on the ferry patiently. It was just huge with many different multi-leveled areas. There was an actual theater in an auditorium, also a large screen movie theatre, a couple of restaurants, and a cafeteria. Big open spaces on several decks with indoor and outdoor seating. Large indoor parking garages for cars. Bars, a duty-free shop, massive lounge areas with seating on all floors, and wide open areas for congregation. There were long corridors with windows looking out by the duty free shop, and on every other level as well. It could have taken days merely to explore the whole vessel.

We walked up and down levels, like we were on a museum tour, going outside, rolling up a hash joint while crouching from the wind, and smoking it, getting cold. Waves passed, engulfed under the belly of the ferry. It divided natures' path. The paradoxical tranquility of the loudness of the waters' attack, and the silence of the distance was calming. Cold shoving winds stung with frozen specs of night, glistening, shedding sparse brittle glimpses of light. We went back inside, and found others to stand around with. A group of French students from the ticket agency lobby, getting drunker, and being loud were on the third floor, with cases of beer sitting were they stood, being emptied quickly. There were French and English families that I hadn't seen at the port, claiming most of the seating areas on the lower levels, travelling, not appearing so much for vacation, as it seemed like for personal or business reasons. There was an arcade room, and TV's were set up in certain seating rooms. Children were running around in playland. It was bright, and on one closed section there was an advertisement for a dinner theatre show that was offered on early evening voyages.

We were standing around the French students who were getting drunk. One guy was taking off his hat and putting it on other people's heads. He tried to take Marv's hat off, and exchange it with his, putting his on Marv's head. Nobody ever really gets that close to him without being invited. In a polite fashion, Marv let him know that it was not a good move. He held on to the guys wrist, asking for a reason to snap the hand from the wrist. His eyes were delicate, no pressure being indicated whatsoever from Marv, but the Frenchman couldn't even move around or struggle, he was held in his place by sheer power. The Frenchman who still had some wit about him, realized the accuracy of Marv's grip, his body language, and his stare. He shook his hand as Marv let go of it, he put his hat back on his own head, smiled like a loud drunkard and went to get another beer, swallowing the rest of the one he had in his hand as he walked away. He was lucky to leave unscathed. We went to the top floor, sitting a while in the stairwell, playing music and smoking. We were moving along steadily, the ship dizzily holding a constant fussing tempo. Like white noise, it over took my unconscious mind. Bass draping vibrations as loud as a house fan in a small room, but more four-dimensional, everywhere, the floors prickled and shook. Up on the top floor, a window played darkness along an unseen coast. We stared at it, standing still. It settled our moment with a candled quietness, Marv was the only moon we could see, not quite full yet, just shy a bit in the upper left corner, but surrounded gloriously by rings of purple haze. His eyes were tinted yellow. Deep inside of him an Indian lay sweating in a ceremony; One hundred degrees or more of hot rocks, burning.

A long grave form of a person, with an austere face, and a misogynic crease on his forehead he let out as a breath, "Alright..." as content pleasure rolled and tingled his skin.

"Yeah, this is a nice ride, huh?" Jules raised his voice but was tired looking in his slacking posture. He wasn't looking at anybody, probably not even paying attention to what he was saying. He was with an empty stare, blinded by a dead light. He leaned to one side, not bothering to scratch the itch that tore at him on the back of his neck.

Underneath a solemn face I deliberated, "Full day!" like an interruption, trying to cover up my insecurities with a stretch, but my backpack held me down, "And tomorrow isn't going to be easier, but at least it'll be more fun dealing with the French." My face changing, now undisguised. I shouldn't have said anything. Luckily Arlo didn't speak up. He knew not to spoil the moment anymore than I just had, we let it pass.

For seconds, all of us forgot any implications of the days ahead of us. Then all together while looking around at each other, we burst out laughing at the French train conductors who's path we would cross soon. They were sure in for a bit of a stir at least. We laughed for a bit more, talking a bunch of nonsense, but relaxing, happy. "The next couple of days are gonna be perfect!" Arlo finally broke.

"Yeah, perfect days," I said, "like when all the coincidences fall into place, and everything that's supposed to happen, happens."

Marv stretched out his words, "Yeah, like a carnival of synchronicity!"

"Yeah, that's some crazy energy." Jules agreed, sighing. It was late and we were tired, or we would have started taking the Sloth for granted, kicking him around like the donkey, just for fun of course. After all, he survived his first day on the dirty road of the poor travelers. He was soon to become another 'Brother of the Brand'.

When lateness dropped to its' final temperature, and it was time to sleep, we sluggishly found a somewhat empty section on one of the top floors. It was the lobby seating room of the movie theatre. We sat in seats at first right next to each other. It was like being in a San Francisco handicap cat burglar line up. All of us nudging for elbow room on the armrests. Pecking words at each other like chickens, grunting, and snorting, then someone farting and causing a ruckus. Marv was writing in his journal, Jules was strumming on his guitar, lightly, and Arlo and I were trying new rhythms softly on the drums. I was whistling and Marv was letting out a moving hum, in waves of feathers from his lips. Arlo was smoking a cigarette, his smoke getting in my eyes, bringing on tears. An employee had rolled in a cage of blankets for all to use. He looked at us stupidly concerned, because we were morons, we didn't just look like them. He left quickly. I didn't bother getting up to get a blanket. Eventually we all fell asleep in our sitting positions.

As night came on and it was barley comfortable, hotness enveloping me as fit as a suit, sweat encasing me, making my confinement within the space unbearable, I jumped up half asleep with no other intention but to rearrange my sleep to the floor. They all followed me, one by lonely one. Our first night out, not having to worry about sleeping on the street. This was the good life. Not really having to sleep with our eyes open. If we didn't make this ferry where would we have slept in England? At Flora's? Yeah right, in my dreams. I took a sad desperate breath, weazing in and out, like a dry tear not coming out of my eyes. Missing this ferry would have thrown off our timing, I thought. I rolled onto my side, my hip straining under the pressure, no soft cushion or bed to dampen the resistance from the plain floor. Arriving into France in the morning was a good thing. We could jump trains during the day more easily, or hitchhike. For if we arrived at night, where would we have caught a ride in France? Only Jules could have gotten a ride at night on a dark road in a foreign land. The rest of us would have been lost to the dust of the moment. Because of our time schedule we had to buy tickets, but it was worth spending some money on a ride. The film festival ceremony would have been over by the time we got there had we missed this ferry. And for some reason, I had a feeling that we needed to be there on time. I didn't know why, perhaps hearing Arlo in the car early, talking about our soon to be grand success was getting to my head. However, everything was going smoothly so far, but who knew how it would all end.

II Chapter

It was a daring day. The dawn had broken, rising me from my helpless inner haven. I woke up sober, My eyes still crusted shut, but, at the very least of my situation, I knew where I was. Yet, under the quilt of the early morning arousal, I lay momentarily isolated, unable to fully think or comprehend, hiding from the waking awareness around me. I took in a breath from the life of the new day, and then I tried to push it all away, what it was that always scared me into not wanting to wake up. There was much to look forward to, the words formed bleakly in my mind, 'We had made it to France'. The excitement of a new day provoked me. I opened my eyes, forcefully, to the sunlight, blinding me, and filling the space around us all. I blinked continuously, holding my hand in front of my face as a shield, trying to adjust my eyes to the light. I stood up trying to support a stiff and sore neck with but just a halfless smile and a snort of stale, yeast dirty breath. There was nothing else, except what would only add to the sour dilemma of my straining pain. Thank God I was young, because in a couple of moments I wouldn't feel any more pain at all. Delusions of courage would rise from the strength of the feeling of a new day, that would act as Anastasia among my physical being.

Barely rested from inadequate sleep, my bones creaked. I was sore, especially my hips. I felt like an old lady that had given birth way to many times to way too many unappreciative children. I stretched and yawned, arousing myself, scratching incessantly at my head, loosening some of the dirt out of my hair. I looked over to my mates hoping to find my lost inspiration. Arlo was gone, but his stuff was still around, lingering close to Jules. Foolish

77

was he to leave it all unattended, I thought. I cracked my back and neck, ahh, it was a crescendo from the percussion of my body. Arcing my back felt so good. I was waking up with wider steps towards coherency and awareness. I looked around, not however investigating the scene, but more to acquire points of reference for my frame of mind.   The big cart of blankets was still sitting there, dead. I wanted to take a blanket, but I knew, I already had too much gear. We were now in the French time zone. England was but a forgotten memory, and through the grand viewing window, which stretched the eight or so feet from the ceiling to the floor, I could see the shore of St. Malo, crawling steadily toward us, getting bigger, consuming the horizon.

Jules was sitting still, with the emphasis of someone recently dead, hoping that someone else would come along and fold down and close his big bright unblinking eyes. I couldn't even tell if he was drawing breath. Physically, he didn't seem aware of my curiosity for him. He seemed to be somewhere else. But that's just how he is in the morning. Marvin on the other hand, was moving around, rocking up and back, a cradle motion, perhaps to move the blood around in his system. We were inadequate bandits at the moment, unable to respond to a threat if it came along. But it was ok, we were safe at the moment. I was vibrating all over from the monotonous drone of the ship, so I stood up, limping, because my left foot was dead from sleep in its sandal. I stretched my body to its peak and yawned loudly, breaking the tension within the confines of Jules' contemplation's. He blinked himself back to reality as I heard him breath deep.

After a couple of breaths, I spoke up, "So, anyone know where Arlo is?"

"He went to use the bathroom, I think. He was gone when I woke up, and
his stuff was tied to me."

"Man, he better not be getting us into trouble already, it's too early," Marv stated coldly, apparently still cranky tired.

As we were talking, Arlo, clean, with fresh smelling breath, but with a face still unshaven, rolled up onto the scene, smiling and drinking orange juice, looking quite reputable, with the audacity of a proper tourist passenger. Relieved to see him, not only because he was still in one piece, but also because he wasn't being dragged about by the authorities, for some mischief he had caused. I stretched again, and yawned awoken delight. Jules and Marv now both rose as well, stretching, slowly accepting the day. Through sips of orange juice from a thin straw, Arlo tried to smile, but had to stop because the orange juice spilled out of his mouth, running down his cheek. He didn't wipe it away, but started talking hurriedly, telling us the facts.

"Fellas, we'll be docking in under an hour. Yeah, France, baby! We made it! Anyway, there's a cafeteria on the lower level, I stole this from there," raising his small mostly empty carton, "I can go get you guys some if you want?" Impatience starting to rise from him, he tilted his head to the side, his forehead wrinkled as he ran a hand through his short wet hair, he sighed fervently "Well?"

"Slow down, Arlo, let me gather my bearings," I said, sighing louder than he, acting with disinterested provocation as I drew out with a stretch. He sat down upset at being put on a leash, grabbed his drum and started playing. Jules rolled up and lit a hash joint, took a couple drags and passed it around. Breakfast was served.

Thinking for a moment, wondering if we were going to have to show our passports at customs, I asked, "Hey Jules, aren't the French authorities after you?"

From a yawn he said, "Man, are you talkin about Paris, back in March? That situation was so minor, they didn't even record my name!"

"Yeah, man, I remember that!" Marv said as he blew out smoke, "After breakin you out of that holding station, we crept out of the country like pirates, man that was exciting. Yeah, I don't think you have anything to worry about, after all, you said they were nice to you at the police station right?"

"Yeah, they fed me my only meal of that week, and asked me all kinds of questions about the policing strategies in the states."

"Right, what did you tell 'em? That the cops walk the streets with machine guns, stopping and searching vagrant looking folks right on the spot, Yeah!"

"Yeah, I told them Americans lived in fear of their own protection system. Everybody is considered a criminal and an enemy of the democracy."

"You think they really believed you?"

"I don't know, but when they were questioning me, I told them I wanted to defect to France, and they were all quiet, I guess unsure if it was all bullshit. Unsure how to react. Unsure if they wanted me to remain in their country, I mean, I don't even speak French. I told them that the US government controlled the press, and as far as domestic affairs went, publicly, we lived freely, made our own decisions, no one controlling our thoughts," he paused, "yeah right." He said shaking his head

"Well shit man, in Italy, all the cops and security guards at the airports and train stations walk around with machine guns and drug dogs, so they probably figured you were tellin the truth."

"What? What happened? What are you guys talking about? Arlo asked, excited and curious. "Hey, give me a hit of that shit, man!" He demanded.

"Nothin' Arlo, it was nothin, just another adventure that you weren't part of." As I passed him the remnants of the joint.

He grabbed it eagerly and puffed away, "Aw man, I shoulda been there!"

"Yeah but you weren't, and your lucky you're here right now, so when we get to France, don't go getting us into any trouble, we gotta make good time." Marv's eye stare was adamant, not necessarily warning him, but assuring him that repercussion for any mishaps that he caused would be severe.

"Anyway, we should get a move on, I think its time to get the fuck outta here." I blurted.

After standing around for a time, our court closed its session, then we quickly used the bathroom and headed down to the lower levels, we were docking momentarily. With the morning rituals finished, it was time to control and manage my wits. I was high as hell, and feeling great. I had a nation ahead of me to conquer. I looked out into France. What a perspective of life I was seeing. It all looked so clean from afar. Excitement started to pinch me. The ferry was lowering the platform for the cars to exit. People were ushering themselves out single file. Marv was warming into the day, his harmonica was on his lips, fluttering notes zealously as he carried along. Arlo and I were tapping away lightly on our drums, as we all walked step by step into France. The other people around us were quite friendly this morning, smiling, seemingly appreciating our commotion. Jules was still silent, not fully woken up yet. St. Malo, France, not a place that we intended to spend time in, but regardless it was accepting us so beautifully, in its nice attire. Smiles on our faces showed our gladness to be there, making us all trickishly courteous to each other.

Joking with, "Excuse me, Sir!" and "Oh, Pardon me," emulating proper English, bumping into each other.

Arlo began to laugh, he couldn't take it anymore. This was happening to him. Pretty extravagant! It all was looking that way. It was brought on by the water front landscape. It seemed to say that somewhere, seductive French women, in loose flowing dresses walked over small grazed hills. Which to me, were rock faced mountains, that thrill seekers scaled without safety ropes. Wow, At that moment, this place was so much more intense than my hometown in America. As we moved along I felt the rush and energy of the surrounding ado running through my veins. We were all escorted to and through the ports ticket agency, where custom officials stood around, hawk looking, some of them in red beret caps, and hands folded behind their upright backs and tight linen uniforms. I thought that we were going to get stopped and searched, but no one was being asked to declare anything. It was more like crossing a state line. That was a good thing because, hash was still sitting in a ball, in my pocket. Of course it was a small little black ball, that wasn't even wrapped in plastic, or in a cigarette case. It was sitting in with the lint, dirt, and sand from previous beach visits. Considered trash in my pocket to the unkeen eye. It was still smokeable though, at least for us.

Walking through the agency most people were acting as if they had done this a thousand times. Cell phones rang in French style ringing melodies, in the hands of leaned over executives in overtly strict tight suits with short pant legs and raised brown socks, pushing their way through the pomposity of the pandemonium, boldly leaning into it head first. The lobby lay full of the possibility to rent a car. People were waiting, aroused from a full night of better sleep than I had. Hugs were being handed out among awaiting friends and family. Roars and laughter built up in distinct locations, then quieted to the existing murmur. We walked outside, I guess we started looking for a cab or the shuttle bus to take us to town. Yeah right, I was considering hard, the notion of stealing a car, but that idea simmered down quickly because of the intuitive feeling in my gut, and perhaps also, because of the fact that there were a lot of cops rousting about.

It was a day notorious of light. I wished I had sunglasses to go with the feeling the situation warranted. My eyes were uncomfortably blinded. The parking lot was full of sleeping cars. Was one of them ours? How about the little red one over to the side, melting into its spot? I caught it through a glance. Forget about it I thought, stick your thumb in the air I contested to myself, someone will give us a ride. 'Hey how about you, cop, sitting there, reading the paper in your air-conditioned car. How about a ride?' I didn't even bother to bother him. People were being received, others delivering themselves, minivans packing in families; too many people with too much stuff. If we had split up, we would have each gotten a ride easily. Marv almost went with that decision; I saw him at a distance, searching, about to jump into the still open sliding door of a moving minivan. I asked a Frenchman which way the town was. He was so rushed he didn't even stop or say anything, he just pointed. So we walked into that direction.

A castle looking wall with a huge iron door with little doors in it for cars to go through chaperoned us for the time being. The pier was set into the peninsula, and it was great scenery of the fresh vivid land as it came to a meshing stop against the edge of the water. An old aged man and woman walked along with us. Ancient looking abodes in a cobblestone facade were set in deep along enclaves in the wall. The elderly couple that walked with us were German, and unaware of the distance of the train station. However, they had wheels on their luggage, enabling them to just push along the weight. They pointed out the abodes, full two story homes, that were set back at a distance from the road, built out of and within the little hill wall made with cobblestones, high with an archway. A fat well treated chain held our movement to an orderly fashion, leading us along, it was used as a divider from the slate walk and the roadway. The wind, unbelievably mistaking its course, was blowing warm, rushed, current over us. The Germans stopped to talk to someone packing up a parked car, they were going to get a ride. Such was the luck of life.

We walked on, to the train station, which wasn't close. We were far by the outskirts of the little town, it was a hot morning and kept getting brighter. Which way were we supposed to go? I thought. My gear started to bother me a little. I jumped up and with the momentum, I shifted my backpack, unsuccessfully, on my back. I kept moving, still with the same comfortless feeling of the bag. The day was already becoming full of itself, bragging about its potency. It grabbed me and held me in its confines. It was the first time on this mission that we had walked. Was it going to be the last? Doubtful, I thought. I was being weighed down, baggage is always heavy, no matter how light it is, I thought. Marv was wearing sweat stained, tan, khakis pants, and shoes that stunk profusely, constantly being noticeable.

"Marv man, I feel sorry for your feet, I can smell your shoes from here," and I was ahead of him, saying this without looking back.

"I feel sorry for your feet!" He said cheerfully with non-dull emphasis and the smirk of the just.

Arlo started laughing out jists of words, high from an endorphin rush. I looked down at my feet and suddenly, I felt sorry for them too. They looked in need of attention. I walked on with my head down, thinking about the weight of the bag on my back.

Arlo started making conversation, "Man my bag is heavy. Is anybody else's' bag heavy? Shit, it sure is heavy." But he wasn't acting as if he was complaining, he was sort of laughing. "Boy is it hot. France sure is hot. God I'm sweating already. How far have we walked? You guys think we're close to the train station? Man my bag is heavy."

"Well then throw some of your shit out. I mean what the fuck did you bring along? An iron for your clothes?" I yelled at him.

"I'm not hot," Marv said happily. He was wearing a black wool jacket, his blood was revving hot under it, but he didn't really look like he was sweating. He wouldn't ever admit to any pain or discomfort he was feeling, ever. He was a true force of power and reliability. He could probably carry us all on his back, along with all the gear, if he had to. He walked on gleefully, probably thinking he had just come from a good night of sleep. And comparatively, it was better than sleeping out on the streets of Ports Mouth.

Jules spoke up, "Do we have any booze left?"

"I got some," Arlo said, jumping at the chance to be heard. He pulled out what was left of a pint of tequila from his back pocket. Almost falling over when he shifted his bag for the reach into the pocket. "I found this laying on a table on the ferry, in the cafeteria.

"Are you really going to drink that shit Jules?"

"Why not?"

"Have you had any of it yet Arlo?"

"Sure, it was like half full when I got it. I've been drinkin it casually. I thought you swore off tequila Welton?"

"I did, I ain't drinkin any of that crap that you stole." My back started to strain and spasm, "Man, my fuckin bag is heavy now to. Why did you have to bring it up." But perhaps it was the weight on my mind that was creating the uncomfortability. I rearranged my bag on my back, but it didn't do any good. I felt like I was the only one of us who was sweating. I ran the back of my hand over my forehead, dripping beads of sweat to the ground. I was breathing hard.

"Give me a swig too." Marv insisted.

After pulling hard on it, Jules passed what was left to Marv. He finished it off and gave Arlo back the empty bottle. "Thanks." He said, and put it back in his pocket. Marv looked at him strangely. "Well I'm not going to litter, I mean we ain't exactly on the streets of London. I got some respect."

"Yeah right." I said, as we all kept walking onward. With every step, I was slouching closer and closer to the pavement, to the point where I was practically crawling on my hands and knees. I must have looked like a desperate turtle with the fear of trying to cross a busy roadway, with the big bag on my back, my shell, and the dead slow crawl on all fours, toward my destination. I was leaving a trail of sweat, like a river, in place of my footprints. But within moments, my sweat in my steps was being evaporated into the French breeze. It was hot and I was concerned dearly about my state of uncomfortability. But there was nothing I could do but continue moving along.

As we neared the town I was sure, absolutely positive, that my backpack was severely too cumbrous for me to go on. I couldn't take it anymore. Salty sweat poured into my mouth and eyes, leaving me helpless, with tear filled and burning eyes. I felt the insanity that a lunatic must feel in the impossible situation of trying to escape the callings in his mind. I searched with breathless gasps, suffocating on the dry air, for a remedy for my frailty. It was hot, I was heaving and sweating. Why had I made the damn bag so heavy? What was even in it? It suddenly became a long desolate walk. I was complaining in my mind for a rest stop. Although it was cheery scenery, it was still a burden, we had no ride, not even our donkey would carry my gear. My mouth was dry, feeling like I had just eaten some sand, latching itself into all the crevices of my mouth. I was in frantic need of some sort of replenishment, but as I looked around, making haunting howling and screeching noises that could only come from a dying beached whale, nothing could be found that would diminish the perimeters of my quandary. I stopped walking, choking on dry coughs, and dropped to my knees, raving mad with stupid laughter. I was out of control now, rolling around, something was going on, I thought. I was hyperventilating, and my eyes were about to burst. Marv, Jules, and Arlo stood quietly, looking at me, not quite with concern, but more with what seemed to be, impatience and disgust. It took me a while full of sweat and tears to calm down. As I did, I started ripping open my bag, mumbling, desperate to throw every thing away, even my clown shoes. As stuff, Pablo my puppet, and clown gear was strewn across the floor, I came across the object sitting at the bottom of the bag that was not mine. I pulled out the heavy instrument that placed the burden of unnecessary ballast upon me!

"What! Fucking what? What the fuck?" I was attacked and satiated with delirium, I couldn't even see straight as I caught onto the scenario. "Who the hell put this fucking watermelon in my bag?" I looked up to them, the sun behind them, a halo whitening their background. A fallen angel I was, crying pleas for help to the Lord's keepers of the knowledge and facts of reality. Searching them all indiscriminately, one by one, for the culprit. They all looked at me silently. I was breathing heavy with salty burning sweat in my eye. Arlo started to laugh, then Jules and Marv joined him.

"I told him not to do it, but he wouldn't listen," Jules said innocently, controlling his laughter, "When you were in the bathroom on the ferry!"

"What?" Arlo said nonchalantly, " I thought it would be a nice surprise. You know, some watermelon late in the day in France. I was gonna mention it when we were waitin on a train on some platform that we got through off onto, and I figured you wouldn't mind carrying it after all, I didn't even think you'd notice the extra weight-

I didn't even wait to think about it, with limp strength I heaved the dense watermelon toward the trio of insipid onlookers and it hit the ground and splattered into sections and pieces well before the desired target. They didn't even flinch. They laughed at me, not even getting hit by any of the spewing remnants. I moved toward Arlo quickly. He was guilty and I was going to sew some repercussion onto the jacket of his anima. Huge feelings, desiring to strike down with force upon came roaring at my mind, he started running before I even moved.

"Hey man, we could have eaten that, why'd you-" and just in time, Marv moved out of the way of punches, flailing arms, and screams from my rebellious lunge toward Arlo. He was small and quick, well ahead of me from the get go, still with his backpack on, and his drum held in his hands like a football. I was chasing him around for a while, I stopped, panting, leaning over with my hands on my knees, coughing, about to throw up. Marvin and Jules came up running and throwing some of my stuff at me. Passing me and laughing, following Arlo into the victory of the joke.

"Oh, you son of a bitch!" I yelped, as a clown shoe hit me in the thigh.

I picked up my clown shoe and ran back to my bag and started shoving articles into it quickly. Ha, ha! The joke was on me. That's ok, I was going to get all of these guys, one way or another. I looked up, and they seemed about a mile up the road, still running. I was sweating hard now, and breathing heavy. I wiped some hot sweat from my forehead. My hair was soaked, water trickled down my spine, lounging casually in the crack of my ass; it tickled. I zipped up the bag and pulled my backpack onto me and picked up my drum, mumbling incoherently about revenge. "I'm gonna get you Arlo," I said out loud, "You're gonna have to do something really embarrassing to yourself, like pee your pants in front of some girls or somethin if you wanna be even after this." I hiked my pants up, lifting myself somewhat off the ground. I started running away from the scene of disaster, stopping quickly to scoop some of the melon out of the carcass piece that lay right side up. It was hot, already instantly retaining the heat of the burning sun. It was mostly liquid in my hands, melon juice dripping all over, seeds falling everywhere.

I was jogging for a while, now, sticky on the face and hands, making my situation wander into the apparent disconsolate impasse of my momentary existence. Haphazardly, I broke down and started to walk. I breathed heavy, my lungs wearing thin. The boys were no where in sight, neither was the station, I carried on, spitting out a seed that dislodged itself from a gap in the deep back of my mouth, where a tooth once lay proudly. I lit a cigarette and smoked it, relieved of the weight of the watermelon, wondering if in my rushed attempt at escape, I had left anything necessary laying about, tempted to stop and check my bag, but I didn't. I finally reached the station. The boys were sitting on their bags in front of it. They stood up and gave me a round of applause as I walked up to them. I didn't stop. I passed them rudely and then turned around in a military fashion.

"I'm going to get you Arlo, you better watch."

"It was just a joke, take it easy," he said with a winners smile, in the winners circle.

"Ha, ha, ha, then, but don't go gettin yourself into a situation where you need me to get you out of it, cause then I'm gonna let you suffer." I said over my own breath. Then forgetting about it for the time being, not even being a sore loser, but sucking up the nonsense mutiny against me. Besides there was work to do now, we had to get on a train that was heading South. They were congratulating him on his joke as they put their gear back on, but they didn't take it any further. I was laughing to, but only on the inside. I smiled a disturbing looking grin at no one in particular. A melon seed in my mouth, found its way to the foreground of my attention. I rolled it around and into position with my tongue, and I spit it at Arlo, hitting him right above his eye, in the nest of his right eyebrow.

"Ouch," he screamed and jostled his head, as his hands went directly to his eye and head and started rubbing away the sting.

"Nice shot, Welton!" Marv rejoiced.

"Damn, that was a shot to put a bet on," Jules said.

"Yeah, well, don't think that my revenge is over, Arlo, 'cause I got somethin planned for you, boy do I ever," not even knowing what I was talking about, bluffing innocently.

His eye teared and he smiled, "That didn't hurt!"

"I'm not trying to hurt you, I'm just gonna get you, when you least expect it, I'll have the last laugh."

"Ha-ha!" He said, pissing me off even more.

"Let's just get on a train before somebody sees us and wants to question us about tickets."

"That's a good idea, hey Marv *man,* take us to our transportation," Jules rousted through a smile with non-condescending tranquility, knowing that Marvs' insight wouldn't steer us in the wrong direction.

"And so I shall. Let's see, hhmmmm, let my sense and wit taste the licit way of our kismet, let us find our way." he pleaded. And with that, Marv set out like a bloodhound inhaling the aroma of the day about us. Nobody else besides us was around. It was an outdoor station, on ground level. The floor was terracotta tile, eccentrically broom cleaned to a nice and neat fashion. Trains were sleeping on the dead end tracks. It was really quiet and peaceful. It was France. Birds chirped away in French tongue, with righteous attitudes over domain or food. Basically, I had no idea where I was or which way to go.

I kept on thinking that we were going to end up getting on the wrong train. Arlo was bouncing, being the smallest of us, and the lightest, he started floating more toward the lead as we walked, as naturally as could be. There was a totally illegible and un-updated train schedule board. We paid it no mind. Blindly we chose our train by its general look and feel. Marv started to veer closer to one sitting two tracks over. Arlo reached up and opened the doors, and let down the steps. We climbed on like companions to the prince of all the Hobo's. As we chose a traincar, and worked out our seating, we opened up the creaky tight windows and started smoking a hash joint that Jules had rolled while they were waiting for me to arrive at the station. The trains weren't even turned on yet.

I kept asking the same questions over and over, "You think we're on the right train? Does this feel right to you Marv?" Looking around, peering out the windows with full uncertain eyes, "You think this one is heading South? I don't know if this is the right train. Where the hell is all the other passengers? Does this station even operate anymore?" I catechized with frustration and paranoia in my voice. No one was listening to me. They were all talking and blowing out clouds of saturated smoke, laughing away the moment.

"Arlo, man, what else did you steal from that cafeteria?" Marv asked, while leaning back in a slouch in his seat.

"Yeah, you got any food for us? And don't try to hide it, cause we'll search ya and beat you down!" Jules inquired, leaning over him, inclosing him with his shadow.

"Naa, That's everything," Arlo said, nonchalantly, puffing away at the joint, trying not to get excited or spoil his bluff, "I shoulda stocked up some more, but where was I going to hide everything. It ain't easy being mischievous, you know." He proclaimed, like a professor. They were ignoring me, so I sat back into my seat, giving up on complaining.

"Fuck it," I said to myself, "What does it matter anyway."

Eventually more people started climbing aboard. Old ladies, three of them, soaked in French attitude, glared, getting all the impression of us they needed from the noticeable tracks of wet sweat and sticky fingers drenched with dirt that we or at least I, left where we had roamed on the traincar. A more youthful teenage local girl would have made our acquaintance, but she was held to a reserved fashion, because one of the older ladies, perhaps, would have told her mother she was cohorting with a bad crowd. The conductors got on the train and looked at us. They were running a little late or they probably would have checked our tickets before starting to depart. They ran to the beginning of the train. The train woke up quickly and started to move, stretching out as it rode along. The wind blew loudly through the window. The hot current splashed onto my face and through my beard. It was refreshing, like a shower, I scratched at my chin, my beard was stiff and prickly, I would need to shave before reaching Cannes, I thought. We had passed through the town and were out on the barren land. I hoped that we could get far on this ride. And literally, as I thought about it, a conductor came onto our traincar. He came up to us, first, out of all the other passengers.

"*Biglettes*?" He queried with a lack of innocence. His face solid and determined in appearance. No one answered him. He stared at Marv, and he stared right back at him. The conductor nodded his head, answering the question for us. He figured out our scheme relatively quickly. We had made it two stops, and were going for the third. We became overtly silent. He asked us again for a ticket. We just nodded no, not saying anything. Arlo shrugged his shoulders as if saying 'What do you want from *us*?' Then the conductor tried another approach.

"Money?" He said seeming confused, in English, while holding his hand up and rubbing the thumb and forefingers of his hand together, as if we didn't understand his interpretation of the word.

We all nodded no, still silent like caged rabbits. Arlo shrugged his shoulders again, and rolled the lines on his forehead around.

Then in a French accent, and a sigh as he swirled his head on its axis, his oversized conductors hat wobbling around the rim of his head, he said, "Ok, come on! Off! Off! Come on! Off!"

We had to get off the train, obviously. We got up, pack up our stuff groggily and headed toward the exit doors without saying anything. A second conductor came up and questioned his buddy about us. In their slang French lingo, they agreed together, that we should be asked to leave if we weren't going to pay for our tickets. They tried to talk to us in French, not most likely about the weather, I presumed. My partners in crime all pointed to me, as if I was to be addressed for our party. I grandly spoke up, clearing my throat and standing up straight, with a pride that seemed like I was attempting to deliver the inaugural address to the emissaries of the French magistrate. I told them bluntly, in Spanish Italian, with some French condescendence in my hand gestures, "Nous no tienemos el dinero!" What dialect I thought, my mother would be proud. I smiled greedily and winked at them. The conductors' frustrations elevated. They were both breathing heavy, upset at my ostentatious narcissism.

The second conductor then said in broken but somewhat perfect English, "Eif you getz caught by authoritie , an' you piss dem off, they vill

88

take your tings anz' arress you." He shook his head, and then sung out in a beautiful melody, "Is de law!" As he pointed to my drum in Marv's hands. He was generally sad for us in a paternal way. Hoping that we would wise up and worry because of the inference of his comment.

Not even silence rose from our tight sealed lips. I couldn't believe that anybody would want our stuff. Jules tightened the grip on his guitar case and hid it behind his back. The train slowed down for its scheduled stop. We got off the train quickly, on this narrow platform, with trains passing on both sides, occasionally, some at high speeds. Ah, the speed line, less stops, covers more land quicker. Would have been nice to be on that one, first class, watching a movie in air conditioned filled and saturated dense air, ah, delicacies satisfying needs of comfort. The speed train passed us quicker than it took the thought to end. The platform shook, and the wind circled crazily. I held on to Marv, for fear of being lifted off and taken away by the current of the trains' passing.

"Welton, relax man," he said.

"Sorry." I said with shattered Epicurean melancholy.

"Hey dig this fellas," Arlo exclaimed, suggesting us toward good looking girls standing on the platform, "I think today just got a little bit more interesting!" He was waning with eagerness.

"Yeah, maybe we can get a quickie before the next train comes!"

"Your such a Neanderthal, Welton."

"I'm a Neanderthal? Have you noticed yourself lately in the mirror 'Sloth'? I mean your not exactly ready to throw on a tuxedo."

"Dude, your not either, and you smell a lot worse than me."

"Yeah but at least I don't try to hide my short comings and if-"

"Alright fellas, lets relax ok. We got a long day ahead of us. You guys can argue later." Marv butted in and settled us both down.

Jules just laughed, "You guys are acting like a couple of fags," and he pushed us all along toward the girls.

I looked around, out and over the stations' lines of demarcation, to the town. This town was big and bland, seeming more industrial. Big warehouses cluttered the district circuitously to the station. However most of the noise I could hear was coming from the un-still fluttering among the waiting passengers. There were a lot of people on this platform heading south. There were several American travelers, with brand names on their backpacks, shorts, and sandals; girls and guys, easily spotted and denoted as Americans. Also there were French locals, dressed in youthful fair student garments, laughing about in French, loudly and boldly. We walked right up to and started talking to the cute American girls. Intrepid stances in our rock-star posture, Jules holding on, loosely to his guitar case, exposing it to the girls' view, we were more than bragging like gorgeous surfer studs, trying to play some stupid role, Arlo and Marv, unconsciously careening the drums that they held. I watched it all, taking it all in, waiting to see what would come about. In our desirous attempt to flirt with the girls we insouciantly seemed distant and uncaring. I started to get nervous, I scratched at my beard roughly. Arlo took them under his wing more than the rest of us, he started to bloat out an epitome monologue of our adventures, trying to impress them. The girls had Euro-rail tickets held tightly, in plain view, in their finely manicured hands.

"We're going to Barcelona," the prettiest of the three interrupted quickly, not really caring where we had been.

"Yeah, we have a couple of friends there, that we met in Paris. We all studied abroad there this spring." Another of them, who was just as attractive, proclaimed inculpably, yet seductively. The three of them looked at each other, smiling soundlessly, sharing untold secrets of their capers in Paris.

Must have been nice. American girls with tenderly wet panties, sexing and making little French boys cum quickly all over Paris. Ah, Paris, what a place to have discrete sexual rendezvous. Shit. The heat was pouring onto us, making us all glisten. My hands were still sticky from the melon, I couldn't escape it, and now I was becoming sexually excited. I looked at all three girls up and down. The third girl who wasn't doing any of the talking was staring at Marv. She looked good. She seemed real shy, but she had a look like she needed little tempting. Her freckled face had a glaze of sweat all over it. I saw Marv lick his lips, he was staring right back at her. He smiled at her, and she smiled back with a soft laugh then looked down at her feet. She shifted her weight on her feet, nervously. She looked back at Marv, who hadn't taken his eyes off her, still smiling. Marv was lucky, his overwhelming presence and aura attracted everyone to him. You could tell that he was a decent honest gentleman. He must have at least one or two women in every country he has past through.

Arlo was still engaged in inquisitive conversation with the other two girls. Jules had drifted into his mind somewhere, probably saying Suzettes' name over and over in his head. What dedication he has, I thought, he wasn't trying to be aloof, he was trying to be loyal to his girlfriend. He is so beautiful, he could have any girl he wants. Probably all three of these girls at the same time, but he has consistently remained faithful to Suzette, despite the fact that he has been literally propositioned by almost all the girls we met in London. Good for him, I thought. I reflected on the obvious fact that none of the girls were checking me out. I'm such a waste, I thought, a lame desperately horny waist. What was even worse was that I was getting a rise in my dirty pants, so I started counting in my mind, in Italian, to forget about it. There was no other way to solve my immediate problem. These girls didn't seem interested in me, they didn't even seem interested in Arlo either, but I don't think he figured it that way, so he kept on harassing them, asking them question after nagging question. I looked down the platform, checking everybody out. The conductor was walking casually toward us. I was hoping that he wasn't going to ask us for our tickets, even if he was genuinely going to try and help, by making sure we were waiting on the right platform, he would have accidentally caught us.

Nervousness and worry began to seep into my mind, causing spontaneous heart murmurs and physical spasms. Blood rushed throughout my body, energizing every impuissant muscle, I squeezed my body tightly to hold onto myself, lest I accidentally flail and hit someone near me, and causing an unneeded commotion. Sweat, with leaps and bounds out of the open faucet of my pores, soiled my reddened face. I bit down on my lip, almost ripping it off my shadowed mouth. I just stood there, still, looking down, getting hit by the heat of the sun, hoping not to catch the conductors' attention as he walked by us. Arlo was still talking loudly with the girls. Marv and Jules were looking at him, with perfunctory peculiarity, barely engaged in the conversation, trying to remain anonymous to any momentary attention to or from the passing conductor. See, the trick is to get on the train, and stay on as long as you can. But if the conductor found out you didn't have a ticket, and weren't planning on paying for one, then he wouldn't let you on the train. Then you had to leave the station and walk, hitchhike, or steal a car, at least to get to the station at the next town. It's a real situation, causing me to believe that travel should be a free privilege granted by the governments of our unified world. I can only just imagine if it were so.

A wind pushed on us from the north, the train was veering close. Exclamation sought forth through nerved muscles, I jumped, excitedly, in the place of my space, eager and glad I hadn't caused a fatal disruptive scene. The train came along in a cloud of heat and exhaust, we all got on; animals onto the steel arc. The platform conductor signaling to the train conductor when we were all aboard. What a process. The girls we were talking to went to find seats. We stopped in the entrance platform of the train. The girls headed straight toward the conductor on the train.

Our choices were limited to one option, "Duh, which way?"

"Ahhh, hhmmm, why don't we go," pausing, acting as if he was really thinking about it, staring in the direction the girls had gone, "Um, that way."

And Marv turned and pointed into the opposite direction that the girls had gone. We waited to move however, until the train started moving. Like releasing gas, it pushed itself off and out.

"That's a good call, Marv," Jules worded with extreme care, swinging his guitar as he turned around within the cramped space of the entrance platform.

"Ya think?" Marv asked as Arlo slid the traincar door open.

"Those girls'll probably wonder why we didn't follow them," I said through a doleful breath, looking in their direction.

"They're definitely going to wonder why we didn't follow them," Arlo's ego ejaculated, "Come on."

We walked down the train, passing seated passengers, a true invasion as if we were bumping and grinding in a night club on our way to the bar. I started to cajole with Arlo from behind him, pushing him onward, sweet talking to him.

"Come on baby, give me some sugar! Ooooh, you so cute!" as I ruffled my hand threw his damp hair from behind him, "I love you daddy!" He threw his hand back to knock my hand off his head.

Ahead of us, Jules laughed, then he added, "Yeah baby, you are cute! Come home to momma baby!"

Then Marv who was walking down the isle directly in front of Arlo stopped just as I pushed and shoved hard up against him, squashing him between us, almost falling on a roused passenger of elder age.

"Sorry, oh I mean, *pardone moi*!" I gleamed, as we kept on walking, completely in the way of everything and everyone's' comfort. Irritating the passengers moment as we past them. Leaving behind a brutal scent that quite possibly could have caused nauseating discomfort.

"Aaaah," Arlo laughed, happy like a dog that we were playing with him.

We reached the front of the train in this fashion, Jules not really having anything to do with it, just walking ahead of us.

"Hey, Jules, you think we should send Arlo back there to get those girls for us? I mean what the fuck? Are you interested? Or are you gonna be a bore on this trip. We gotta get us some girls to eat, right?"

"Ha-ha!" he smirked, then taking a second to think about it, unsure if he wanted to talk about it, he said, "I shoulda broke up with Suzette before we left huh?"

"Shit, why didn't you? You know you're gonna wanta fuck around, and besides it's not like you were gonna marry her anyway!" I detested.

"Ah, Jules, forget about her, man, did you see those chicks checkin you out? They were practically fighting each other for your attention!" Arlo proclaimed.

"Yeah well, that one chick was checkin Marv hard, I thought she was gonna drop the ball right on his lap. Marv man you shoulda taxed that a little." Jules shyly tried to divert the attention away from himself.

"She was a little too young for me, besides, I like older more mature women!"

"Shit, there's gonna be a lot more women in Cannes, with even less clothes on, and probably a lot easier to get with than those broads!" Arlo stated bluntly.

"Yeah, man, I think everything is lookin good!" I said eagerly, still horny, "after all we deserve some fun!"

"Yeah like we didn't have any fun in London," Marv said sarcastically.

"Ha-ha!" Arlo mouthed.

The train was mostly empty toward the front. We stood in the last entrance and exit platform of an empty traincar, awaiting our soon to be, asked departure.

"Marv let me have my drum."

"Here ya go kid! But don't go givin' me a headache now!"

"Oh *seniore*! But of course not, I just wanna hold it."

The door was slid closed separating the traincar and the platform, but you could see well into the car and down the line of cars pretty far. Tension saw itself fit to disturb us, wonder made us curios as to how far we could get out of this ride. It was hard to feel at ease. No one really said anything important. I looked out for the conductor. A figure stood in the isle far down toward where we had gotten on the train. You really had to look hard to see him, but I knew it was the 'conductor'. I noticed the skies turning gray outside, it was going to rain. The French countryside was so much more inviting than the English. It was more interactive, rolling over endlessly, pleasant, in my eyes, 'almost' romantic. It did make me wish that I was travelling in veiled tryst, sitting closely, tightly, side by side, hands feeling hands and soft skin of a clandestine lover. It must be the air in France. They must mix it with the mist and sweat of sex, after all, sex sells right? My libido called out more and more with desperate salacious intent. I tried not to think about it. On the outside of my mind, time passed in a boring haphazard fashion. More than several stops came and went. Then as expected, but probably a little late, the conductor entered the last train car, obvious but slow, trying to be nonchalant, he was coming toward us. No one moved. He was frail looking. I felt the train starting to slow down.

"As luck would have it, we're coming to our stop." I gasp under my breath, unable to commit to any excitement.

But then, all of a sudden Jules proclaimed a hum for us to tune to, "Hhhhhmmmm, me, me, me, me, me!"

Jules looked about us, and I nodded to him, egging him on, unsure where he was going, but following him. He cleared his throat and put his hands up, index fingers pointing to the sky, about to begin the symphony.

"Jules man, that's funny, I get it, you're the conductor, not this fuckin French guy!"

He smiled, and began moving his hands up and down in a four count tempo. Instantly, we became the instruments of his orchestra. I realized the potential of our defeat, as we all came together, with like-mindedness into the scene. Arlo started whistling an improvised concerto and tapped bass on his drum, according to Jules' hands' instructions. The 'train conductor' could hear it through the door. He slowed down a bit.

"Ooh, that sounds good Jules," Arlo avowed. Then Marv started humming along with Jules, fluting notes intermittently on his harmonica at Jules' command.

Our song rose, with crying intensity, in more than just mathematical degree. "Ahh, I see, Yup! Whatta buncha of silly char-acters we are! Duh!" Came purporting out of my mouth in dumb clownesque disguise. "We're aaaa regula opus production!"

The conductor stopped as if we were in a dark alley and he was about to get mugged. I crept out into the spot light of our stage, with a stupid face and a grin that couldn't hold my tongue in my mouth. Arlo was still whistling, madly, behind me. I could feel the momentum of energy coming off of Jules' hands as they swung feverishly about in steady rhythm. We were casting out such aggressive yet kind vibes.

"Give it to him Welton," Marv shouted, as he started to clap resolutely.

The traincar door, made of glass, being the only thing separating us from him. He was about seven feet back. I lunged and slammed myself against the windowed door. He jumped back a bit in shock and froze. My back pack and drum not getting in the way at all, but moving with me with conceding degree. I peeled myself off of the glass sinisterly, my eyes locked onto his. I could see some worry creased within the glare on his forehead. But in his eyes there was a sudden stillness that froze him in his place, there was a lack of ability to do anything about the fear growing in this situation, casting out from behind the blank white of his eyes. I laughed for a second, braking from the scene to ponder the thought, he was a deer, addictively trapped in the aberrant drawing from within the spectrum of the headlights of an oncoming car. Sucker.

I held out my hand and Marv pranced into my strut. Jules and Arlo started banging their feet on the steel floor of the platform, vibrating mad echoes through the door. The conductor was dizzied about from the waves, the knocking, and motion of the train, he grabbed onto the nearby seat to hold himself up. Marv and I danced, kicking legs and jumping on each other, completely flexible and still retaining our agility, even with our cumbersome backpacks on. Marv, spinning me around, like a high heeled girlie, squeamish with giggles, accelerating me, banging on my drum as it passed around in the circle as well, then letting me go. Jules and Arlo now doing some sort of tribal dance song, a frenzied sort of humming and whistling and catcalling, drum banging and foot stomping. Marv did an American Indian call of attack. It was loud, I was dizzy, spinning on my own, viciously, falling slowly to the ground, starting to cry and tear, extravagantly, overzealous screams of defeat. The conductor had, not just a look, but a physical posture that evinced that he feared some internal miscalculated devastation. His face manifested uncontrollably, a look of being perplexed beyond all reason.

I turned grotesque, vomiting foam drool with the words "Nous no tienemos pas les biglette's!"

With this punch line, cries and shouts poured out of Marv, Jules, and Arlo, roaring loud for a time, then sedating tranquil but in a disturbed murmur, on and off. My hands waved in the air above seeking redemption, whining un-affably and screaming for the pain and the suffering to end. All over the place, chaos lurked, bouncing off the walls, attempting to shatter the glass that separated his freedom from us. Marv grabbed me by the ear and pulled me up to a stand. Depressing cat cries from Julian and Arlo stopped to a silence. The air became cold and mute. My hearts' beat, vociferated through sharp ripping breath. The conductor was motionless, in shock. I could only imagine how he perceived us to be; luned tribal bandits. The train hovered, slowing down, barely noticeable through the fogged mindful of the moment. Marv and I back away towards Jules and Arlo. I whimpered as Marv pet me, reassuringly, looking at the conductor, staring defensively. The train doors opened up and sucked the stale silence out of the traincar exit platform. Marv escorted me off, I still perceived to be defeated, as Jules and Arlo got off the train, but first taking a full moment to stop and stare at the trembling scared, frigid thin conductor, pale in his stance, who would now probably have nightmares. I started walking with better posture rising to the joke of the scene, and then we all started laughing at our craziness. Walking tall and high, wondering where that had come from.

"Aha ha ha ha ah ha he heee he, that guys never gonna forget us!" Arlo said through the loud impetus of our rejoicement.

"Marv man at the end you should've put out the hat!" The train doors closed as we jumped and skipped up the platform, the train started to move.

"That would have been funny." Jules hiccuped, "If we charged him for the show."

"Ha-ha."

Through the window I saw the conductor sitting down in a seat, holding his face in his hands, maybe he was crying. We laughed and laughed, inspired as we bounced along. Other passengers on the train rolling past us were looking around curious at what they had heard but did not see. I laughed excited laughter. As we walked along still full of explosive energy, we passed a waiting platform conductor. He didn't know what was going on, but he had the question of wonder on his kind face.

As I got up close to him, I stopped and said still laughing in bursts, "Ah, Bordeaux!" Not looking at him, but swaying my arm to the landscape. Smiling and walking on past him, my mates agreeing like tourists to the beautiful city of Bordeaux.

"Bordeaux? No! No es pas Bordeaux!" He said with concern.

"Oh! Yesssss! Bordeaux!" Arlo spoke suddenly and vehemently. He started clapping excitedly, a round of applause for our arrival.

The conductor tried to speak up above our turmoil, but he was being purposely ignored, and misunderstood. I wiped some sweat from my brow with the back of my hand, then I scratched at an itch that lay hidden, deep within the burrow of my beard. Marv put his hand on the conductors' shoulder, startling him a little, "Senoire! Grazias! Muchas Grazias!" He was acting as if the conductor had done us a favor.

Arlo closed in on the poor troubled guy, who was having a hard time trying to correctly organize the circumstances. He didn't hesitate to offer his gratitude "Bordeaux es belle! Me gusto mucho! Grazias!" in like American Spanish dialect, or what we called 'Spanglish'.

"No, no, no, Il no es pas Bordea-"

"Si es Belle Bordeaux!" Jules added, as he used his guitar case to point to the dead scenery around us, "Vamos! Nous semos 'Miestros de la Musica'! Tocamos en Bordeaux! Muchos dinero!"

Jules and Marv were absolute, pointing toward the exit and telling the conductor over and over, "Bordeaux! Bordeaux!"

I started banging loudly on my drum and singing, " Bordeaux! Es belle Bordeaux! Bordeaux! Bordeaux!"

"No! No! No!" He kept saying to the four of us, trying to rise above the noise from the drum, while we completely didn't understand him.

"Si, Senoire! It's ok, es Bordeaux!" Marv kept reassuring him, as he jumped up and down like a schoolboy, casting wild shadows of excitement.

We concentrated our movement toward the exit from the train station, laughing out our joy all over the place. "Muchos dinero para la musica, aqui en Bordeaux!" Marv said happily. None of us were even speaking proper Spanish. We were mixing this guy up pretty good. He kept shaking his head, saying something apparently important about Bordeaux in French, and he used the word 'no' way to many times, but we didn't understand him, so we kept on walking, sluggishly, toward the exit. I couldn't keep a straight face as I kept walking, "Yeah fellas, this is Bordeaux alright. Look at it! It's even more beautiful than they said it was. Man were going to love this town!"

Wishing that I could have said it in French so the conductor could understand. You couldn't even see a town, and the station was pretty simple looking. The conductor now started to insist on something. He was doing a pretty good job of understanding our problem, but it was hard for him to get us to realize the paradoxicality of the situation. He ran up and grabbed me. I stopped and turned.

"Que es?" Ou es Bordeaux?"

"No, no, no!" Cried the little platform conductor, pleading, "Il no es Bordeaux! Ayyee, no es Bordeaux!" Attondrez aqui." Cursing himself in French, No es Bordeaux!" He said.

We kept acting as if we didn't understand him, and that this was Bordeaux. We almost made it out the exit door, heading toward the town. He got all flustered, his face reddened as he took a stand, deliberately blocking our movement through the exit door. He was holding his hands up, signaling us to stop, as we looked at him curiously. He took a couple of breaths, as silence set into the scene. We looked at him with stupid wonder, as to why we couldn't go to Bordeaux. He calmly tried to explain to us in French and brightened hand movement that we should have never gotten off at this stop. He pointed toward the exit and said, "No es pas Bordeaux! Es Savaney! Savaney!" He begged, hoping desperately that we would understand.

Still with mild attempts to leave Jules asked, "No Bordeaux?"

Finally a smile came across his face, "No! No es Bordeaux! Es Savaney!"

While still looking at this guy, Arlo tried to interpret what he was saying, "Guys, I think what he's tryin to say is that this isn't Bordeaux."

And the conductor shook his head up and down, agreeing with Arlo, "Si! Si! Es Savaney!"

Marv started to act like he was upset, he moved in closer to the worried conductor and asked, "Es Bordeaux?"

"He shook his head side to side, sadly, "No, no es Bordeaux."

"Oh," I said, "This isn't Bordeaux, I think he said this town is called Savaney," as I pointed to the town. Then the conductor smiled because we started to understand our mistake, "Si! Es Savaney!" He cried.

We gave up, and showed our believe that we had gotten off at the wrong stop, "Damn, so we got off at the wrong stop. How could that be?" Jules asked.

"Well it's not my fault!" I said obtrusively, trying to instigate concern within the conductors mind.

"Man, now what?" Jules asked, seeming upset. The conductor kept looking at us, wondering god knows what.

"Senoire, quando per le train para Bordeaux?" Marv asked.

"Oh!" Then he started talking wildly yet melodically in French, then he pointed to his watch, and he managed to inform us that the next train would come in about two hours.

"Two hours? Ahh, man," I said acting terribly upset.

The conductor shook his head, feeling sorry for us with tenderness in his eyes.

"Americans." I said, shrugging my shoulders in a dumb way, making my backpack swing up and down, while pointing to all of us.

All the boys laughed sorryness, supporting our claim. We now turned a bit uneasy and acted like we were wondering what to do. The conductor stood, seeming upset for us because we had gotten off at the wrong stop.

"Oh well, I guess we have to wait for the next train." I said, as exciting winds casting forbidden glimpses of life brushed up against me, making the hair on the back of my neck stand on end.

"I guess so," Jules said, "Lets roll a joint!"

"Ssiiick! Good idea," as Arlo looked around, "How about over there, under that canopy!"

Marv looked over and assessed the scene then said, "Sure!" Then he turned to the conductor and said, "Senoire, nous," and he pointed to the spot we had picked out, "over there para el train. Si? Dos hueres!"

The conductor smiled and said, "Si. Si…" With an entire ending of his sentence in French in which went completely ununderstood.

Casually, we went and sat down on the platform and started waiting. We all took our backpacks off, instantly. I stretched out. We were laughing at what we had done so far. "So, Savaney, France! Nice place!" Arlo said as we all got comfortable.

"Yeah, it's not bad. But we're still far from Cannes, and we gotta wait two hours for the next train."

"I wouldn't worry about that Welton, we're making great time." Jules said as he began the process of rolling the joint.

The conductor who was still standing there, where we had left him was talking to himself, probably saying something in French like, 'How could the train conductor let us get off at the wrong stop?' Pissed that somebody wasn't doing their job correctly with foreign passengers. He was really nice to us and genuinely upset, probably because of the long wait ahead of us for the next train. In my mind, I was giving everybody a high five, even the conductor, who in my fantasy daydream, was just as excited for us because we had fooled him!

"Thank God for the language barrier," I said.

"No shit," Marv said, "Hey, Welton, how's' about findin us some fluids to drink."

"Sure! I'm sure I can come up with somethin. I mean after all, we're in Savaney!"

"Ha-ha!" Jules laughed as I got up for the search.

"You want me to go with ya?" Arlo asked.

"Naa, just wait till I get back to smoke that and watch my bag."

Nobody replied as I looked at them sternly, so then I set out for my mission. I walked toward the conductor, standing by the exit and nodded to him as I passed him. I didn't feel like getting into a conversation with him at all, it would have taken too long and it would have been mentally painful to try and interpret him. As if I interrupted him, he straightened up, and calmly started walking toward his office, smiling and nodding his head. I walked out of the train station and saw a petty looking restaurant, sitting quietly yet pleasantly all by itself across the street. I veered over towards it, in the hopes of getting us some replenishment. All I had for use was just a few English pounds, if that. Excitedly, I slid through the outdoor seating arrangement, and through the doors. Before I even looked around I asked the hefty bartender in English if she accepted the English Lb. She didn't say yes. She scolded me in French and some English about getting my currency exchanged at the border. It seemed that this old fat lady at the bar really didn't want to sell me anything. She stopped talking to me, and gave a glance over to the one well groomed patron standing without notice or care, over to the side of the bar. I noticed surprisingly, that she was surrounded by platters of food, all along the bar. The intensity of the food dripped all over me, making my concentration stray and my stomach growl viciously. The delicious odor was overpowering. I wanted it all to be an illusion. I closed my eyes and begged.

Then, slowly, I opened them, and the food was still there, "Damn," I said as I gave up the thought about eating, and then carried on about my business. Not using my nose to breath in, "Soda!" I exclaimed.

She didn't answer me, she looked down and continued polishing some glassware. I waited for a time, she ignored me heavily. 'Ohhh', I started thinking, 'it turns out that I'm the illusion', I said in my head. 'Huh'. So sitting there in my mind, I kept thinking, that if I was an illusion, I could casually walk over to the bar and start eating some food, and nobody would notice. Well why not, I thought, and so I did. I walked over, but probably stumbling overtly and salivating, making a nuisance of a noise, because now I had realized how hungry I was. This got the attention of the bartender and she reached out, before I was within even five feet of her, leaning on the bar greedily, and said, "Hey, no! It is not for YOU!"

I stopped, cut off from thinking, 'Not for ME?" I felt like slapping her, but I backed away thinking, she's right, it's not for me? So why did I come here again?" Trying to think where I was and how I'd gotten here. I scratched at my beard, slouching in a daze.

The bartenders nerves calmed, as she realized my timidness, she leaned back. Then through a few more strokes on the glassware with the rag, and through a couple of blinks of the eyes, eventually, perhaps just to get rid of me, she pulled two measly sodas out of her cooler. They had probably been in there for a while, but they were still warm. The little differences. She wanted to charge me an ungraspable amount of money. I accidentally, through my disgust at her price, snorted in a breath of air through my nose. The smell of the food drew my head down toward the bar, I had to yank it back, lest it fell onto a platter of food. I started to loose my concentration, I had to get out of there quick, for fear of an attempt at a blatant robbery of the food. Who was all this food for, I thought? I pulled out of my pocket, some sand from my last trip through Spain, some disintegrating paper with illegible scribble on it, the little hash ball, in which she noticed and scrutinized offendedly, and some pounds, but mostly pence.

I counted out what worked out to be roughly four pounds. I didn't want to give it all to her, so I tried to argue with her, over the price of the sodas, using barely understandable words, unintelligibly, from three different languages. From what I gathered, she wouldn't accept anything less, and she tried to blame the grand expense on import tax. I was excited, breathing and snorting, unable to stop myself from smelling the food that I was practically rubbing up against. I had to get out of there, I was sweating fast beads of sweat. I ended up dropping the coins and some sand from the Spanish Costa Del Sol into her hand. I had lived two weeks once on about five pounds. I felt like I just burned money in a fireplace, for two sodas. After she took the money, she drew back, appearing haggled, as if I had brought her some kind of direct offence, she wanted me, not in her eyes a quality customer, out of there. It must have been the contrast that I, a dirty poor American with no money, was surrounded by.

It was a dark restaurant covered in mahogany; cold. More so, than the brisk French air which was coming through the open patios. Hence, the French door! The floor was all slate, with wide elegant stone moldings. There was no brunchtime customers, except for the one rich eccentric looking older gentleman. Who stood still and silent throughout my whole exchange, uncurious. I couldn't tell what nationality he was, except that he looked like he was expensive. He was tanned dark, wearing a bright white suit. He had big yet well-maintained eyebrows floating still and plain like clouds. He wrinkled his forehead and strained his eyes to see the newspaper in front of him more clearly. He was drinking this tight espresso with a pound of sugar in it. I saw him pouring it in, scoop by scoop, must have been six, maybe seven full scoops of sugar. He was standing, delicate in his movements, as if he was holding himself back from lashing out, by a stool at the bar. Platters of food arrayed in combinations sat, all along the bar waiting for what appeared to be, all the customers to come out of the bathroom and fill the space around this gentlemen, the fat lady and I, to eat. The smell of the food kept on driving me delirious. My mind rambled to itself, completely free from the grip that held it in control. Perspiration soaked my face. The instance reminded me of a poem Marv had construed. It is called, 'DIET, Did I Eat Today?' I took a breath through my nose, and it brought me back into the scene. The now re-noticeable opulence of the place was drastically augmented because of my being there. From my smell, to the sight of me, enhanced by my drastic character traits and personality, splashed against their canvass of serenity, peach trees, and country side picnicking, it was obvious that I was the one who was completely out of place, I agreed to myself. I appeared like a bum waiting for a food hand-out. 'I'm outa here', I thought.

Without soreness, and not looking at the food that was greedily teasing my olfactory system, I picked up the sodas to go. I looked over to the man at the bar, in some hopes of an offer of farewell. The gentleman at the bar looked with wide eyes at the newspaper. It seemed like it was the only thing interesting to him within the world around him. He didn't seem surprised at all to see me, nor even curious. He went about his newspaper and breakfast. I let out a deflated breath full of suggested debacle. I was run down looking to say the least. Seemingly to the fat girl with the loathsome look on her face, the only thing keeping me together was my youth.

"Yep," I said, "I'm a nuisance!" And I turned to escape their boring regular course of daily events. I bowed with soft benevolence to the gentleman. He actually smiled and nodded. He bit into the corner of his croissant and accidentally bit his napkin, which wouldn't get out of his way. Ah the little things in life. He must have felt a twang of anxiety. So be it. I walked back out into the rest of the world, somewhere in a little town in France. At that moment, it was the most perfect place in life, I thought. For a couple of moments, I stopped taking life for granted. It was becoming one of the greatest days of life, a day to write about in my journal.

I got back on the platform, smiling, and passed around the sodas. I didn't mention anything about the food that I saw. However, Marv could sense that I was covered in a fragrance that I rarely wore, he sniffed at me with the intensity of a dog sniffing at a trashcan.

"Another round of breakfast?" I inquired as a joke.

"Well it wouldn't be a real breakfast without some..." and he paused to reach into his back pocket and with a sly look, he pulled out a half full pint bottle, "Jack Daniels!" as he held the bottle up for all to stare at.

"Nice, Jules! I'm not even going to ask where it came from, but I'll take some." As he threw me the bottle, he must have been hoarding it for days. We were the only ones on the platform. "How about that joint?" I asked.

"Marv, light that shit," Arlo said.

"Cool!" And we all drew in close for the smoking ritual. We sat around smoking a couple of joints and finishing off the bottle of JD. It was casual but a tiresome feeling grew out of the strain of waiting. I looked around to see if anybody else was waiting for a train. There was nobody in the station, except for the conductor, he was typing away on his computer. "Here we are humbly straying away in a down- beaten and glitterless effulgent fashion," Marv blew out the words to the sky, helplessly speaking themselves out of the smoke, "Our borrowed cards, being laid out on destinies' table, what a game to be sitting in on, what a desire to be fulfilling, ahh," he breathed, "What curious time we spend making this of ourselves to pass the hours." Jules looked up at him smiling and shaking his head.

"I should have asked you to help me write my book!" He laughed as Marv passed him the joint.

"I don't know who to write," he laughed.

"Ha-ha!" I said.

Arlo asked, "Welton, wanna play a game of chess?"

I looked over to him and said, "Sure! I'll get the board! But the loser has to do twenty push-ups!"

"I'll do some even if I win!" He said.

"Don't you mean *when* you win, Arlo!" Jules said, instigating him.

"Oooh, I see! You got your money on him do ya Jules?" And I looked over to Marv, who was nodding his head in frolicsome disbelief. "Eh Tu Marv? Has everyone abandoned and turned on me?"

"Welton, beat him then!"

"Well ok then, I will!"

And so to pass the time we played a couple rounds of chess. Of course I beat Arlo three games in a row. It didn't take long. Occasionally a car would drive by on the road by the restaurant. God knows how many cigarettes and joints we'd smoked during the games. The day was delicate, as it passed us on, with soft winds, but there was a hint of foul weather stirring in the air. We were all eager to get to Cannes, and waiting for a train seemed like that last thing that we wanted to be doing.

"So Arlo that's sixty push-ups!" I figured.

"Yeah, yeah, yeah," he said as he took a hit off another joint we'd rolled.

"Come on Arlo, I'll do some with ya." Marv stated, as he got up and started to stretch.

"Yeah, I'll do some too," Jules said, as he got up and took off his shirt. Taking steps backward, avoiding our campsite and all our gear that was spread out all over the place.

"Man Jules, your one pale ass bastard." I said as I looked at his dry white skin.

"I'm gonna get a nice tan in Cannes."

"We're gonna lay on the beach all day!" Marv said, as we all got down to do some push-ups, even me. We grunted at the labor, proclaiming our manhood. I felt like we were cell-mates in a prison courtyard in Alabama, with our shirts off, getting tuff on each other, pumping iron.

The wait for the train seemed to grow longer as the day went on. We kept pushing-up.

"You guys think this guy understood us when we asked him when the next train is goin by?"

"You think he meant to say two days?" Marv asked through expected laughter.

"That would be just our luck, huh, and this guy would probably let us sit here, for two days, waiting for the fuckin train." We all laughed stupidly, at our supposed dumb luck.

"Why don't we go check the board?" Arlo said.

"That's a good call, come on!" I said as Arlo and I got up to head over to the station office.

We were in the office looking at the schedule board and a train route map of France, fantasizing about being on the speed train, which didn't even stop at Savaney, when Marv came in to use the bathroom. The Buzzer for the bathroom door didn't work, and the conductor had to come out and give him the key.

"I'm going to clean up," he said. He had some soap, a razor, his toothbrush and toothpaste in his hands.

"That's a good idea," Arlo said as I agreed. We went back out to the platform to get our toiletries out of our bags. Jules was laying around writing something.

"Thoughts with passionate sway come so easily to you, huh Jules?" I asked him as I grabbed my toothbrush and razor from my bag.

"I wish writing was easier," he said.

"So do I. So does everybody, I think."

"What about what you wrote this semester?"

"Man, that killed me, all those hours in my mind in that attic. I don't think I'm recovered yet from pulling all that shit out of my mind and throwin it down to paper. I mean, I think I'm a little burnt out."

"Your not burnt, Marv is burnt out." Arlo interrupted him.

"Well whatever, cause if you sell your script for big bags of money, you can afford to be as stupid as you want." I grunted, trying to reassure even myself.

"Yeah," he paused, "I gotta see what I got us into here, this might be a big waste of time."

"Dude, relax, would you rather be workin right now mowin lawns or," he started to raise his voice, "are you like totally excited that you're taking us to the party, sssiiiiiiiiiiiccccckkkkkk!" He yelled and screamed, getting excited, "it's fuckin great. You gonna shave, yeah?" Arlo asked Jules breaking up our conversation.

"Na, not today, tomorrow I think."

"Watch the gear, will ya!" Arlo said as we headed back into the station.

We had to knock on the bathroom door. Marv opened up the door with soap on his face. We walked in and set up shop by the sinks. Arlo threw down his toiletry bag, and unraveled it. It was spread out like a 6 foot hoagie on the long countertop. Cleanliness on the road isn't easy, all of us realizing that we had to grab the chance of a nice bathroom when we could. The three of us commenced the shaving process, quite enjoyably because we were in this really big and clean bathroom. We lined up and lathered ourselves up like jocks in the locker room.

"Shit, I don't think it's gonna be easy to cut this beard off." I said, "Maybe I should use scissors on it first?"

"Just cut that shit off, Welton, so what if you get a couple cuts on your face, you're ugly anyway, the cuts won't stand out."

"Ha-ha! I'm prettier that you Arlo." We looked at each other, it was funny to say the least. Scraggly looking faces barely covered in white soap. "Then again, you're kind of cute with that soap on your face."

Marv wasn't paying attention to our conversation. He was concentrating on shaving. "Man, fucking Cannes!" Arlo said, as he let out a scream. "We're making great time getting through France, fellas!" We continued the process. Three dirty faces slowly coming clean. I ended up, cutting myself, minutely by my right sideburn. Arlo had this really intricate routine. He went through two blades on one shave, one for each side of his face. He used both hands ambidextrously, He switched hands when he switched sides. He talked a little in this low mumbling voice every time he shaved. It sounded like prayer. Marv and I looked at each other through the mirror. He shrugged his shoulders, not bothering to ask Arlo what the deal was. I didn't ask either. I splashed tepid water on my face and dried myself off with my shirt.

"Not bad," I said, as I looked at myself in the mirror. "I feel like a sixteen year old hotty blondy, big titty virgin baby!"

"Yeah like a chronic one handed finger nail biter!" Arlo said.

"What's that?" I questioned, it even got the Marv's interest.

"You know like a girl who's a chronic masterbater, she's always bitin on that finger that's got her pussies taste on it."

"That's fucked up." I said.

"Actually, no it's not Welton, it's like those high school band girls man, ridin home on the bus with them after a concert, we'd be fingerin them in the back of the bus all the way home. They would let anybody do it, you just had to be the closest finger."

"Damn, I missed all that."

"That's because you weren't cool enough to sit at the back of the bus, jerk-off." Arlo laughed at me.

"What ever. I got plenty of pussy in high school." I said wondering how old I actually was when I finally lost my virginity. I went over to use one of the toilets. The first toilet I came across was clogged with something dirtier than any of us. "Shit! Damn! Marv did you do that?"

"Hells no, that shit was there before I came into this joint yeah!"

"That's disgusting." I said as I entered another stall. Inspecting it first, however, making sure it was clean. Marv finished up and walked out of the bathroom. Arlo and I followed, briefly behind him. Marv walked over and inspected the map and train schedules. There wasn't anything of importance on it for him, either way you looked at it, we were waiting on a train that was heading South, or most likely, the first train that stop at this station. No map could ever route out our path. We traveled on the wings of chance. That's how we found ourselves here, in Savaney! Marv smiled at the conductor, who was looking at him, noticing something different about him. Perhaps, Marv had shaved in his bathroom, he must have thought. He was definitely wondering if we had made a mess for him to clean. We actually kept it clean though.

"I wanna tell this guy that his toilet was clogged before we went in there, but I think in the end, he probably won't understand us, and it'll turn into a big ordeal, trying to converse with this guy."

"Yeah, fuck it Marv, I mean, he's probably the one who clogged it!" Arlo jumped.

"Yeah right, it's not like there's anybody else here!" I said, agreeing with Arlo. Marv realized it to be a futile attempt as the conductor sat looking at him curiously wondering what we were saying.

Marv gave up trying to finish his next sentence in mid-sentence, smiled, put up his hand and said, "Ah, forget about it." He gave the conductor back his key and we followed him back out to the waiting platform, smiling to the conductor as we left. Jules was outside laying down on the platform playing his guitar, looking at the newly arisen detrimental forecast of the overcastting sky, smoking. Shirt unbuttoned, looking beautiful like he was in a postcard. The day had hastily turned into a gray that threatened rain. The wind even felt a little bit heavier. I looked at Jules, he was lighting another joint. He brought about bounteousness to even the worst of environments. He was sitting on top of and around our camp of gear, playing a tune that I hadn't ever heard him play before, on his guitar, hash falling out of the joint and burning a new hole in his shirt. It was hard to be worried about what was going to happen next, I felt a sigh of relief come over me. Arlo, who was standing next to me, pulled out his wallet to get his calling card. There was a phone outside on the side of the station office. Still with his toiletry bag in hand, he started to call Natalia, his supposed party girl lover from the house.

"Is she at Jays' house?" I asked, hoping that I wouldn't have to talk to Cherissa.

"Na, I think she's staying at Kathy and Melanies' place. Man they got a nice place. Those broads got some rich daddies. You ever been there? They got the place for the rest of the summer, and I think they're gonna just hang out and party until they get thrown out."

"I ain't never been there, but I hit that shit once!" I said, with a mysterious sly smile.

"You did? Who Kathy? Melanie?" He asked, completely interrupted, almost dropping the phone.

"Melanie! Are you crazy? I wouldn't touch Kathy with your dick. Yeah we did it, in that employee bathroom, on the second floor cafeteria, one night after theatre class. She's fuckin hot. She came all over my face. We did all sorts of shit for like three hours. But she wasn't cool with it, afterwards. She was upset because I was cheating on Cherissa. I told her that I would break up with her but she told me not to bother. I think she started dating that English dude, in our literature class. Man her pussy tasted good." I said, reminiscing and instantly getting erect, "She loved it. I loved it. She's a really good lay. She got a soft tight pussy." I was getting lost in the dream, about to cum in my pants, "I almost got her clothes off the night of that wine and cheese party we had a couple of weeks after, but it was too risqué for her, right in Cherissa's bed. Besides, I think she was way too drunk to fuck anyway."

"Damn, you lucky bastard. I would've loved to fuck her."

"Yeah I bet you would." I said through a snort, "Give my love to the girls." I said, as I walked off to put my toiletries away. It was probably better if I didn't talk to any girl right now, in my excited condition, I thought.

The weather started getting terribly rough, the wind began to blow with an aroused pace. Arlo came back relatively quickly from his phone conversation appearing distressed.

"She didn't seem like she wanted to talk to me!" He said sadly, looking at the ground. "She got off the phone right away, sayin she was practically out the door. Actin real weird!"

"Maybe she was rollin, or baked! You know it's completely possible that those girls are totally fucked up this early in the day." I said trying to cheer him up.

"She said to say hi to you Marv." Arlo said exhaustively out of gas.

Marv's eyebrow raised, but he didn't look up.

"God, you're not going to cry? Are you Arlo?" Jules asked him. He was looking severely sad and hurt. He didn't answer. He just turned and walked down the platform a ways and sat alone, ruined. All by himself, with his toiletry bag in his hand, he sat down on a step and seemed to be crying, with his head in his hands.

"Shit, what a pussy!" I said as I lit a cigarette. Now. the sky was overcome by a darkened gray. It was becoming more and more dismal in the air around us.

"It's starting to rain." Marv observed. And as if the weather was waiting for him to say that, enormous roaring thunder began striking down upon France. It rained hard, heavily, but on and off, in bursts. The wind picked up aggressively, as the air became solemnly cold.

Jules mentioned through a breath, "Somebody should go and sort Arlo out."

"Not it!" Marv said.

"I'd be delighted to take on this task!" I said with faking conviction. "Besides, Marv you probably shouldn't get involved. I mean, how many times a day did Natalia ask you to fuck her?"

He smiled, and shook his head unable to count the endless amount of times. There was nothing he could say that would cheer Arlo up. The girl Arlo loved and raved about constantly was in love with Marv. The three of us looked at each other.

"Marv you slut!" I said.

"Hey we're all sluts here!" He argued.

"I wouldn't have it any other way!" Jules said as we laughed at each other, forgetting about Arlo's misery.

"Jules your not a slut," I said then, "man, Cannes. Can you imagine!" I kept on going, "Your gonna see some sluts there," still unbelieving that we were actually going there.

"It's pretty sick huh?" Marv said.

"We gotta work and make some money. We're gonna be out of hash pretty soon, and that's not to mention booze and cigarettes." Jules proclaimed, firing out his statement.

"We're gonna make plenty of money, don't you worry about it Jules, just leave it up to Raymond and Pablo, and just keep the music comin."

"Yeah and besides, if we get desperate, we can go into the heat on Arlo's credit card!" Marv said completely as a joke.

"Ha-ha!" I smirked then I changed the subject. "Are you really gonna sell your script Jules? I mean that'd be real cool if somebody bought it, like for money, yeah!"

"No shit." He said.

"What's it about?" Marv asked quietly.

"It's a long story." Jules deflected the question. "Speakin of which, Arlo's pansyness is a long story and you should go get him Mr. Spells." Jules said.

"Yeah, get a move on 'cause I think the train should be comin pretty soon." Marv agreed with him.

"Be right back, with or without him!" I said as I darted down the platform. The wind was blowing stinging little raindrops upon me as I passed out from under our cover from the station platform canopy. I hustled down the platform toward the steps that Arlo was sitting on. As I neared him, I noticed the train coming in the distance. "Shit, we gotta move." I said to myself. I started yelling to Arlo, who wouldn't budge, or even look at me. I started running toward him with quicker faster movements. The rain was coming down hard now, I was getting more excited, because the train was arriving. For a second I could have sworn Arlo wanted us to leave him there. But then I thought however, that all he wanted was some answers, to the mysteries of life, and some beautiful girl to love him. We were both naked to the rain, getting soaked with wetness, life couldn't have been any better.

"Arlo control your God damn emotions, bub. Life ain't fair for anyone. What makes you think you got any special privileges?" I told him, "Now get your sorry ass up and move, damn it! The trains comin!" He was acting like Billy from Kurt Vonnogets novel 'Slaughter House Five'. "I don't have any answers for you man! Cry it out and go with the pain, but you'd better start walking or you gonna have a lot more time to sit on these steps and indulge in your loneliness. I'm outa here!" I turned around and headed back up the platform, moving quickly. By this time, I wasn't only out in the rain, I was a part of it, dripping and shaking it off of me like a wet dog. It was amazing how the weather changed quite instantly, I thought.

Marv and Julian were waiting like passengers for the train. Marv mimed like he was looking at his watch on his wrist and upset that the train was late. They had their backpacks on, the guitar was all packed up and they were holding Arlo's and my gear. The rain was hauling down with dense strength. I was shaking it off my arms, flapping them, applying for take off. I wanted to scream out, 'whhhraaaaaapppppp! Yap yap yap!'. But I didn't, I stayed on the ground. Jules and Marv were under the platform canopy, but still from my distance, I could see that they were nevertheless, getting wet. I on the other hand, or rather, at a further end on the same hand, was undoubtedly soaked. I wiped some water off my face, when all of a sudden Arlo came running up beside me, and advanced so he was kind of looking back at me. He started preaching to me as if all of a sudden the answers came to him and he needed to get them off his chest.

"Yeah, yeah, you see," confident in his deliverance of his news, almost staged and thought out. Trying to say it as if he was an actor in a movie shoot. Or some profound character in this book, "Cannes has never seen the likes of us! We're gonna take the place over. And forget about that broad Uncle

Lefty," as if I was the one who was hurt over her denial of me. I must have brought about some reality on his naivete, "We don't need her!" He said.

I stopped him short of his speech by saying, "Yeah forget about her, that's what I've been sayin. Your gonna get yourself three girls everyday in Cannes." Trying to reassure him, "But one thing you shouldn't forget about, one thing your gonna need is that razor and toothbrush of yours!" I laughed and kept running.

He looked down to his hands with a shocked double take. "Oh, shit! My bag! It's on the steps!" And with that, he turned around and in even faster speed headed back to get it. I ran on. I have to admit he was quick because before I got that much further up the platform he had already gotten his bag and caught up to me. He even had a smoking cigarette hanging from his greedy looking smile.

I was breathing heavy, but I managed to say with a grimace, "You're a dork, Sloth." I had the feeling that Arlo didn't really care if it was Natalia that loved him, he just wanted some attention, or pity, as if he was a loser with no girls. He wanted someone to love him. I didn't care if I cheered him up or not. I should have told him to go cry on his mother's shoulder.

The conductor was up ahead, exposed to the rain, holding his hat down on his head and leaning into the wind. He had a piece of paper in his hand and was waving at Arlo and I. I was trying to remain as nonchalant as possible, slowing down as we went to pass him.

"He's just making sure that we don't miss the train," I said to Arlo as I smiled to him and shook my head up and down in agreement. He put a piece of paper in my hand and was yelling something to us in French over the sound of the storm. I took the flimsy wet paper, thanking him, but not looking at it, and I just kept going. Arlo and I had about ten seconds to go until the train would arrive and stop.

Marv called out, "Come on, lets go!" As we hurried along through the clouding moisture. We needed to be ready and undisturbing to the flow of the train. Marv and Jules both had a look implying that they would have left without us. Probably sharing some inside joke about sticking me with Arlo. I jumped and hurdled over puddles and practically leaped into the straps of my backpack just as the train pulled up. Arlo was right behind me.

"Marv you got my drum?" I asked through an exhausted breath just as the doors of the train opened.

"Yeah! Help him out, Welton," as Marv noticed Arlo somewhat struggling with a strap, "Get his drum."

I picked up Arlo's drum and we walked onto the train, forgetting to wave goodbye to the platform conductor. "Man I'm fucking wet! Thanks a lot Arlo!"

"Sorry man, but if it makes you feel better, I'm wet too! Let me get my drum."

I handed him his drum and I wiped my hands on the orange padding on the walls in the entrance platforms. We were standing by the restrooms, sweating out rain and, at least I, was breathing heavy. The doors of the train closed and the train started to move.

"See ya Savaney!" Jules said as he waved goodbye.

Drizzle splashed on the window as we leaped over the valley. It was gray out but it was clearing up in the foreground. I paced around in what little space there was to move in the little entrance platform. You could see very far down the corridors, even through the tinted glass doors on this train. About ten cars down, a conductor was walking our way.

"Here he comes," I said, shaking some water off my left arm with a swat from my right hand, spraying and spattering it onto Arlo.

"Let's go find some seats!" Marv said.

We walked into the other direction of the oncoming conductor, to the front of the train, which was the way in which the train was moving. There weren't that many passengers on this train. Those of them that were there were for the most part French citizens going on daily routines. "To the head of the train then mates," the pirate in me shouted as we passed a fragile French couple. I smiled, making the only noise out of all of us. No ostentatious travelers were found sitting in seats flamboyantly, as we headed forward. We were the only ones who got on the train at our stop, and the conductor saw us get on for sure. From how it appeared we stuck out oddly enough. So we moved, trying to get ahead of the conductors' pace. Getting through the aisle was always somewhat difficult when you were hauling a lot of gear. Especially because I was feeling the restraint of the soaked tight attire that I was carrying on my person. There were many empty seats. The few passengers that were there seemed alert, waiting for their stop to come upon them.

An old lady in a pale blue dress, hiding a girdle, festooned and perpetuated by the authenticity of France, held herself high in a cloud of elevated deportment as we walked by. We were like an intrusion, walking deceptively, with all our stuff, on the prowl. None of us, my comrades, or the seated passengers, attempted to introduce an exchange of pleasantries. Both parties of course for different reasons, and be that as it may, we were all upon the same agreement of how the moment should be. I was always careful not to

bump a passenger hanging out a bit in the aisle. Unless of course it was a
sweet female that drew me into her magnetic field, then still it would have
been with tender tendencies and a soft longing brush of our arms and hands.
Not any luck of that kind of humble exchange around here, I thought. The
kinds of intercourse that indulged the imagination with sensual curiosity, that
left you wondering if you had just past your destiny or soul mate. They
usually never went any further than that moment, but they created a lasting
memory, full of what ifs and I should have's. How sweet and nostalgic life can
truly be, in the right frame of mind, I found myself thinking. "Are we there
yet?" I asked, not expecting an answer, trying to brake myself out of my
thoughts. "Marv, are ya sure that this isn't our stop?" I asked as the train
slowed down for a stop. No one answered, and the train kept moving on and
on.

We reached the first train car and sat down in seats in the center. Arlo
threw his bag in the over head cargo. I still practically had mine on my back.
We had made a couple of stops since we got on and other passengers got on
and off. During this, I could still see the conductor about four cars down. He
seemed as if he knew exactly who was supposed to get on and off at the stops.
No one came into our car. Two windows on the left side behind us were open
and the breeze was coming in, loud and whizzing so we had to speak up.
Although no one spoke except for simple chatter, we were all a little worried,
we had just wasted two hours and we didn't want to get thrown off the train
so soon. It wasn't cold, but I was chilled. I looked out the window, the skies
had actually cleared up. I took my back pack off and threw it on a seat next
to ours. Even though we were the only ones on the car. We still sat two to a
seat facing each other in the center of the traincar.

Arlo and I sat with our backs facing in the direction we were travelling,
which also faced the way that the conductor was coming. In front of me, Jules
sat facing me, with Marv to his left. Jules and I were in the seat by the aisle, I
could see our reflection in the window. They were vague, almost ghost like
fading in and out as we passed changing sceneries of different hues. It would
have been nice if we faded out as the conductor came through our traincar.
We were on the right hand side of the train. There was only these two seats
on both sides of the train in the center of the car that sat facing each other, all
the others sat facing in the direction the train was travelling. We were totally
cool.

Jules spoke up through a blank stare of wondering what to do, "I'm a
half of a second away from getting up to get my guitar back out of its case," he
said as he let out a breath.

"Now that's what I'm talkin about!" Marv said, "Arlo, roll a joint!"

Then in perfect harmony, indiscriminant noise broke out following his statement. It came from the sundry wears and tears of the traincar and its ingress/egress system, introducing an entrance into our traincar. I could see the cognizance in both Jules and Marv's faces', that they grasped that the conductor had arrived upon us. Marv shook his head side to side, "I knew it! You can't have any fun anymore," he said sarcastically.

He was a little French man, who held onto himself through shallow light steps of cautious advancement. His face showed two intertwined eyebrows and a severe wrinkle in his forehead, he seemed intimidated by our presence. Somehow he seemed alert to the pain he suffered due to the advanced stresses of his metier. The pain brought on by his right to dictate authoritative power over any and all patrons of this train; his domain. He was flittery and jumpy, I was hoping my estimation of him was accurate, I was hoping that he was someone we could take advantage of.

He said, "Biglette! Biglette! Ou es! Ou es." Holding himself tall, trying to stand with importance.

My partners in crime did not speak. Arlo looked at him with a blank face. I smiled at him. Jules and Marv didn't even make a move to turn around. So used to this mundane scene we were, my boys didn't even flinch. He looked back and forth between Arlo and I.

"Passaportes? Biglettes!" He said, acting as if he was getting frustrated.

He looked at Arlo and the stare broke him out of his silence, he said, "No parle francias!"

The conductor shot a comprehendible answer back quickly, "Ticket! Ticket!" Then he went on in French, but we all heard him say ticket.

Arlo said, "OOOOhhhhhh," and he laughed. "Ticket! I get it!" laughing at the guy, "Sure, I got one." And he started to feel on top of his pants front pockets.

I just kept smiling. I had the wet piece of paper that the platform conductor had given me in my shirt pocket. The conductor was talking flipidly in French. I knew that this guy spoke English, but he refused to out of arrogance. Marv was casually, yet, not really looking for his ticket, somewhere on him, or in between his seats. Jules wasn't even moving, let alone pretending to be looking for a ticket. The conductor was looking up to the ceiling, arguing to himself loudly in French, expecting us to be listening to his scolding. He spoke up louder, trying to be heard over the sound of the wind coming crashing through the open windows into our steel terrained sailboat . I couldn't take it anymore.

"I got it!" I said without even looking for it, interrupting the conductors French gala. I was still sitting there, hesitating my move. The conductor stopped talking.

"Well thank God," Marv said, "The last thing we need, is to have lost our tickets, Yeah!" He clasped his hands together, wiping them clean of this occurrence.

"I know yeah! That would have sucked." Arlo said, "It's one thing to lose your mind, but I mean your ticket!" He said as he looked at the conductor.

"Thank God!" Jules said.

"So I'm glad that's settled," I said as I wiped my brow with my hand, looking at the confused conductor. Then we all became silent, none of us looking at the conductor.

He waited for a good seventeen seconds, I counted them, then he said, "Biglette! Ou es? Ticket! Ticket."

"Didn't you give him the ticket?" Arlo asked.

"I thought you gave it to him!"

"Me? You said you had it!"

"I did?"

"Yeah you did, Welton!" Marv said, getting in on it.

I sat thinking for a second, wrinkling my face, trying to remember, then I looked at Jules and asked, "Jules did I say that?" He nodded his head up and down.

"Oh I did? I guess I did."

"Biglette! Ticket! Biglette!" The conductor interrupted.

"Here!" I pulled out the piece of paper the platform conductor had given me, I gave it to the conductor and said "Biglettes," and pointed to all four of us. "Cannes France." He looked at me with a figure of disbelief. Arlo shook his head, reassuringly, up and down.

"There ya go fella." Marv said.

"That's a bonafied biglette," Jules snickered.

The conductor held the folded, moist piece of paper in his hand carefully and delicately, scrutinizing upon it with every crevice of his optical orifices, as if it was the blessed bread that is symbolically embodied by the legend of the body of Christ. Yet his mind showed on his face, disbelief and horror. How could it be true that this is our ticket you wonder? I found myself thinking in my head. He didn't even have the gal or nerve to tear it open greedily, in an authoritative obtrusive fashion. He was physically quite dainty in his movements. After several tender steps of unfolding the piece of paper, then sensitively analyzing it, cautiously, with an attempt of understanding it, he began to mumble to himself in French. A minute bead of sweat swelled up in a ridge on his forehead. He started shaking his head from side to side, through a roar of French symphonious noise, his voice rising to the challenge of the strain in his throat caused by having to speak English. "This is not ticket!" He screamed, "No, no, no, no. Biglettes! Ticket. Give it to me! This is not ticket." He was starting to breath heavy. It was becoming a bit embarrassing. He mumbled songlike consistently in French.

"Take it easy man," Arlo said, "You're getting needlessly excited. That's our ticket all right." A stop came and went. The conductor looked around him, checking out the people waiting on the platform. The train carried on, covering ground.

"Yeah, We got it in Savaney, we paid for it."

"Money? You have money? You must pay now."

"Hey," Marv started to act upset, straightening up somewhat in his seat, turning slightly around to look at the French guy. The conductor took a step backward, and gulped. "That's our biglette, ok."

"NO! No is ticket." Then he said, "Passeportes, passeportes." Along with some more stuff in French.

We kept delaying, replying no, both verbally and through shaking our heads side to side. Jules was pointing to the piece of paper in his hand and kept saying the word biglette through a crack of a smile, trying to impersonate the French tongue. We were all trying to talk over the sound of each others' voices. The conductor was so flustered, he was sweating hard now.

"Give me back our ticket," I said as I reached out and grabbed our ticket out of his hand. The conductor choked on a shocked breath, behaving with vigorous insulted disposition, so typical of French character. He took another step backward. He seemed like he felt appalled at the disrespect he was getting from us. It became quiet, no one spoke for a good eight seconds. We all leaned back and started acting like we were enjoying the ride. As if we thought everything was ok, assuming the role of legal passengers.

Arlo asked the conductor, "How far is it to Cannes, France. Will we get there by tonight?"

The conductor started yelling in French, he kept shaking his head side to side, waving his hands in the air, then he turned around and walked out of our traincar. I could tell, not from what little I knew of the language, but from obvious body language that he was going to get someone with more authority than him to deal with us. I looked at my comrades, none of us moved.

"Arlo, for a second there I was gonna tell you to give him your now four day old all day pass for zones 1, 2, and 3." Jules said as he laughed.

"Ha-ha. I think this guy is goin to get reinforcements." Arlo said.

"No shit, yeah." Marv said, "How the fuck are we supposed to get to Cannes with all these interruptions."

"The fucking French," I said.

"Hey, Welton, what was that you gave him?" Jules asked.

"I gave him something?"

"Ha-ha!" Arlo spat out as we all laughed. I looked at the piece of paper.

"It's directions to Bordeaux."

"Bordeaux?"

"Yeah, that conductor in Savaney gave it to me."

"I guess he didn't want us to get lost."

"I guess not."

"How could he expect us to stick to an outline in this improvisational state of mind that we travel in!" Arlo flared. Jules lit a cigarette.

"Give me a drag of that shit," I said.

"We should be smokin a joint, yeah?." Arlo said.

"I know!" Marv agreed.

"Let's hold off on that for a second," I said through an exhale of the cigarette. "Here," I said as I passed the cigarette to Arlo, "Take a couple drags of this." Sweating now, almost internally, I started to get worried. "This ride is coming to an end. I got a feeling that this guy really might do more than just throw us off the train. You know, like those stories of people getting deported for stunts like this. Or like what that one guy told us that they could confiscate our stuff." I had a feeling that what we had was the only real stuff that meant anything to all of us. Our clown gear, our puppets, and instruments, and most important, our sleeping bags. How were we to survive with out our tools of the trade?

"Shit, here they come." Arlo said. I looked up to see the conductor come in with another conductor of roughly the same build. They were engaged in conversation. Jules dropped the cigarette to the floor and smothered it beneath his worn out boot as they entered our traincar. A cloud of still smoke sat in the winded blown air, refusing to leave our presence. I coughed and swallowed, clearing my throat. The one guy we had met was explaining to the other guy that we had no tickets, that much was obvious. They came up to us, arrogantly.

The new conductor said shyly, "Tickets?" I stood up and drew a breath, I gave him the printout of our route that the platform conductor had given me. The wind was blowing hard on the back of my head. I didn't have any facial expression. The conductor took it with wild curious acceptance. He looked at it and after a spell, he said, "Oh no, no," getting upset, wondering what was going on. Marv and Jules both turned around in their seats. In French he tried to explain to us the situation. I sat back down.

"No, no, no, no es pas *il biglettes!*" He kept stammering about. Throwing his language around as if attempting to simmer down a room full of fattened beaurocrats. "No tickets, No!" And then in quite comprehendible English he repeated several times, "This is directions to Bordeaux. Directions, directions, not tickets."

I rather enjoyed listening to his un-understandable song of French than his English. I was thinking, could he really believe that we were really this stupid? I mean even with the stereotyping Americans get overseas. Didn't we know that the piece of soggy paper wasn't a ticket?

All of a sudden Arlo stood up, "Hey, we paid for these tickets." And he pointed to the piece of paper. Then he nodded his head up and down, adjusted his shirt with his left hand and sat back down with a smile on his face. The conductors stopped talking and looked at each other. Then the second one got the bright idea to ask us if we had any money.

"This is going to get ugly," I said underneath my breath with my eyes cast to the floor. I took a second and looked up, "Alright, that's it, I've had it with the French, you know what, you can keep our ticket! We're outa here, damn it."

"That's right, we don't need this shit." Marv said. "I mean, after all, your country owes us so much money, and then you think you can treat us this way, just wait till our embassy hears about this, the train authorities selling poor Americans false tickets."

"Yeah, your gonna have to do more than just donate a friggin statue to our country when this hits the newspapers. It'll be the biggest scandal since the 'French Fry'," he got all exaggerated like and then said, "you know that shit *ain't* French." Jules spoke up furiously. Arlo looked at him with wonder. I stopped myself from giggling, and then I realized I shouldn't have. Marv started to act mad and upset, riling us up.

The conductors weren't going for it, they kept nodding their heads, unsure of what to do, but still holding their ground, "Passeportes, passeportes." They both started to say.

"I ain't givin these guys my passport, come on fellas, we'll get better treatment from the Spanish, at least there's still some decency left somewhere in Southern Europe." I said, insinuating a sneer at the Frenchmen. In unison, we threw up our hands at the French and made loud noise and ruckus, stirring wildly and rising out of our seats. Arlo reached for his gear in the overhead compartment. I put my backpack on and strapped in my drum ready for the brake, this wasn't going to be pretty. Marv was already moving down the corridor toward the exit. We brushed passed these two guys, almost knocking them down into the seats. I grabbed our ticket out of the one guys hand, almost ripping it. I looked out the window, we were heading into a town, passing little houses stacked in rows and some industrial warehouses. I couldn't see our reflections in the window. The first conductor we met, said something in French, with eagerness to the other conductor. They started yelling at us, one of them ran passed us, and continued running up ahead. Probably, he was going to get some reinforcements.

As he was moving along, Marv kept yelling, "No passeportes, no passeportes." I looked at my mates. The level of intensity was up to a maximum. It was enjoyable and riddled with fear at the same time. The train was pulling into a station, at the time I didn't even know the name of the town we were getting off at. The other conductor came running back up, yelling at this conductor who was guarding us, now even more excited for some sort of a bust. The were saying something about the police, and now they were smiling and yelling to get everyone's attention. The doors opened and we walked off the train, the conductors following us at first, not sure what to do. Obviously the police hadn't arrived yet, and without reinforcements, these little Frenchmen were scared of us.

We started walking toward the station exit, the conductors started yelling, don't let them get away, somebody stop them in French and English. Other passengers travelling and exiting along with us looked on as if we had just robbed the train of its diamonds, and we were on the run. The scene was drawing heavy, very pulp fictionesque. An older French woman, civilized, looked on us with wide worried eyes. She grabbed her daughter and pulled her closer to her as we walked by, hiding her from the spewing disaster of the crime scene. I didn't look back at the conductors who were following us, yelling, but letting us get away. I kept walking. I could tell, that at any moment, someone was going to start running. Then as if our opponents made a move to take our queen, the police showed up. There must have been ten of them, about six uniformed guards, and four or five under cover cops. Then one of the two little French train conductors who had followed us reached out and grabbed my shoulder. The moment hit. If we had guns, we would have started spraying everybody down right now, civilians and all. I pulled away and kept on moving. I had the feeling that Arlo had slithered away unnoticed in all the excitement. I could see Marv and Jules almost out the door. The cops rushed us, as the train conductors were yelling in French to get us, pointing at us and holding onto their hats through the wind of the excitement. 'There they are', they must have been saying in cartoon French 'Seize the criminals'. The cops barracked our movement, lining up with stern unfriendly faces. We were forced to stop the movement of our odyssey.

The undercover cops looked at us blankly, scrutinizing us. Passengers of mostly French descent were staring in awe at the Americans. The train conductors celebrated the capture, and scolded us hard in French. They told the cops what was going on, probably telling them to stiff us with a hard fine. They spoke quickly through victory smiles, trying to add as much color to the situation as they could. They spoke over each other, trying to add all the pertinent information to the list of laws we had just broken. They then ran back to the train, which was being held up due to our interference and brushed along with body language and hand movements, all the passengers, trying to dismiss all the commotion. The cops stared at us, unsure of what to do, unable to question us abruptly because of the language barrier. I gave the one cop, with this flaring mustache, who was assuming the role of leader, the paper with our route on it and said "biglette."

I was wondering if this guy was going to think that we really were that dumb. None of us spoke. He looked at the piece of paper and then he shook his head.

He asked, "Bordeaux?"

"Si, Bordeaux, si, oh yeah, es Bordeaux? Biglettes para Bordeaux!" We all talked over ourselves, pointing to each other.

"No, es biglettes," the leader said. Some of the other cops peered over his shoulder to inspect the piece of paper. Then they agreed with him that it wasn't a ticket.

"Hey, we paid for that in Savaney, for all four of us to get to Bordeaux, now if you French guys are trying to rob us-"

"Or better yet blackmail us-" Arlo blurted out, sneering and snorting.

"Yeah, extortin us into buying another ticket, I heard about this routine," I said shaking my head in disgust at the head cop, "we have no choice but to call our embassy, alright. Where's the phone? Is there a phone here?"

"What's the number damn it?" Arlo begged the cops.

"So, is this Bordeaux?" Marv asked.

"Bordeaux? Jules inquired, "Es Bordeaux? Ahhh, que belle, Bordeaux! We made it!" Jules and Marv started patting each other on the back. The uniformed cops looked at us, completely unsure if they wanted to take the time out of their day to kick the shit out of us, and they probably would have been allowed to do it.

The leader looked around and asked, obviously, if any of his mates spoke English. No one had a reply. Then a smaller more timid and reserved undercover cop asked, from over the shoulder of his leader, if we knew any other languages.

"Ah, Io parle Italiano." I said proudly.

"Oh bueno, blah, blah blah," he chattered through a smile, but I couldn't understand him. He was mixing it up with French, and I wasn't particularly fond of breaking the communications barrier. The leader looked back and forth to me and him, hoping that a resolution would surface.

"No, no comprende que dice," I said. "Do you understand him Marv-"

"Nope!" He said without fail.

The leader let out a sigh. We were still standing in the corridor, taking up a lot of space, turning passerby's into rubberneckers. The leader shifted his weight on his feet, then he said something in French to most of the other cops, and they dispersed without question. Just the leader and his little Italian speaking buddy were left to deal with us. They motioned for us to follow them, and we did, happily. We were taken into this office, passing all sorts of curios train employees. In the office with the door closed, we stood, cramped as usual, while they tried to explain to us that the piece of paper wasn't a ticket.

"But Senoire," Marv said sarcastically, "Es biglette."

"No, no es biglette," The mustached agent replied.

"No es Biglette?" Marv asked.

"No," the mustache shook from side to side, "No es biglette."

I grabbed the piece of paper, and looked at it, counting how many words were on the page, then I spoke, "Guys, I think that this isn't a ticket."

"What! It's not a ticket. Oh man, now what are we gonna do." Jules said through somewhat of a frustrated lisp.

The French guys were seeming saddened by our situation, then the leader asked, "Tienes passeportes?"

"Passports? For what? We didn't do anything wrong, we got ripped off in Savaney, we paid for that piece of worthless paper," Marv said, as Arlo agreed with him with body language, holding his hand out and rubbing his fingers together, symbolizing money.

"It's ok, no worry, give passeportes." He smiled

"Shit, we might as well give them our passports, I mean I think they got us." Arlo fussed.

"Yeah well, we'll see about that," I said as I started taking my backpack off. It was more of an ordeal gearing down to get at our passports than it was to actually go through the process of getting busted. We all had to reach somewhere secret to pull this vital piece of information out. I was wondering at that time what else was going to fall out of any of our pockets. I reached into my dirty smelly inside pouch held on by a string around my neck, snug underneath my arm pit practically mended to me. Marv pulled his out of his hipsack around his waste. Jules had his pushed and into his bag, stuffed with all his writings and thoughts. No matter what he was looking for in that bag, it always seemed to be sitting right on top so he didn't have to dig through to find it. Arlo carried a travel planner with storage compartments and a calculator. They took our identification with eagerness. They recorded our social security numbers and wrote our names down on the bandits to watch out for this summer list. They talked amongst themselves as they scrutinized our pictures and names.

"Tienes dinero?" They asked.

"Seniore, nous pagar para el papel con todos nuestro dinero." Marv said.

"Well put, I think your picking up this French language quicker than you thought you would."

"Hey what can I say, I'm eclectic."

"Ha-ha."

Jules then asked, "Queres que nous tocamos la musica?" It had worked with the cops in France on our last trip, we played them a song to avoid a fine for hitchhiking on the super highway. Anything when you're low on cash to get by helps.

"Oh, no no no," they said, "Dinero, Dinero."

"What, like a pay off? Sorry, no dinero." I said. I could tell that they were pissed that we couldn't pay their fine. The Italian speaking cop started to insinuate, by pointing to our stuff, that he would like to confiscate something of value.

Arlo stepped up a bit and said, "Let's just play them a song and get the fuck out of here."

"Good call, Arlo," I said as Jules, with diligence, started opening up his guitar case. He laid it on the ground and unlatched it. Arlo grabbed his drum, and before any one else could say anything. A loud egotistical shriek came out of Marv's harp. The Italian cop jolted his hands to his ears and let out a shriek. "That's good, sing along," I said trying to encourage them. Song was underway, Arlo was tapping some background beats to the cries of the harp. I assumed a face of clownesque sadness, implying please don't hurt

121

us. The leader cop didn't really want to be amused, however he took it in good faith. They let us play for about a minute until they quieted us down with hand motion. Employees in the hallways peered through the windows of the office.

"Ok. Ok, ok," came the words out through the mustache. Then he started calling out our names to hand us back the correct passports. We all went silent, Jules put his guitar away. We held out our hands instinctively when our name was called. The last passport, he held up, and as if he was a tenor from an opera doing the announcements for a basketball game, he eloquented out, "Marvelous Ellowin." We all giggled a little when hearing this.

"Marvelous?" Jules and Arlo questioned him.

"I thought your name was Marv?" Arlo quirked.

"It is," Marv answered, trying to avoid getting into it but then he said, "It's short for Marvelous." He said through a cool un-helpable smile.

"Really? That's cool that your parents named you Marvelous."

"Yeah. Actually my parents wanted me to be born black."

"What?" Arlo asked. Jules laughed. I already knew the whole story and actually it was true, Marv's parents were way too cool to be republicans.

"Seriously, its not funny, they always tell me," and he quoted with his hands, "I wish you were born black, kid, my mom would say to me." The officers stood there wondering what we were talking about. I started to move for the door. Marv gestured to the cops goodbye. And with all this behind us, we thanked them and walked out of the office. The cops followed us out. By now, station employees had gathered to view the aftermath of the great train smugglers. News had in an obvious fashion passed quickly down the gossip lines amongst the station employees.

An employee who had been standing outside the office was told to escort us out of the train station. We waved to the cops and left.

"I'm glad that's over with, so let's get on the next train outa here," Arlo said as we walked away.

"Wait a second, let's think about this for a minute." I jumbled the words out through concerned frustration, that was slowly making its way to the foreground of my attention.

"Yeah?" Arlo asked.

"While we're at it, let's find a place to roll a joint, Yeah?"

"Good call, Marv, but let's check this out first." Jules added as he veered toward a ticket window, following the station employee. Apparently in France, you had to pay for transportation. It turned out that we were in

Nantes, France. The train station lobby was pretty big, giving the impression that its capabilities were well beyond the call of tourism to the town.

I asked the ticket agent, who spoke English, "How much is a ticket to Cannes, France?"

After checking her computer she said, "There are two trains leaving for Cannes," she glanced over to a watch on the counter, while tapping away on the keyboard, "one is leaving in twenty three minutes, and another in three hours and twenty three minutes. The prices are the same, at exactly," and she worked it out in her mind for me, "sixty five American dollars apiece. We accept travelers checks."

"Damn," Jules said over my shoulder.

"Travelers checks, " I said under my breath, and let out a snorted breath, "What ever, thanks, we'll be back for the train in three hours," I said.

"It departs at six twenty three this evening, from platform 12, if you take that train, you will arrive in Cannes in the early morning of tomorrow."

"Thanks," Marv said as we walked away.

"Lets go smoke a joint." I said as we turned and walked away.

"Why don't we just get on the next train, yeah? We got this far. I mean what are they going to do to us?"

"What disheartening news, for fucks sake," Jules wimpered out. He turned his back on us and moved a few feet away, stalling his thoughts.

I looked at Arlo, "It's not what they are going to do to us Arlo, it's a question of timing. At this rate, we'll be there in two days."

"He's right Arlo, we gotta think about this," Marv said as he plotted and pointed out the perfect spot right outside the train station to stop and roll a joint. We walked over, passing Jules, he followed along behind us. We all took our bags off and sat on them, except for Jules. Arlo broke out the hash and started rolling it into a joint.

I looked at Jules, he seemed worried. "Hey Jules, what's the problem, huh? It's all good, I mean we're gonna get there, don't worry." I said with a bland attempt to cheer him up.

"Yes, it is true, Julian," Marv let out, "it's never seen easily," he paused, "the distance is so far away, so hard to see," they both looked at each other sincerely, "but it doesn't mean it's more difficult or harder to accomplish, it's just more uncertain and that definitely doesn't mean it's wrong."

"What about hitchhiking?" Arlo broke in, getting Jules off the hook of having to respond to what ever the hell it was that Marv was saying.

"That's a good idea, but we'd probably have to split up, and that can get out of hand. I'd rather stick together and do this the right way." I said to Arlo.

Outside it was full of life, some European tourists but mostly a lot of teenagers and youthful smiles along the way. It seemed like it was a big town set up within the limits of a confined area, leaving a lot of the space on the outer limits of the town, unused. There was an oversized roadway, and there was a steady flow of car and pedestrian traffic, right outside the train station.

"You know, I'm willing to bet that we could make the money we need and then some, in about an hour, in this town."

"You think?" Arlo asked as he lit the joint, puffed on it, then passed it around.

"Sure. Look around. All these people walking around, it stopped raining, what else can you ask for?"

"You know, I bet you're right, Welton," Marv said as he took a drag from the joint.

"I could play a few tunes right now," Jules smiled, then laughed at us, "so whatever, but if we're gonna do it, we gotta go find a good spot."

"How about right over there," I said as I pointed over to a wide median where kids were sitting on a bench. Marv passed me the joint and looked over his shoulder to assess the spot.

"That looks perfect he said, as he stood up and unzipped his backpack. Then like the rainbow after the storm, out came Raymond.

"Oh, shit, here we go!" Arlo said, getting excited. "Welton, you wanna do that clown routine with me?"

"Um, let's work the puppets first, I think they are gonna do better here."
"Yeah I think you're right," Jules said as I passed him the last hit off the joint.

"Alright let's go," Marv said, as he put his bag on and started manipulating Raymond.

And instantly, people started to notice the little black man being walked down the street. We all got up and followed Marv. People started pointing at Raymond.

"Man I hope the cops don't flag us."

"Don't worry about that, we'll send them over to see the train cops and tell them that they gave us permission."

Raymond was a spectacle and people stopped in their places to stare at him. We reached the spot, and took it over. Putting our bags down and tying them together. Marv had already dropped the hat onto the pavement and was already surrounded by some people checking out Raymond. He was waving and hiding behind Marv's leg, peering out then walking over to the hat and leaning on it, tapping his foot. Then he looked inside the hat and started shaking his head from side to side. Man, Marv is so good at manipulating Raymond with such delicate and intricate movements. It's as if he really is alive. Then again, he's well built too, but still, Marv has mastered his movement capabilities. The people standing around got the idea easily that Raymond was looking for money in the hat. They seemed like students and they were talking to each other and laughing, some of them were calling some more of their friends over. Then as if we hit on the slot machine, coins started to get pitched into the hat.

"Geez Marv, you don't even need us."

"Yeah right, should I even take out my guitar?"

"Well we gotta have something for Raymond and Pablo to dance to," Arlo
said as he started beating, tribal like, on his drum.

I started accompanying him with the beats, and it was sounding really good
and tight. A bigger circle started to form around us. More people stopping to look, mesmerized by Raymond, then reaching into their pockets for change, and throwing money into our hat. Some of them walking off, but many off them sticking around to enjoy what they were witnessing. The drums were calling peoples' attention from further away, and they came over to see what was going on. Jules electrified us with some sweet riffs. People were moving with the wave of the music. Raymond was dancing and jumping and shaking hands with people. Everybody was giving us money. It was great. Marv was smiling and dancing with Raymond. Little children ran up and pushed their way to the front of the crowd. Their parents threw money into our hat. The crowd started taking over part of the street. It wasn't good to have too big a crowd, because then actually, less people threw money into your hat.

"You guys, lets bring this up then cut it, ok?"

"Yeah, let me get Raymond to climb this wall, then he'll fall, then we'll end
it." Marv said as he started walking over, through the crowd, to a three feet high wall. We rose steadily the speed of the drum beats. The guitar riffed up and down some scales. Marv jumped up and stood on the wall, while Raymond climbed away, struggling to get up the wall. People loved it. They were in awe. Then all of a sudden, a little kid ran over and grabbed Raymond and helped him climb up the wall. Marv was in tune with it and accepted the

kids help. People started clapping, and yelling and laughing in French. Raymond straightened himself out, dusted himself off and stuck his hand out to shake the kids hand. Shyly the kid shook his hand, then ran back to his mom through wild applause from the groaning crowd. The music was in a frenzy, at its highest point. Then Raymond started clapping, He jumped up in a styly fashion, stalling in mid air like a witch, and then came down and bowed, just as the music stopped abruptly. The last note from the guitar, lingering in the air, holding everyone's attention in a sealed and elongated moment. Applause grew and roars from the crowd didn't die down for some time. They loved it. People ran up to throw money in our hat. Telling us fantastic things in French. We sat still, smiling and thanking everyone. Marv jumped down from the wall, and walked Raymond over to the hat. We waited for the crowd to die down.

"I bet we just made at least one ticket," I said to Jules as he lit a cigarette.

"Shit, that was cool." Arlo said.

"Yeah and it's only gonna get better." There were people standing around

trying to communicate with Marv, asking to get a better look at Raymond. Marv was kind, thanking them, bowing Raymond. People started to walk away, Shaking their heads, and happy to have witnessed such delight on such a nice day. The crowd died down and we were left unbothered by those still hanging about.

"Marv lets empty the hat."

"Here. Let's give it a minute before we go for round two, and break out Pablo."

"Hey Arlo, there was a board on the floor where we were smoking that joint, go over and get it. Raymond and Pablo'll do their little teeter board act."

"Cool." He said as he ran off, beating on his drum, attracting attention.

"Yo, there are a couple bills in here."

"Well how much do we have?"

"I don't know, I never did understand this currency."

"Well alright, we'll keep playin around, until we get tired, and if we don't have enough money, we'll just leave Arlo behind." Jules said.

"There ya go Jules, now you're startin to think like me."

"Yeah that might get you in trouble if you're not careful." Marv said.

"Break out Pablo and let's see what kind of trouble *he* can get us into." Jules said, winking at me and blowing me a kiss.

"Sure. Hey, was there any Americans in that crowd, Marv?"

"I don't think so."

"I bet this place isn't even on the map."

"Probably not the tourist map. Like those little towns in Southern Italy with Cathedrals and Coliseums grander than those in Rome, except built by the Moors, thus unable to be exploited as their own creations, and only a matter of time until they're demolished, in this day and age."

"Yeah, what a shame."

"Hey you guys," Arlo said as he came running up, "You know what I was thinking? I was thinkin that maybe there's a council travel somewhere in this town, where we can get our tickets even cheaper."

"How much cheaper can they be?"

"Well, when I went up to Christiania, the tickets through council travel where half the price of normal tickets."

"Really? That sounds good to me. Arlo why don't you go ask someone in the train station if they know of one in this town."

"Ok, here." And he gave me the board that he had gone to retrieve and he turned around and ran down the street to the train station.

"Looks like Arlo is coming in handy after all."

"I told you he would." Marv said.

"Well lets just see what he comes back with. So I'm gonna play the drum and we'll use Pablo when Arlo gets back."

"Sure, are you guys ready."

"Yeah," and Jules started to strum softly on his guitar. I started to play along, quietly, and Raymond started to move around. Raymond just stood and waved at first, grabbing passerbyes attention, then he started tapping his foot and lifting his leg. He moved around. The people walking by stopped to look at Raymond, they all threw money into our hat. It was so easy. More people of all types stopped and drew around us. How fascinating it must have been for them to see us, Americans, living on their street. Raymond waved at everyone, kids in the crowd waved back. Marv walked Raymond over to an empty baby stroller being wheeled about by an attractive mother. The little boy was standing beside it, unsure of what to do. Raymond started to climb into it, and the kid started crying. The crowd started to laugh unanimously, and then the kid started to punch Raymond. The crowd became even more crazy and the kid started screaming and crying and Raymond ran away to hide behind Marv. People literally lost it. Those of them that had already given us money, reached into their pockets to give us some more.

"Jules, this is working out great," I said over the sounds of the music.

"Yeah, what would we have done without Raymond."

"I know, it would have been a lot harder to make money."

"Hey fellas, bring the music up."

"As you wish, maestro," I said as I started beating harder and faster on my drum. Jules moved fast through notes, with somewhat of a bluegrass country style. The crowd was big, and getting bigger, making it impossible for the people in the back to see Raymond.

"Marv we gotta end this, remember keep it short and simple."

"Yeah fine, give me a drop off point." And with that, I did a drum roll, Jules tweetered a note, and Raymond did a little style jump into a split, and then we cut it. The crowd applauded and laughed. Kids were jumping up and down, asking their parents for some money to throw into our hat. People started to leave, but everyone put money into the hat before they walked away. It was a beautiful thing.

"Geez, I think we have enough for three tickets fellas and something to drink and eat, if we leave Beeeeeezleeeey behind."

"Ha-ha, very funny he said as he came walking back up to our circle." Playing a beat while bustling through the crowd.

"I was just kidding Arlo, anyway what's the verdict?"

"Well I was right, there is a council travel but it's on the other side of town. But the good news is that tickets are about twenty five dollars cheaper apiece."

"That's fucking good news, I guess you're coming with us Arlo," Jules said. "Did you get directions on how to get there?"

"Yep." He said. I peered into the hat.

"Well it looks like we have a lot of money here, Marv what do you think? We got over an hour until the train, wanna got get the tickets now?"

"We should count the money first and see if we have enough."

"Arlo you know how to count this shit, right?"

"Sure." People walked by, wondering what kind of show we were doing, staring and pointing to the sleeping puppets.

"Well get to work then. And do it in your bag, we don't need to draw attention to our profits. Marv you should put Raymond away while he counts this, cause' he's gonna draw attention to us."

"No problem, I'll roll a joint."

"Jules man, I could do this for the rest of my life. Shit people work harder for less money. We got it good."

"Yeah we're a good team."

"You can say that again," Arlo interrupted, "We got enough money here to buy four tickets without even going all the way to the council travel."

"Really? Did you count it all?"

"Just in bills we have most of it yeah! Looks like we're actually going to eat today." And he handed Marv the hat with the coins in it. Then he folded the bills up and gave them as well, to Marv.

"Damn…Marv what do you want to do?" I asked curiously, stalling to scratch at some dead skin ashing itself off of my arm.

"Should we send Arlo to get the tickets, and we'll work some more?" Jules coughed out.

"Actually we should all go, you never know what could happen to him."

"Alright then, lets get a move on." And we all got up and threw our bags on and started walking, following Arlo. We turned several corners and walked down little streets that were packed with people. Several of the people we passed greeted us like we were all friends. They must have been part of the crowds that gathered for our show. We kept on walking. Tables were set up in these little cobblestone streets and it seemed like all the people of the town were out and about, mingling. Intricate nicnaks were being sold by old ladies with leathered skin and discolored scars. It seemed like the street vendors were set up to cater to groups of tourists, and it was the season for travelers, but I didn't see too many tourists. Those of whom I did see, appeared to be German. We didn't run into any Americans. We found our way well enough through the town. There were very sweet clean looking shops layering the facades of crooked buildings in these small streets. It was almost as tight as walking through the aisle on a traincar.

"Arlo are we there yet?"

"Are you sure you know where you're going Mr. Euro-rail ticket?" Jules demanded, poking him from the back with his guitar case.

"The girlie on the phone said it's right next to that church," and he pointed to the tip of a churches tower that seemed to be about ten streets away.

"I guess that's easy enough."

"Yeah but how the fuck are we going to get back to the train station?" Jules asked.

"I think I remember the way," I said.

"This is a cool town," Marv said, admiring the authenticity of the cobblestone streets.

"All these little towns are like this."

"I know, I just happen to feel really comfortable right now."

"Well shit, the last time we made this much money in such a short time was in Rome, back in January."

"Yeah you remember that Welton."

"How could I forget." And all of a sudden when we turned the corner, we got the full view of the church that had guided our way.

"You seen one church, you seen them all." Arlo said.

"I bet you never even been inside a church Arlo," I said.

"Hey there it is, council travel, it looks the same in every friggin country," he said, dismissing my religious comment.

"Alright." Marv said as he walked up and opened the doors for us to enter.

Upon entering, the beautiful girl behind the counter looked up and asked if she could help us, in English.

"Yes, actually, you can help us-"

"What my friend here means," Jules said, interrupting me, knowing that I would have asked her for a different kind of help, "Is that we need four tickets to Cannes, France."

"Oh, Are you all students? Under twenty six years old?"

"Yes."

"Very good then." She said as she looked up the information on the computer. "Did one of you call here early?"

"Yes," And Arlo pushed ahead of us, knocking us out of the way with the bulky boldness of all his gear surrounding him, and with his chin to the ceiling he said, "It was I! Was it you, that I was talking to?"

"Yes and I am sorry, because I gave you a bit of miss-information. I quoted a price for tickets to Marseilles, not Cannes. It was a mistake, it will be about another ten American dollars apiece for tickets to Cannes. I am sorry."

Great, I thought, another forty bucks down the drain. And then I realized the correct answer, and I interrupted what Arlo was about to say, probably something along the lines of 'well honey, do you take Visa?' and said to her, "Well that's ok, we're not in the habit of paying for tickets anyway actually, so I think that Marseilles'll be good enough for us. We can walk to Cannes from there."

"To Marseilles then, you wish me to make four tickets?"

"Arlo are you coming with us?" Marv asked without expecting a reply, "yes four tickets then, and I hope you accept change." He said as he pulled out the weighted hat and dropped it onto the counter. It must have been the heaviest paper weight she had ever seen in her office. She looked at it for a second and smiled. Then she went to work on printing out our tickets. She grabbed the hat to count the money. It took her about ten minutes. There wasn't enough money in coins so Marv had to use some of the bills that we had been given. We were left with some money left over. At least enough for cigarettes. We would have to make more tomorrow if we wanted to eat in Cannes. After our transaction was over, we thanked the lady and went on our way. I'm glad I didn't try to haggle her into accepting blame, for her mistake about the extra ten dollars apiece that we would have to pay. Us, the weary traveler who walked all this way to the council travel, causing us to miss our first available train, thus throwing off our precious timing. And us, only having enough money for what she had quoted, but now having to pay practically the train stations' price, I bet I could have convinced her that she was using a technique called false advertising to lure business her way. I probably could have easily made her realize that this mistake, in favor of the customer, was something that her company should be willing to reimburse us for. But she was real pretty, and I wasn't in the mood to debate and after thinking about it, I decided that a walk from Marseilles to Cannes could turn into an adventure and a half if we chose the right house to stop and break into, uh, I mean check out. As for now, I was more hoping that we wouldn't get lost or sidetracked on our way back to the train station, it would complicate our timing.

As we were walking this really drunk girl befriended Arlo. She wanted to play his drum. He let her tap on it as we walked. She almost fell over onto an old ladies table. She almost knocked over this expensive looking lamp. She took up a lot of room swaggering, in the little street. More room than we did with all of our equipment and backpacks. We didn't have time to deal with her. The old lady yelled out something and reached to balance out her toppling lamp.

"Arlo why don't you walk her home?"

"Ha-ha." He said, as he tried to say goodbye to her, but gone was the moment of his escape from her. She wouldn't leave him alone. She kept talking to him in French and saying 'hello how are you!' over and over. She didn't even give up, after several attempts of communication and Arlo ignoring her and smiling politely. Before we turned the corner onto a bigger avenue, Arlo stop and turned to her, he grabbed her by the shoulders and held her still, then he put his hand up and had his palm facing her, he looked into her eyes and said, "Stay." Then he nodded his head up and down and turned and started walking.

"Arlo, is that how you get rid of all of your girlfriends?" Jules asked.

"Yeah right, like wait here, I'll be right back." The girl stood there, wobbling and hiccuping trying to regain her thoughts.

"That's how he's gonna get rid of his wife and kids one day, when he's tapped out all of daddy's bank accounts. "

"Ha-ha," he said, taking it, "Hey lets catch that bus," he said as he started running toward it. It was just starting to depart. We all yelled at it, and ran toward it. Backpacks shaking vigorously up and down as we hustled toward the unstopping bus. The bus driver stopped proceeding, but rolled slowly as he opened up the doors to let us on. He was still in motion as we clumsily got on the moving bus. It was kind of like being on a treadmill. We paid our fare with stupid smiles.

"I could get used to this paying for transportation stuff. Nobody bothers
you, or haggles you when you pay. It's weird." I said.

"Yeah, well don't get used to it, Welton. Remember who you are, you fuckin criminal." Marv said.

Jules was staring at us, my eyes locked on Marv's, the silence within the pause causing a dramatic fear to stir up in the winded, rushing air. "Shit, Marv, is he really a criminal?" Jules asked sincerely, "Let's get the story straight, cause to me it sounds like hearsay."

"Man how many laws did you see him break in London, remember Jules? Breaking and entering, theft, assault with a deadly weapon-"

"It wasn't really a deadly weapon, and besides that was a self defense situation, and I never got caught for anything so, technically, to the naked eye of the law, I'm not a criminal, but if a psychologist where to analyze me, they may say that one of my personalities has a criminal mind." And I raised my eyebrows up and down, smiled insanely without showing any teeth, my reddening cheeks pushed up against my opened wide eyes, staring at Marv.

"Whatever, mister I was born to fuck my neighbors wife and steal his car."

"Marv what's gotten into you man, why you workin him so hard?" Arlo
asked. But before he could answer him this guy on the bus jumped into the middle of our huddle. He had his hand out and started asking us for money.

"This guys' out of his mind," I said. He reached out to touch my drum. Marv grabbed his wrist and held him at bay without any effort. I pushed him back but he was being held into place by Marv. I put my hands around his neck. He tried to resist and brought his free hand up to his neck. My left hand felt him swallow, and his eyes reddened. My right hand clasp his hand down around his own neck. He was trying hard to breath. I could feel the look from some other passengers on the back of my head, It felt like every one else was scared of what was about to happen, except for me. I smiled at his staring blank eyes and the vigorous snorts coming through his nose.

"I think we should kick this guys ass, and take his clothes. Do we have enough time for that?"

"I don't think so Welton."

"Well he's real fucking lucky then." I squeezed my grip on his neck tighter,
and he squirmed, but couldn't move because Marv was holding on to his one wrist. Then I let go of him and stepped back. I leaned back, the weight of my backpack and the movement of the bus forcing me to shift my feet to regain my physical balance. I would have liked to have taught this guy a lesson, perhaps show him the truth about humiliation. The bus made a stop and Marv walked him over to the door. The lad left willingly. He was glad to have control of himself again, he checked his wrists' function and rubbed his neck as he exited, not daring to look at us. Everyone around us stared at the floor.

"Man why'd you have to go callin me a criminal. You know it's you who provokes me into being bad."

"What ever-"

"Hey the train stations up ahead." Arlo interrupted, "let's forget about this shit ok. We're here to have a good time, not to argue or kill anybody, right?"

"I know, I just hate paying for tickets."

"Welton, this is the only ticket that I think you've' ever paid for, or at least full price for, and you've been travel throughout Europe for a year man. Relax I think it's ok." Jules said, trying to reassure me.

"Yeah you're right, I'm the man."

"Well I wouldn't go that far." Arlo said as we got off the bus and headed for the train station.

"Ok then, I'm the man's buddy," I said through the noise of the train station as we walked through the doors.

"Yeah and I guess I'm the man," Arlo said, bolting ahead of us, "Cause I
know which platform our train is leaving from." Arlo held his ticket up high and mighty, for all to see as he moved. It appeared that what had happened to us recently was instantly forgotten. We were now reputable passengers. No one seemed to hold a grudge or even seem to remember that we were the great train bandits. Taking Arlo's advice we walked over to a platform and got on a train, waiting to depart.

"We made good time, this train leaves in ten minutes."

"If nobody checks our tickets, I'm going to be pissed."

"That'd be funny, huh, all the way to Cannes."

"Shit with our luck, they would check us at Marseilles."

"Now that would be really funny."

We found seats on an empty traincar and sat down in separate seats. Jules pulled out his guitar and started tuning it. More people boarded the train and then it departed, rolling out of Nantes, heading South in France. We made several stops at small towns and several other people got on the train, some of them sat in our train car. One of them was a strange sort of a man. He sat at a distance from us. He kept looking at us through a curious bright but soft stare. Jules and I were sitting facing his direction, sitting in separate seats. I could see him at an angle. He was listening intently to the music coming from Jules' guitar. Arlo was rolling a joint. The guy smiled at me, delicately, the way a holy Hebrew man would have. I smiled over to him and waved my hand, asked him to join us. He was a thin, shy moving dark skinned man, very quiet and soft, with light features and a wise chin. He came over and sat down next to Marv. He nodded and I reached over to shake his hand. Every one else followed my doing, except for Arlo. He lit the joint and puffed on it, then motioned to pass it to him. He accepted it kindly, and smoked away at it. He smiled, exhaled then passed it to Marv. He motioned to Jules, if he could play his guitar.

"Si, si," Jules said as he flipped it over and passed it to him. He pulled it into place, calmly, strumming incredibly softly, almost inaudible over the obtrusive sounds and noises around us. He played beautiful soft music with three simple chords but it was like a new light being shined on us. It was archaic and full of an ancient aura, the way he gave life to the guitar. He smiled as we encouraged him on. He stopped and reached into his pocket. He pulled a ball of hash and handed it over to Marv.

He said, "We smoke." And he nodded his head and continued playing the guitar.

"Alright," Marv said, "This is my kind of stranger." He started breaking up the hash and rolled up a cone style joint. We smoked it and laughed, but ironically enough, none of us attempted to communicate verbally. The fellow gave Jules back his guitar. He looked outside realizing the train was slowing down. He nodded to us and put his hand out to shake our hands. We all threw our hands at him. The train was coming to a stop. He went to get up. And I nodded to him. Marv went to hand him back his hash, but nodded his head side to side, implying that we should have it.

"Thank you, Marv said." He smiled and waved goodbye, as he walked toward the exit doors.

"He was very nice, huh Jules?"

"Ah man, I think that was Jesus Christ!"

134

"I bet he's from Arabia."

"He had that cool, indistinguishable look goin on. I bet he spoke better English than us, and graduated from London School of Economics."

"He left just as innocently and mysteriously as he came to us, like he was an angel." We sat back until the next stop talking about him, and as if we switched the channel on the television, a new scenario headed our way as we reached the platform for the stop. A very long platform but a simple looking train station. I saw an endless group of jumping, screaming caroling, school of children waiting to get on our train, taking up practically all of the platform. The doors of the train opened and kids, running and screaming, just poured in from both sides of the train. They took up about three train cars, and it felt like I was back in my old circus days.

"Here we go," I said, pure activity and entertainment for the rest of the ride. These kids are gonna drive me nuts, if they ride with us all the way to Cannes." All I wanted to do was sleep, I was tired, and I wished I had something to quench my thirst and ache. The kids were annoying, running up and down, in and out of traincars, no chaperone attempting to settle them down. This wouldn't have been legal in the states. "Are you even allowed to transport this many kids at one time, on the public transportation system?" I asked. "Shouldn't there be someone yelling out names, making sure they haven't lost one of these little tikes?" The kids sitting in our traincar started singing. Some of them in seated sections were playing on miniature board games. One little girl was drawing on the seat with a crayon. Jules still had his guitar out, and a little girl looked over and basically demanded of him to play his guitar for her, in French. Jules smiled and complied. He started playing the chords he had just heard our hash Angel play. A little girl came over and sat next to Arlo, she started tapping on his drum. Neither of the three adult chaperones on our traincar seemed to object to the children befriending us. One of them was smoking a cigarette probably wishing she had a cell phone so she could talk to her boyfriend.

"Welton, you should clown up for these kids."

"Yeah right Arlo, Are you crazy? I'd be stepped on, pulled, and pinched, all the way to Bordeaux." I said.

"Come on. Do it for the kids man."

"I can't believe I'm even considering this." I thought to myself out loud. But then I thought of the time my boy Kenny had this whole arena trapped in a moment of laughter, back in the day, in Detroit. What a crazy clown of a person he is I thought. I let out a breath, a burst of inspiration hit me. "All right Arlo, but if this turns out to be a bad idea, I'm making you get off at the next stop." I jumped up and grabbed my bag from over head. Jules was teaching the little girl how to play the guitar.

"We are decent people." I said. A little boy walked over with a bag of candy and offered all of us some of his candy. He was talking through a smile and asking us a whole bunch of questions that I couldn't understand, and that he definitely assumed that I did. The little girl saved me by telling him that we didn't speak French. He got a concerned look on his face, wondering looking, then he walked away and sat down in a seat, not facing us. The little girl started to try teaching Arlo some words in French. I chewed on the candy, the sugar was good. I pulled out my nose, my clown shoes, and some red makeup. Some of the closer kids drawled in closer to get a look at what was going on. I pulled off my sandals and threw them in my bag. The kids saw my clown shoes and started to get loudly excited, yelling out the word clown in French. The chaperones, fragile young ladies, looking worn out from the day, wearing glasses and formal dresses, noticed the stir and started to seem a little unsure of what was going to happen. I put my finger up, symbolizing that every one should wait, and I went to the bathroom to change.

I love putting on my clown shoes and every time I do it, I feel like I should be wearing them more often. When they were on, still in my dirty pants and shirt, I looked at myself in the mirror. I put my nose on, and then I saw the clown in me come to life. The stupid smirk hit my face. I studied my eyes. They were glowing with envy over myself. I loved the feeling of being a clown. "Yup ahh, I'ma clown for life, ahhh yuppa." I said in my goofed voice. I stepped out of the bathroom, first giving a trumpet call to get everyone's attention. I could hear Arlo play a drum roll. I stumbled out and hit the wall and fell back into the bathroom. Marv's harp went "Wanb wanb waaaaannbbbba!" Nobody could see me in there, but I was still accentuating all of my movements. I shook my head like a dog and pulled open the door, and hit myself in the head, knocking me against the wall, still all alone in the bathroom. I heard a stir outside. The guitar went all the way up a crazy scale. Finally, I opened up the door, and peered out toward all the children, who by now had gathered up in the aisle around where I was about to walk out into. I jumped out and dusted myself off, and started walking goofily, bent over, legs reaching up and tucking under my chin for a beat then down in front of me, toward the children, down the isle, with a stupid smirk and a weird look. There was a change in the tempo of the murmur, and all were standing still, staring at me.

Little boys and girls started applauding. I walked down a bit passed the children standing in the aisle, then tripped over my own feet, and tumbled head first into a sitting position in a seat. There was shocked noises coming from the children, wondering if I had hurt myself, but I could hear much more laughter at the stupidity of my fall. I started standing up, looking dumbfounded, wondering what happened. "Huh?" I said. Then, Marv threw the hat up and it landed squarely, on my head. Roars off applause came from everyone, even me, exaggerating it, allowing my claps to get flamboyantly out of hand. I started laughing like a moron as the kids giggled at me. They loved it. With my hands and arms still throwing claps at me, sometimes hitting myself in the head, I started to sink into my stance. All of a sudden Arlo threw a jellybean which the kids gave him, into my mouth. I actually caught it, by complete accident. There was no way he could have had that good of an aim. I got excited and laughed, not like a clown, but like a person, unable to stop a burst of shocked laughter come out of me. I looked at him and he was smiling so hard at his luck that he couldn't stop himself from laughing either. I rubbed my stomach with my left hand, showing that it was good, saying, "Mmmm!" through the voice of some silliness, and then I said, "you lucky bastard!" with more of a 'nice shot' sort of tone and implication.

I started to bark like a seal, and flap my arms around, sitting like a trained animal for more food. Now, Jules from two seats down started throwing some candy at me. I missed the first two times, then the third time I grabbed it with my hand and a snickering look and then shoved it into my mouth. I started to fake like it was some kind of venom I had swallowed, growing more excited and rushing up and down the isle with all the kids I passed, hanging on me. I ran up to one end of the traincar and as I did, I looked up, my eyes looking everywhere, but then suddenly something so familiar, almost to the point of causing me nausea drew me completely out of my next the thought. I focused on and saw with a frozen look of being caught, the conductor standing in front of me, looking at me. I stopped, turned pale, ready to run or fight, feeling like I was really in trouble now. Seconds passed, I could now feel my sweat covering me and I was breathing heavy. It became so silent that I could tell that the kids where wondering if I was in trouble, or maybe them too for some reason. Then a realization hit me. I snorted, playing over the truth of the facts in my mind. I started laughing out loud, thinking to myself that I had a bonafied legitimate ticket for this ride. I started laughing louder, slapping myself on the knee, not stopping, but growing it and making the laughter bigger. I laughed at him, he was looking at me with a decent smile, "I'm not in trouble," I tried to say through unstoppable and real laughter. The children started laughing back up again. I started crying from joy and I started clapping. "Now this is comedie," I said, still laughing, turning around and walking toward the happily reassured children. The conductor seemed pleased at the scene, he didn't even ask me for a ticket yet. Me and my posse fit right in with the kids. Cool, I went back to work. I was sweating and out of breath. I looked up and saw Marv standing in the aisle, miming like he was casting a fishing line into the ocean.

"Here boy, wanta cookie? Beep beep!"

"Oooooohhhhhhhhhhhh." Came a screech out of me. I instantly became the fish, swimming with my cheeks sucked into my mouth, and my lips puckering themselves over and over, toward the bait. I took the bait in a gulp and Marv snagged me, raising his imaginary fishing pole. My head yanked up and I started moving in toward him, putting up a struggle, as he jerked about, having a hard time reeling me in. I struggled and kept coming in closer, losing the battle, until finally I gave up and sat with a sad face hanging by the fishing string, as Marv held me up as his prize.

"Gotcha, you drunkin fish." Was all I could hear Marv say over the bubbling children. Then Arlo jumped up and he mimed like he was taking Marv's picture. Marv stood back as if the flash blinded him, putting his arms up to his eyes to block the light. And in that instant, Jules reached up and with an imaginary scissors, cut the string that I was hanging from. I was free. I looked at Arlo and he took the picture. It's still a lasting memory in my mind to this day. I turned to run down the isle toward the conductor who was still standing there watching and actually approving of us. The place was packed with children, in the aisles, standing on the seats, the noise was beating in my heart, my mind was in a murmur; if I was more in tune with my God, some of those kids would have been plastered to the ceiling, like balloons filled with helium held back from floating any higher or away. I started moving but in slow motion. The wind coming through the various open windows was dying down inside the traincar. The train was reaching a stop. How far away was it and who's stop was it, I thought. I needed to end this, I was getting tired, and besides I kept remembering that I wasn't gonna get paid for this. My facial expressions contorted wondering why I was in slow motion. Then I saw the door of our train car open and two wide heavy set ladies wearing what seemed to be aprons came through yelling and sweeping some kids down the aisle with their hands. One of the ladies blew a whistle and all the kids shrieked. I jumped and screamed to an alert military fashion, saluting. The kids were applauding, loving the whole thing. Even the conductor was applauding. We were coming up to what I had hoped was their stop. The conductor turned toward the ladies, yelling and dictating quickly in French, understanding that he needed to help them organize the unloading of all the children off of the train.

Play time was over, I broke out of character and stood where I was, resting. Allowing the adults to handle the children. Other adults came running into our traincar screaming. I was panting heavily. Everyone realizing all of a sudden how much of an effort it was going to be to gather all these children together for the move off the train. One of the ladies looked at me and double taked. She started laughing and saying something like 'what the fuck is the clown doin here?' in French. I smiled at her and started to move toward her. I was actually relieved that the lights had gotten turned off on our show. The children where now pretty much paying attention to the adults, who were doing an excellent job of concentrating the children. The show was over, so quickly, so abruptly, as if it never happened, so unlike having an actual ending. The kids were still singing and pushing each other, some still uncontrollably looking at me, all of them being shaken around and startled by an adult chaperone. I walked right passed the adult lady and nodded my head as I passed her. I walked straight into the bathroom, sweating hard and panting. I was as high as could be. I loved it. I looked at myself in the mirror. I wasn't such a bad guy after all. My eyes were swirling different colors of joy. My clown nose had snot running out of it. Whhhhheeeeeew," I screamed through gathering breathes. I unzipped my pants to take a piss, getting an intense view of my penis surrounded by the big clown shoes. I loved it. I could hear all the children leaving the train. What a long day I was having. They sang and bounced their way off the train. I was calming down. The noise outside died down, then I felt the train pull away. I de-geared, taking my nose off, and loosening up my clown shoes, relieved that the kids weren't out there. I walked back out into the traincar. The conductor was gone.

"Welton, man, that was awesome." Arlo said as he handed me a burning joint.

"Does any body have any booze? Where's that bottle of JD? Is that what we were drinkin?" I asked, feeling some strain in my back. Outside, night crept, falling without letting on to anyone that the day was over. I was feeling happily tired.

"Sick!" Arlo said as he pulled out a half bottle of gin.

"Oh shit! Where did you get that Arlo?" Marv asked him.

"One of the chicks watchin the kids gave it to me on her way out."

"No shit." I said as we all laughed. Marv rolled up another hash joint.

I grabbed the bottle from Arlo and raised it to the ceiling, "Cannes, tomorrow baby." I cheered assuringly and I took a swig, then passed it on to Jules. We rolled legitimately through France, sometimes fast, sometimes slow. Now it didn't matter, come day light we would be in Cannes.

"Did that conductor even check our tickets?" I asked as I put my nose and shoes back in my bag. I put my sandals on slowly.

"Yeah I sorted him out, but he might come back and ask to actual see our tickets."

"Did you show him yours?"

"Yeah," Marv said.

"I betcha he doesn't come back to check. We could have gotten away with only buying one ticket for this ride I bet."

"What ever. Anyway that shit was cool huh Welton?"

"Hells yeah, we got a bottle of gin out of it."

The train came to a stop and an American Girl traveler got on our traincar. It was casual, I was tired from my exercise.

"Arlo another night out on the street for you huh?" I asked.

"What can I say, we are pretty lucky 'Estranieros'!"

"Yeah we are," Marv said without looking up from what he was doing. I lit a cigarette and sat back in my seat. Marv was writing something in his journal. I drank deep gulps. Jules strummed on his guitar and blew out clouds of smoke. The wind was wizzing hard, and the couple of other straggling passengers had closed the windows by their seats. Arlo struck up a conversation with the girl. She was sewing beads onto a hemp necklace, she seemed like a hippy and she was wearing Birkenstocks. She was going to Marseilles. The train made more stops and it got busier with people on our traincar. I wasn't going to let anyone sit next to me so I grabbed my bag from overhead and put in on my seat next to me. I pulled my hat down over my eyes and attempted to fall asleep with my legs intertwined in the straps of my backpack and drum.

III Chapter

I got up, it was early morning, the train was shaking along. I walked, a starved frail feather of a man, pulling myself along by the support of the seats and unstable and shaking wobbly arms, to the entrance platform to smoke. A tired, solemn wake, I was uncomfortable from sleeping on the train. A yawn broke from my conscience. I had slept, awoken throughout the whole time. Direct and focused determined beams of light peered in on a waving frequency, shadowed out by the scenery of mountain side in front of it, through the windows, disabling my attempt at concentrating, forcing my eyes to squint. I stopped off in the bathroom to brush my teeth. A closet of a room, shaking me in my place, the water from the faucet was non potable. Regardless I brushed my teeth, feeling tired but proud of it, as if I had just come from saving the world and I hadn't had just sleep in days. I could barely see into my own eyes through the mirror. A bell rang somewhere on the train. The thought of Cannes enlivened me and brought on a smile and some nervous excitement. I became aroused and excited that I was alone. I finished myself off, carrying away in my mind in the bathroom, realizing where I was; along the French Riviera. A picturesque scene that imposed imaginings of chariots, and motorcycles, and tanned naked heir Goddesses with white and blonde wreathed hair, rolling down the beautiful winding road of the mountain side; water splashing, creating a music and a harmony not of this world on the rocks below. Immaculate houses of mad fortune and cleanliness, sitting perfectly, like champion Great Danes. The experience of it, being all that is up close and personal with the pure and the conveniently privileged, the real proper and justs' of life, doesn't everyone want to be a part of it I wondered?

I walked out of the bathroom feeling relieved. We were about two hours from Cannes, it was about 5 am in the morning. Standing now, on the platform smoking, wondering about the rich and the famous, I looked at myself in the window reflection. From what I could see, it wasn't that bad. I was a seeking being, curious about life and the existence of it, and I was confident that I could find what it was that I was looking for. I only hoped to have enough patience to be always looking for it throughout all of my life, and never giving up the search, knowing that I may perhaps never understand it or be able to do anything with it even when I found it. Maybe I'll understand it all in the moment of my last breath of life I started thinking. Then Arlo came out interrupting my thoughts, to take a couple drags of smoke. As well, he was tired from the lack of sleep. There was something beautiful about the moment. The sunrise on the southern coast of France. Four horsemen riding throughout the night, upon a virgin land, to reach a guessed fair lady. What wild delight I felt. Our story at that moment was lyrics in a song. It was just cold enough to give you goosebumps, only because it was still somewhat of a dark morning. However, it was warm, and the air was quickly getting more dense with warmth. We went back into the train car smiling,

"Welton, you've gotta accept the fact that we are pretty fucking cool right now."

I grabbed the bottle out of his back pocket, smiling at him, as his physically little head turned around to look at me while he walked. I took a healthy swig thinking that the French Riviera would be cool even if we weren't here. "I'm glad we still have some of this left." I said, not bothering to tell him that it wasn't us that was the cool part of this whole experience. Everyone else was starting to wake up. Marv was writing something in his journal. Julian was laying on the floor, smoking a cigarette. The American girl was sleeping on a seat.

Jules got up to sit on his seat and look out the window. He started to reach for his guitar.

"Hey Jules," I whispered, sitting down in the seat next to him, "Can you believe this? Wow. I never been to Cannes, I can't believe it." He was tuning his guitar nonchalantly, going over some chords at a barely audible level, the cigarette's ashes falling all over his shirt. He let out a sigh.

"Yeah, it's pretty crazy huh? The film festival, jeez. I'm scared to ask myself why I'm goin there?"

"Jules that should be something I should be askin myself, I mean shit, if the right person there spots you, you're gonna be like asked to become famous man, They're gonna take one look at you and say 'Wow' hunny where have you been hiding yourself, come here sugar. You don't have anything to worry about. And shit, you got even more to offer, you're tryin to pitch a script yeah? That's gonna happen. Somebodies gonna be interested in what you have to say, trust me. Scripts get bought at places like this, and that's what your hear to do. What the fuck are me, Marv, and Arlo doing goin to Cannes is the more appropriate question."

"Whatever man, it's so hard to get it together."

"Jules your talkin like a beautiful blonde baby complainin that guys don't take her seriously. You got it together, just don't let it get away from ya. Besides it's early in the game, we are still young and healthy and were goin to Cannes so you can't help it, any way you look at it your gonna have a good day today."

At that moment I hoped that the train didn't accidentally derail and kill us all, proving the wrongs of my truth's to me. Marv stood up with his journal in his hand and started preaching, "Laughter of the child, grows deep from the enjoyment of birth. The womb, once so caring and decent. How we all know our ironies. Guilt and fault living among the freedom of our will. The kingdom of those who come to be, is found by all who don't see what it is that God is really doing. The blind and the blissful are truly the happiest of us all. To give up the greedy search without finding what you know to be," and he paused, the stillness became awkward then he continued, "is the acceptance of the truth." And he started laughing, the train started to shake and lean, we were heading into a turn. The American girl peeked her head up from her sleep with a question mark tattooed within the wrinkles of her forehead, being stirred and woken up by Marv's excitement. Through a devilish laughter he spoke, taking his time in his pauses, "In a past life, I was born and then betrayed in that house," and he pointed to a beautifully structured and antiquated house set into the rocks of the mountain, just as we were passing it. We all looked out the window to see what he was talking about, and we all got a grande view of the consuming alcazar. It was an unbelievably, overpowering and breath taking view of an edifice chateau and the screaming wet water beyond it, all of it being bent and scarred with age. Marv sat back down and started writing, laughing to himself. No one could mutter out a word. The American girl laid back down to hide from us. I looked at Marv, who was busily writing away in his own world deep in his mind, was he reading thoughts from all of our minds I wondered.

I took a sip of the gin and said, "Arlo roll a joint." Just to brake the intensity of the early morning moment.

"Already got one rolled," he said as he started lighting it up.

The American girl poked her head up once again, this time she talked, asking, "Did we pass Marseilles?"

"It should be comin up any time soon." Arlo said as he passed me the joint. She wanted a hit off our joint. It was smooth of Arlo not to hand it to her. He probably hit on her last night and she denied him, cause I'm sure if she had any interest in him, he would have definitely passed it to her immediately. She sat there and watched me pass the joint to Marv and then it went to Jules. It was so completely smoked by the time Jules got it, it would have been embarrassing asking her if she wanted a hit. There was nothing left to smoke. Jules dropped the remnants of the joint on the floor of the train. The girl turned around and started digging into her bag. The door of our traincar opened and a lively conductor came walking through. Not checking our tickets. The girl asked him how much longer it was to Marseilles. He implied about five minutes. What was she doing going to Marseilles, I wondered, a city that's considered to be the most dangerous city in the world. The conductor kept walking on, through to the end of the train.

"Man if that guy checked our tickets, I would have kicked his ass and locked him in the bathroom." I said. The girl started packing up her stuff and moved to the door,

"Good bye," Arlo said.

"Bye," she said, insincerely with a false smile. We all waved to her as she left our traincar, being cordial. Marv stood up and stretched.

"Cannes, Jules here we go, Yeeeeeaaaaahhhhhh!" He screamed. The train started to slow down for the stop at Marseilles. The sun was up and it was a warm beautiful day outside.

"We are gonna be famous," Arlo said.

"You already are famous," Jules said through a relaxed breath of laughter.

The train dropped the girl off in Marseilles and then it cruised us straight to Cannes.

"Only in *his* mind Jules, don't let his ego get to his head. Arlo remember, this party was gonna happen anyway, and nobody invited us, understand that. We really can't afford to even go to Cannes the way the rest of the people there are going to experience a vacation to the Southern Coast of France for a film festival."

"Yeah but we're goin aren't we?"

"True, we are goin," Marv said, interrupting us, "And I think that we are gonna have a fine time Welton, stop bein such a defeatist."

"Fine! Let's party then," I said, a bit insulted, but I raised the bottle of gin to my lips and finished off the rest of it in a big gulp, then I burp long and loud.

Jules got up to stretch and use the bathroom, Marv started packing up his stuff. Arlo took a walk through the train. I waited nervously but patiently to arrive. I smoked a cigarette. The day just kept getting better, the closer we got to Cannes, the more the sun warmed up the day. The air was fresh and breezy, smelling of coastal waters. The conductor came through our traincar again and implied that Cannes was momentarily up ahead. Jules and Arlo came back and we gobbled up our gear and moved toward the exit. I left my ticket on my seat.

"Here we go, fellas."

"I hope they let us work, I mean we are definitely going to need some money." Marv said. The train came into the belly of Cannes, France. An emptiness consumed the quiet station. From entering through the town on the train I noticed that it appeared more like a small village town than the crazy party beach town everyone said it was. It perhaps was one of the richest little towns in Europe with a massive call of tourism each year. You could tell that there was vast support to keep everything here well maintained. In a normal little village town, if a thing had broken, it may have stayed broken for quite a while, eventually being labeled romantic or historic. Where as here, there were festivals to be upheld for. Everything seemed nice and neat. From my first impression, I could not imagine that it would have such an outlandish turnout of such various sorts of people. Nobody was around. I was feeling a little incoherent, hungry past any decent stage of nutrition, and I hadn't had any coffee to wake up yet. The train stopped and let us off. We were the only ones who got off at this stop.

How unusual I thought, then I asked, "Jules did we miss the festival."

"No, it's tonight."

"It's a little weird huh, nobodies around. I would have figured that there would be a lot more people showing up."

"It's probably still too early in the morning." Marv said.

The station was sleeping, With two sides of the little city on each side, with the beach in front of it. We walked out of the station down this side street toward this broad space where half withered wagon carts with long radiuses and finely spoked thin wooden wheels were set up. They were pushed together underneath this vast canopy.

"Some sort of market?" Arlo asked. A couple of old peasant women were setting up fruit to look presentable in one of the wooden carts.

"Fruit market, it looks like," Marv said as we walked by the market and toward the setup along the beach for the famous, well actually more for the tourists that were here to see the famous. Research tents, standing tall and open were set up, creating a separation between the town and the beach at the entrance to the beachwalk. The research in the tents was being conducted by all different associates of different media bureaus, radio, TV, news and entertainment agencies. Standing satellites, imported and rolled in upon large diesel trucks, were grounded connecting radio and TV transmissions to the other side of Cannes, for all the world to see. Just personnel staff and market analysis people were hanging about, checking equipment and writing things down. It was too early to actually grab a victim for their research, and we definitely weren't the research type, so we walked around these tents, as they hid the view ahead. I came upon and saw an enjoyable greeting. The Cannes beachfront, wow is it pretty, not too glitzy as I had imagined. I dropped my backpack and took off my shirt.

"Check that shit out fellas." Arlo said, standing in awe.

"Wow." I was only able to say as I stared at the beach and the calm water tenderly perpetrating it. I felt the sun on my pale skin. I started to sweat, and instantly, I was tanning. We were now realizing where it was that we were. Cannes, France.

"We made it. I hope this is what heaven looks like."

"This is awesome, and we got here cheap too."

"Yeah but it took us about two days to get here."

"So what. We're here and we're early even."

"You know what Marv, you're absolutely right, we are here. I'm goin in the water."

"Everybody is still sleeping. I bet nothing is even open where we can get some coffee."

"Do we have enough money for coffee?"

"Yeah but that's pretty much all we have money for, unless we get hit with mad tourist prices. Then we probably only have enough for one cup." We were excited but it was still too early for everyone else.

"Well what ever, I need to clean up anyway," Jules said.

"Yeah right, I mean after all, supposed celebrities are goin to be throwing money into our hats here. The least we could do is try to look pretty." I said. It was hot. Sun came down spoiling any attempt to be sad or lonely. Inspiring visions of possibility and creative imaginative excitement.

We bounced, throwing conversation in the air as if we were important, and we had arrived late.

"Which way to the loo? Where's my chauffeur?"

"Jeeves, get the car, we're moving," Marv egged on. We walked by the beach, the sounds of the sea meeting the sand was tremendous. It had been a while since I could hear this nature. Water crept onto the small but long beach. Hotels and restaurants stood all along divided by a slate walkway, which was where truck food vendors were setting up. You had to walk down these long steps to get to the beach. The walk way was up about ten feet from the sand. The city was still asleep, just a few morning joggers were moving in the distance. Three or four older expensive ladies laid out on the beach, separated by competitive strategy, at far distances, hoping to capture the more perfect tanning rays of the sun. Hoping to make them seem more youthful than the other, just as rich, but aging ladies of their high society day. Perhaps also, they were trying to avoid the mid-day beach chaos that would attack them here, later. And this, I could understand, because I don't really like to be crowded in on a beach. A beach is one of the best places to sit, for a while, as if I were in a church, Gods house, ahhh nature. We walked down a ways on the walk, listening to the ocean. A change comes over everyone when they are near a grand body of water. The Mediterranean sea. So calm this morning. Everything seemed easy.

"I gotta clean myself up," Jules said again innocently.

"Funny Jules, you don't look dirty. Arlo looks dirty."

"Ha-ha." And we followed Jules expecting him to know where to find a bathroom to use. We turned in towards the inner sections of the town. Little roads towards this pleasant square, turning and bending up and down. There was outdoor seating available for a fine looking McDonalds. There was also these little quaint benches around a fountain pool.

"I'm gonna go use this bathroom, I'll be right back." Jules said.

"Sure, we'll wait here." We went and sat around the fountain.

"I gotta do somethin about my foot situation," Marv said.

"What do you propose, Mr. Ellowin?"

"I'd like to get some sandals to travel in."

"Yeah, with what money?"

"Not money, ingenuity!"

"Oh, I see. Need any help?"

"I think I'd work better on this project alone, Mr. Spells, besides I gotta have my lawyer on the outside of the scene to come and bail me out, if I get into trouble."

"I seriously doubt that you'll have any trouble, Marv."

Arlo was looking back and forth between us. "What's he gonna do?"
He asked curiously.

"Actually, you should probably take Arlo with ya, he's better at that
sort of mischief than all of us." I said.

"What makes you think I'm going to acquire sandals in an unsuitable or
ill-timed fashion."

"Hey what ever then, I'll watch your gear if you want." I said, laying
back, with my chest to the sky. Down the little cobblestone street store owners
were out, setting up for the seasons business. Some, but very few tourists were
out.

"I'll be right back then yeah." Marv said.

"No problem, we'll be here." Arlo said.

"You think this town is gonna fill out Arlo?" I asked.

"Man are you kidding? This place is gonna be a mob scene later on
tonight, and probably for the rest of the week."

"Yeah I guess you're right, I mean it's fucking Cannes, what am I
thinking."

"Hey, we should definitely hit the beach soon."

"Yeah, but if there's a lot of people out we should busk, we could use
the money for tonight."

"Yeah, but I can use my credit card if we just wanna take it easy
today."

"Arlo, that's nice of you, but we are taking it easy, even when we're
working. I think we'll be cool without the card, but if you want I'll ask Marv
what he wants to do when he comes back." I grabbed my drum and started
banging on it. Arlo picked his up and we started to do some rhythms
together. It sounded good. Some more people started to show up, mostly
women were moving about, all of them with barely any clothes on. Jules came
back from the McDonalds.

"Man Jules you clean up real nice."

"Thanks," he said over the sound of our drums.

"Is it me, or are there only women out here right now?"

"Maybe there's no men here!" Arlo bustled.

"I think that it's only chicks out here doin some early morning bikini
shopping." I said.

"Yeah, their husbands are still sleepin in the hotel."

"Where's Marv?" Jules asked.

"He went to get some sandals." I said, "Arlo this sounds great, keep
goin." Implying the sounds of our drums.

"Thank god," Jules said, as he started rolling up a hash joint, "His feet were killin me."

"I know right, those fuckin hiking shoes with worn out and holed souls."

"They could have used that odor in the gas chambers."

"I bet."

"So what are we doin?" Jules enquired.

"Waitin for Marv to get back, he'll be right back."

"Then are we gonna wait for him to smoke this?" Jules asked.

"Nope, fire that shit up." I said as our drumming came to an inconsistent stop. Arlo and I drawled in toward Jules.

We sat around lazily. The day was picking up. Eventually, Marv came back with a smile on his face and new sandals on his feet.

"What'd you do, bargain for a cheap price?"

"Nope, I traded something for them." He said with a slithered smile, looking back and forth to all of us. "Let's just say that the lady store owner thought I was real nice."

"She could smell that you're feet were in need huh?" Jules said.

"I didn't take my shoes off there, I left then tried the sandals on. I threw my old shoes in a dumpster near this jewelry store."

"The smell in the dumpster'll probably push all the customers away today."

"Yeah the guy saw me throw my shoes away, and I bet he can smell them now, hesitating going in the dumpster to remove them from his corner."

"If he goes into that dumpster without a gas mask, he's gonna pass out and die in there." Arlo said.

"I know, I'm gonna write about it later, call it, 'Shoe Cemetary'." Marv said as he scratched at his chin. "Anyway, we should get a move on cause it's getting busier and we need to make some money."

"Arlo said he was treatin today." I said as we were gathering our stuff.

"Yeah, you don't wanna work today, Welton?" Marv asked as we walked to the busier beach front.

"I'll work, I don't give a shit, but if he wants to buy us some booze for right now, why not." I said, just as we walked by these two beautiful girls. One a foxy looking red head, and the other one, a short hair blonde with a massive chest.

"We're gonna make enough money for booze in a half hour, Welton, let Arlo hold onto his wallet until we really need it." Marv said, slowing down and veering over to the girls. Jules followed almost automatically. The girls were setting up a video camera, facing it against a blue backdrop.

"What are you ladies doing?" Arlo asked, with their somewhat tan uncovered backs turned to us, taking it for granted that they spoke English. I was willing to bet that everybody here this week would be speaking English.

The girls turned around and started smiling when they saw us. "We're doing a promotional package, a collage for the year 2000. Kind of like everyone getting along, you know, peace and harmony across the world." The blonde said.

"Like a peace treaty?" I asked wittily.

The red head laughed, then she asked, "Would you chaps like to say something to the world?" They were English probably working for the BBC.

"How can we say no to that." I said smiling hard at the red head, enjoying looking at her.

"Great." The blonde said and she reached into a duffel bag and pulled out some paperwork. She handed us all some forms to fill out.

"Hey you should let Raymond and Pablo say peace for you." Jules said.

"Good call, Julian." I said,

"Who better than them to do it." Marv added. The blonde looked at us, wondering who we were talking about.

"We're gonna let our puppets do this, ok?" I asked, not waiting for a reply but dropping my bag and pulling out Pablo. The girls gathered round, quite impressed, they liked the idea. Marv pulled out Raymond and the two puppets ran around chasing each other and playing tag. I ran Pablo around and hid behind the red head. She laughed. I accidentally brushed my hand up against her thigh, man she felt good. Pablo reached up and offered to shake her hand. She bent down willingly and shook it, saying, "You're cute."

"He gets that all the time," I said. "And you know, it's not their first time on TV either."

"Really?" The red head said. "Well they'll be the perfect spice we need for our collage then." Marv walked Raymond over to the seat and he climbed up. The blonde was mesmerized, stalling what she was doing, just staring at Raymond.

"He moves rather well," she said.

"Yeah, a friend of mine in Amsterdam built him. He's great, ain't he." Marv said.

Arlo started to get antsy, getting jealous that he wasn't involved in the scene with the girls. He turned to Jules to say something but Jules had been confronted by a babe. A French girl who spoke English rather well, and loud with strict pronunciation. She was asking stupid questions, beating around the bush. Instead of asking him to take her to her bed, she was asking him where the beach was. You could see the beach. She was wallowing around, twisting her hair, definitely into Jules' fine looks. Man girls just throw themselves right at him I thought, what a lucky bastard.

The blonde girl said, "We'll use these mics all right?" And she handed Marv and I the mics, and stood there. We were standing with Raymond and Pablo in the chair up against the backdrop.

I asked the red head who was coming in close to fix the puppets into the scene, "Can you clip this to my nipple for me?" Inviting the stinging pain.

She gave a shocked look, turning her head to the side and widening her eyes. Was I the first to invent the nipple clip mic, I thought? "Where else can you clip it," I said. She started to get excited, looking my pale limp chest up and down. Was she personally interested in this kind off kinky thing? Whatever it was, I liked her and would have enjoyed knowing her better, but good things don't happen to a nice guy like me. I'd have to be a smoother talker with serious wit to get this girl, I thought. None of which I had, I was a low life homeless boy drunkard. What are you gonna do? The blonde girl went behind the camera as the red was clipping the mic to my nipple.

"Does it hurt?" She asked.

"The only thing you could do to me that would hurt me is fall madly in love me."

She smiled and laughed, but still looked into my eyes, probably wondering how serious I was.

Raymond said, "Come on Pablo lets get this over with." The red head backed away as the blonde zoomed in and barked out some commands.

"How long does this have to be?" Marv asked as she directed us to inch the puppets into the frame. People were now walking by in crowds. The day was well underway.

"No more than fifteen seconds ok? Ready and action!" The blonde said.

"Hi I'm Raymond," Marv said, waving Raymonds hand to the camera.

"And I'm Pablo!" I said as Pablo did a little dance.

"We're here today to ask everyone to be kind to each other." Marv said, as Raymond put his arm around Pablo.

"Yeah, can't we all just get along." I said with some exaggeration, as Pablo reached over and hugged and kissed Raymond. Then they both started dancing and waving good bye. The blonde broke away from the camera.

"Ok that was great, thanks a lot," She said as the two girls came up to get the mics and shake our hands.

"No problem," We both said at the same time. Arlo walked in to interrupt us.

"Fellas there's a lot of people out here, we should go find a place to work." Jules was still talking to the girl that confronted him.

"Where are you ladies gonna be later?" I asked.

"Oh, I'm not really sure, but I think I'm going to be pretty busy with this today. We aren't exactly here on vacation, we have a deadline for this." The blonde spoke for both of them.

"I see," I said as I wrapped Pablo up and put my bag on. Marv was packing up as well, and he kept Raymond out. "Well thanks," I said. Trying to look one more time into the red's eyes. She was diverting her attention, playing with some cables.

"Oh, thank you," the girls said as we started to leave. The red giving a quick unimplying glance. What a sweet daydream the red head was.

"Look out for our infomercial sometime in the year 2000." The blonde said as we were walking away.

"I'll probably be dead by then. Fucking deadline." I said underneath my breath.

"You just might be Welton," Marv said, "But what are you gonna do."

"Drink and fuck some other chick, that's what I'm gonna do."

"Yeah," Arlo said. Jules walked behind us, calmly, he had taken off his shirt and was looking pale. Now, more toward the beach, which had gained tremendous popularity since this morning, everyone was outside. People were in the water, ladies sat on hotel terraces and had breakfast. Everyone was smiling, the rush of the new day was on. The beach was a little crowded, except at a moments flash, you saw a crowd of people running toward this one identifying Female, laying on the beach. Cameras bopping up and down. People screaming like the roar of the titans. Everyone on the walk stopped to look, asking themselves curiously, at the growing mob.

"What's goin on over there?" I heard. "Is it somebody famous?"

"I think it's Robert Dinero." I said to someone over my shoulder.

"Robert Dinero's on the beach!" I heard someone scream, then people started running down the walkway toward the crowd on the beach.

"I think it's a porn star," Jules said.

"How do you know?" Arlo asked.

"I heard about this, they come here and try to get famous or at least increase their popularity in the business." Apparently, supposed hard core porn stars were on the beach getting photos taken of their enormousness. Or maybe they had a nice smile! Chinese thin guys ran, leaping over their associates, practically throwing sand at each other, in an attempt to steal shots with brand new cameras. Perhaps Sony CEO's really did let looser than American CEO's when on vacation. It was a mad rush, harder than that of the tides' waves attacking the sand shore. Bombardment and total chaos over big tits. Who knew, who was who, here? Anybody could have been anybody, if you didn't really know who was who and what they looked like. It was definitely funny; fat perverted looking heavy stomached guys , grunting, all running to circle around bib tittie girls for photos. People trampled over others who were laying out, outright stepping on them, kicking sand on them, there was no holds barred, From my distance I saw only the mob surrounding the girls with enormous breasts. Everyone shooting off photographs. What amateurs. Richer more dignified vacationers staring from afar, one guy with binoculars. Others with telephoto lenses being upset at the mobs interruption of the view. What a time we were living in.

"That's pretty funny huh?" Arlo said.

"Yeah man, I wish I had big tits." I said.

"We should go busk," Marv said. We were standing there, Marv and I holding the puppets in their sleep mode.

"Lets walk down a bit." Jules said. So, we decided that the beach could wait, even though it was hot and we wanted to enjoy the water. Besides there were a lot of people walking around at this time of day and we needed some money.

"Arlo, we'll play on the sand later. We'll lounge and drink, I promise." I said.

"That's cool, I'm with it. I understand that our funds are short right now, and it would be nice to be able to buy some spirits and cigarettes on money that we made." We walked on to find a spot to work.

"Now you're talkin like a true blue collar civilian." I said. It was heavily crowded the further we walked down the walkway, and already there were other buskers out. Taking up the best spots to work. Mostly the white angel statues and musicians. We had found a spot but it was too small for the four of us so we decided to split up in two, I got stuck with Arlo. Marv and Jules took the spot and Marv pulled the well worn gray hat off my head and placed it on the ground, in front of Jules. "Arlo's got a hat," he said. I did him a favor, as I heard him and Jules exchange conversation, I went clownesquely over and placed a fluorescent scarf, orange being what had worked the best in the past, under his hat, Which was actually my hat, but everybody proclaimed it as theirs. Raymond jumped to life. Jules opened up his guitar case and people already started dropping money in the hat. It was amazing. We captured the French franc, because everyone had already exchanged currency, but there was no end to the different types of currencies our hats had seen in our days of busking. The walkway around Marv and Jules was alive with human rubbernecking traffic. Arlo tried to readjust his backpack and had knotted himself into it and his drum. He tried to unknot himself. Marv tuned Raymond's dance to the sound of the guitar. All the passing people stopped to share the moment with us. Most left money in the hat. I was standing there waiting for Arlo, thinking that I should wake up Pablo. A good looking hunny stared at Jules, watching him move the strings of the guitar, creating such harmony. He was smoking on the job in the sun.

Marv asked, "Jules where the fuck would you be right now if you weren't having fun in Cannes?"

"Probably pumping gas somewhere in Rhode Island." He said as he puffed away on the guitar. I tied together Jules' and Marvs' backpacks, so no one could run off with our stuff.

"Yeah," Marv said, running Raymond around, chasing a little boy around his mommy, "I'd probably be serving someone a tuna cooked medium rare, asking if he wanted another Chianti." Being in France, on vacation, was nice. It was actually fun to busk, none of us minded it at all.

I added to the thought, "There'd be a lot more serenity to that kind of job Jules, as opposed to that other job you said you had, driven three hours each way commuting from Boston to New York four days a week." The crowd died down for a second.

Still strumming the guitar, but talking casually and looking up in thought, "No shit," Jules coughed, "Yeah, I was so sick, my throat was so sore I couldn't even smoke a cigarette. It was that job I had with that film company man, they worked me over, treating me like shit. Making me do all the vexatious work that nobody else wanted to do. They took me totally for granted. I literally had to eat shit from a bunch of bastards who thought so highly of themselves. I couldn't take it."

"Hey it was the bottom rungs of the film industry. If you ever climbed that ladder, you'd be just like your old boss was to you. It's the years of misery, stress, and frustration that add up, and then finally when you get your day in the sun, you get just as stubborn and greedy as everybody else. If you can stay in the game for that long, you wanna insist that everyone else know you're the man." Marv put down Raymond and helped Arlo untie himself. I took the moment to show off. I unstrung Pablo and he jumped on the sleeping Raymond. Beating him up as he was on the ground not in Marvs' hands. He was working out Arlos' knot. People laughed and pointed at Pablo and Raymond. It was a promising day!

"I don't think I was born to like or enjoy stress, and I went to the hospital back then and they said the reason I was getting sick was from stress."

"That's why you're at this film festival with us and not that film crew, Mr. Shivers! I said as I bowed Pablo and then I smiled at Jules.

"I used to feel back then, that I had totally deserted myself. My life was a belligerent mess of a frustration." Jules almost cried, slowing down his strumming and lowering his head.

"You were like that puny little assistant in that movie 'Swimming with the Sharks!" Arlo broke in from a confused and tangled daydream.

"Arlo, that movie hasn't even come out yet." I said shaking my head wondering if anybody was paying attention to anything that they were reading. "Besides Jules if you sell this script that you wrote then you won't have to climb a ladder or eat any top executive stool, you can just live off the money somewhere in Spain and continue writing, yeah?

"That's the plan I think." He said with some uncertainty.

"Jules, I'll get those guys to buy your script," Arlo yelled out stupidly. We all looked at him, standing there, straight-jacketed.

"See you guys later," I left, grabbing Arlo saying, "Don't worry Marv, I'll untie him." Arlo was mesmerized or in a daze, I couldn't tell, "Arlo are you cool?" I asked as we walked away. "I mean you're pretty fucking knotted up in your own gear. You know they wouldn't tolerate this shit in the army."

He shook his head. "I'm cool, I just got into a daze that's all. It's not every day that I go to Cannes, it just overwhelmed me a little. I'm fine now."

"Yeah you are. So we gotta find a spot." I assured him, pulling a strap loose and freeing him, physically from his dilemma.

"Yeah!" He said starting to bounce as we walked through the people. I was going to break him in to his first real time busking. Vacationers, and tourists passing us by as we walked, looking at our drums and Pablo. Arlo was tapping away on it getting everyone's attention around us. He was bouncing along, happily. We walked on. I started explaining some rules to Arlo. He wasn't listening, and I didn't care if he heard me, I just had to say certain things for the record of course. Kids always turning to look at Pablo as I carried him along, as if he was on a leash. Women and men as well stared at the three of us. We walked very far down until our gear had become to heavy. We forced a spot between some tourists sitting on the edge of the walkway by the steps to go down to the beach. Arlo put out the hat and then dropped his bag and sat down. I put my bag and his up against the wall and told Arlo to sit on them both.

"Here, wrap my drum strap around you, bro." I said as I unraveled Pablo, and jumped up on the ledge. It was even hotter out now. Children, people alike, everyone walking by noticed our display. Arlo was playing a kind beat on his drum. Pablo, although constructed in London was still a work in progress. He was cute though and could hang better than Arlo. He wasn't as well built as Raymond, but I was currently in the process of building a better body for him. He seemed at times to have cerebral palsy, if he wasn't manipulated within a certain correct degree, he would walk as if he needed the leg cages that Forest Gump used as a child. But he still attracted customers because I knew how to be friendly and pleasant. The puppets are one of the more finer displays of busking. There are so many various sorts of street artist that most would say anything would sell on the streets, because people are suckers. But every one truly did like the puppets. Especially Raymond. I mean wow, our buddy J.P. in Amsterdam constructed a work of art. But as well, it was also important who was manipulating the puppet.

For instance, when Raymond was in Marvs hands, he was a wand in his grip, moving, alive, with a heart beating, displaying feelings and rhythm. You really do have to see it for yourself. It is amazing. All street buskers made money in Europe however, especially the fucking white statues, standing there, still as can be, moving slightly and elegantly when someone dropped money into their hat. Tourists are suckers for that kind of crap art. Then you had the kinds of tourist people that were interested in us because we were Americans and street performing, not necessarily interested in the art we were doing, but the lifestyle we chose on our travels. They could tell that we were of at least proper descent, even though we were dirty, and we weren't staying in a hotel room. You could tell this because we were still carrying our backpacks instead of having left them in our rooms. Some people, respectable family types, stopped to ask us questions about where we were from, almost proud of the future of Americas youth, sleeping on the streets of Europe working for pence.

There was no telling the types of people that had wanted to gain entrance into our world. And that was what was such an amazement to me on this trip. People didn't make me feel like I was as much of a bum as I thought. So be it. Pablo, Arlo and I kept busking. Pablo was playing around with a little girl and her father. The girl was shy and the dad was laughing, pulling out a bill to throw into our hat. As we busked, a British girl took it upon herself to meet me. She was dazzling and rare, with short hair and nice tan. She came over, with her friend and put money in the hat, then she started talking. I didn't stop working while I talked to her, looking mostly at my puppet and the reactions of children and passerby when Pablo waved and bowed. He was sort of idling because I was however trying to make conversation. She asked me where I was staying, her breasts beading with moisture upon them. I told her bluntly that I was probably going to sleep on the beach with my friends and I pointed to Arlo, who smiled at the two girls. Her friend was acting as if talking to us was a waste of time. The British girl rather boldly invited me to sleep with her this evening instead of on the beach, she told me her hotel and room number. I was having a hard time believing that this was actually happening to me.

Arlo skipped a couple of beats on his drum. I told her to come find me on the beach later. Kids started surrounding Arlo. He was giving them attention, letting them play his drum, doing some light but interesting clown antics. The girls' friend started pulling the sweet short haired girl away from me. A little girl child started tagging and dancing with Pablo, picking him up. I had to take him out of her hands. The British girl talked over the noise of the children, saying that she and her friend were going to the awards tonight. She giggled. Her friend started pulling her away with harder attempts, she waved and her eyes blew me a soft seductive cat kiss. I knew I would never see her again. I can't believe she invited me to her hotel room. They left, and I knew that she was just teasing me.

I didn't think a moment more about her. I didn't even bother remembering her room number. She was going to meet some guy tonight who would take her to Montecarlo in a limousine and drop 25 maybe 30,000 dollars gambling on her. After all, guys like that were here right now. I was in an expensive playpen and I was the guy cleaning out the urinals. She would come back to her hotel room tonight with some rich guy and find me with all my stuff, wasted and dirty smelling, trying to hold onto a smile on my face with less than a zero sense of broken confidence, waiting at her door and she would call the hotel security to get rid of me. So I was better sleeping on the beach with my friends, and not in some French prison cell for some type of public nuisance or vagrancy violation.

We had been there about an hour, and I stopped working Pablo and lit a cigarette. Arlo spoke up, "We got enough money here for a bottle of gin."

"Let's go get it then," I said. The hat was sufficiently heavy, and I was betting hard that Marvs was fuller with heavier more meaningful coins. So we decided to go find Marv and Jules and maybe get some lunch. It wasn't as much fun being separated. We walked back the way we had come to catch up with our other two amigos. There were a lot of other buskers out, perhaps too many. Face painters, balloonists, statues, musicians, etc. etc. Arlo pitched some of them some coins as we walked by. And too, many tourists, families and couples all looking well groomed and detailed with sheik beachwear. We found Marv and Jules in a different spot than we had left them. Already, they had sandwiches that they had bought from a food truck vendor. They had even bought two for Arlo and I. They were lounging out on their stuff, under the shade of a palm tree on this grass patch by the walkway, by the port o potties. It was a good spot for busking, a lot of traffic. They had even taken a trip to the spirits shop and sorted us out with booze and cigarettes.

"We figured, that you didn't make any money because of Arlo, so we bought you guys some food." Jules said to me.

"Ha ha." Arlo said. We sat down, and attacked the food. I was starved, when was the last time I had eaten, I wondered. Our hat was significantly lighter than theirs. They had even had an ice cream cone to eat already. We sat and felt proud, picnicking. People stood by us, waiting to use the port o potties. Looking at us and our instruments and puppets and big backpacks and sleeping bags and stuff. We were a world. Passing around another bottle of JD, drinking while the puppets slept.

"This is a great spot to busk," Arlo said.

""I know yeah," Marv answered him, "All these hot chicks standin around checkin us out, waitin to use the loo, and the walk by traffic is close enough to draw the crowd."

"I've found that the bathroom area is always a good gathering spot." I said through a gorged mouth full of food. Then out of thin air, flashed a light, the sun became brighter. A French guy, tall, thin, confident, yet not arrogant like so many northern French came up to us, staring at our instruments, and smiling. He was excited, treating us like a grand discovery. He made me feel like he was lucky to have met us. From what he implied, he was from Cannes. He was debonair, handsome, and young, yet he seemed down to earth and rebellious in his choice of lifestyle, more like he was a beach bum but with a tremendous air of class. He was staring hard at our equipment, having a more than sincere and most intense respect for my drum, as much in awe of it as the tourists were in meeting celebrities. He was humble with us, not like so many other French I had met in my time. He happened to be a drummer, and he asked to play my drum. I gave it to him willingly. He was one of the only outsiders to ever touch my drum. He played it very well, and afterwards he implied that it needed to be tightened, in non verbal communication. It was busy out and the people constantly gathered around us, to wait in line for the toilet. He gestured he would come back to tighten it later. We said goodbye, not disagreeing with his departure. He left to walk among the tourists.

"Let's work some more, and then we'll go lay on the beach," Marv said. "We should make some more money today, cause these people will be spending a lot of money and they'll be hesitant to hook us up tomorrow."

"No problem," Arlo said, as we prepared to busk.

"I'm not puttin on my clown gear, yet." I said. Truthfully it was easier to simply use the puppets. It was draining to put full on clown routines on the streets, and the pay off wasn't as good as it was with the puppets. If I had had the energy of six men, I would have clowned up, but I pulled out Pablo and brought him to life. Raymond was a bit tangled up. It happened, sometimes you could spend an hour trying to untangle him. Once I was close to cutting the strings on Pablo. Anyhow Marv detangled Raymond, lucky for Raymond. We busked for about an hour. People dropping money into our hat generously. We weren't even doing much. Pablo and Raymond would chase each other around. They would both conspire to trap a child walking by, and draw him or her into play. Raymond jumped into a stroller as a daddy was walking it. The child ran over and saw Raymond in his stroller and started crying. His mother came over and put money in our hat. She stopped to stare at Jules, strumming with ill-frivolous swagger. Arlo gave a little roll of the drum. She smiled and put some more money in our hat. She was pleased with helping us. We weren't beggars. We were performers. Even though we were hanging out looking like characters without respect or decency, still we gave children a story to experience with the lividness of puppetry. Not on a stage, but right on their level in a neutral environment.

Most people were so stunned when they came across us. Younger children sometimes couldn't tell if the puppets were real. As well, when dogs walking by noticed the puppets they became instantly curious and frustrated, unsure what kind of animal they were, moving and acting alive. They barked and attempted to play with the puppets backing off at moments then jumping to prance on them. So much more interactive the streets were as opposed to the screen displays that all the people were really in Cannes for. How ironic the situations of life are sometimes. I put Pablo down and sat down and started playing on my drum.

Arlo picked up Pablo and started manipulating him, at least standing him up. Jules stopped playing song, and started trying to figure out a riff of chords. He was focused into his guitar and concentrating. Marv walked Raymond out to the walkway ledge and let him look out to the sea. Everyone walking by stopped to check out Raymond. Arlo was walking Pablo slowly, trying to jump him over a curb. I tapped away on the drum, bored a little bit. Some girls who didn't speak English came over from where Raymond was and asked if that was his hat. Arlo brought Pablo over and he covered the hat so the girls couldn't put money in it. It was a funny move, keeping people gathered around the hat and drawing more attention to it. He moved Pablo out of the way and stopped looking up as if it was over. I would have taunted the girls for a little longer. It's what you call milking the scene for all that its worth. It also allows time for more passersby to stop and witness, drawing them in. What a game it all is. I stopped tapping my drum and took Pablo out of Arlo's hands. I walked him out a bit and jumped him up and tried to climb him onto me. I was standing there in the crowd that had stopped and Pablo fell off of me on to the floor right in the way of a little girl that was walking by. She wanted to smile and laugh but she walked around him nervously, she kept on walking. Her mother and father both wished she had interacted, they both stopped and tried to encourage her to shake Pablos hand but she moved quickly ahead. I walked Pablo back in, standing under the shade of the palm tree, and just idled him. Jules had figured out the riff and had put some words to it. His world was being explained, a story of a long ago time was being told, as if it was a pink floyd song. Nobody was even listening to his music. The sun was full of power and it was hot.

I'm not gettin out of the shade." I said through sweat dripping into my mouth. "It's unbearable."

"Neither am I," Arlo answered me, over the music Jules was playing.

"Where's that bottle, or is it finished already?" Arlo asked.

"Here," I said, as I passed it to him.

Marv was still out on the walkway with Raymond, in the heat, and every once in a while some one would walk up asking us if that was Raymond's hat. I imagined that we must have looked funny to those people, all of us sitting their lounging while Marv and Raymond did all the work. Marv was out in a crowd being passed by. He had a layer of tanned sweat covering him. He probably hadn't taken a really good look at himself in the mirror in months. Rushing every time he was in a bathroom, uninvited, when was the last time he had his own running water toilet in an apartment or house, probably last semester in Italy I thought, well then again, maybe not even in Italy. God only knows where the crust laid on his body, and all of us as well. Why would any lady get so close as to taste the skin of any of us. Marv danced talking with his body in harmony with Raymond. He looked above the crowd around him, over to us and saw me looking at him. He smiled, then he yelled out, "Welton check this out," and he jumped up on the ledge and started preaching out words to get the attention of the people that they were already giving him and Raymond. "Ah ha ha ha ha ha," he laughed like a man full of rage, "OK ladies and gentile men, come on round and see, it's the amazing and the thought provoking, what else could it be! Ah ha hah ha ah wa he he eh ha ha!" He laughed, "Step right up and get your mustache rides, come on now, mustache rides, step right up," He laughed through his words.

I heard an American girl, who had stopped to look, say, "You don't have a mustache!" in a high pitched squeal.

I could tell that Marv was way too sophisticated to actually show her the mustache he was actually talking about. He smiled, then he said, "Well, little darlin, you're right! OK, how about this then; Ladies and gentile men, step right up, that's right, absolutely nothing for sale, for only one dollar! That's right people, absolutely nothin, for only a dollar." People stopped in their walk to stare and wonder, he went on, gathering their attention, "That's right, I could sell you nothin," he said while staring into the eyes of a weakly tanned man with his arm wrapped tightly around his young pretty girlfriend, "Absolutely nothin, for sale, for only one American dollar yes that's right,"

"Where in France Yankee, you're going to get the franc." I heard someone yell.

"Ahhh," Marv laughed innocently, "How could I forget!" Then he straightened up, and cleared his throat. He pulled his harp out and started playing a breezy styled introduction of a melody. Then he went on, implying in his gestures, quotes from an old book, "To ease into the sigh of the unknown, not knowing where it is, ha ha ha, my next home. And, how I will awake tomorrow, an empty stomach, sand in my glands, I roam the lands, with my fellow nomads. A foot step ahead of yesterday, ha ha ha ha ha," he went on, people actually staying where they were, to listen to him, "The Cannes film festival's 50th year anniversary, May 12,1997, what a glorious day to be in Cannes. To witness the famous rejoice in their granted appreciation. I, standing in the distance, unfamous, unrevealed, not afraid to stand alone." He smiled, holding in his breath for a moment, "Dirty and worn, laughing internally about my journey. I stare and wonder when will my film come alive." A passerby egged him on, someone started clapping. Jules backed him up with agreeing music, "Its never in the obvious or is it?" He asked the crowd around him. "Ahhhh, that shit don't phase me." He said, throwing out an arm, Raymond swinging on his strings, temporarily dormant. "Discover your character. Be yourself." He protested, physically taunting the crowd, "On the streets, strangers eyes meet. Don't neglect your instantaneous thoughts, I smile at all who enter my aura. I hope you found what you sought to see, while watching me. Ah ha ha ha ha aha!"
Then he bowed and jumped down from the ledge. Jules twiddled on a couple of notes then ended the music. People clapped and as he walked back toward us, some of them, teenagers, patted him on the back and walked with him.

"Marv, what was that?" Arlo asked.

"Arlo, that was life man, don't you understand?" I said.

Marv was sweating and smiling. People came over to put money in our hat. Marv set Raymond down.

"No preacher on the streets ever got any money for speakin the way you're gettin it Marv."

"I'm hot, we should go to the beach. I think I've had enough for right now." He said, ignoring my obvious comment.

"That's a good call," Jules said. "We're filthy and covered in stench, not like I mind or anything, but it would be good to get into that water."

"Ah the water, let's move." I said. Then we all motivated the move and started packing up. "This crowd grew today, huh?" I said.

"Yeah, I got to admit, the cash rolled in," Jules said as he was putting away his guitar. With all the excitement going on around us, it was always necessary to keep an eye on the hat and the gear. The hat, full of money, is out at an arms reach from the passerby's, and usually there was always a disrespectful bastard out there, thinking to rob us. Someone who is worse off than us. Someone could just grab the hat and run, and sometimes it happened. We usually trust blindly and assume the people around us mean no harm, but like a serrated knife or a fishing hook, sometimes, someone stupid, who doesn't know who it is that he is dealing with, tries to rob us. And then it's war. It happened several times, in Spain, mostly Barcelona, all those fucking heroin junkies. When we caught up to them, Marv and I paid them some pain, while Jules stood guard over the gear. You have to protect yourself and your profits. Isn't that the story of life?

"Man we have a lot of money here, even some American change. Where are we gonna exchange this shit. I can't believe how much we just made," Arlo said after counting it.

"Great, let's go spend it. And if we can't exchange, throw it out cause I'm not carrying it." Marv snorted.

"Add this to the money we made earlier and we got about two hundred dollars." Arlo excitedly stammered as he put the hat into Marv's backpack.

"Really?" Jules wondered.

"Yeah, really." Arlo jumped with exclamation.

"Well what are we gonna do with all of it. I mean even if we wanted to get a hotel room, which I'm not sayin we do, but if we did, we have the money for it, but I think they are all booked up." I spoke up calmly.

"Damn, I guess we're not gettin a room tonight. Shucks." Arlo said, as he strapped his bag to his back.

"Let's buy some more hash." Marv said, "we're running low on the supply."

"It shouldn't be to hard to find drugs in this town, but it'll probably be more expensive."

"Give me a swig of that JD," I said. Jules passed the bottle over to me, "Damn Jules you finished the whole fuckin thing."

"Sorry man, let's just buy some more."

"Well of course we're gonna buy some more, and speakin of which, we should smoke a joint before we roll to the beach." I said

"Yeah, it might be uncool smokin on the beach this time of day."

"What time is it?" Arlo asked, even though he had a watch somewhere in his backpack.

"Who cares. Where we gonna smoke this?"

"Let's roll that shit up right here." Marv said.

"Ok." Arlo said, as he dropped his bag, sat down and pulled out the hash. We all sat down again and encircled him. People were standing around us, waiting in line for the bathroom. Jules started mumbling something about our girls from London meeting us down here sometime, but none of us paid him any mind. We smoked in the most blatant fashion, uncaring about doing something illegal. Activity of all sorts going on around us. After our smoke break we geared up and headed toward the much needed nourishment of the beach. It was time to party. We stopped to get a bottle of gin now, and some more cigarettes on the way.

"I'm gonna lay on the beach and get some rest and tranquility and let the sound of the water cool me down."

"Shit, I'm goin in the water," Marv said.

"Well so am I, but, the sound man, it moves me, you know." We walked down the platform steps with all our gear getting in the way of everybody, and moved as if we were conquering the land. Still, spontaneous crowds drew together shooting photographs toward the sand every few moments. Porn star babies getting their pictures taken all over the beach. I stopped every while as I walked on the sand, letting my now barefoot feet absorb the heat from the burning sand, glad to be on the beach in Cannes for this party, and not because of the war against the Germans, not so many years ago. We found a suitable spot and degeared ourselves, stretching and sitting to relax.

"Wow, look at all these people." I said, looking around, feeling a bit out of place. We were sitting around, Jules and I still in our long pants, drinking the bottle of gin that we had bought. Crazy shit was going on around us. Groups of fraternity looking Americans acting up around dark Europeans taking in sun, with silent rich looks without facial expressions through the dress of expensive sunglasses, all clashing. While at the same time existing and balancing each others' energies out, then there was us, with a pile of gear that took up more space than the four of us did, making a home on the beach. We looked like we were about to go and start asking people on the beach for change. Every one around us was a tourist and there were no locals spending time on this part of the beach.

Jules looked up and smiled to the sun, "Arlo, let me see your sun glasses." He said. Arlo took them off and gave them to him.

"Thanks," he said, putting them on and laying back to fall asleep.

"Are you gonna wear them?" Arlo asked wondering if he was getting them back.

"Yep," He said without moving his head from its position, then he smiled and started to laugh.

"What's so funny?" I asked.

He turned to me and said, "Man the chances of me dyin today is pretty fuckin slim."

"Ah ha ha," I thought, "That's probably true, but you never know, well, I guess then now that I think about it, the chances are pretty slim, but it could still happen. And besides, cemeteries in France are usually only open in the early daytime, they're all probably closed by now, you couldn't even die and rest in peace right now even if you wanted to, so fuck cemetaries."

"Welton, don't I specifically remember you sayin, that you liked to sneak into cemeteries, scale the walls late in the night, and creep," and I quote, "'with heavy breath', into the lonely wake of the moonlight?" Arlo asked without a hint of gloom, repeating what I had said once verbatim.

"That's beside the point. All I'm sayin is who wants to live forever anyway." And I brushed him off with a wave of my hand and a quicken in my pace to readjust myself on the hot sand.

"Is that what you've been tryin to say?" Arlo asked, unsure whether or not I was contradicting myself.

"Sort of, I mean check this out, Marv was sayin that once he saw this old man die-"

"Was it your grandfather?" Jules asked Marv without turning or even moving.

"Na, it was just some random guy. I went into a hospital once when I was really young and when I was wanderin through it, I came across this old man in a room, tryin hard to stay alive."

"Was it someone's private room?" Arlo asked curiously.

"Yeah, it was just some old man. I sat in there and waited for him to die. I saw the whole thing. I must have been in there for like a good eight hours."

"Didn't anyone say anything to you, like what the fuck are you doing here little boy?"

"Na, the doctors and nurses all thought I was part of the family and after a while some of the older family members started sitting with me, wondering which grandson I was. I just wanted to watch him die, you know it was when I was real young before I was even attracted to the thought of taking peoples lives away from them. It was the first time I saw death."

"Yeah any way you said he was hooked up to all those monitors, screaming and beggin for his family to take him out of there, bein shot up with drugs and hoses in all his crevices hooked up to machines that beeped." I quirked.

"Yeah, he was beggin and screamin all the way to the end to get out of there and go die in his bed at home. But nobody was doin nothin. The family just stood there and watched him die, a physically poor old man unable to believe his days were over. His kids were just waitin, they seemed so impatient, eager to start spending the life insurance money and abusing the inheritance.

"Shit when I go, man I want be out in the woods somewhere, in warm weather, passin on into the light, leavin my body to decay like a wild animal, concieving myself anew," I threw my right hand around in a circle and raised my eye brows, "into natures world of life. Now that's my point Arlo." I nervously bellowed.

"Yeah you're a true dinosaur. I'm goin in the water."

"Don't come back," Jules said as Arlo got up and ran and dove, childlike into the water.

Jules was looking good. His jeans were rolled up as far as they could go, up above his knees. His feet buried in the sand, and his stomach all oily shiny and white. He reached into his bag and got his journal. He fell prey to his pen as he wrote something down with a smile.

"Marv, pass me that bottle." I said.

"I'm goin," He said, staring out beyond the horizon, unmoving and without a flinch from the layer of dry dusting sand around us being stirred by the breeze.

"Yo, Marv," I said, finally reaching over to grab the bottle sitting beside him in the sand, "listen, you better come back, yeah. There's still a lot we have to do." I said, still looking at him hoping he wasn't going forever, where ever it was he was planning on going. I was thinking that for sure, he was planning on going somewhere out of the reach of what my imagination could handle, my stomach tightened as nervousness awoke from it's sleep within my conscience. He wasn't planning on inviting me, let alone anyone with him, and I kind of wanted to keep him around for at least a little while longer, there was so much more that I could learn from him. He kept staring, Jules looked up from his writing. I took a breath and then I took a big sip from the bottle.

Marv straightened up, put away his glasses and looked over to me, "Welton, how far do you think I can get without getting caught?"

"Further than the prophesy and those that prophesized, had speculated, supposed or imagined," Jules broke in before I could even process the question. Marv laughed, shaking his head in joy, and stood up, the sun umbrellaed from my eyes, I looked up to him, easily.

"This won't take long then. I'll just head down to the Suez canal." He said and turned and processed in pharaoh Egyptian style, as if he was floating, being carried by an invisible force, to the water. He passed Arlo, stopping him from his commotion of splashing in the very shallow end. He kept on walking through it until he was submersed. The wind was breezy, not quite cold. Jules and I were staring at him, catching a glimpse of his head every once or twice with the movement of the water. Arlo looked toward where Marv went down, standing in less than knee high water, broken out of his playtime splashing, confused and scratching his head. Then, Marv was gone. Jules and I sat there for the next couple of minutes, looking for Marv silently.

I took a sip from the bottle and passed it to Jules. "He better come back," I said.

"He will," He said and drank. Arlo came running up to us, panting and wild eyed.

"Hey, did you guys see him come up anywhere? I didn't see him come up. Does he know how to swim?" He was looking back and forth from me to Jules. We were sitting there casually unconcerned. "What the fuck man, is he cool out there or what? Should I go get a lifeguard?" He asked somewhat impatiently.

"Relax Beezley," Jules said, "Marv has gills."

"What?"

"Yeah, he breathes water sometimes, it's cool man, there's a lot of people out there that can do it."

"You guys are fucking with me. Where the fuck is he" He said, looking out to the water then sitting down in the sand.

"Don't worry about it Arlo, if he doesn't come back, he said you can carry his stuff for us." I said slapping him on the back of the head.

"He'll be back," He said confidently, as he shot up and pulled the sunglasses off of Jules' face. "Ssssiiiiickkkkk!" He quirked as he laid back down in the sand.

"What a day," I said, looking around, taking it all in. No office cubicles, no ties, everyone spending their lives in this one moment. I felt cool, like I was part of something. The enjoyment level around me was in a calm and content mood. Everyone soaking in the tranquility of the sun, the beach and the Mediterranean's' movement and sound.

"Marv's like another fish in the water." Arlo said. Pretty girls in a group, walked by. It was hot, the sand was dry where we were sitting.

"It was such a good call to come to Cannes." I said as I got up.

"No shit," Arlo said. I walked down through the crowds of tourist families and children, to the water. The sand, more moist now was welcoming me. I felt the cool water encircle my feet. As the two energies mixed I felt new sensations surging electrically up my spinal chord. At that moment I was completely content with everything. My life was a permanent vacation right now, nothing holding me back from reaching my greatest goals, passing my time here on planet Earth in a completely agreeable fashion. I was so glad to be alive and happy. I smiled as little boys and girls ran passed me, throwing buckets of sand at each other and diving into the shallow water. I stood there for what seemed like a century. My shadow had moved distantly around me. Marv suddenly reemerged slowly out of knee high water, right beside me. One of the little girls playing near me, screamed out in shock, completely surprised by him. As was I.

"Jesus, you scared me," I said, as he stood up out of the water. "You're crazy man. I didn't see you come up for air once and you've been out there like at least a half hour. What did you do, swim to Majorca.

"I told you I'd be back, if I would have went there I wouldn't have come back." He said.

"How do you do that?" I asked.

"Do what?" He smiled, not giving me a chance to explain myself, he walked past me saying nothing, he went up to our camp dripping, stopping and briefly exchanging words with Arlo and Jules. He opened his backpack and took out Raymond. He walked him to the water and jumped him up over the tide coming in.

"Raymond loves the water huh?" I asked.

"Who doesn't," He said. I looked back to our camp. Arlo was talking to Jules, hiding from the sun, behind his sunglasses with his arm around his drum like it was his girl friend.

"I'm gonna go for a walk." I said.

"See ya," he said, dancing Raymond around, drawing in the attention of all the children in the water. They veered closer toward Marv. I walked back to Jules and Arlo and put my sandals on. I told the fellows that I was going to walk around a bit, as it was too hot for me on the beach. I left without objection, and walked along side of people on the beach. I mostly noticed the more finer looking ladies, those of whom usually were seen motionless, holding sun on themselves, or spraying themselves with water, readjusting. There were plenty of beautiful girls, I could have one right? I walked up the ramp to the slate walkway. It was still busy, and others were out there busking, playing music, some statue buskers were drawing a big crowd. I walked around happy, not looking so bad, already tan, light roughage on my face. People past, men and women holding hands vacationing, perhaps honeymooning. Outdoor terrace waiter's finely dressed, sweating, hustled foods and cooled down and refreshed drinks. Children and families were eating pastries and drinking café's. I walked a lone path, swaying, moving around people as they came at me.

I looked for her, my destiny, as if this was the moment. There was a roar of commotion on the beach that startled the attention of the passerby's around me. Everyone stopped hoping to see a star. It was another sweet-body girl, laying in the wake of the sand offering herself to peoples cameras. I resumed on, not letting anything get to me. I would find her, I was patient. People were sitting and watching everything, others walking, it was a paradise but not like an ancient rock, but more like glamour held on stilts concealing the natural beauty the plainness of the scene had with the impressiveness of the types of people the festival had brought. How much more beautiful this place would have been if it was a lost world, if there was nobody here, a truly abandoned paradise left in time. And me, a survivalist, unknown to society, drifting and searching for nirvana, coming across this place, so far distant from home, yet finally finding a nostalgic comfort in this great world, here, in this place. It was a daydream that left me wanting to go discover a rainforest, never to be heard from again. But not as if I had disappeared, but more as if I had never really existed or impressed myself into peoples psyche, not having anybody wonder what ever happened to me. Talked about, in underground circles of curious landlopers, vagabond wayfarers and soul searchers; a fairytale mythified legend that inspired those with the right frame of mind to test their courage and invite their fears onto the battlefield.

I ended up walking over to where the stars would be entering the awards festival later that night. Empty now, looking easily infiltrated, I thought about sneaking inside, just to see what it was like, but I didn't. Outside it was clean and set up with intrepid disposition, it looked like there was about to be a very good party tonight. I thought about everyone who would be there, supposedly, the stars that would be out tonight. I didn't know any of them, but I had seen them while looking up, to the big screen. I made a promise to myself that one day, I would be one, a star, a universe of conversation, attention, and ego... damn I started to get frustrated. I threw my hand out, "One day, I'll be going to this party, legitimately," I said out loud to myself. Lifetime dreams past before my eyes, wind blew fate into places that were unexpecting it to show up. How was my life going to turn out, I wondered? Would I be ever be able to sustain happiness in my life? Was just a couple of moments of joy all anyone could ask for? Did I have all of them already? How do I kill my fear inside me, I asked myself, screaming the question to myself in my mind. My thoughts were tainted and tarred by the experiences and things that weren't so good to me, that have come across my path, so much more often than the finer things in life. Did I really want to be famous I wondered? Do I really like people that much as to offer them an invitation to assume that they were my best friend? Isn't that what happens to movie stars, they can't even walk down the street without somebody jumping all over them with attention. Would I even be able to sit through a whole awards ceremony even? Did I have the patience to make it as an actor if I tried, or would I forever be an extra on the set? What else could I do with my life to make money in society, work at a supermarket? An office manager? What I wondered will be of me? I couldn't figure it out. I let it go and looked around. I lit a cigarette. "Good luck sellin your fuckin script to these people Jules," I said out loud through dense smoke.

Near me, there were mostly just preparation clerks and red carpet. I leaned on a metal barrier that would eventually separate the merge of the impatient people. Tonight the world was going to recognize artists for greatness. I took a drag of my cigarette. Where was I going to be? Does the greatest man that ever lived truly pass away unknown? What is it that I wanted out of life? I truly didn't know. My thoughts were somewhat superficial in thinking I should waste the summer away travelling Europe, especially the way I was doing it. I didn't know, I couldn't figure it all out. Depression started to cough inside me. I walked away. Smoking, not nervous, more disdained and upset. I started to walk back to the comfort of my comrades. Hot and sweaty, I pulled the bottle of gin out that I had snuck away from the fellows, and took a scolding swig. I played a reoccurring tune in my head, singing 'goin down the road felling bad...'. In a way, proud to be me, even if I was a nobody. I walked back by the scene at the beach, already used to it.

I was on the slate walkway, staring out to all the people on the beach. People walked by me, surrounding me and each other, taking a casual passage in Cannes. I was looking forward to spending a couple of days here. We could make money, and more and more interesting characters were for sure, going to show up. A baby girl and her family walking by recognized me as one of the puppeteers from earlier. They were from Belgium, and the father spoke some English. A short and well proportioned, yet still heavy set man, with a dark black mustache and thick clothes on, he said that the marionette was a very popular theatrical art in Prague, Czechoslovakia. I told him I hadn't been there, but perhaps was going to make my way up there. I thought for a second that I could leave now if I wanted to. I was staring at his much younger bride and was thrilled at our connection. So radiant were her eyes. From what I could assume, the little girl asked her mother where my puppet was, and it was going to get into a huge diplomatic translation thing so, with non verbal communication we agreed to depart, saying goodbye. I headed back down to the beach, making my way through the beached people, finding Marv, Jules and Arlo surrounded by a group of others still with their backpacks and gear.

Marv was juggling, passing clubs with one of them. Tools like that bond people, creating an instant camaraderie between people who know how to pass juggling clubs. I walked up to the group. Another guy dropped his bag and took out his diablo, a large yo-yo type piece that can be manipulated by a string tied to two sticks. A dog came running up on the beach to our group. I bent down to pet it.

"Who's dog?" I asked stroking the dog and letting it lick my face.

"Mine," The guy with the diablo said. "That's Lanmer. I'm Peter."

"I'm Welton, nice to meet you. You speak very good English, where are you from?" I asked.

"I live in London for almost three years now."

"Wow, with your dog? I thought it was hard to get him in and out of that country."

"It is," He said, "But I sneak him in and out." He gestured. He reached into his bag and pulled out a can of dog food. Lanmer was right up on him, sniffing the food. My stomach started to growl. He fed his dog. The beach itself was so hot, it was sweating. Jules was sitting down, next to Arlo, who was tapping away on his drum. Families around us had nonchalantly moved further away from us, but it was still relatively crowded on the beach. "I am staying on the beach with these people," implying the two others, a girl sitting next to Jules and the guy juggling with Marv, and the dog he was with, "but I am traveling independently for three weeks now, only with Lanmer."

"Great, how long have you been here?"

"Two days, it has been very quiet, very nice, but today, almost everyone of these people arrived. The party is on tonight," He said as his dog was licking the food off his fingers.

"Yeah," Jules butted in, "He said that nobodies given him a problem about sleeping on the beach and they all slept right down there last night," He said to me, pointing to Peters friends, then down away on the beach.

"Really? Nice. That sucks that all these people are here, huh," I asked Peter, "It must have been great yesterday, all alone out here."

"Yes, very calm, beautiful." He got up and started manipulating his diablo. "But perhaps today is better to make some money!"

"Yeah, probably. I saw a lot of buskers up there." I turned my head looking at the rest of his group. Marv was still passing clubs with the blonde haired boy, much taller than he, and doing nice tricks together. The physically strong looking girl was sitting now, moving next to Arlo, who had given her my drum to play. They both started doing a rhythm together, slow but decent sounding.

"Hey, how about that gin in your back pocket, is it empty?" Jules asked.

"Did you guys smoke all the hash?" I asked before giving him the bottle. And Jules pulled out two joints he had rolled. "We still have a little more even." He said.

"Well fire that shit up," I said, pulling out the gin and sitting down next to him, then taking a swig. Jules lit up a joint as I passed him the bottle. We shared it with Peter and his friends, all of us introducing ourselves to each other. Marv and the blonde haired boy, who's name was Celene, continued to juggle, but they took hits off the joint. The girl, who was Celene's girlfriend, was Disuvera. They spoke no English whatsoever, and I had never heard of the country they were from. Apparently it was a part of ex-Yugoslavia somewhere. Cool. We hung out for a while smoking the rest of the joint, then they rolled a couple joints also. They were smokers like us. I got up to play with Peters diablo, I had used one before. I could still do some tricks. Peter looked at what I was doing.

"You are good," He said.

"I haven't really played with one of these in a while. It's hard to make money with this on the streets, unless it's part of a show."

"Yes, I know. I am not exactly a street busker, but I am travelling as cheaply as I can. Not paying for my passage, getting thrown off of the trains, like you, yes?"

"Sure, who has the money to travel." I insisted.

"I come from Italy, from Capri. I am from Belgium. I stopped off here in Cannes to see what was going on." He was simple and kind hearted looking into my eyes as he talked and listened. Probably easier for him to travel illegally, less noticeably with his dog only, as opposed to the four of us all together, traveling without tickets. He said he had had some pretty smooth rides straight through. Getting lucky he figured. The blonde haired boy, Celene, who was quite muscular and his girlfriend, who was even more muscular than he passed around a bottle of water. They seemed very humbly. We smoked our last hash joint with them. The muscular girl, Disuvera explained with practically sign language that she was getting more hash that evening. She asked us if we wanted to get some hash with her. The blonde boyfriend was quiet, she did all the nonverbal talking. Peter, who kind of understood them, did some translating. He was going in on it with them. I didn't think it was a scam. We took the money right out of the hat, using the bigger currency. Arlo made the deal with the girl, and Peter went with her to get it. Peter left his dog on the beach, all by himself. He was running all the way down the beach, he kept running until you could barely see him. Peter said that the dog would be back. The blonde boy sat down and looked blankly. All of a sudden the sleeping bag that was laid out on the beach, in which we were all sitting, started to move. I yelled out that there was a crab, the only logical thing on a beach. It turned out, the blonde guy had a pet with him as well. He was travelling with a rat. It was a rat, not a mouse. He picked it up, put it to his face. It looked like he was going to take a bite, but he started kissing it. Marv was amazed. He proclaimed that he had found the perfect travel pet. A pure animal lover. Marv asked to see his rat, talking to himself with playful imagination.

"Ma, I don't know where Welton is, shit gets lost, anyway Ma, I got a rat, Ma! You gotta check this out," He yelled in excitement.

"Yeah, she'll love that." I said. Jules was lounging enjoying the scene.

Arlo commented on the rat as well saying, "Man, that's a way to pick up the chicks, using a rat."

"Damn, if you got a pigeon, you'd have the perfect hobo circus." I said.

We sat around with the rat, no one talking, feeling a bit inconvenienced because Celene couldn't understand us. Marv and I passed some clubs, Celene watched, nodding his head at the tricks we were throwing. I could tell that he wanted very much to say something. Crowds started move up above on the walk. Restaurants lit up, attempting to attract a tourist in for dinner. The beach was starting to thin out. I was drinking the bottle of gin easier today than I had yesterday. Rodanto the rat scuttled around in the sleeping bag. Then Peters dog showed back up and came over and sat by Jules, the rat, and the Blonde boy Celene. Arlo was using the diablo, picking it up quite easily. There was nothing else to do but live for the day. Disuvera and Peter came back with the hash. We celebrated vividly. More like a haze around us than smoke signals, we danced and kicked sand. We rolled up some hash

joints and drank the gin. It was a lazy atmosphere, toasting to the visible moon, we sat around taking open eyed naps. Marv was over a bit laying in the warm sand, on his back. Arlo was more toward the water, with his hands behind his head, on a mound of sand that he pushed up. Celene, Disuvera, Peter and I smoked some more. Peter passed me the gin.
We were lounging fully. Marv got up and went back into the water. Arlo followed him.

Jules asked, " Welton, you wanna play a game of chess?"
"Na,"
"I will play," Peter said.
"Yeah?" Jules asked, "Ok." And he got the game out of my bag and set it up. I got up and stretched, then I pick up Peters diablo. The rat was sleeping near the tone belly of Disuvera, who was laying in Celenes arms. The wind blew mildly, as the onset of the days change occurred. The two ex-Yugoslavians seemed like brother and sister. They were dark, I imagine not having left the beach in days, They looked totally settled. They had a big blanket, a rat and some hash. All they were missing was a tent, a barbecue, and a cooler of beers, but then again, they weren't American, so they probably weren't missing anything, and after all, they had a rat. I never really got around to fully understand why Celene and Disuvera were here, with the rat. They weren't vacationing, it was more like they were living here on the beach. Maybe they had broken off for a time from some gypsy tribe. Who knew what their story could possibly be. Peter beat Jules at chess. He asked if I wanted to play, I said no, and they played another game. Marv and Arlo came in from the water. They were pretty much dry, having walked on the beach for a while. We smoked some more hash and laid around.

"The scene is dyin out, we walked all the way down the beach. It's desolate down there, maybe we can sleep there later tonight." Arlo said. We sat around doing nothing in particular, having that almost comfortable feeling you get when you're at your mother-in laws house for some holiday. It started to get later in the day. It was a good thing because the sand had cooled off. Peter was petting his dog while beating Jules in chess. The beach was severely less cramped now. People had left, apparently to begin the preparations for the evenings events. "People are starting to show up on the walkway in there dinner gear."

"Yeah, I gotta get mine out of my bag."
"Yeah, Welton you should put that on."
"I will. Anybody got an iron?" Peter was trying to understand what we were saying, looking back and forth between Jules, Arlo, and I. "It's a joke Peter. We're making fun of the rich people."

"Oh, or are you laughing at yourselves and *your* entourage," he said quite seriously, insinuating everyone of us.

I thought about it for a second, "Yeah, it would be cool, to be goin to that show tonight, huh? Like the way cool guys do it-"

"Like Jack Nicholson for doin Easy Rider." Arlo broke in.

"Yeah," Jules said, exhaling some smoke and staring into nothingness.

"Well, what if you were that cool and you just didn't know it." Marv interrupted our rap.

"What like suppose you were addicted to heroin and you didn't know that's what you were addicted to, would you be able to beat the craving?" Jules asked.

"Man, exactly, it's all about feeling important about yourself. Giving yourself the respect that you deserve, cause like lets face it, we are pretty fuckin cool dudes." I jumped up into a squat position getting excited, "Man these people are gonna realize one day that they were once the same kinds of people like us, with the same ideologies and radical beliefs and they're gonna realize that they gave up feeling what we feel and they lost some intuitive keenness and some actual contentness, the last real thing they had, you know! And now, for them it's too late, they can never again regain that innocence they once had like when they were a child. They can never be anything but what they are in their expensive dress, and cruise vacations. But us, or at least me, even if I become one of them, I will never be like them, cause I'm never gonna forget what it's like to feel like me, ever."

"Damn," Arlo said leaving a staleness in the air.

After a second Jules spoke up, "Yeah how many of those people have ever swam with the dolphins."

"How many of them even came out of the air-condition today?" Marv said.

"Yeah, yeah, yeah, I bet there are some people in this world that have never seen the sun." I said through a goofy smile.

We all started laughing, even the ex-Yugoslavians who were somewhat paying attention to our dialog but whispering to each other about other matters every once in a while. Then Peter said, "It is quite possible to avoid the sun completely in London."

"That's true huh." Arlo said calming us all down to a simmer. We hung out on the beach for a little while longer. Everyone lounging. Lanmer was all tuckered out from all that he did today. Marv was like a wolf looking at the moon, sitting still, for a waiting nature. Jules and I shared a cigarette as Arlo started to revive and get antsy. Noises started to arise more vibrantly above on the walkway. The day was running later and more people started showing up walking on the walkway toward the event in evening wear. We were one of the last ones to leave the beach, dressing and putting on our luggage, we were a bit sluggish.

"We are going to check out the festival." I said to Peter.

"Very good, it will be nice. Very attractive people will be there."

"Yes, are yougoing?" Jules asked.

"No, I will be here, it is not for me. I prefer more the stillness of the night tide."

"So do I," Marv said. People were in the fancy restaurants in suits and dresses worth more than I would spend this year, or in their prestigious hotel room getting into dresses like that. "But, I want to see what goes on for myself."

"Yes it is very curious and interesting I admit, but I am not interested. We will stay here tonight. Come back to find us." Peter said.

"Sure we will. It was nice hanging out with you guys," Arlo said, starting to get up and stretch, fixing his hair casually. The beach scene was dead, however wind current off the water was still blowing warm. Everyone else was going to the show. We packed up our stuff, and slung our backpacks onto our backs. We said goodbye to the ex-Yugoslavians in one simultaneous blurb, insinuating that we would see them soon. It was a casual farewell. We walked along the beach to the platform.

"So Jules," I said starting to get nervous, "What's this gonna be like?"

"What kind of question is that? I mean can you actually expect me to know what's going to happen next?"

Then I thought about it, "Sorry, but man it's gonna be cool-"

"Yeah," Arlo broke in, feeling the knot in his stomach as well, "We should see if we can get a shot of us on that big TV screen out in front."

"Yeah, like a panning crowd shot and then focusing on all four of us standin there like we're folk singin circus boys, waitin for the bus on a lone hot desolate unshaded country road in Idaho."

"Yeah, We should bust out a routine." Marv said. And it hit me in a shock. I hadn't thought about busking this crowd for some reason. Why not, I thought. We walked over, up, and among the massiveness of the crowds, everyone was trying to get as close to the entrance as they could. I saw all the pretty people walking in a wave of traffic. I stared at the naked back of a revealing red dressed and clean shouldered, tanned and tall brunette walking in front of me. I started to giggle in my mind.

"Marv, you want in on the old dead and alive gag? What do you think, we don't even have to put a hat out." I knew he wouldn't anyway, and quite frankly we both thought it to be a cheesy idea to send Arlo around through the crowd with a hat to pull money out of the people standing around for the performance. It wasn't our style.

"You bet. Nothin too fancy, I'm low on energy from today."

"Yeah right, I bet you could probably carry a half ton of bricks to Barcelona right now. But ok, I'll keep it light. How's the modo go? Get in, get the laugh then get out."

"Yeah, unless we can milk some of it."

"Sssssiiickkkkk," Arlo broke in. Jules was walking silently, smiling and looking down, blowing smoke from his cigarette onto the jacket of the man directly in front of him. Several girls had positioned their pace to be walking directly beside him. The three bright red from the sun, blonde and smiley girls in colorfully patterned and showy dresses kept poking looks at Jules wondering who he was. He smiled at them innocently and kept dredging along. Cannes, at this moment, made me feel important about myself. I slid, quite mischievously; with bold hard movements, into our awaiting supposed treasures. Jules looked without blinking the whole time. Walking peaceably along. He had an innate smile, not appearingly, but showed vows of pure devotion to simplicity and kindness. He showed no sign of fear, and had no reason to bluff his truths. His presence attracted everyone. In our eyes, he already was famous. We were fortunate to be at the hottest spot in the world that night and we were accompanying Jules, a prince, soon to become a king. The burden of my backpack was feltless. I saw life almost four dimensionally. Anxiety stirred and the situation was heated, but I tried to be cool.

Calming my steps so as not to run up into the person walking in front of me. We were a bit spaced out, but you could tell that we were there together in the crowd. I looked over through the crowd, where Marv was, and I saw Arlo, he looked like he was trying to be cool, noticing that it was the kind of scene were you had to play real tuff, at any social gathering, everybody likes to look good right? Everyone checks everybody else out. Arlo must have thought they were all looking at him. Actually he had this weird way of looking like he had some value to him. He bounced and jazzed along; excited. Marv was indifferent, worth so much more than any one could ever understand. He was beyond the whole scene, still probably, playing cards with the sun, he and the dolphins conquering her brightness and most likely cheating, innocently. He was tight and steady, rolling along. The lines became jammed. There was no movement, traffic, engines revving, it was getting darker, overhead lights were on. Tired of standing still, everyone around me noticing my moldy body odor smell, I initiated a turn down a little walkway by the back end of the port-o-potties.

We entered through to a tent, not really through an entrance, more from the side making our own entrance, almost unrevealingly. We wandered longly, down a tunnel like tented hallway. Stands holding well brillianted frames with thick black and white photographs of all the stars in all of their great moments, off screen, were all along the tent corridor. It was quiet in the tent, like a grave or sanctuary almost. So powerful the photographs were, even more potent than the actual moment itself, I imagined. I thought about what it must have been like for one of them to see themselves in such grandiose photographs. "Damn," a bit upset, "I ain't never had no photo taken of me like that," I said arrogantly distraught.

"It's so quiet in here." Marv said. Not to many tourists were in this tent because they were all in line. I walked over to stare at a picture of Joe Pesci, standing like a tough guy with all the Good Fella boys behind him. It was such a powerful photograph. It saddened me a little at that moment, thinking that my life would never be that great. Marv was shuffling behind me, staring, impressed more in here than out there, seemingly.

Jules fit right in, we joked saying, "Jules we should leave you in here,"

"Yeah right, he's like a fucking black and white photograph."

"You're as radiant as anybody in these pictures." He didn't say anything, hiding his embarrassment.

"Hey you guys remember that picture that Jim took of you guys in that pub in London?" Arlo asked. "That shit should be hangin in here."

"Yeah it should." Marv said, "I think that's the only picture we have of London."

"It's probably the only picture I have period." I said. I stopped short for a second and thought about it. "That really was a good picture of us," then I started to feel better, having something beautifully taken of me, with my comrades, kind of like the Good Fella crew. Just different levels of the game I guessed, I was now definitely feeling better about myself, I was in pictures.

"These are just people in these pictures, just like us," Arlo said.

"Sure, but the difference is like how much respect would Bruce Willis get if he was just some guy named Bruce who worked down the corridor from your cubicle at his day job." Night time came quick, yet it was still full of light out side.

"It depends on how many chicks he was screwin around the office."

"Yeah but still you know what I mean right?" I said.

"Sure we do Bruce." Marv said, pushing me a little and laughing.

"Ha-ha." We moved, a little shaken and impressed, but gleeful. Outside the night of the awards was upon us, we managed to cut through to the front where people were actually waiting in the staged off line. Time came for the evening festivals to begin. It was a big moment for us, we thought we were going to go to Cannes and get famous, but secretly, I think we all knew we were walking out of here losers like we walked in. And here we were about to get it. All those who could afford tickets stood in queue. Organized penguins with there knock out dates. Others stood a distance away, watching them, watching us, we watched them. In my peripheral vision, I saw a man tossing a diablo smoothly three stories high and landing it perfectly on the string. In my center view was the enormous television so all could see which star was entering into what I have no idea or could imagine. All of us where standing in check with our gear on taking in the scene. Thousands of people from all over were here.

Reporters ran to catch the first glimpse. More people were showing up, we had to pay attention, cause we had a lot of gear and we were in a tight space. Every once in a while a local would come scurrying through the crowd, worse dirtier than us, all undecent like and definitely working, attempting to do some sort of pickpocket job. We worked our way up in front of the big screen. The guy doing the diablo show kept throwing it high in the air and catching it. He yelled and tried to jeer the crowd. He had a hat out up close to where the lines of people passed. Huge crowds of zigzagging lines were all approaching like snails to the bright red carpet. Women in ten thousand dollar dresses were eagerly going into the party. Us, dirty, not invited, just standing there, hoping to at least brush up against the soft silk of a strapless dress. The gurgle of the masses casting symphonized blurred out rhetoric. People spending thousands of dollars that week. More money than I had ever seen. Too many people were standing around in line. We stood in the crowd that was just there to see. There was a guy, he was flagrant, colorful, and simpletonlike. The way he pranced around and glared his blinking eyes showed that he had a lot of respect for himself, taking pictures and then offering to sell them to the tourists at a later date in his tent.

He came over and gazed at Jules, "Ooooohhhh, sweetheart, I'm tellin you baby that you are beautiful." Jules fell silent and drew the hat on his head tighter over his eyes, covering his cards. With a full on fairy English accent he persisted, "What are you doin baby, can't you see you're on the wrong side of the barricades here!" He laughed at his own humor and looked at us standing there, a posse, "Ooohhh I see, these here are your friends. You must be bad guys. You boys look too rugged for me, but you baby," pointing to Jules, "You all right. I see, you boys look dangerous, mmmmmm, like the untouchables." Bending his hand at the wrist, straightening out his finely soft fingers, and creasing and the skin on his forehead. He started laughing, loving our physical charisma and with intensity the man made space to take our picture. Creating space around the standers with flagrant boyance to the fluidity of the insecure crowd around us. We were momentarily infamous, everybody around us stood for less than a blink to watch the flash that cast double images of us into the horizon. We were so cool at that moment. In Spain on our last trip Jules, Marv, and I had earned the title 'Estranieros', which meant something completely different in Spanish than it does in English; 'Strangers'. And now, the four of us, I felt that we were again, like Greek explorers in the odyssey. The effect wore off long before our fifteen minutes of fame were up. We told him we weren't going to buy the picture, and he said that it was fine, somebody else would.

He laughed saying, "Somebody is sure to discover him for sure," he said implying Jules. Then he walked on, taking pictures. We stood for a moment, all of us for sure looking at ourselves wondering if we were that cool.

"Yo Marv, lets go break in on this guys space," I said implying the guy with the diablo.

"Sure. Arlo, listen we need you to watch our gear. And listen watch out for that little sneaky guy runnin around here, smellin like a dumpster. He was eyein us."

"No problem," he said as I handed him my drum. I dropped my bag and switched quickly into my clown shoes. Marv was doing the same thing. It was nerving to have to gear up so quickly. We handed Arlo and Jules our backpacks. We moved through the crowd.

"Let me get this guys attention," I said.

"I think we should just bust into his gig, He's not even doin a show, he's just throwin that thing up in the air."

"Ok but like I said, lets be quick about this, I don't wanna be standin out there lookin like an idiot, like this guy." Implying the diablo man, "These people aren't interested in second rate personalities. Their lookin to meet Robert Dinero."

"Completely brother. They got the awards ceremony on their minds. We'll just give them a little taste, some pre-show flavor."

Then we put our clown noses on, and wham, "Duuuhhh, I'll go that way!" I said, crossing my arms and pointing in both directions.

"OOOOOOOOOOKKKKKKKKK, hhuuh huh uh huh!" Marv said and turned around and accidentally slapped me as he did. Some people around us started noticing us. A man with a plain shirt smiled. His girlfriend who was more normal looking than him kept staring up to the red carper. We moved separately across from each other outside the diablo mans circle. Then as he was idling the diablo, screaming at the crowd to check him out, we simultaneously walked into his circle from opposing ends. Me, moving slowly like a robot. Marv, wandering in looking lost, looking around for me. The diablo man noticed us and became silent. Realizing quickly that he was being intruded on. I looked to see if he was going to object against it. Then Marv was coming out of a trip, he yelled out, "Heyyyyy!"

I looked up and got excited. We waved to each other and smiled. We kept waving and then he implied that we should shake hands. The diablo guy started yelling out to get the crowds attention, still idling his diablo. We both stuck our hands out and walked in clown like fashion towards each other. I could tell that the diablo guy stalled slightly, unsure what to do. Apparently not used to having his show interrupted by another show. But he gave us the space, he probably could tell that we were professionals. Marv and I walked with our hands extended out as if we were walking up to meet and shake each others hands. Then as if we didn't notice we walked directly passed each other to the end of the circle. We both turned around being confused. Then we noticed each other again and happily started walking back toward each other, then passing each other again and walking to the opposite ends of the open play space. I looked into the crowd with a crazy clownesque face. People were actually checking us out. What else are they gonna do I thought, this is a captive audience I said to myself in my mind. I turned around, I saw Marv spin around and overspin and start walking into the crowd. They pushed him back into the circle. I heard the crowd near him chuckle.

He turned around in quarters. Stepping and turning, pulling his leg up and placing it in a turn then swinging his body. Then we noticed each other and this time we came toward each other slowing, unsure, but still with our hands out. Then the diablo was getting thrown up in the air directly behind us over and over. We reached each other and smiled. A woman, who was probably bored, in the crowd started clapping and yelling, "Go clowns go." I went to shake Marv's hand and he instantly bowed. Then we apologized clown like. Then he put out his hand and I bowed and curtsied. Then we started to get frustrated and did this stupid miss action, building it up until I was going so fast Marv stepped out of the picture. I started hugging myself as if I was greeting someone, shaking my own hands. Marv looked at me like I was the strange one. He looked out to the crowd, then he implied with a big swirl around his temple that I was crazy. He got a bright idea and then came around and kicked me in the ass. I rolled forward, tumbling and landing facing the crowd. Someone yelled out, "That's not funny." I kept going.

I got up and started chasing Marv around kicking him. But I started slowing down and running out of gas. A robot who's battery died. Then I drooped, standing there, game over like. The crowd jeered, liking my ability to do slow motion. Usually this is where money made me start up again, but Marv came over and pulled the string in my back, like a lawn mower. I tested him a little, not starting, then he kicked me in the butt. I started to move but in slow motion. He got a bright idea. He pulled a round balloon out of his pockets and blew it up. Then he snapped his fingers and got my attention. I started staring at it eagerly as he rocked it back and forth. I was hypnotized. I stood on one leg and started barking. The crowd kind of laughed. He started manipulating it as if it was some tremendously heavy object. Pushing it along. Pulling it. Struggling to turn it over and over. Sweating and showing that the balloon was arduous to move. It was a really nice effect and Marv could do it well. The trick is to keep the balloon still. The crowd all turned to watch what seemed like a heavy object in his hands. He carried the balloon, tugging at it, letting it take him several steps backward. Then finally reaching our exit, me following him the whole way in quirky slow motion, spinning a mimed crank with my left hand in normal speed, and bellowing like a sea otter. Some people actually applauded. It was the balloon manipulation that got those people interested not the clowning.

"Nice movement with that balloon Marv," I said, sweating and panting.

"Thanks, I've been practicing." He wasn't out of breath and didn't seem to be sweating. Arlo and Jules came up to us through the crowd. No one came up to shake our hands or congratulate us. The guy with the diablo started filling his space. Trying to make sure that we wouldn't come back out for an encore. He threw the diablo and started running around, jeering.

"Did they show us on the big screen?" I asked Arlo.

"Na, but that was some cool shit. I saw a lot of people staring at you guys."

"Marv that was really cool with the balloon," Jules said, "People liked that shit."

"Thanks." He said, taking off his clown gear.

"All right." I said taking off my clown nose and getting my backpack back from Arlo. We degeared right in the thick of the crowd. "So what are we doin?" I asked, "Do we have a chance of sneakin into this joint?"

"I seriously doubt it." Arlo said. "I would love a job bein an extra in this crowd, you know, when a star goes to the bathroom, some nobody goes and sits in his seat, to make the audience seem full for the cameras. That would be a cool job. Imagine who you would sit next to." Arlo said.

"Yeah, just imagine," Marv answered him. "Let's move outa here," he said as he put his backpack on and grabbed my drum from Arlo.

"I wouldn't wanna be sittin in there, fuck these people" I thought I heard Jules say but I let it go without comment, I didn't even stare at him. Wasn't he tryin to get in there I wondered?

We moved closer to the road where cars were coming in. I started to enjoy it a little bit, being a part of this pseudo classed crowd. A limousine pulled up and let out Danny Devito. Both him and the car about the same height, but Danny with much more energy. He jogged along walking quickly, waving and smiling and saying Hi. What more could he do? We cheered him on. He seemed like a lot of fun. But what do I know what he's like in a business deal or as a friend. Jules yelled out over the noise of the crowd, something personal to Danny Devito. In his steps he stopped for too quick a second to let it register, Nonchalantly looking around to see where it came from. Then he dismissed the whole scene and moved onward to his duty as a celebrity. We sat around talking excitedly about the stars.

Arlo asked, "Hey Jules what was that you yelled to Dan?" Marv looked at him, being curios as well. I leaned in, earnestly wondering as well.

Jules said, "We spent time in the same neighborhoods. It was nothing, just a catch phrase."

"Oh," Arlo said not pushing it any further.

"Is that the dude your mom almost got on?" I asked, "Cause if it is, your mom has great taste." I said. They all looked at me. "What, she would have been lucky to get a catch like him right? Well dressed, rich, famous, and funny! He's the man, I wish he was my dad." Nobody said anything to me, they just kept staring at the limos. Other people poured out of the long limousines. It started to get boring just standing there, on the outside looking in, so we decided to move.

"This sucks." Jules persisted, but not becoming upset.

"Fuck this, we don't need them to boost our egos," Arlo said.

"Man," Jules let out a sigh but didn't say anything more. He became withdrawn. We walked along the roadway where more limousines were lined up. Dark locked windows staring at us, our reflections only in the mirrorlike window, not inside the car. There was this big square in front of Planet Hollywood. We settled there for a bit. Crowds were gathered on the outside patios of bars and people were standing around in the square and on the streets. A big bus almost ran over a drunkard. A waitress was outside talking to some other girls, we approached them and started them up in conversation, they were polite and going back inside. They said that supposedly Bruce Willis was in there with Sylvester Stallone. I folded, I let out a breath and I started realizing how heavy my backpack was.

I had the sudden impulse to call a friend of mine in the United States. Months ago we had planned to travel together this summer, as that he was graduating from school and his parents were going to give him a present of some money for a trip to Europe. He was going to photograph our journey along the way. He was at the time I had know him an aspiring photographer. I borrowed Arlo's calling card and spent several minutes trying to understand the phone over the ambiance outside the booth. Finally a connection through was made.

Terrance, my friend was actually home, I didn't even think about what time it was in America. In a wide open space right by the Planet Hollywood in a lone phone booth I listened to Terrance's tale. It turned out that he had failed out of school this past semester. His life falling prey to the intricacies of harder drugs. He was in a rehab now, outpatient, working and with all intention from his parents, grounded. It depressed me. What had happened? He had the ride of his life in front of him. He was supposed to graduate and he could have traveled, his parents paying for his travel expenses as a present, but he got screwed up with drugs, failed out of school and now was in rehab. I was upset, Terrance would have gotten so much out of this experience. I came out of the phone booth, completely beat. Everything around me was falling apart, while everyone else seemed to be achieving their greatest enjoyment.

I told Marv the woes and troubles Terrance was having. He didn't seem surprised. Jules and Arlo were sitting on a bench talking to a group of local teens. They were telling them which sections of the little city were more dangerous, and suggesting where not to sleep. They were kind and used to travelers like us in their town. We sat around for a while. It was late, I had just witnessed true success of others, I was a bum with nowhere to sleep. Why did my comrades want me with them on their travels across Europe, I had too much for one day, but a film festival will do that to you. Many people were out drinking. Beautiful women being talked out of their panties from expensive looking suggestions from, classy men in nice clothes were all over the place. In between all the couples, there were dangerous types out, being controlled by the patrol of the French law. It started to get a little seedy.

"You guys wanna go back to the beach and see what Peter and the two Slavs are doing?" Arlo asked.

"Sure," Marv answered him. We walked through crazed and stirred crowds, alcohol influencing everyone. Toward the beach I saw bright pants and shiny shirts and dresses reflecting the waters glimmer on the beach. People were walking, silhouetted against the water background. Women swaying hips and holding in their hands unlaced high heels, while men walked near them tearing at a rounded bottle of champagne. Everyone was laughing and screaming. The party was in full swing. A guy ran and tackled a girl. Another guy picked up a girl and brought her kicking and screaming and threw her in the water. She came out running after him and jumping on his back hitting him. I was unsure if they were friends or if that had been their first introduction to each other, and it could have very well been.

"There they are over there." Arlo pointed. We walked down onto the beach, passing all sorts of well dressed and aggressive people. We walked up to Peter and the Slavs. They smiled at us and welcomed us to sit. We threw our bags down and started rolling up hash joints.

"How was the festival?" Peter asked.

"About as crazy as it is here." I said looking around at all the nighttime action on the beach. A couple of guys were playing tackle football, some girls were drunk and dunking and pushing each other in the shallow end of the Mediterranean, accepting the fact that they were ruining there dresses. We were camped out, with all our stuff in the middle of it all. Luckily no tuff guy tourist came up to us asking to smoke some of our hash. I wouldn't have offered any to anyone. A guy was making a beautiful sand castle type world near the walkway, and from above, people were pitching money onto the sand around it. Somebody came running along with a piñata hooked up on a string to a long pole. Another guy was chasing him with a plunger, swinging it.

"Shit's flying off that plunger," Arlo said.

"That's funny." I said. A girl was running down the beach casually taking off clothes and turning around, taunting a guy following her, pulling off his shirt. They ran down a bit, fully disrobing in the distance then laying down, and definitely fucking.

"Yo, check that out." I pointed at their silhouette in the distance, she was on top of him, arced back and moaning, "Right out in public like that, damn, that's some cool shit. "He's fuckin her. Shit. Arlo that's what you're talkin about right?"

He turned his head to scrutinize the distance, "Yeah."

"Well then what the fuck are we doin. Let's get some of that."

"Where?"

"Yeah right, I guess that's the closest we're gonna get to getting laid tonight."

"Maybe not," he said as a group of girls walked by, "Hey ladies," Arlo said, getting up and walking over to them nearer to the water. Bouncing and happily herding them in. After talking to them for a minute, he brought them over to our group. They sat down and we all said hi. They were from Norway, not speaking any English. We passed around several joints. They weren't that pretty, but a couple of them had some sex appeal. Then some of their guys friends ran up yelling and drinking from bottles of beer and champagne, laughing and wrestling in the sand. One guy stood over us and told this story in Norwegian that made all the girls laugh. We even laughed, even though we didn't understand him, but he must have thought that we did. I kept nodding my head and agreeing with him. He laughed to himself then ran and jumped in the water. Some of the girls followed him, taking off their dresses and going in the water in their conservative looking underwear. We sat around aimlessly for a while, smoking.

A shady looking guy with a dreaded out Mohawk goatee was prancin about at casual speed, doing a two step and pivot move, prowlin with tinted antique fighter pilot goggles on, sayin 'yeah yeah oh yeah', and laughing to himself, staring from just outside the scene on the beach. An American in khaki shorts and normally bright white, but now bruised and brightly sunburned skin was running around with keys in his hand, held high above the crowd, yelling, "Keys? Did anybody lose keys to their hotel?" He was frazzled, trying to remain anal and focused, probably not used to being so drunk. The plunger was in full force, chasing around a girl now who was running with the piñata. It was a paper mache fish, painted silver with big bulby eyes. A guy on the walkway was letting girls do shots of tequila, sucking lemons out from in between his open shirted and really well muscled pecks.

The plunger was sloshing around in the air. The piñata carrier and the guy chasing her ran by, right near us. Mostly likely specks of shit sloshing onto everyone. "There's shit coming off that plunger," some one in the crowd yelled.

"Oui, Le merde." I heard. I was sitting there in a drunken stoned happiness.

"I think I just got hit with some shit." Arlo said, wiping his head.

"This is getting out of hand, I can't believe I'm here. What the fuck am I doing here." Jules said in a muffle throwing some of the blanket over his head for protection from the flying shit and the outside scene around us.

"You're here babe and don't worry man tomorrow we're gonna sell that script of yours." I tried to cheer him up.

"I'm tellin ya, it's cool, this place is gonna serve its purpose for you Jules" Marv said. He was getting a shoulder massage from one of the Norwegian girls.

"It is quite normal, this kind of extravagance, in France," Peter said.

"I'm gonna take a walk. Will you watch my stuff Welton?" Marv excitedly asked.

"Sure." I said as Marv got up with the girl who was giving him a massage and they walked hand in hand down the beach. "Nice." I said to myself out loud. Arlo got up and ripped his shirt and pants off and went running and screaming naked into the water where the other Norwegians were playing in the water. They all moved over to him, yelling and praising him and splashing water at him. Jules, Peter, the two Slavs, one Norwegian girl, Lanmer and I sat there barely talking, just taking it all in, looking around. This girl isn't into it, I was thinking. She seemed shy. Disuvera passed around a hash chillum. The rat stirred under the blanket and came up for air. The Norwegian girl looked at it hard, then started talking to herself and getting hyper. She got up and started running from the beach screaming.

"I guess she is afraid of rats." Peter said. Celene looked with a smile quietly, then he shrugged his shoulders and took a hit off the chillum.

"Oh well, that sucks for her." I said as el Rodanto settled into a nest in the blanket. I started to feel like I was procrastinating. I stood up and stretched. Arlo came back to the camp wet and naked, not trying to hide himself, but trying to attract girls attention with his visible package. He stood near us, dripping water and letting it all hang out.

"Arlo put your pants on, you're not gonna attract girls with that thing, you're gonna get us in trouble with the cops."

"Yeah, you're like a target with that thing out."

Disuvera was checking him out bluntly, then she said something to Celene, who laughed. Arlo looked at them and said, "What, what are you guys talking about?" Curious like and getting frustrated. Celene shook his head, implying nothing but Arlo insisted, "What." Celene smiled and brought his hand up and put his thumb and forefinger about an inch apart, implying little dick. We all laughed, and Disuvera pointed to Celene and put both hands about a foot apart implying big dick. We all laughed, "Oh ha ha ha." Arlo snickered, "You go in the water and see how much you shrivel up." He said. Celene tried to apologize playfully. Arlo put his pants on shrugging it off. The Norwegians came in from the water holding their clothes. At least they had underwear on. Two of the guys patted Arlo on the back. The girls dressed then they left practically without saying goodbye.

"This party is just beginning," Came the sound from Jules, but perhaps with a distressed intonation." I stared in tired silence for a second, then a yawn hit me.
Jules went back under the blanket, encouraged to lay his head next to the rat on Disuvera's lap. Celene even insisted. "I'm getting cranky I think." Jules exhaled solemnly from on her lap.

"The sun," I said, pointing up then tapped my hand down, "Today," then I blew out a sigh, shook my head side to side and wiped my brow, "It was very hot."

Celene started shaking his head in understanding. He said something to Peter, then he translated as Celene reached over and put his thumb on my arm and depressed. His hands were strong, bold exciting with firm movements. Then he let go, showing the contrast of white to the immensely red skin, "He says that you are sunburned and that you will be sore tomorrow."

"Yeah, the sun wore me out today, it's our first day out in the sun on the beach, by the end of the summer I'm going to be darker than Celene." I said to Peter.

"Yes. He says that you have the kind of pigment, skin that takes to the sun rather well."

"Man, the sun was so hot today," Jules snored out from on Disuveras lap under the blanket. The party had picked up, every once in a while some distinguished looking couple would fall flagrantly to the ground near us, kicking up dirt.

"Yo, it's gonna be a nice day tomorrow." Arlo put in from his silence, sitting with his hands wrapped around his knees.

"He takes to the sun well, look, he's not even sunburned, he's just dark already," I gestured over to Arlo. Celene looked at Arlo and shook his head, staring, almost jealous like over Arlo's dark coat. Marv came back with the Norwegian girl, hand in hand, carrying her shoes, silently smiling. She looked around, Peter implied that her friends had left. She smiled and nodded her head and whispered into Marvs ear. She kissed him on the lips then she waved to all of us and left grabbing her shoes from Marv, not letting go of his hand till the very end, still holding his gaze in her eyes until they could no longer distinguish the features of each others faces because of the distance and the darkness. He didn't sit down. He turned around and looked out to the water.

"Marv, not to bust your groove or anything, but where are we gonna sleep tonight. Cause if we crash out here, we ain't gonna get any proper sleep, and then tomorrow will be a lazy day."

"We'll go find a nice place. A cemetery."

"That's a plan." I started to get excited. "Yes."

"Cemetery?" Peter asked curiously leaning in.

"Yeah, that's his favorite place to sleep." Arlo broke in through a yawn.

"Actually, my favorite place to sleep is with my face in-between a girls thighs," I said laughing. Peter smiled.

"Ha-ha," Jules jumped from beneath the blanket, sitting up.

"But, cemeteries are cool places to crash out to. My head on a shallow based tombstone, high as hell, hangin with the dead. Aahhhhh," I leaned back a bit getting nostalgic, "Echoing my drum for the silenced prayers." It became silent for a second, it was weird, the whole beach stirred in a stale moment, every one calming to a murmur as if the music stopped, the juke box was in between CD's, everybody unsure for some reason. Then it picked up, a girl screamed and ran tearing off clothes into the water.

"I say we roll." I stretched, "Peter, are you guys gonna sleep here?" I asked looking around to see what of mine was laying about.

"Yes, it will not be like sleep until six thirty or so, after the sun has come up. Then we will sleep." A couple of guys dropped down quite near us and started doing push-ups. A really old looking short man in a zoot suit walked up to the pusher-uppers and started singing to them, almost as if he was conducting them in some strange French way.

Marv stared at it all, then said, "Yeah, I don't think we're gonna hang for the sunrise. But we'll catch up with you guys tomorrow." He turned back around and starting to gear up. Jules realized the stir in the moment and he perked up, picking up his backpack, or office and initiating the good-byes, nodding to every one.

"Ok, we're out, see you guys later." Arlo said, shaking every ones hands and packing up securely. Jules kindly passed his good-byes around. I jumped up and grabbed all that was mine. We calmly went on our way to find a place to sleep. Jules started walking ahead of us, dodging all the night time beach traffic. A football game on the beach was going on in the distance. Jules turned around to us and he had a tear in his eye, "I can't take it anymore. I'll be right back!" He ran off. I started to follow him, starting to yell, but Marv grabbed me and held me back.

"Let him go man, he's gotta sort somethin out. It'll be cool, he's coming right back." Marv assured me. I saw Jules hit the ground in the distance and dump something out of his office. He sat over a handful of stuff, staring down at it for a while, then he lit it on fire. We all stood there among all the commotion staring at him.

"Hey, what's he doin? Is he burnin his guitar?" I started to get worried.

"He's burnin somethin." Arlo replied.

"That's his fuckin script he's burnin isn't it? Marv, what the fuck is he doin?" I screamed, jumping a step toward him, crazy traffic going on in front of me, blocking my view of Jules.

"Is it?" Arlo all of a sudden became concerned.

"Hey, it's his to do what he wants with." Marv rebuttled us.

"Is he fuckin crazy. What the fuck is he doin?" In the distance he stood up, now facing a hulking fire on the beach. "Jules." I yelled, trying to run to him but Marv stopped me.

"Don't Welton. Didn't you see him. He doesn't want anything to do with this film festival crap. He thinks he made a mistake coming here."

"Hey be careful what you wish for I guess," Arlo interjected through staring around at all the drunken girls around us, not really caring about Jules but seeming more interested in the girls with little clothes on.

"Here he comes, don't say anything Welton. He doesn't need to deal with it right now." I couldn't believe Marv was just going to let him throw away everything he had been working on for the past couple of months. Slowly, without me noticing anything else around me, I watched Jules come back to us. He had tears in his eyes.

"Jules, are you ready to go now." Arlo asked boringly, his body language telling that he was upset that he wasn't playing in any of the games on the beach, pissed at having to sit on the sidelines.

Jules was smiling with a drunken red joy flushing on his cheeks, as if he had just gotten laid, "This film festival isn't even reputable anymore, it's just a glamour thing." He turned and looked out beyond the waters edge. Marv walked up to him and patted him on the shoulder. "I mean all these blockbuster hits with crazy action goin on, not even a good plot in these films, just movie stars."

"I know brother, there is no more integrity in the major market film industry anymore," Marv said. People ran buy us yelling and screaming. There was a mix of different languages in the air. We stood around it all, in the eye of the storm of it, not being affected by any of it.

I spoke up, now understanding that all this superficial extravagance was unimportant to Jules, there was no piece of mind for him in that scene, "They'll take your story away from you Jules, maybe it's better that you didn't give it to them." But did you have to burn it I asked myself in my head.

"Yeah it is Jules, fuck these people. They would have turned your story into a circus," Arlo said, now more upset that everyone else around us was having fun, turning his head side to side, not even really paying attention to our conversation, just trying to act as if he was part of a crowd at a party. So many good looking girls were walking by, back and forth on the beach, in groups, men sauntering slowly behind them.

"They would have missed the point entirely if they would have tried to make a movie out of it." Marv said.

"You guys are right," he said, "And you know what, I don't even think that this whole run was a waste of time either. I feel pretty good. It's like I have this pot of gold, or like a bucket of chocolate, I wanna hoard it, greedily, all to myself. I don't wanna share it with everybody, I wanna only share it with the people that were a part of it. It's like my girlfriend, this story that I wrote, I don't wanna share her with anybody. I wanna stay in my bedroom with her for days at a time, hiding from everybody, not letting anybody into our world. Only the two of us crying and loving each other. It's too intimate for anybody else's eyes. That's how I feel about what I wrote this semester, it's mine."

A long silence fell over us. I could barely notice all the other commotion around us. I just stared out to the water, thinking on what Jules was saying.

Arlo finally broke in on all our thoughts. With nervousness in his voice he asked, "So what did you write about Jules?"

He laughed a little and then smiled again, "It was about somethin I saw happen in Russia in '93, somethin I was a part of, and it's mine," he said confidently, nodding his head, "Yeah, I'm keepin it for myself, that's why I burned it. Fuck this film festival and you know what?" He said getting excited and moving around, his guitar case flailing about, "I'll sell these fools somethin next year, a story about some fucked up dyslexic janitor cleaning the dorms at Amsterdam University. Somethin from my imagination that's not even personal. That'll be ten times more worth it than giving them the blood that runs through my veins. This," he said, holding up a piece of burnt paper in the air that was now mostly ash, "This is mine." And he put it into his pocket to disintegrate with the rest of him. "I'm not sharing it with anybody, I'm keeping it for myself."

"I would do the same thing Jules," Marv answered him.

"So would I, but I wouldn't make such a big deal of it," Arlo said.

"That's cause you have a little dick, you can't really afford to make a big deal out of anything." I said to him, pushing him now.

"Ha-ha," He gibbered and started to move around. "Now can we get the fuck out of here, this place is depressing me."

"Sure, lets go get some sleep." Jules nodded his head and started walking through people. We followed him, spraying sand in front of us from our marching. Not even glancing around at all the fun we were missing out on. We hurried off the beach, trying to avoid the commotion. Speedily and in an escape like fashion, looking down and being quiet, we hurried down the walkway and turned down a little unlit cobblestone street.

"These are the kinds of streets where people get mugged. We should have stayed on the beach." I said, worrying a little. Squinting to gain more focused sight.

"Don't worry, Welton," Marv assured me. I was run down and maybe a little depressed on myself. We walked a long time down so many long unlit roads. We just walked toward where our minds said the exit signs were. We got even more lost, totally an un-rememberable distance away from the center of town, all of us completely unsure as to its direction. The roads seemed to wind together, and with our tiredness, and grogginess, they all appeared to be the same road over and over. There was no cemetery to be found, and we couldn't find a decent place to sleep on the streets. There was always a reason why the spot was no good. But determination and common sense made us carry on. We walked through different little streets, up hills and back down little alleyway roads. None of us saying anything, but all of us glad that we were away from the commotion of Cannes. I'm sure one of us was wishing that we had gotten a hotel room, a nap and a shower. I'm sure none of us wanted to be carrying our backpacks right now I thought. We came across a little grass park, that divided two roads. It had a bench or two that made it look quaint. There was shrubbery and a tree.

"This spot looks great." Finally giving up looking for a better spot. It worked, we were tired and worn drunk. We had been down a long road the past couple of days. The sun beat us all down. Was it like Homer and The Odyssey? Was I on a voyage to happiness? We laid out our sleeping bags quietly. Not making commotion. With slit eyes I looked around for any lurking danger. It seemed well enough. The grass we laid on was moist. I put a plastic bag around my drum. We talked a bit, looking at the stars. There was no heaven that I could see. Stars where winking at me. It was a living organism up there, and I was a part of it. I started to fall asleep as cars past us by on the roads occasionally.

"Welton this isn't exactly the rose gardens of Vondel Park in Amsterdam, is it?" Marv mentioned through to my mind from a couple of sleeping bags over. It was a road divider, with tall fat bushes surrounding it, a couple of benches and small trees, like a median. A car could have came crashing at the right angle between the trees and run over us. We let fate take its course. All of a sudden I heard voices, then some people showed up and their dog was barking more out of wimp curiosity then fierce angry determination. A French poodle came over sniffing. None of us moved. I could tell that he was on a really long leash. The people were over to the distance. The dog peed on the bottom of my sleeping bag. Soaking it and wetting my feet and legs.

I kicked my legs and the dog jumped and bark. The lady, talking to another lady didn't notice, or chose not to notice her dog peeing on me. The dog knew the little grass park well, it had been there before, I wondered if I was sleeping on the remnants of the dogs recently previous visit. I exclaimed in a grunt, startling the dog, "Yah, Yah," Shooing it away but not getting out of my bag. The pee soaking through at the bottom of my bag, "Shit," I snarled. Marv didn't move, it was apparent he had sensed out the situation before me, and saw it not as a threat to the rest of his sleep. He started laughing under his sleeping bag, figuring out what had happened, and by the commotion and odor of the urine. Arlo slept in-between Jules and I and he raised up, checking to see if his bag had gotten wet, staring now at the barking dog. The owner pulled in on the leash and was holding her dog at bay, in French, looking at us disapprovingly. She started yelling something at us. Arlo waved and said, "Buenos noches." in Spanish. She left with her friend, snickering, avoiding the situation. Arlo laid back down. Everyone started to breath normally again, then they all started to laughed at my misfortune, "Ha-ha!" Jules wheezing and coughing under his bag. "Great." I said not doing anything about it. I actually kind of liked it, it was funny, and ironic, almost expected and natural. We were laying there laughing casually when all of a sudden a car came roaring around one side of the bend, screeching to turn. I froze. Another car came following it, just as fast, around the other side of the roadway, too tight into the turn, ramming into a bush taking it out of the ground and speeding away with it. It was loud and I could smell the burning gas and clutch surrounding us.

"Okay," I said.

"We are out of here.!" Marv exclaimed. No one disagreeing, but jumping up quickly and rolling up our sleeping bags and strapping on our bags.

"Quick, before they come back." We hurried out of the middle of the street and left to find a safer place. "Maybe that's what that lady with the dog was saying to us." I said. Jules was walking fast, ahead of us, still sleeping probably.

Turning, picking, and choosing our way for us. Quietly escaping, we kept on, into our hard luck story. We past some vast estates and small houses coinciding peacefully. "I can't believe we can't find the cemetery." I yawned, all of us carrying our sleeping bags, mine all unrolled and me stepping on it, all most tripping into it as I walked. Trying to keep the urine soaked end furthest from my face. My feet being moist, attracting and holding the dirt from the road through my sandals.

"How about right here?" Jules asked finally, like a dog locating the perfect spot for him to do his business, we crept into a driveway. Like Arabs, we tip-toed to this back parking lot. The building hiding us from the road was

192

an apartment complex. It looked more like a dorm than anything but there was ample space to sleep.

"We are so far from the festival, I bet none of them over there never even get out this far into Cannes." Arlo said as he picked our spot. He wisely chose a section not on the driveway, where a car couldn't run us over as it pulled up into a spot. We let Arlo sleep on the outside. I slept on the inside end, closest to the building on the side of us. We were on this little blacktop hill under a tree. There was a metal post that protected the tree from bumpers, and it served our purposes of auto protection for the evening. I rolled out in my sleeping bag, the bottom of it still wet, none of us spoke, not even in a whisper, less someone hears us and tells us to move on, it would have been a burden to seek other shelter. This was far from town and very safe, just a little bit uncomfortable. No one complained. Was it only I who saw our lame predicament. Now, in lue of all I had seen today, did I still like myself I wondered?

I laughed and said, "Arlo tighten your backpack's security string to yourself," not commenting on it being his first night sleeping on the streets. Jules fell asleep quickly, sleeping soundly and snoring. Marv was an owl in the tree, hooting. What was going to come to be I thought? Would my mother approve of me now? I felt so many random thoughts. I wanted to meet my beautiful girl soulmate already. When? Where was she? And do I deserve her? What is God I thought? What is life? What have I made with the life I have been given? Did I have problems? None so far...thanks. Where are my creations, where are the songs, can a fool stand on his hands that long? Where do my thoughts come from? What will I be? Envy to the guitar and the sounds of music in the ear. I could get better at life if I tried, right? Thoughts, clouded out physical uncomfortableness. I wasn't worrying, I was wondering. The inner peace of sleep, a resting room to lay in, found me walking accidentally into it. I was always hesitant to go in, but softly, stepping with the delicacy required to get into hot bathwater, I drifted off to much needed and tired sleep.

?